## About th

CW00520352

David Ahern grew up in a theatrical family in Ireland but ran away to Scotland to become a research psychologist and sensible person. He earned his doctorate and taught in major universities but could never explain to his granny why he didn't own a stethoscope.

Finding the challenge of pretending to know things exhausting, David Ahern shaved off his beard and absconded to work in television. He became an award-winning writer, director and producer, creating international documentary series.

For no particular reason, David Ahern embarked on writing the Madam Tulip mysteries and enjoys pretending this is actual work. He lives in the beautiful West of Ireland with his wife, two cats and a vegetable garden of which he is inordinately proud.

To find out more about Madam Tulip and David Ahern, visit
www.davidahern.info

*Also by David Ahern*
MADAM TULIP

# Madam Tulip

## and the

# Knave of Hearts

DAVID AHERN

MALIN PRESS
Ireland

MALIN PRESS

First published 2016

This paperback edition published 2016

ISBN 978-0-9935448-2-8

Malin Press, Ireland

Malin Press is an imprint of Malin Film and Television Ltd

Registered in Ireland 309163

*Dedication*

For Sheila, aka Beezie


*Acknowledgements*

My special thanks to the wonderful people who generously read
and commented on the draft:

Ces Cassidy (editor-in-chief), Aisling Chambers, Sheila Flitton,
Stephen Flitton, Anne Kent, Patricia Mahon, Breda McCormack,
Iris Park, Wendy Smith.

# Madam Tulip

### and the

# Knave of Hearts

# 1

The one thing psychics rarely do, and for the best of reasons, is foretell their own future. Even if they're tempted to have a go, against all the advice of the ages, they need to be at least half awake. But on the day the arch gracing the stage of Dublin's Palace Theatre came tumbling down, Derry O'Donnell, actress of some talent but limited luck, was sound asleep.

Fortunately, the collapse happened at five a.m. on a Saturday, so no one was hurt. The stagehands were long gone, and actors rarely work at five a.m. At five a.m. and for that matter at eleven a.m., especially after an opening night party, actors don't do much of anything at all.

Around noon Derry O'Donnell opened a tentative eye, groaned, then remembered to be happy. The opening night had been a triumph. She knew that, because in the theatre bar after the show her friends and fellow actors had clustered round offering not the miserly and noncommittal 'Well done,' but the coveted and resounding endorsement, 'Darling!'

Derry smiled to herself, basking in the recollected glory of no fewer than three curtain calls. Her part was a satisfyingly chunky role, and she reckoned her performance had been good—not brilliant, but more than okay for a first night. Much more than okay. She smiled again then reminded herself sternly that the most important thing was not her own performance but the excellence of the play and the quality of the whole cast. For at least one full minute she maintained this pious fiction before admitting to herself she was lying through her teeth.

Derry's plan, if you could call anything so vague a plan, was that after several coffees to dispel the effects of an unwise quantity of wine at the after-show party, she would venture out to get the papers and see what the critics had to say. She was sure they'd love the play, a comedy satire crowd-pleasingly named *The Dead Politician*. But what would they say about her performance?

Derry had just opened her second eye and had made the first experimental moves of her head from left to right, then up and down, when her phone rang.

'I don't believe it!' said Bella.

'Um,' said Derry. 'Who?'

'Bella!' said Bella. 'Lucky no one was killed!'

'What?' said Derry, uncomfortably aware that whatever synapses connected her ears to her brain were still rubbing their eyes and wondering what day it was.

'The Palace!' said Bella. 'The proscenium arch fell down! The ceiling collapsed and the stage is in bits. It'll take weeks to fix. Months! Imagine, it could have happened during the show!'

'In bits?' said Derry.

'Total bits.'

Derry frowned. The second day of a widely publicised run of a guaranteed crowd-pleaser was just the time when a stage was absolutely not optional.

'They'll have to cancel!' announced Bella.

'They can't!' said Derry.

'They'll have to,' countered Bella. 'Do you think they're insured?'

Derry thought about that. The theatre might well be

insured. The producers too. But she was certain the actors were not. She mentally slapped herself for being selfish and stupid. The crew, the cleaners, the staff who manned the box-office, many had families to support. Derry had no one to worry about but herself. When you looked at it that way, reviews didn't seem to matter so much.

'Derry,' said Bella. 'I really am sorry.'

'Thanks.' She knew Bella meant it.

'Oh, by the way,' said Bella, 'your review was terrific.'

'What?' squealed Derry. 'Where? What did he say? I can't believe that monster Farrelly said anything good—'

'Twas he,' said Bella. 'No, really. Glowing. Do you want me to read it?'

In the universe of unnecessary questions, where all redundant queries answer themselves for all eternity, the most unnecessary is when one actor asks another would they like them to read aloud a glowing review.

Certain words stick in the minds of an actor to be cherished forever. They include *powerful, charismatic,* and *definitive*—all in this case deliciously applied to Derry's performance—and *stunning, hilarious and tour de force* describing the production. The show was going to be a hit.

Or was.

Of course, now it wasn't.

Even as Derry was talking to Bella, her phone pinged several times announcing missed calls. Derry didn't have to look to know who were the callers—her fellow actors, the director, maybe even the producer—though not likely yet; he'd be either hiding or having a nervous breakdown.

'At least you got the review,' said Bella. 'The evening

papers will be full of what happened.' She paused. 'Shame. All that publicity going to waste.'

# 2

At six thirty that same fateful Saturday, Derry sat in a spartan hotel meeting room. Right now she should have been getting into costume for the show. Instead she, the rest of the cast and the theatre staff were perched on orange plastic chairs while the theatre manager delivered the appalling news. The theatre would be closed indefinitely. The building was sound, but the stage area and auditorium could be out of commission for a long time. In fact, the theatre might close for good, as nobody yet had the faintest idea where the funds for an expensive restoration would come from.

The room sat in deathly silence as the manager handed over to the show's producer. He looked shell-shocked, possibly wondering who to fear most, the anxious crowd in front of him or the bankers whose calls he had dodged all day. Answering the obvious questions took no more than five minutes. No alternative theatre could be found. Every venue in the city had shows in for the entire season. The room lapsed into despairing silence.

The meeting ended, the Producer thanking everyone for coming, as though they had done him some kind of favour. For a while, small knots of people stood around whispering, but most quickly drifted away. The whole awful business had taken less than thirty minutes.

Derry couldn't bear to talk to anyone. She slipped out to a nearby bar where Bella had promised she would be drinking in sympathy.

Dublin city centre was doing what it always does at seven o'clock on a Saturday night—putting on its finery, doing its hair, having a quick belt of something strong to counter the outrageous cost of drinking in the bars, and heading out to clock the Talent. The aim is to end the night in the most sociable way possible but without being accused of having absolutely no taste whatsoever.

On this fateful Saturday evening, as Derry and Bella sat side by side in silence at the back of the pub, neither were the least interested in the Talent. For Derry, this wasn't unusual—in affairs of the heart her recent history had been, to say the least, complicated. But for Bella, abstinence was a gesture of solidarity with a suffering fellow actor and best friend. Derry fully appreciated the sacrifice, though she did notice that a rockabilly band setting up on a little stage in the far corner had caught Bella's attention, much as a small scampering furry thing catches the attention of a terrier. Bella emitted little humming noises, tuneless but expressive.

'What if it stays closed?' said Derry.

'Naw,' said Bella, her attention fixed on the cute guitarist waiting with charming helplessness for the bass player to show him where to plug his instrument. 'Come on, it's a landmark. You can't close the Palace.'

Derry remembered the stunned face of the theatre manager and the frightened looks of the staff. 'They weren't saying, but I think they know it's bad. More than just a quick fix. How can they keep people on without shows to pay the bills? Poor Jasmine and Lorna.'

In traditional Irish lore, naming a person, living or dead, will conjure up their presence—a good reason to be careful if your circle includes anyone you would prefer not to knock on your door on a dark night. But in this case, the spirits summoned were benevolence itself. Jasmine and Lorna were Wardrobe Mistresses of the Palace theatre. Or, Derry reflected gloomily, soon to be ex-Mistresses.

'Thought you guys would be here,' announced Jasmine, her vast bulk blocking the light, her frizzy red hair alarmingly backlit. She turned to the elf-like Lorna by her side. 'Would you do the honours sweetheart? You guys okay?' she asked Derry and Bella, indicating their half-empty glasses.

The question was of course rhetorical. Penniless practitioners of the theatrical arts will go to extraordinary lengths to avoid bankrupting themselves buying a round of drinks. Actors have been known to feign epilepsy with all the conviction of a trained professional. Such excesses are met with general disapproval. Faking a call from one's agent should suffice and would add to one's cachet, neatly killing two birds with one stone.

'No, we're fine, thanks,' said Derry, sticking to the script.

Jasmine squeezed herself into a chair. 'Banjaxed,' she announced.

Derry and Bella nodded silently.

'At least Wardrobe was alright,' said Jasmine. 'No costumes damaged. I hear management's not too worried about the building, but the stage will cost a fortune to repair. Meanwhile, we're all on the scrapheap.'

'Surely they can fix whatever it is in a month or two?' said Bella.

'Uh-uh,' said Jasmine. 'That's not what I hear. Could take yonks. And where do they get the cash?'

Lorna slipped in beside them, delivering a foaming pint of beer and a demure glass of port. Lorna was so beautiful, delicate and eternally youthful, she made Derry think of fairy raths and changelings.

'Thanks, hon,' said Jasmine. She sipped her port while Lorna took a mighty swig of her beer.

'You've heard of sugar-daddies?' enquired Lorna sweetly. 'How about a sugar-momma?' She turned to Jasmine. 'We could try.'

Jasmine scowled. In a competition to recruit a suitable sugar-momma with an eye for the girls, oodles of cash and a penchant for paying other people's electricity bills, Lorna would win hands down.

'Only jokin'!' said Lorna, with an innocent smile, fooling nobody.

The bar was filling up. The rockabilly band would play within the hour if, rumour had it, someone would volunteer to fetch the drummer's drums. Meanwhile, what was there to talk about? Every stab at conversation turned once more to the Palace. So intent were the four on their own miserable thoughts, they didn't notice the shambling male figure edging its way to their table in an approximation of the urge to socialise.

'Well banjaxed,' said Frankie.

The four nodded.

'Mind if I join yez?'

Any other person would take the shrugs that greeted Frankie's polite request as an unambiguous and resounding *No*. They might also detect a subtle nuance signalling please go away, and on your way out tell anyone without halitosis and with two atoms of charm to come on in. But subtle nuances were as lost on Frankie as the aroma of distant hamburger to a cactus.

Frankie, the Palace's stage-door keeper and general dogsbody, was said to be older than the hundred-and-fifty-year-old building. Rumour had it that Frankie had been conceived backstage during dress rehearsals via the hurried congress of a pantomime dame and a chorus girl trying to win a bet.

'Bella!' said Frankie. Frankie counted himself Bella's friend since the first time she played the Palace. Bella had thought it politic to buy him a drink, not realising she was only the second person to do so in the whole of Frankie's adult life. The first was an American graduate student who imagined that Frankie could give him priceless insights into the lives of Ireland's theatrical legends. He soon learned that all Frankie's stories were about how he had saved said legends from destroying their careers through the barely sentient idiocies that were all you could expect from actors.

'Is that last orders they're calling?' enquired Frankie.

'Frankie, it's not even eight o'clock, stop worrying,' said Lorna. She answered sincerely, as if the question had been a genuine enquiry rather than a cue for someone, anyone but himself, to go to the bar for another round.

Jasmine gazed dotingly on Lorna, as if struck afresh by the innocent and uncynical nature of her partner of two whole years. 'You really are a sweet girl,' she said. 'But you shouldn't talk to strange men.'

'She's known me for six years!' protested Frankie. 'Since she was two.'

'I said strange, not unfamiliar,' said Jasmine. 'You'd better hurry and get that drink before the bar closes.'

'How time flies when you're having fun,' answered Frankie. He got to his feet. 'Do you know what it is?' he asked, in that rhetorical way of the true Dubliner. 'No one uses their heads in this gaffe.'

'Except you Frankie, is that right?' said Bella, her steel tooth glinting.

'It's as well someone has a head to use, let me tell you,' retorted Frankie. 'The only difference between today and yesterday is we don't have a stage. We have a theatre; we just do not have a stage. No stage, no actors. Sounds like heaven to me.'

Derry laughed. 'Come on, you can't have a theatre without actors!'

'Haven't we got two great big eff-off bars?' replied Frankie. 'What do we need actors for? Sure they only clutter up the place. Drive you to distraction with their whinging.' He vanished into the crowd until all that could be seen was his head bobbing up and down as he tried vainly to get noticed at the bar in a scrum of six-foot men with quiffs.

'He's right about one thing,' said Bella. The others stared in astonishment. The idea that Frankie could be right about anything made the head reel. 'No, really. Everyone is being so negative. What we don't have is—'

'Jobs?' Derry couldn't help adding. Ungrammatical, but justified under the circumstances.

'This is all so negative,' repeated Bella. She thumped the table. 'I mean come on, you have to say No to Negativity! Frankie the old shyster said it right. If the rest of the theatre is okay, management can open the bars. Make a few quid. Pay the staff.'

'They could do it,' said Derry thoughtfully. 'Keep the doors open, pay some salaries.' She was shamefully aware she sounded less than wholehearted. She should have been celebrating this new hope for the theatre staff without privately lamenting that, however many bars were kept open, no actors would be paid. Maybe Frankie was right about the whinging. She tried again. 'That really is a great idea! And whenever they fix the stage, the theatre would be ready to get up and running.'

Gloom settled once more as all realised that keeping the building open was only a good thing if the stage could indeed be fixed. That could cost millions.

'Arts Council?' said Derry.

Jasmine shook her head. 'You'd spend six months filling out forms, then get the price of a few cartridge refills—maybe. Haven't they salaries to pay?'

'Their own,' snarled Bella, whose antipathy to the arts establishment was well known. In her one and only featured profile in a national newspaper Bella had famously described the arts bureaucrats as 'a crowd of wankers who think drama is role-playing ethnicity awareness in a five-star hotel.'

'The government?' suggested Lorna.

Bella's lip curled. 'Aye, they could sell a few spare Mercedes.'

'But Bella is right,' said Derry. 'We should be thinking positive. 'Why not ask people to give money? Dubliners love their theatres, right? Back in the States people make donations. Rich folks give millions to the Arts.'

The idea of rich Irish people contributing millions to

11

anything much beyond a penthouse in Monaco and a private jet made the others purse their lips. Scepticism was in the air.

'Ordinary people would give. Honest. I really think they would,' insisted Derry.

'Someone could start a fund,' said Bella.

Jasmine snorted. 'Someone would run off with it.'

'Don't be so cynical!' said Derry. Being mostly American, she was shocked at how the Irish vastly preferred to believe the worst of everybody, and would continue to do so until the facts proved they didn't know the half of it.

'You put together a committee. Make a plan,' Derry continued. 'Then you try to get loads of publicity. Like a campaign.'

Derry felt justifiably proud of this businesslike observation. In the years since she graduated in Theatre Arts from Trinity College Dublin she had won many plaudits for her acting, but none at all for her commercial acumen. Most of those years had been spent flat broke and with her mother subsidising her little rented apartment. That same mother, the wildly successful owner of modern art galleries in New York, London and Dublin had more than once referred to Derry as 'my artistically successful, albeit penniless, aging, unmarried daughter with questionable fashion sense.' Derry had been outraged. The part about the fashion sense was totally untrue.

'What we need are some fund-raising events,' added Derry, slipping comfortably into the persona of marketing guru extraordinaire.

'What, like a marathon?' asked Bella, feeling no need to disguise her horror at the thought of running for anything other than the last taxi at five in the morning.

'Um, can't see that, exactly,' admitted Derry. An actors' marathon seemed as unpromising as a truck drivers' beauty contest.

'Raffles?' suggested Jasmine.

'The prize could be Frankie,' said Bella, sniggering.

'That's cruel,' Lorna observed, making the others feel guilty. 'How about Burlesque?' she said, casually. 'It's very popular just now. Art form, really.'

'Art form my arse!' snapped Jasmine. 'A degrading spectacle for disgusting men. And women!' she added darkly, glaring at Lorna who wore her innocent-fawn-in-the-woods expression.

'How about a street party?' suggested Bella.

'Meh,' said Jasmine. 'Can't see the neighbours making cup-cakes.' The neighbours of the Palace Theatre were mostly bars catering to stag parties—hordes of drunken revellers whose uses for a cupcake could prove unorthodox. 'And if we had free drink we'd have a hundred thousand Dubs at the door. Plus hangers-on.'

'I've an idea,' said Derry. 'We could have an art exhibition. Hey, maybe my mother could do something. Like a celebrity artists' show. Famous people paint a picture or draw a cartoon, and sign it, and we sell the works for gazillions.'

Derry felt sure her suggestion was inspired. In fact, it was almost certainly proof of a heightened and well-developed creativity, as might be expected of the ex-supporting female in the almost-successful comic masterpiece *The Dead Politician*. She wasn't one bit surprised when the others failed to laugh derisively. Instead, they scratched their noses, frowned and wiggled their eyebrows.

'I like it,' said Bella.

'We could have the exhibition in the foyer and an auction in one of the bars,' added Jasmine.

'Is Management going to go with all this? Sounds like the lunatics have taken over the asylum,' said Bella.

'Money talks,' said Jasmine.

No one doubted she was right.

'Derry could tell fortunes! Madam Tulip would make a packet! Ow!' Bella rubbed her shin. 'What? I mean, like, what!'

Jasmine and Lorna looked away tactfully. Although sworn to secrecy, they knew something of the dramatic events of early summer. To help Derry make some desperately needed cash, they had helped her create Madam Tulip, a fortune-teller who would entertain at society events, parties and celebrity gatherings. But, for Tulip and Derry O'Donnell, what had started as a simple way to make some money had turned into a nightmare.

Madam Tulip was a source of great professional pride to Jasmine and Lorna. They had deployed all their skills in costume, hair and makeup to help Derry create a sophisticated, if amply proportioned, character who would inspire respect and confidence. That Derry O'Donnell was uniquely qualified was even more satisfactory. As the daughter of a seventh son of a seventh son, Derry had powers of perception that could only be described as psychic. But Madam Tulip's first gigs, a celebrity charity event and a famous supermodel's birthday treat, had each ended in a horrible death.

Not once in the months since had Derry O'Donnell reprised her role as Madam Tulip. Her beautiful costume with its pearls and feather headdress had lain unused, carefully packed in the closet of her little bedroom. To her intense relief, neither had Derry experienced again the strange premonitions and obscure visions almost routine during that time. Perhaps the gift had left her for good. Maybe that was for the best.

'I must bring you back the costume,' she said.

'No!' said Jasmine. 'You don't mean it. It was the shock. Bad associations.'

'Negative vibes,' added Lorna.

'And we know about those,' said Bella darkly. 'I keep telling ye; what you have to do is—'

She didn't get a chance to finish. The other three chanted in unison. 'Say No to Negativity!' They raised their glasses and clinked.

Strangely, almost at once everyone seemed to feel a little better. Only then did Derry realise that for months she had been living in shadow, hardly aware of an indefinable sadness. And now, on a day that should have been nothing but misery, the shadow was gone.

# 3

'Darling! I just heard the news! You should have told me! I'm appalled!'

Impossible to tell whether Vanessa was appalled by what had happened to the Palace Theatre or that Derry hadn't instantly called her mother so she could in turn phone her friends with hot news.

'I would *sooo* have been there for you!'

'Hi Mom,' said Derry. In a more cynical mood, Derry might have reflected that Vanessa's version of *there* could mean an exhibition in Los Angeles or a weekend party in an English stately home; and if you happened to be invited too, well that was just awesome. 'Where are you now?'

'London, sweetheart. And to think I was feeling guilty about missing your wonderful opening night. But there's no need now, is there.'

'No, I understood. Dad couldn't be there either; he's in England too. You didn't meet up?'

'England has sixty million people darling; your father could avoid me in a room of ten. Has he called you? I need to speak with him.'

Derry refused to be drawn on the subject of her father. Jacko and her mother had been divorced for years but still acted like besotted high-school teens or deadly enemies, according to some weird chemistry Derry could never fathom. Jacko was a hugely famous though permanently broke artist, and Vanessa was still his agent, a source of inevitable friction. In Jacko's mind, agents and their galleries were the real-life inspiration for Dracula and his castle. In Vanessa's mind, artists were impossible children who would starve out of sheer incompetence if someone didn't take them in hand.

'How was the exhibition?' Derry asked, prudently side stepping the subject of fathers. Vanessa had a new show opening at her gallery near London's fashionable Bond Street. Her exhibitions were a cultural event, and her clients French tax exiles, Russian oligarchs and British aristocrats with property portfolios worth more than middle-sized countries.

'If I told you who showed up, you would not believe me in one million years!' Vanessa's voice quavered with the irresistible urge to tell.

Derry debated with herself. The script demanded she beg to be told who was this wonderful personage. On the other hand, with Vanessa you had to grab what little victories you could, because you would never win big ones. Vanessa had thoughtfully left a conversational space into which Derry was expected to insert her question. Derry declined, instead leaving silence to fill the void with nothing at all.

'Hello! Can you hear me? Hello?'

'Here Mom,' said Derry, allowing herself a smile.

'Did I mention we had a special person show up?'

Derry couldn't find it in her heart to take a hard line; her mother was a maniac as a parent but a wonderful person if you took the broadest view.

'Who was that?' asked Derry.

'Well, if I said that she said, "*We* enjoyed the pictures very much indeed," you'll know who I mean!' Vanessa's voice rose to a pitch she normally reserved for describing stupendously large sums denominated in dollars.

'I'm sorry?' said Derry. Usually she had no problem grasping what her mother meant, especially when it followed the strict formula indicated by *you'll never guess who*.

'Honey!' said Vanessa, her exasperation bordering on a plea. 'I said, SHE said "WE enjoyed" et cetera! SHE! WE!'

'I'm sorry, Mom, am I missing something here?'

'WE ARE NOT AMUSED! FRANCIS DRAKE! GOOD QUEEN—you know!'

'Oh,' said Derry. For once she was genuinely impressed. 'That's really something. Did she buy a picture?'

'That is not the point! Of course she didn't. She already owns half the pictures in England. Where would she put more for goodness' sake? Do be sensible, darling.'

'Well congratulations, anyhow.'

'Thank you dear. Now. This business of your theatre falling down—'

'It did not fall down, Mom, not all of it, just the ceiling over the stage.'

'I hope it's not bad luck,' said Vanessa, showing no interest in fine architectural distinctions.

'I don't see what other kind of luck it could have been,' said Derry, unsure where this was heading. A lifetime's experience of her mother's byzantine thought processes had taught Derry to be vigilant. 'The stage staff are probably out of their jobs. Some have families.'

'You do seem to have had a lot of bad luck lately,' Vanessa followed up. 'Are you sure it's not… you know… *you*, dear?

'Mom!'

'What about that awful business on the boat. That was you too!'

What can you say to the accusation that two unfortunate things that occurred in your life were suspiciously connected by the indisputable fact that they both happened to you?

'I've always said we make our own luck darling. This acting business, and that silly fortune telling scheme—let's face it, you tried,' continued Vanessa, clinching her case.

Whenever anyone says you tried, they usually mean you failed. Derry had no doubt failure was what Vanessa implied.

'I did well!' insisted Derry.

'Did you get paid?'

'Yes!'

'Really? I thought he was dead.'

'Mom! That's… how can you say—?'

'Did you get paid or did you not? I enquire in the spirit of a supportive yet focused business mentor. I presume it was a business darling and not a means of whiling away the idle hours?'

'I got paid for the first part, the celebrity auction at the castle. It was a huge success.'

'Oh darling,' said Vanessa with a sigh. 'I do appreciate your determination. But it's time for real life. Remember what we talked about?'

Derry could hardly forget. Her mother was determined she should give up her acting career and become her Public Relations person in New York. The prospect was horrifying. Derry loved acting more than she had ever loved doing anything. Acting involved speaking the most wonderful lines ever written, bringing people in imagination to magical places, moving them to laughter and tears. Acting also involved dressing up, lots of makeup, showing off and—with luck—being hugely admired by loads of people all at once.

'Mom, how could I live in New York? Or London? I've been here so long now. Dublin is my home. All my friends are here.' Although Derry was American by birth and upbringing, her father Jacko was Irish. Derry had grown up between New York and Ireland, and when her parents divorced by mutual and friendly consent, and with barely concealed sighs of relief, Derry had moved to Ireland to study drama.

'What is it with you young people?' declared Vanessa. 'Friends are for Facebook. And if you must have real ones, you can Skype.' She paused to let her words sink in. 'Did I mention I was talking to Meryl?'

No need to wonder which of the planet's millions of Meryls Vanessa meant. 'She said—and she was quite adamant about this—"over thirty years of age an actress is invisible; producers just don't want to know." From the horse's mouth, darling.'

Derry guessed that to be quoted so freely, Meryl must have bought paintings from Vanessa. Whether she would have liked being quoted as a horse was more doubtful, but Meryl had made a point it was hard to deny. As an actress, the older you got the more unemployed you got, unless you were very lucky indeed.

'That is not true,' said Derry, who knew perfectly well it was true. 'Meryl is proof. Age hasn't stopped her getting wonderful parts.'

'*But do we know what she has to do?*' enquired Vanessa darkly. 'One hesitates to imagine.'

The thought made Derry's mind swim. She was about to protest the implication was outrageous, but Vanessa had moved on. 'I didn't want to bring this up again after your awful experience, but it's for your own good dear—'

A diversion was called for. And right now. 'I have a publicity idea for your gallery, Mom. You want to hear it?'

'Oh,' said Vanessa, in the tone she might have used if her Persian cat had suggested a menu to include cod roe and lightly smoked ham. 'I suppose so.'

'We're planning some fundraisers to pay for repairs to the theatre. Raffles, marathons, that kind of thing.'

'Marathons? Those appalling shorts!'

'That's not my idea, Mom. I'm thinking of a celebrity art exhibition. You get famous people to make a little drawing or painting and sign it. Or they donate a painting from their collection. We have a show at the theatre and auction the pictures. The whole thing organised by your famous gallery.'

For a moment, silence. An uncanny state of affairs in any conversation with Vanessa.

'The press will go wild,' added Derry hopefully. 'Famous people love the Palace. It's a landmark.'

'Hired,' said Vanessa.

'You like it?'

'Why didn't you tell me?'

'Mom?'

'Nobody tells me anything. Did your father know?'

'Mom?'

'Why should I be surprised you may be clever? I am your mother. Darling, that's brilliant! You can start tomorrow morning.'

'Mom?'

'You needn't worry about getting up early, I know you acting people don't like that. We can pretend we're on New

York time. Your first proper job, darling. I can't believe it, you're going to be useful!'

'But Mom—'

'And I thought I was going to be hiring you just to keep you off the streets. Welcome aboard darling! Must rush, but I'm so excited we'll be working together at last! Call you tomorrow, New York time.' She laughed happily. 'You will so enjoy your new job, sweetheart. And I promise, you will meet *such* interesting people.'

Before Derry could say another word, Vanessa was gone.

# 4

Vanessa was right about the interesting people.

In its long and colourful history, the Palace Theatre had seen its fair share of big personalities. But the egos gathered for the Save Our Theatre Celebrity Art Auction could hardly have been contained by a building ten times its size.

Ever-expanding bubbles of self-regard filled the crowded bars. The President of Ireland was busily claiming that the Irish invented Music Hall, in fact invented music. The Arts Minister was refusing to be embarrassed that his government wouldn't pay for the theatre to be restored and instead congratulated himself and his party for several centuries of Irish literary achievement. So many celebrities turned up no one could be rude to the harassed bar staff in case they turned out to be a Somebody. The event promised to be a roaring success.

Derry parked herself on one of the bar's plush velvet banquettes at a table reserved for Vanessa's guests and observed the crowd. She had nearly worn her favourite dress, a 1950s Audrey Hepburn rockabilly number guaranteed to wow the cognoscenti, but had changed her mind at the last minute, nearly making herself late. Instead, she was resplendent in a silky black Victorian garment, full length, sleeveless, with ruffles down the front. Vanessa had frowned. She could recognise designers at a thousand yards in near pitch dark, but the Victorians didn't go in for ostentatious labelling. 'You say it's an antique dear,' she said, 'but how are we supposed to know it's not just old?'

For the three weeks building up to auction day, Derry had worked for Vanessa at her mother's Dublin gallery. The experience left her feeling like she had just stepped off one of those crazy spinning machines they use to train astronauts. A typical day with Vanessa started with her being pained that you hadn't done something she hadn't asked you to do. Next would come a stream of instructions overflowing with pronouns. 'It's being picked up by the couriers at three—can you look after it dear? He'll be testing the fire-alarm at four, can you let her know?' Vanessa would then disappear on some urgent mission, leaving Derry baffled. Derry knew that somehow she would have to tell her mother she couldn't go on. She might end up tossing burgers, as Vanessa had so often predicted, but at least with a burger you knew where you stood.

All the same, Derry's sacrifice had been worthwhile. Her idea for an auction had blossomed into collective action. It seemed everyone who had ever worked at the Palace was lending a hand. Jasmine and Lorna were showing the VIPs to their tables. Bella was selling exhibition catalogues for an exorbitant price while flirting shamelessly with guests she deemed musically credible. Bruce Adams, Derry's actor friend and fellow American, was placing pictures for sale on the display easel and removing them with all due ceremony as each was auctioned off. Six foot four with chiselled chin and toned physique, impeccably dressed in dinner jacket and bow tie, Bruce was a magnet for the eyes of middle-aged women in the audience. Perhaps they failed to discern that Bruce's recreational interests lay elsewhere. Then again, they may not have cared.

Presiding over all was the regal figure of Vanessa, exquisitely clad in Dior. Her hair was a work of art, and her jewellery glinted with that smug assurance hinting at loads more at home. She stood on the auctioneer's podium with the poise of a President of the United States giving a press conference. Gracing the front of her lectern was the eye-catching logo of her Caravaggio Galleries, a shameless and largely successful grab for whatever credit was due. Derry protested, but Vanessa said something about synergy, and how the distinction between public and private, business and charity, giving and receiving was so last century. Hadn't Derry heard of social entrepreneurship?

Vanessa was expertly wooing the crowd. One after the other, at bewildering speed, she despatched paintings, cartoons, drawings and collages—each sale accompanied by rounds of self-congratulatory applause from the room. The pictures were mostly signed by names familiar to anybody who read the Sunday supplements, but a few were donations from established artists of real fame. One of those artists, a painting of whose had already sold for a respectable sum, was now threading his way towards Derry's table at the back. He was tall and well-built, with a mane of wild hair, and wore a green riding cape, a broad belt and an oversize tin star saying 'Sheriff.'

Jacko O'Donnell waved airily to the President, oblivious to whether or not the President waved back, before squeezing in beside Derry on her velvet banquette. Jacko's only concession to the crowded tables around was to refrain from lighting the cigar he waved expansively, but he seemed to enjoy spreading alarm and disapproval.

'Hi Dad,' said Derry, giving him a kiss. 'Hey, thanks for coming.'

'Wouldn't miss it for the world, dear child,' said Jacko,

plonking his cowboy-booted feet on the table. 'You look marvellous, but I came to admire your mother. Normally art dealers do their lying, cheating and larceny behind closed doors. This is like seeing a zombie in daylight—you don't know whether to laugh or run.'

'Stop it,' said Derry, lifting Jacko's feet and dropping them where they belonged. 'You promised you'd be good.'

'Good? Isn't the Pope persecuted with people telling him what a saint I am, to be sure, and I should be canonised tout suite. I told him I'm not interested 'till I'm dead; then he can do what he likes.'

'Mom has done an amazing job,' insisted Derry, loyally. 'Doesn't matter how important the bidders are, they eat out of her hand. She's raised a fortune.'

As Derry spoke, Vanessa proved the point by winding the room to fever pitch over a nondescript watercolour of a castle painted by a prominent British Royal. Until now, Vanessa's voice as she introduced each picture had been carefully modulated—for the professionals, deep and venerating; for the amateurs, comical and just on the right side of condescending. But if a voice could be said to curtsy, bow and simper all at once, that's what Vanessa's voice was doing now as she announced that the Royal Picture had been generously donated by the Dowager Countess of Berkshire, England.

'Such an honour!' crowed Vanessa. 'Graciously signed with His Very Own Hand,' she added, as though the Royal in question usually delegated the actual signing part to a minion, but in this case went the extra mile.

A reverent hush greeted the bidding. The offers came briskly. A modest sum might acquire a painting by a future King of England (if the other contenders for the throne had some terminally bad luck).

'I've never understood why the Irish are so keen on the British Royal Family,' observed Derry to Jacko in a whisper. 'You know—all that bad history. You'd think they'd have a grudge.'

'Sure what has history to do with it, at all?' replied Jacko. 'Isn't it a grand show, with all the parades and marriages and scandals galore? All paid for by the British taxpayer, God bless them. We Irish say thank you very much; do carry on.'

As Vanessa brought down her gavel on an impressive winning bid for the Royal Work, Jacko showed surprisingly few signs of outrage. Derry expected disparaging remarks about the style, the technique and the subject, or at least a suggestion that someone should have a quiet word with the perpetrator, Royal or no Royal. But Jacko seemed strangely unperturbed.

'*Your* picture went for a fair price,' observed Derry, wondering if there lay the secret of her father's good humour. Jacko had turned up too late to see his own work auctioned, perhaps deliberately.

'Fair enough,' said Jacko. 'Can't complain at all, at all,' he added. Derry found herself thinking of a fox emerging from a hen coop covered in feathers and grinning. The image, vivid and startling, gave way to an especially smug-looking owl that blinked. Or was it a wink?

'A telephone bid?' said Jacko.

Derry nodded. The bidder who bought Jacko's painting for a healthy sum was indeed an anonymous telephone caller. A suspicion dawned. 'You didn't! Your own picture!'

'Certainly not,' protested Jacko, prepared to be offended.

'Who then?'

Jacko pretended to whistle an imagined tune.

'Mom bought it herself?'

'Supporting the market, my dear. Can't have a picture of mine sold on the cheap because a room full of gobshites can't tell the difference between a work of art and a souvenir of Buckingham Palace. Nothing illegal as long as the picture's not bought back for more than the reserve price. Which in this case it was.' He wiggled his eyebrows.

'I thought she was looking a bit shifty,' said Derry thoughtfully. 'I imagined it was because she meant to claim her commission, charity or no charity.'

'Take it as a compliment to your integrity that she didn't ask you to make the fake bid. She knew you for an honest soul. Art is a dirty business, as you will discover now you're Personal Assistant to the dark side. But vice wilts in the pure light of virtue.' Jacko put on his most pious expression. If his daughter was virtuous, the laws of inheritance would award himself a good slice of the credit.

'Wow, she'll have to write a cheque to the theatre fund.'

'And to yours truly. No way out of it.'

'She won't be happy,' observed Derry.

'And that's not the only cheque coming to yours truly,' said Jacko. His eyes sparkled. 'I think I've sold the Corrib Series.'

'Hey, congratulations!' said Derry. And congratulations were deserved. The Series was a collection of six pictures with an eye-watering price tag, but which Jacko believed with justification to be his best work. 'Who's the buyer?'

'A German billionaire,' said Jacko, rolling the syllables around his tongue like a Belgian chocolate. 'He's off on his yacht for a month, then he'll do the deal.'

'But aren't the pictures in London?' The pictures were prominently displayed in Vanessa's London gallery and had been for some time, as even the gallery's richest patrons winced at the price tag.

'True, that's where Herr Billionaire saw them; but then he jetted over to my studio, wondering whether the services of a dealer were needed at all.'

'You can't cut out your agent!' said Derry. 'Even if she is Mom. And look what happened—'

'You do me an injustice, child,' retorted Jacko. 'How could I deny a sucking leech her meal of an artist's precious life-blood? Anyhow, the pictures are, as you say, in her gallery.' He eyed Derry speculatively. 'A favour to your old Da? When the deal is done, they'll need to be packed and despatched to Herr Billionaire. Would you see to it for me? I know you'd look after them, not like the ham-fisted interns Vanessa takes on because daddy's got a title.'

'Sure I would,' said Derry. 'But Mom hasn't said anything about me going to London. Anyhow, I don't think I'll be in the job for long, to be honest. It's... not been easy. I've only been doing it for the sake of the auction.'

'Ah,' said Jacko. He gave a Derry a sympathetic look as though reading her mind, which of course he might well have been doing. As the seventh son of a seventh son, Jacko had what might be called paranormal powers if they were any use at all, which they rarely were. Jacko had been known to lament that his more or less pointless supernatural talents mirrored the story of his native island—abundant creative gifts in art, poetry and music, when what was really needed was a drop or two of oil and a sovereign wealth fund.

It was thanks to Jacko that Derry had what modest psychic powers she possessed, and Jacko seemed to operate on some wavelength she couldn't tune out. Or maybe this unavoidable empathy was just family stuff, and everybody did it. As a child, you learned to read your parents thoughts as the quickest way to get out of trouble or get that cool red bicycle for Christmas.

'So what are you going to do with all that cash—I mean if the sale goes through?' asked Derry, avoiding the tricky subject of her nonexistent career as Vanessa's PA.

'Aha!' said Jacko. 'Oho!' he added, in case any doubt remained that he was mightily pleased. 'Can't say.'

'Oh come on!'

'I'll give you a hint,' said Jacko. 'Once upon a time in the far West, there were the O'Donnells—warriors and chieftains of the Gaelic nobility. Have I mentioned this before?'

'Not more than a thousand times,' answered Derry. Suddenly, she had a startling vision of Jacko wearing a coronet, being serenaded in a medieval feasting hall by an incongruously large-chested harpist. Incongruous because, as far as Derry knew, harpists in old Ireland were always male, while this one most definitely was not.

'Don't tell me you're going to buy a title! I don't believe it!'

'Certainly not! Sure why would a direct descendant of the third greatest of the O'Donnells need to buy a title? I believe the English invented titles because you couldn't tell an English noble just from the look of him.' His grin grew broader. 'Another guess?'

Derry never did get a chance to guess again. In the room, the crowd fell silent as Bruce reverently bore a small painting to the display easel. You could tell from Vanessa's dramatic pose that here was a star piece.

'Oho-ho!' whispered Jacko under his breath, his eyes fixed on the stage.

'Here we have a masterpiece,' breathed Vanessa. 'Mr. President, Madam President, Ladies and gentlemen, I present to you an exceptional picture by a Russian master of the avant-garde, Sikorsky's *Man in Reverse Order*. I would love to tell you by whom this marvellous work was most generously donated, but the donor insists on remaining anonymous. This is an exceptional opportunity. I'm starting the bidding at twenty thousand euro.'

The sum was far more than anything yet sold. But no hands were raised. No cards were waved. Was that because the Russian avant-garde was just too avant-garde for the rich and famous of modern Ireland? Or was it that the genius Sikorsky was far too dead to invite the buyer to parties?

Vanessa lowered the bidding to fifteen thousand euro, but still no takers. 'Ladies and gentlemen, only three of Sikorsky's paintings have reached the open market in over eighty years. This is a truly exceptional opportunity for the connoisseur collector.'

'Any idea what the reserve might be, at all?' whispered Jacko.

'Not a clue. Are you bidding?' asked Derry, astonished. Although Jacko had quietly acquired numerous works by painters he admired over the years—mostly, she suspected, by challenging the owner to a drunken game of chance—offering to buy with real money and at a public auction was unprecedented.

'Let me tell you,' said Jacko, 'there's more geniuses amongst those Russians than in the rest of the world put together. I'd never sleep again if I missed it. And that's a fact.' Derry saw that Jacko was genuinely troubled.

'Then why not bid?'

'Wouldn't I be afraid I'd bankrupt meself? What if I get carried away? Go on, help your old Da out. Just this once. Take a little peek?'

'No,' said Derry firmly. Jacko had a regrettable habit of trying to recruit Derry's modest but respectable powers as an aid to winning bets on horses, dogs, boats or anything that moved from A to B fast enough to collect a crowd. To his eternal frustration, Jacko's own psychic powers seemed to fail when he gambled. So disastrous was Jacko's record that his friends reckoned his uncanny ability to lose money at the racetrack could only be accounted for by supernatural agencies sympathetic to bookies.

Again Vanessa extolled the genius of the late Russian—the profound insight, the incomparable compositional mastery, the inevitably increasing asset value. Still the room was silent but for the rustling of expensively dressed bottoms on velvet chairs and the secretive craning of necks as the audience tried to spot anyone with the remotest idea of what they were looking at.

'The reserve!' whispered Jacko, desperation in his voice 'I need to know what's the cheapest she'll let it go for!'

Derry's lifelong mission was to learn as little as possible about her mother's business of art galleries and auctions, but she did know about reserve prices. The auctioneer always set a secret price below which they wouldn't sell. Instead, they would withdraw the piece or buy it themselves. Extracting the reserve price from Vanessa was about as likely as getting details of her Swiss bank accounts or the name of that wonderful little man who does marvellous things with her hair colour and keeps secrets better than the CIA.

'No!' repeated Derry. 'Absolutely not.'

'Not even for the Da who bought you the reddest red bicycle in the whole of New York for Christmas when you were six?'

'Hey!' said Derry, recognising an underhand tactic when she saw one. In matters psychic, was there such a thing as hacking? 'Dad, come on. Just make a bid; it's all for the theatre fund anyhow. Pay the money! They could tear the place down, and it's been open since 1842. Or was it 1852?'

'Eighteen-fifty-two, you say?'

Derry felt weary. 'What's the difference? It's old.'

Jacko beamed. 'You're a darling!' He gave her a smacking kiss on the cheek before ostentatiously holding up both hands, palms open, all his fingers raised. Vanessa frowned, anxiously scanning the room for other bidders. But even Vanessa couldn't pretend not to see a hairy man in a green cape, with both arms in the air and a triumphant grin.

'I'm bid ten thousand. Any advance on ten?' announced Vanessa.

But no advance came, and Vanessa failed to rustle up even one more bid to beat the low-ball that hit her secret reserve smack in the middle of its carefully concealed forehead.

Vanessa slammed down her gavel with unnecessary force but managed an urbane smile as Jacko stood to receive the respectful applause of the room.

'Congratulations?' enquired Derry.

'Did you see her face? Ha ha! Bang on the money! You're a star!'

'I didn't do anything!'

'What's the difference!' announced Jacko.

'I'm sorry?'

'What's the difference? What you said.'

On the scale of one to ten in the impenetrable fog of O'Donnell family life, this one was at least a nine.

' "This place has been open since 1842," 'quoted Jacko. ' "Or was it 1852? Oh, what's the difference." The difference is, of course, ten!'

Derry stared. This had to be the most far-fetched proof of a psychic event in the history of far-fetched proofs. 'I didn't mean that!'

Jacko smiled. And again Derry saw in vivid Technicolor that smug-looking owl who blinked.

Or winked.

# 5

Only a handful of items remained to be auctioned. By now, the audience was ready to bolt for a convenient restaurant or any nightclub promising free champagne. On the podium, Vanessa had expertly read the signs and was racing through the sale.

So transfixed was Derry by Vanessa's mastery of the auctioneer's art that she almost failed to notice a startlingly beautiful woman waving to her from across the room. Smiling a perfect smile, the vision made her way through the crowd, heading for Derry's table. Heads turned to follow her movements. The face of almost every man in the place wore an idiot grin. Wives frowned and searched fruitlessly for something in the apparition to criticise.

Marlene O'Mara, the internationally famous model, was a world-class beauty. You couldn't help feeling that when Nature put her together, Nature was in an especially good mood and on top of its game. 'Derry! Honey!' cooed Marlene, clasping her in a huge hug.

Jacko stood, gallantly offering Marlene his seat. But Marlene had no need of Jacko's seat. Bruce was following urgently behind, a chair perched upside down on his head. Marlene graciously allowed Bruce to place the chair, and he stood beaming as she took her seat. To say that Bruce was in love with Marlene could never be strictly accurate, as Bruce was entirely dedicated to his orientation, but he seemed just as bewitched as other males. To Derry's eyes, Marlene looked happy—surprisingly so given the appalling events of only a few months ago.

'I asked Vanessa would she be my manager, she's such a genius,' said Marlene, laughing. 'She said she'd love to, but the other geniuses would be jealous and throw a hissy-fit.' She turned to Jacko, 'Did she mean you?' Incredibly, Jacko simpered—an extraordinary sight, like Henry the Eighth clucking over someone's embroidery.

On the podium, Vanessa was making a gushing speech of thanks. She announced the impressive total of funds raised for the theatre and was greeted by the hearty applause of a roomful of people thinking mostly about alcohol and food.

'Must go,' announced Jacko. 'I'm expected at an important barstool. Will you do me a favour, Derry me darling? Will you get the Sikorsky sent on to me? I'm headed back to Galway in the morning, and your mother might accidentally forget I ever made a bid. Never, ever trust an art dealer.' He beamed, hugged Derry, pecked Marlene demurely on the cheek and was gone.

'I'm so happy your Dad won my little donation,' Marlene said smiling.

'You gave the Sikorsky?' asked Derry. 'That was so generous. I didn't know you were an art buff.'

'Not me. Wouldn't know a Matisse from a string vest,' said Marlene. 'I bought the picture from your mother. She got it from a Russian dealer. It's got some kind of certificate saying it is whatever it is; that's all I know.' She paused. 'I owe you such a lot.'

Derry couldn't think of anything to say. When you nearly get yourself killed saving someone's life, you can't rightly shrug and mumble it was nothing. Or not without sounding like a jerk.

'Your show was pulled, right?' said Marlene.

'For the foreseeable, anyhow,' said Derry.

'At least you've got work with your mom, I hear. She's thrilled to have you. She's acting like she's just in the nick of time rescued you from the gutter.'

'Problem is, I don't want to be rescued.'

'I kinda guessed,' said Marlene. 'Anyhow, it's a waste. We all know where your talents really lie. You can't turn your back on your gifts. It's like me—I don't know—being a plumber.' She smiled brightly, as if resisting a powerful urge to become a plumber had been one of her better decisions.

'All my agent can think of is making a new showreel,' said Derry. 'As if actual roles are out there.'

'I don't mean acting,' said Marlene, tossing her mane of blonde hair and frowning picturesquely. 'Madam Tulip! I've been telling everybody about you. How amazing you are, and how you see stuff and everything. Anyhow, you can't let me down.'

'I'm sorry?'

'I've booked you, well sort of. Not me. The Countess.'

Derry was lost. 'Booked?'

'Sure. I got you a gig. Dowager Countess of Berkshire. She was the one donated the royal painting. In fact, your dad's Russian picture came originally from their collection too. I told the Countess all about Madam Tulip. And I've a job for your friends in Wardrobe.'

'Can you start from the beginning?'

'I've got a model friend in London called Charlotte Harvey-James. Her Dad's the Earl of Berkshire and her great-aunt is the Dowager Countess. They live in a great big stately home called Sorley Hall and have pots of money.'

'What's a Dowager?' asked Derry.

'Something to do with being a widow,' said Marlene. 'Octavia is her real name. She must be nearly eighty now, but she's full of beans. Main thing is, she used to work here.'

'What, like here?' said Derry, astonished. You didn't imagine a Countess doing time in a theatre bar.

'As a chorus girl. Back in the Sixties. She says the happiest days of her life were here.'

'What, happiest like before she married a Count?'

'Earl. The English don't do Counts. That's the Italians. But yes. Pure coincidence—I was telling her about the awful things that happened to us, and Madam Tulip and everything, and how then you're in a show and the roof falls down. And she looks like she's been hit by lightning. She goes, 'The Palace Theatre! I don't believe it!' And she tells me how she ran off to Ireland when she was eighteen to be a dancer and what a great time she had.'

'So the Earl sees her in a show and marries her? That's like out of a story; you don't believe that stuff actually happens. Like Cinderella.'

'Not exactly. Her father was Sir Somebody-Somebody, so she wasn't what you'd call a peasant. She says that's why she ran off—pure boredom with upper-class airheads who thought pouring champagne down their trousers was a good way to get introduced. You know they still do that?'

'So she donated the royal watercolour.'

'That's it. I told her about the auction, and she took the picture straight off the wall and she says, "Why don't you give them this. Everybody loves a Royal." And I go, "Hey, isn't that worth a lot?" And she says, "Sure, but he can't paint for nuts, and I can't stand it. When he drops in, I'll tell him it's out for cleaning." '

'He just drops in?'

'Sure. He has the estate next door at Fotheringham. He turned up a couple of times while I was there. He and the Earl talk paintings. And compost—he's into gardening. Has his bodyguard carry plant cuttings in a big bunch in his arms. He looks so embarrassed. Cute though.'

'You said there might be jobs for friends in Wardrobe?'

'Oh, sure thing. Charlotte is having an engagement party. She wants everyone to come dressed as characters from famous paintings. Her fiancée, Torquil, is going to video everything. He wants to be a film director, but so far he's only on YouTube.'

Derry didn't know too much about engagement parties. Most of her friends, if they hadn't forgotten to marry, usually forgot to get engaged.

'So I had an idea—tell me if it's stupid, okay?' Marlene smiled her dazzling smile. 'Usually, if you're having a themed party, people hire their costumes—there's a great little place in Chelsea. But my idea is we get the costumes made-to-measure.'

'Get them made! Isn't that going to cost a fortune?'

Marlene looked puzzled. 'Of course! That's the point! Derry, you are *sooo* naive! The guests pay for their own costumes, okay? If it wasn't expensive, how would you keep the guest list small? This way lots of people are relieved not to be invited. Win-win, see? I've mentioned it to your friends already. They're up for it.'

'Jasmine and Lorna?'

'They'd get a budget for each costume and nearly three weeks to do the job. They get a good fee, and there'll be a healthy donation to the theatre fund.'

'You've mentioned it?'

'Sure. They were thrilled. They're checking it out with the boss. So what about it?'

For a moment, Derry didn't know what Marlene meant.

'Madam Tulip! Octavia is mad to meet you, and Charlotte loves the idea of a fortune-teller for her party. And Bryony, her sister, is totally into spirits and druids and stuff and wants you to teach her how to read a crystal ball. See? Everybody wants you. Say yes.'

'I… don't know,' said Derry. She had grown so used to thinking of Madam Tulip as an episode in the past—closed, an unsuccessful experiment.

'Octavia says I'm to ask you how much you want. So I'm asking. How much?'

Now Derry was flummoxed. Were aristocrats always so blunt about money? Were models? 'I don't know. Honest. Not a clue.'

'Why not make it the same as last time, plus say twenty percent, seeing as how you're more experienced now. Plus expenses. Okay?'

'Really, I—'

'Come on! Or do you want to stay working for your mother! Or sit going crazy waiting for a call from your agent. You'll get a load of work out of this!'

Marlene had a point. Out-of-work actors were a menace. Derry didn't need psychic powers to foresee she'd spend the next couple of weeks telling herself she'd soon get a call from her agent. Then when she didn't get a call, she'd phone her agent every second day until she was begged to stop. Then she'd start worrying about the rent her mother used to subsidise and now wouldn't, so she'd try to get a job waitressing. But she mightn't even get that, as actors were known to be unreliable, dropping their shift at the first promise of an audition. And all the while, her non-acting friends would avoid her because they couldn't stand hearing the same whining complaints about the State Of The Arts Today when they knew the actor meant the state of their own employment prospects. The whole sorry tale would end with Derry going on demonstrations against the government's arts policy then sitting over cheap coffee with half a dozen fellow actors all competing for sympathy.

'Two grand?' said Derry, mentally closing her eyes at the audacity.

'A day? Fine. Sterling, of course. Plus expenses—you'll have to travel to England.'

Derry nodded dumbly, certain that any word she said would shatter the dream into a million pieces, and she'd be back on the protest march shouting 'Art is the Voice of the People' as if anybody believed it.

'Two days, plus two travel days at half rate would be normal. Five K.' Marlene added, 'It'll be fun. I'll text Octavia now. She'll be thrilled!'

Derry sat staring at Marlene open-mouthed, like a goldfish in a tank vaguely wondering when the room lights would go on.

# 6

When Immigration Control at Holyhead's bustling ferry terminal singled out Bruce's van for inspection, Derry guessed the cause was its colour, a violent purple. Touring musicians, festivalgoers and men offering to tar your driveway for a large sum paid in advance will all tell you that as soon as the human brain dons a uniform it takes a jaundiced view of unorthodox colour schemes.

In fact, Bruce was not responsible for this particular crime against good taste and public order. A purple van is a cheap van, affordable for an out-of-work actor, and although he was out-of-work Bruce was not unemployed. Actors, like the rest of the population, must eat, pay the rent and maintain their blood-stream alcohol at a tolerable level. To these ends Bruce was a furniture removal man, a computer tech, a lifeguard, a fitness coach and a nightclub bouncer. Right now, he was a transporter of theatrical costumes to an aristocratic engagement party, and chauffeur to Madam Tulip, fortune-teller to the rich and fashionable. Or would be, thought Derry, if they ever got out of the ferry terminal.

The two uniformed Border Control officers were polite but firm. Derry and Bruce were to step out of the vehicle please if they didn't mind. They were escorted without fuss into a nondescript office and invited to sit at a table. Opposite sat a middle-aged officer with dark circles under his eyes and dandruff in his thinning hair.

The officer pursed his lips, inspected their passports and asked about their business in the United Kingdom. That

Bruce and Derry were Americans didn't seem to be the problem; Britain allows Americans to visit without a visa. Perhaps Bruce's obscure but adventurous past as a US Navy SEAL had sparked official interest. Whatever the cause, Bruce was ushered into another room, while Derry remained sitting across from the tired officer. He resumed flicking through the pages of her passport before returning to the interesting entry Occupation: Actress.

'Been on the telly?' he enquired.

'Oh, a few small things,' answered Derry modestly. The officer's face fell. Perhaps he had been hoping to change his wife's view of his job from 'mind-numbingly boring but suiting his personality' to 'hob-nobbing with the famous.' Who knew but a sprinkling of stardust might revive the matrimonial interest for a night or two?

No actor welcomes disappointment from an audience, even an audience of one immigration officer with a dysfunctional body-clock.

'Have you seen *The Elizabethans*?' asked Derry.

The officer perked up 'Oh yes. Well, not actually, but my wife wouldn't miss an episode. You were in that?'

'Sure,' said Derry, airily.

'Shame it's finished,' said the officer. 'It were a good 'un, so the wife says. Must be hard when a big series ends, like. Do you get redundancy?'

For a moment, Derry was stumped. The idea of an actor getting redundancy payments was startlingly original.

'Goodness me, no!' Derry laughed, hopefully underlining how amusing was the idea that any actor featured in such a prestigious series would concern themselves with pin money.

'There's always the next role. And a few days to recharge the batteries are more than welcome.' She smiled brightly. That her batteries had been recharging for several weeks now and looked likely to be on the charger for the indefinite future, was neither here nor there.

'It must be nice to be famous,' said the officer, his expression wistful.

Derry's conscience stirred. Perhaps she had overstated her importance. 'Really, if you blinked you missed me,' she said. Satisfied, her conscience rolled over and went back to sleep.

But surely, false modesty is as great a fault as vanity. In *The Elizabethans*, Derry had several lines in four episodes. In fact, far from blinking, to miss her you would have had to shut your eyes for seconds at a time. In any actor's book, such a role counted as meaty. 'I did think the writing was really strong,' she confided.

'Lucky to do a job you like,' said the officer.

'It was fun to do,' agreed Derry. It was important that non-actors understood acting was a vocation and not in any way motivated by mere cash. Derry's conscience, jolted awake and rubbing its eyes grumpily, wasn't fooled for a minute by this Jesuitical moving of the goalposts. But its opportunity had passed.

'Oh, here's your friend,' said the officer.

Bruce emerged from the room into which he had been escorted, grinning and being patted on the back by a fit-looking young man in civilian clothes, also grinning. Derry's officer looked surprised, then relieved, then disappointed. 'Probably had the same nanny or summat,' he said, rolling his eyes. As he closed the folder in front of him, Derry was sure she heard him mutter, '*Effing toffs, gimme a break.*'

The fit young man shook Bruce's hand heartily as he escorted them back to their van. 'Cool to meet you, dude,' he said, in an accent pure Chelsea. 'Enjoy the party. Any spare earl's daughters, do pass one on like a good chap?'

Bruce laughed, not to be outdone in any competition for chummiest chum. 'Sure will. *Dude.*'

Derry's officer shook his head as though the ways of the British upper classes would be forever a closed book, and it was welcome to stay closed. 'I'll tell the wife I met you,' he said. 'She'll be well chuffed. You wouldn't autograph this, would you, Miss?' From his inside pocket he pulled a grubby envelope and a pen, thrusting them at Derry. She signed her name with a guilty flourish and climbed into the van, waving the officer a sympathetic goodbye. If Derry's fame was to be his only passport to matrimonial bliss, his chances were poorer than he knew.

'What was all that old pals stuff about?' asked Derry, when she and Bruce were back in the van and rolling unhindered out of the ferry terminal onto the main road. She had before seen Bruce treated like a long-lost brother by men in uniform. Except this one had been in plain clothes.

'I thought it was all going to be such a bore, but he was really sweet. As you know, we don't have much time for spooks.'

By *we* Derry knew Bruce meant he and his old comrades in the US military.

'Those guys get you into the doo-doo,' continued Bruce. 'And where are they when it hits the fan? Sweet nowhere, darling, that's where.'

As it happened, Derry was not aware of this alleged fact. On the other hand, a show of ignorance might earn that male look saying *don't women know anything?* So she settled for raising her eyebrows, intimating she knew perfectly well what spooks did and didn't do. Obviously.

'But this guy was cool,' continued Bruce. 'Ex-special forces. Hates being a cop or whatever they call security spooks here. You know we once hit the same LZ in Afghan within ten minutes of each other? How about that! I mean what are the chances?' He looked as pleased as if he had met a friend from kindergarten with whom he fondly remembered sharing a matey bag of jellies.

Before Bruce had come to Dublin as a student of drama, he had been in the US Navy—a member of that elite band known as Navy SEALs, whose members perform astonishing feats of daring. Derry was a little hazy on what those feats actually were, but the job seemed to involve jumping into the ocean in the dark from helicopters, carrying assault rifles, explosives, supplies for three days in the desert, snowshoes, full climbing equipment and their iPads.

'Did they pick up on your passport, or what?' asked Derry.

'Sure. They saw I was an actor, then checked my record and found the other stuff. Maybe they like to keep tabs on us vets, in case we go to the dark side.' He laughed. 'Or maybe actors make them nervous.'

Not for the first time Derry marvelled that no matter what happened, Bruce never seemed to get annoyed at anything.

'How come you don't lose your temper at all this stupid stuff? I mean, like how dumb are those people? Do we look like terrorists? If I were a terrorist, I'd wear Versace and I guarantee I'd sail right through.'

'Uh, training I guess,' said Bruce. He shrugged. 'We don't get mad. I mean if I got mad, maybe I'd kill somebody. Maybe I'd kill everybody!' He smiled and shook his head wearily, 'Man there'd be some forms to fill.'

Derry decided to laugh. It was a joke, right?

After more than an hour rattling along the coast of North Wales, they saw the roadside sign announcing 'Welcome to England.' A flat landscape of fields and farms gave way to industrial parks and yet more featureless fields. Derry found herself faintly regretting she knew little about the different crops farmers grew. But Derry was a New Yorker, and a kind of Dubliner too, and neither breed could readily tell you why fields were sometimes brown and other times not. Derry could, with some pride, recognise cabbages once they got to football size; and of course cows, if you included bulls. But there was a lot to the whole countryside business if you really looked into it, and the only way was to settle for the broad brushstrokes—basically, the whole world was made up of fields, when it wasn't buildings or roads. England, she couldn't help noticing, had lots of all three, and meant to show them off for another four hours.

A turn at driving relieved Derry's boredom for a while, but now, a passenger once more, she felt herself numbed into a kind of motorway coma. She slept.

Derry sat at a table. On its surface lay a board of some kind, like a game board, though she couldn't make out its shape. Four flat pieces, each bearing an image, were strewn at random. Playing cards?

The images were an odd assortment of the familiar and the unfamiliar: a double V, like chevron stripes on a soldiers sleeve; three holly leaves; a dog in profile in a hunting posture; a hand, or perhaps a glove, upright, fist clenched. Now Derry was shuffling the images, deciding where each would go on the… shield, that's what it was—a shield, like a coat of arms. As she neatly positioned the last of the symbols on the board, she felt intense satisfaction, as if she had finished a difficult jigsaw.

Something was different. At first Derry couldn't tell what. Then she saw it—the hand was changing colour. Until now, she hadn't noticed any colours at all; everything must have been in black and white, shades of grey. But just where the arm or glove ended, just where the owner's forearm should have been, was a vivid streak of red, a widening smear like the blood on a butcher's block trailing after a slab of meat. Shocked, Derry jumped back, scattering the pieces on the table, knocking her chair away.

'Up all hands! Shake a leg!' announced Bruce. His voice had the cheery callousness of the early riser victimising a night owl. Nearly six p.m. Derry had slept resting her head against a rolled blanket jammed against the window. Her neck was stiff, her mouth dry. Her dream clung to her, and she had to concentrate to shake it off.

'Where are we?' She reached into the door pocket for her bottle of water. They were still on a main road, but she could see little as the scenery was hidden by a high brick wall running along the roadway.

'I'd say we're five minutes from Sorley Hall. Should be some kinda entrance just ahead on our left.'

Bruce had hardly spoken when Derry saw the wall sweep inwards, rising even higher to frame a massive pair of gate posts. Bruce slowed the van and swung into the entrance.

A black sign on one of the pillars said Sorley Hall in gold letters, with a list of opening hours. On the wall, another sign boasted of an organic kitchen garden, a farm and stables, a tearoom, children's play area and an art gallery. 'Did that say closed at five p.m.?' asked Derry. It was nearly six. As they drove through the gateway, her question was answered by a sturdy red and white boom blocking the drive. Opposite was a redbrick gate lodge like a miniature castle complete with battlements. Bruce pulled the van to the side and leapt lightly to the ground. A couple of minutes later he was back, accompanied by a dour elderly man who raised the barrier and watched with a look of intense disapproval as they drove past in their purple van.

Bruce was grinning. 'Should my feelings be hurt? He said be sure to park at the back, at the farm. The big house is strictly off-limits. I think I get the message.'

Wherever the main house was, they got no glimpse as they motored up a curving driveway at least half a mile long, lined by ancient trees. Ahead were rolling hillocks—natural or landscaped it was impossible to tell. And suddenly they saw the house. Across a stone bridge over a meandering river, the drive led in a gentle curve to a magnificent facade.

'Cosy,' said Bruce.

'Wow,' said Derry. 'I mean, wow.'

You could see why stately homes were called stately. The first impression of the great house was of its sheer size. It wasn't a palace, but it was no modest manor either. Red brick glowed a warm red in the late sun. Serried ranks of windows marched along the frontage, outlined in yellow stone. Capping the lot were battlements topped with steep grey cliffs of slate like church steeples.

The main avenue to the house led straight to its imposing entrance, a broad flight of steps rising to a front door framed by pillars. But the van's way ahead was blocked by strategically placed flower beds and a signpost. The sign pointed left along a neatly gravelled road to the visitors' carpark, the tearoom and the farm mentioned by the gatekeeper. Bruce swung the van and headed that way.

'Man!' said Bruce. 'This is so cool! Like the movies the English make? Butlers and all? This is awesome research. You never know when you might have to audition as some kind of gamekeeper, even a lord, right?'

Derry didn't think she needed to worry too much about playing a gamekeeper or a lord. But the thought did occur to her that she was about to meet a whole family of British aristocrats in their stately home. Weren't the English upper classes famous for being horrible if they thought you were nobody important? Derry shook herself. The fear was silly. This was an acting job; no more, no less. Did Shakespeare worry about being looked down on by dukes and earls? He did not—he thought of the guineas and whatever they had in those days for a bank account. Probably a box at the end of the bed.

Bruce turned the van into a cobbled courtyard signpost-ed 'Staff and Guest Parking Only.' He pulled up beside an old green Land Rover. Once, the complex must have been a working farm complete with stables, cart shed and barn, but had since been converted into visitor accommodation. Just as Derry stepped down from the van, wondering where they should go now, into the yard swung a pristine white SUV. A big black Labrador with a ball in its mouth raced alongside. Dog and SUV skidded to a halt, the driver's door was flung open and down jumped Marlene.

For a moment Marlene stood, hand resting on the door handle, like she was posing for a photoshoot. She wore a tweed country ensemble that had had surely never strayed far from London W1. For a moment she stood relaxed but poised, like she was waiting for the cameras to flash and the photographers to shout their thanks. The Labrador jumped up, begging to have its ball thrown. Marlene ignored him.

'Hi!' she sang. Throwing her arms wide, she strode toward Derry, grasped her firmly by the shoulders and gave her a heartfelt hug. She kissed Bruce on both cheeks, causing him to blush like a boy. 'You got here!' she announced, as though they had crossed a desert or fought their way through a jungle. 'We only arrived from London half an hour ago!'

From the passenger side of the SUV stepped a delicate beau-ty, perhaps in her mid-twenties, almost as tall and slender as Marlene. The girl was red-haired, with misty grey eyes and wore her designer sunglasses perched on her head. She wore smart slacks and a sweater—no nod to the countryside there. Her cheekbones were high and perfectly formed, well matched with the wide and pearly smile she directed at Derry and Bruce.

'This is my friend Charlotte,' said Marlene, introducing them.

The Labrador shifted its attention to Charlotte, earning an abstracted ruffle of its ears. 'And this is Percy—don't mind him, he's an idiot. Aren't you Percy,' said Charlotte, nuzzling the dog. She turned to Derry and Bruce. 'I am so happy you could do this. Great-aunt Octavia will be thrilled. You've got the costumes and everything?'

Bruce threw open the sliding side door of the van to show densely packed rails with their treasures safely hanging, each outfit draped in polythene. Charlotte squealed, holding onto Percy's collar as the dog tried to leap into the van. 'This is *sooo* cool! Torquil will go crazy! He likes costumes so much, it's pervy!' She gave a ribald laugh, throaty and startling coming from those refined features.

'Torquil is Charlotte's fiancée,' explained Marlene. 'I think I told you? He's in film?'

'And you're an actress!' said Charlotte to Derry, as though Derry might be surprised at the news.

'Bruce is an actor too,' said Marlene. Bruce shuffled his feet and seemed to find the cobblestones fascinating.

'Cool!' said Charlotte. 'You two and Torquil will have so much to talk about. He doesn't do theatre, says it's elitist, but he does really admire theatre people. So dedicated.'

Derry wondered if by dedicated she didn't mean poor, but Charlotte was so open-faced and brimming with friendly enthusiasm it was hard to imagine her words had any hidden sting.

'The guy at the gate said to park here,' said Bruce. 'That okay? I can move it if you want.'

'He phoned to tell us you were coming,' said Charlotte. 'He was afraid you'd park near the house and get in the way of the tourists photographing in the morning. They complain if there's anything modern in the way of their pictures. We've had emails from people wanting their entrance fee refunded because they took a video and put it on Youtube, and somebody noticed a satellite TV dish on the wall of the service wing. Thank goodness I don't stay here all the time. In the season it's like living in a railway station.'

Derry's sympathetic look was genuine. 'So how will you manage your party on Saturday? Will you close off someplace?'

'Sort of. We'll have to barricade ourselves in the East Wing and the walled garden. You can be sure some visitor will complain to British Heritage about being excluded. And the Heritage crowd list us on their website and we need the publicity. We have to send grovelling emails and free tickets even if a complaint is silly. But that's Bryony's problem, thank goodness. She's my big sister. We call her The Head Prefect, but she doesn't seem to mind.'

'The van?' Bruce reminded her.

'No, no—Bryony says leave the van. We'll need to sort out where to stash the costumes until the guests arrive. You won't believe it, but around here there's never anywhere to park and never anywhere to put anything. And you're to come and have something to eat first; you must both be starving. Grab your bags and hop in.' She waved vaguely at Marlene's SUV.

Marlene driving, the SUV raced back towards the great house, spewing gravel as it went, Percy the Labrador bounding along beside them. They negotiated a long a narrow lane around the back of the house, before threading their way between two high, stone gateposts into a walled and cobbled courtyard. A sign said No Admittance—Staff Only.

Marlene swung the SUV in a tight circle, neatly avoiding a builders' skip, a cement mixer, stacks of bricks half-hidden under tarpaulins, and a mound of sand. She slammed into reverse, surprising Derry by inserting the vehicle neatly into a space between a magnificent Bentley and a sleek Italian sports car, gleaming red, the sort driven by star footballers. 'Mind those doors when you get out!' warned Charlotte. 'I don't know whose nervous breakdown would be worse if you dinged their car, Daddy or Sebastian. Best not tempt fate.'

They disembarked, careful to avoid inflicting nervous breakdowns on anyone. Derry brought her handbag with her but, on Charlotte's advice, left her costume bag and wig box in the SUV for now. She looked around trying to guess where they were headed. The back of the house, or at least the wing she could see, was much plainer than the front and was garlanded with scaffolding. Facing it, on the other side of the courtyard was a line of pretty redbrick annexes; perhaps once they were servants' quarters, service buildings or coach houses. And in the corner, looming massively over all, stood an ancient tower, brutal and uncompromising. Nothing elegant or aristocratic about this, thought Derry. She paused to take in its massive studded door, and above it— She stopped dead, staring.

Over the lintel, picked into the stone of a giant slab, was a coat of arms: a shield emblazoned with a chevron, a crouching dog, what looked to be a holly branch, and—weatherworn but unmistakeable—a clenched fist upraised.

*Don't be silly!*

Jumping to conclusions was plain ridiculous. She must have seen the coat of arms on the estate website.

Of course.

# 7

'Amazing how old habits never die,' said Charlotte, stopping at a mirrored hall stand and rifling through a small pile of junk mail. She laughed. 'I think I'm still waiting for a letter from a boy I met in France when I was fifteen.'

The others stood behind her, waiting to be led into the house. Percy pranced happily. The hallway was spacious, clearly not the grand entrance to the main house, but impressive—wide and bright, with tall windows and a broad stairway. Corridors led off on three sides. The ceiling was high and ornately plastered, and paintings hung on every wall. Surprisingly, the pictures weren't Old Masters or ancestral portraits, but bright, modern works. Derry knew enough to see that most were abstract expressionists and futurists, a few surrealists dotted amongst them. Someone was a collector. She remembered Marlene saying the Russian picture Jacko bought came originally from this house.

'The family sticks to this wing,' continued Charlotte. 'Sort of like the Alamo; we're hanging on until the last man. Woman too, of course, but we don't count.' She led them down a wide corridor its walls densely hung with yet more paintings. Shooing Percy away, she ushered them into a surprising room. She called it the breakfast room. The impression was of a country kitchen, but much, much bigger than anything you'd see in a cottage or farmhouse. A smart range graced a vast fireplace. A painted wooden dresser displayed colourful plates and pots and a collection of ceramic chickens. Battered armchairs and a settee offered comfort, and in the centre of the room was a huge wooden table big enough to seat at least a dozen people. The real kitchen was off to one side, but through the open door you could see it was fully equipped, and someone was preparing food.

'Throw your bags down there and take a pew,' said Charlotte. 'I thought vegetarian spaghetti bolognese? Is that alright? Bryony should be along soon. I know Aunt Octavia is out, probably making the gardeners do overtime; she has them all believing they work for her personally. Daddy is around somewhere.' She shouted through to the kitchen area. 'How are we doing, Annie?'

A voice came back, 'One moment, my lady. Almost there.'

How strange, thought Derry. Lady Charlotte. She'd never met a *lady* before. Was she expected to call her *my lady* as the voice from the kitchen had? Derry discovered she didn't like that idea at all. She was, after all, American. And Irish. And neither nationality was much given to forelock-tugging.

A thin, anxious-looking woman in a blue housecoat bustled in with plates and cutlery, setting places just for Derry and Bruce. Derry presumed this was Annie. Charlotte, absorbed in checking her phone for messages, made no move to help. Marlene looked on wistfully, and Derry wondered if models ate at all.

'So what do we call you guys?' asked Bruce, neatly solving Derry's problem. 'Like, your ladyships, or what?'

Charlotte laughed. 'Just Charlotte, for goodness' sake.' A relief. But Derry couldn't help noticing that Annie, now delivering pots of spaghetti and sauce, wasn't accorded the same privilege.

They had hardly started on their meal when a girl Derry

guessed must be Bryony bustled breathlessly into the room. 'Sorry I'm late, don't get up!' she said, shaking hands first with Derry then with Bruce before dumping a leather satchel on the floor, pulling up a chair and settling down at the table.

If you didn't know that Bryony and Charlotte were sisters, you could never have guessed. They had the same surprising grey eyes, but in every other respect they were different. Where Charlotte was tall and willowy, Bryony was broad shouldered and of medium height. Where Charlotte was fine-featured, Bryony had that hearty look you associate with women into horse-riding and gardening. Her complexion was tanned by sun and wind. Her hair was brown and tied back in a business-like ponytail. She wore corduroy trousers and a heavy jumper under a sleeveless green, quilted jacket.

'Delighted you got here so early. Evenings are getting dark now; pain in the rear trying to get stuff done. Have to shut up shop soon.'

Presumably by shop she meant the house and gardens. 'Won't you be glad of the break?' asked Derry. 'It must be tough managing all those tourists.'

Bryony laughed. 'Nothing tough about fifteen quid a head. Keeps the damn' roof on. Just.'

From the kitchen, Annie poked her head into the room. 'Coffee or a tea, Lady Bryony?'

'No thanks, Annie m'dear,' said Bryony. 'Trying to fight the caffeine demon. Losing battle. Tell you what, why don't you toddle off now. We'll look after what's left.'

'Are you sure, Lady Bryony?' asked Annie. She was already taking off her housecoat.

'Quite sure,' said Bryony. 'And thanks, Annie.'

Annie left, smiling shyly as she went.

'Eat up,' said Bryony. 'Then I'll show you where you're staying and you can have a lie-down if you like. Unless you want a quick scoot around the grounds before dark?'

'That would be nice,' answered Derry. 'if I could just have a quick brush up first?'

'Sure,' said Bryony.

'I could get on with unpacking the van,' said Bruce, 'Maybe best not leave the costumes overnight.'

'Have you thought where you want to keep everything?' Bryony asked Charlotte.

'Um,' said Charlotte.

'It's alright—that's why I asked they park at the farm,' said Bryony. 'We can put everything in one of the lodges—they've been vacuumed today.' She turned to Derry. 'Has anyone told you the plan? Thought not. Some guests will arrive tomorrow evening. We'll feed and water 'em but, if you wouldn't mind, could you make yourself available for some fortune telling? Say seven to nine?'

'Looking forward to it,' said Derry, smiling. And she found she was, too.

'We'll encourage them to go for it before they're too blotto. Some can get pretty silly, but that's more likely on Saturday. Some people collect friends—Charlotte collects hooligans.'

Charlotte grinned broadly, but didn't deny the allegation.

'Why don't I take you back to the farm and we can unload,' said Bryony to Bruce. 'Then you can bring your van round here.'

'Great, thanks,' said Bruce, beaming. You could tell he thought here was a woman you could do business with.

'Let me do these,' said Bryony, sweeping up an armful of plates and marching toward the kitchen. Derry collected the remaining dishes and followed.

'Hey, let me help with those!' said Bruce, not moving to get up. Marlene and Charlotte ostentatiously checked their phones, their foreheads creased in concentration.

Derry and Bryony exchanged knowing glances and donned their rubber gloves.

~

Bryony led Derry and Bruce out of the house and across the rear courtyard to the row of low, redbrick buildings Derry had noticed earlier. As they retrieved their bags from Marlene's SUV, Derry had to admit to herself she was disappointed. Silly, as there was no reason at all why she should have expected to stay in the mansion.

They stopped in front of what had once been a stable block. Bryony pulled out a heavy ring of keys and pushed open a door painted a cheerful blue. 'You'll find the place comfortable,' she said. 'It's got everything, all the mod cons.' She handed two keys to Derry. 'These are for you—don't lose them.'

They stepped directly into a cosy kitchen-cum-sitting room. No need to switch on a light—a big window had been made from what had once been the stable doorway, and the blinds were up. The walls were a beautiful light green panelling. A little wood-burning stove sat, already lit, beneath a lovely old cast-iron fireplace inset with brightly painted tiles. In front of the stove were placed a comfortable couch and an armchair. The kitchen cupboards and the cooker were functional and tasteful, and off to one side was a small dining table. A painted ceramic hen sat on the mantelpiece beside an old wooden-cased clock. The only pictures were framed sepia photographs of the house and estate. No valuable paintings here, Derry noticed. Perhaps they'd prove too much temptation for the guests.

'I've stocked the fridge with everything you need for breakfast. We'll have lunch in the house if that suits. Coffee, bread, soup, snacking stuff in the cupboards. So make yourselves at home. Two bedrooms…' She paused, giving Derry and Bruce a questioning look.

'Uh, yes, thanks,' said Derry. Bruce inspected the photographs, trying to look as if he hadn't heard.

'Fine, take your pick.'

Derry opened the door to one of the bedrooms. The room was cute—a large double bed, an old oak dresser, a dressing table with a tilting mirror. A wooden seaman's chest sat by a small window. She swung her bag onto the bed with a sigh and carefully placed her wig box on the dressing table. She'd unpack later, though she didn't much like leaving her Madam Tulip costume in her bag.

'Alright then?' asked Bryony, shoving her head around the door. 'Bathroom is to the left.'

'Lovely. It really is nice,' said Derry.

'Why don't you chill out for a little. Unpack and so on. We honestly don't need you to help unload the costumes. Take a stroll around the paths before it gets dark, if you like. Nobody will bother you.'

'Are you sure?' said Derry. 'I don't mind helping. Really.'

'No need. That's right, isn't it Bruce, m'dear?'

'Sure thing, Lady B.,' said Bruce, emerging from the room next door. 'Be done in a flash.'

Bryony and Bruce left, Bruce gallantly holding open the door for Bryony, and Derry was left to her own devices.

After a quick dash to the bathroom, she got a chance to look around. This wasn't bad at all. Comfortable and private, and no need to be politely attentive like she'd have to be in the main house. Derry settled into the armchair in front of the blazing stove, stretched out her legs and gave a contented sigh.

~

Her phone rang. She shouldn't have been surprised. Why shouldn't it ring? She was in England, not Kazakhstan. Even there, she supposed, her phone might ring in a perfectly routine way. But oddly, less than four hundred miles from her little apartment in Dublin, she felt abroad.

She was surprised to see it was her father calling. While her heart didn't exactly sink—she was always happy to hear from Jacko and know he was well—she was aware of a tiny voice in her head saying, oh no, what now?

'Hi, Dad!'

'I can't get your mother! She's not returning my calls!'

'Hi, Dad,' repeated Derry. She could hear a roaring engine and whistling wind. He must have been driving his sports car with the top down.

'It's an emergency! I've left twenty messages!' Jacko roared.

'Hello, Dad. Beginning? Start? At?'

'She has me on the ropes!'

'From the—?'

'Herr Billionaire came back from his cruise. He's decided he wants the Corrib Series!'

'That's great. Cool!'

'But the pictures are in the London gallery, and I can't get Vanessa! What if he changes his mind?'

'If he really wants them, surely he'll be okay to wait a bit?' Derry was careful to sound relaxed, as though she firmly believed German billionaires keen to give you money would be happy to wait at your convenience rather than taking their whims elsewhere.

'Has she gone back to the States without telling me?'

'No, she's still in London. Maybe her phone is giving trouble? Have you called the gallery? One of the assistants will get her, surely.'

'They say she isn't there. They gave me her phone number, like I wouldn't have it already!'

'Seems strange,' said Derry. But there was nothing strange about it. The number of possible reasons Vanessa might avoid her ex-husband and client was as astronomical as the number of reasons her ex-husband might avoid her.

'You're in England,' said Jacko. 'When are you leaving—Sunday?'

'Um… Sunday evening, I think. Not sure what time.'

'Would you do me a favour?'

Here we go. 'I don't honestly know what I can do,' said Derry, keeping it vague. This was no time for initiative.

'Can you go to London and see what's happening? You could get the pictures packed up, like you said. Get them despatched? Will you do that?'

'I've got a lift back to Dublin,' said Derry. But she knew her cause was hopeless.

'Don't you worry about that,' said Jacko. 'I'll pay your flight home. Derry darlin', I need that sale!'

Cornered. Derry had no wish to visit Vanessa in her London lair. So far, she'd managed to avoid telling her mother she didn't mean to carry on working for her. She hoped the business would come up in a phone call rather than in person, preferably when she and Vanessa were in different countries.

'Let me talk to Bruce and see if I can change my plans. I'll call you tomorrow, okay?'

'You're a sweetheart. I knew you'd—'

The call went dead. Derry tried to phone back, but it was no use. An automatic message told her the other party had their phone switched off or were out of range. The pleasing prospect of a meditative doze in front of the fire dissolved in irritation. Derry sighed and got up, her conscience reminding her about her Madam Tulip costume lying neglected and crumpling in her bag.

~

Derry carefully laid out each item on the bed.

First she unpacked her crystal ball, unwrapping it from the richly embroidered velvet tablecloth in which it was cocooned for safety. Next came her antique ten-minute timer, like an egg timer only bigger, given to her by Bruce as a present. The timer let clients know how much longer they had left in their session. Derry had learned long ago that once someone started talking about themselves they wanted to carry on discussing that most riveting subject forever.

Next came two decks of cards, one normal, one Tarot. Then came her costume—dress, beads and long gloves. She inspected her wig and its delicate feather headdress. Both were in perfect condition. Derry hung everything that needed hanging, while laying the rest on top of the seaman's chest by the window.

Opening her overnight bag, she fished out her makeup container, her trusty hand mirror and her face wipes, placing them neatly on the dressing table beside her box of tissues. Like all actors, Derry arrayed the tools of her trade in precisely the same way every time. She smiled. Actors were such creatures of habit. Last came her little box of borage tea.

In a kitchen cupboard Derry found a collection of mugs, each decorated with a picture of Brighton Pier. A job lot at an auction? She chose one, washed it and popped in a sachet. In five minutes she was nestling in the plump armchair by the stove, sipping her brew contentedly. Not exactly the life of an aristocrat, she thought, but just fine for me.

Had she fallen asleep for a moment? Had the borage, that heady and beguiling herb, made her dream? Or had she been mesmerised by the flickering orange of the fire through the glass door of the stove? Whatever the reason, right there, seeming to take shape in the dancing flame, was a book. Oddly, the book showed no signs of burning.

The volume was old and leather-bound, more like a journal than a novel or textbook. As Derry watched, the oversized leaves rippled open showing pages arranged in columns like accounts, the handwriting neat and clerical. Some kind of ledger? She stared hard, trying to make out the writing, but the image blurred then faded away.

Inexplicably, Derry felt a profound sense of loss. A gut-wrenching feeling of bereavement took hold, as if the book was her only possession and was being taken from her. But the book wasn't being taken. The open pages were being slowly obscured by a light dusting of snow. And now the book was gone, vanished under a soft white blanket.

For a moment, Derry thought her strange half-dream had ended. Instead, right where the book lay buried unseen, the snow began to give off some kind of vapour. A gentle steam drifted up. Faster than you would ever expect, the snow was melting.

Once more the open ledger was revealed, emerging from a glistening pool of icy sludge. And now the impossible happened. In the centre of the right-hand page, a spot of the deepest black appeared. As Derry watched, the spot grew and grew, its expanding edge racing to the margins, obliterating the writing. With startling suddenness, a fierce yellow flame burst through the paper, flaring up to engulf the whole page, consuming the book in its own miniature furnace.

You could still see the outline of a book in the black, curled-up ash. You could even make out its separate leaves, seemingly still bound together by the shadow of a cover on the snow. A sudden breeze ruffled the charred and fragile pages, before scattering them in blackened fragments across the frozen landscape.

# 8

Derry strolled along the gravel path leading to the art gallery. At this hour, the gallery would be closed, of course, but her walk was an excuse to again see the imposing facade of the house. The way led through pleasant lawns past carefully tended flower beds—circular, square, triangular. Even this late in the season, flowers were blazing with colour. Derry wondered idly how many gardeners you needed to run a place like this. And beyond, like a vast theatrical backdrop, stood the magnificent mansion of Sorley Hall.

From behind came the sound of tyres crunching the gravel. Derry turned. A golf buggy was approaching at surprising speed. She couldn't make out the features of the driver behind the windshield, but whoever it was took a bend in the path with dangerous abandon. As the machine bore down on Derry, it showed no sign of slowing. Derry frowned and stepped to one side onto the grass. But instead of careering past, the buggy slid to a halt right beside her, weaving as the brakes were slammed on hard.

'Better keep off the grass or James will have your guts.'

Derry opened her mouth to protest, then realised the driver was an elderly woman.

'You're Derry,' the woman announced. 'Jump in!' She beckoned impatiently for Derry to sit in the seat beside her. Derry did what she was told. It hadn't occurred to her to do anything else.

'My dear,' said the woman, 'delighted to meet you. Heard so much. Octavia.'

'Oh,' said Derry. 'Hello.'

'They call me the Dowager,' said Octavia. 'Might as well say Old Hag, but one reads between the lines.'

This woman was nothing like the Dowager Countess Derry had expected to meet. Only now did she realise her mental picture of a Countess had included full evening dress, a diamond necklace, elbow-length gloves and a tiara. This countess was wearing a padded green jacket that had seen better days, a stalker's tweed hat, faded corduroy trousers, and wellington boots. A walking stick was propped by her side like a rifle poking out of a cowboy's saddle holster, ready to deal decisively with any outlaws that chanced to appear.

'Avanti!' cried the Dowager Countess, gunning the buggy heartily, sending it accelerating  down the straight. Derry was thrown violently back in her seat.

'Like a tour?' shouted the Dowager.

Derry fumbled for a safety-belt but found none. 'Yes, please. Very kind—'

'Better you get your tour like this or George will make you do it with him. Lord, he drones on. Believe me, you'll prefer this way.'

'Thank you, I only meant—'

'House,' announced Octavia, waving her arm vaguely towards the grand facade. The buggy lurched alarmingly. 'Big. Old. Lots of rebuilds. Norman castle, Tudor monstrosity, nineteenth-century family house with plumbing. If, that is, a family house can have eighty-two bedrooms. Needless to say, the plumbing still doesn't work.'

Derry gave a combined nod and shrug.

'Built on the backs of the peasants, of course,' continued

Octavia. 'Though by the eighteen-hundreds they were in the West Indies slaving on a sugar plantation rather than down the road shearing sheep. Out of sight, out of mind, what? Over there you can see the gallery. I believe your father is a famous painter. I've met your mother.'

Derry concentrated on trying to look more attentive than scared, while resuming her hopeful search for a seat belt.

'That's the gallery,' said the Dowager, pointing to a high, plain building with irregular windows, the brick a different shade from the rest of the house.

'The gallery is George's baby—Sebastian too, of course. He's George's curator. When he hears you're here, he'll want to meet you. Wonderful young man. Bit of a boffin. Nothing he doesn't know about pictures. Probably knows more about your father than you do.'

Racing past the entrance to the gallery, they swung left making a wide sweep around a small grassy hillock, one of several that dotted the parkland. Derry was surprised to see this one had strange green boxes on top, like beehives, and was fronted by a modern-looking heavy doorway that seemed to lead into the little hill.

'This is the bit I like,' said the Dowager. 'Bryony wants to make it a tourist attraction, but George is having none of it.'

'What is it?' asked Derry. 'Looks like some kind of bunker.'

'Spot on. That's exactly what it is. During the war, the house was taken over by the military. They used to train Czech officers and spies here. Forged passports, that sort of thing. Then dropped 'em by parachute into Nazi-occupied Europe. Never heard of again, most of 'em, poor devils.'

Derry tried to imagine the great house looking drab and military, with green trucks and uniformed men milling about. Hard to visualise, but it had happened.

'So they built a ruddy great air-raid shelter for the soldiers. Under there.' Octavia stopped the buggy in front of the bunker's steel doors, flanked on either side by impressive grey concrete uprights. The mound of grass-covered earth loomed above their heads.

'After the war, the government took it over so the politicians and busybodies from the Town Hall could sit tight and eat baked beans while the rest of us were incinerated by the Russians.'

'You mean that's a nuclear shelter?' asked Derry, amazed. How incongruous. An end-of-the-world bunker in the middle of the idyllic English countryside, in the grounds of a house that made you think of horses and carriages and ladies in crinoline.

'But then the Russians gave up, deciding they preferred capitalist gangsters to communist gangsters. So the bunker went up for sale. Since it was more or less on the lawn and had belonged to the estate before the government took it off us, my late husband bought it. Just used for storage now. But if you hear the sirens go, you'll know where to head.' The Dowager cackled. 'They won't let the likes of me in. I imagine they'll only want breeders.'

Once more, the Dowager opened the buggy's throttle wide. They swept round the back of the little hill, climbing a curving path up an incline toward another small eminence crowned with artfully placed trees. To Derry's relief, the climb slowed the buggy to a walking pace. On the hilltop in front of the trees was a stone-built alcove sheltering a bench.

'Planted the trees m'self,' said the Dowager. 'Forty years ago next year—can't believe it. Sweet chestnut.'

The Dowager paused, gazing up at the foliage, lost in thought, before sweeping the buggy briskly round to face back towards the house.

'The great Capability Brown designed the gardens in 1765. Cost a fortune. Went to pot in the war, of course. I've almost brought it back. Quite proud of m'self.' Again her thoughts seemed to drift to some other time or place. 'Just hope I live a bit longer. Finish the job.'

Now Derry could see why the Dowager had brought them up the slope. From here they had a stunning view of the house and gardens. The setting sun was blood red, making the bricks of the mansion glow, while the windows blazed as though lit from the inside by a million chandeliers. To the left, the river meandered lazily into the distance.

Why this vantage point had been created on the ridge was obvious. The stone bower and its bench were carefully positioned to give the rich and powerful owner of this splendid estate a perfect view of his prize possession. Derry could almost hear his satisfaction: *See how special I am, and how special were my ancestors! And when I'm gone, my descendants will still be here, and this place will always be mine.*

'Beautiful, isn't it?' said the Dowager, her voice soft. She seemed to wake from a dream. 'You must come and visit me in my little sitting room. How about now?'

# 9

'Just you and me,' said Octavia. 'How cosy. The others will be having dinner. My, those girls can eat!'

So much for Marlene and Charlotte's models-on-a-diet act, thought Derry. She needn't have bothered feeling sorry for them. They were saving their appetites for dinner—dinner to which Derry and Bruce had pointedly not been invited.

Derry knew she shouldn't feel annoyed. People could have dinner with whomever they wanted, surely. She and Bruce were only here to do a job. Visiting plumbers wouldn't expect to be asked to dinner, would they? Then she realised she wasn't annoyed, she was hurt. No—not hurt—somehow shamed, like being talked into going to a nightclub with a friend and being refused entry for not being trendy enough or famous enough. A small but brutal reminder the world was nowhere near as democratic a place as you liked to believe.

The room Octavia called her little sitting-room wasn't especially little. Her salon was comfortable yet grand, furnished with fine antiques. Most surprising of all was the arty flourish overlaying the grandeur. A costumier's dummy wore a feather boa and a twenties cloche hat. A jade necklace was draped over an art deco vase bursting with dried flowers and feathery reeds. A richly embroidered throw covered an ample couch. In front of a grand mantelpiece, a chaise longue took advantage of the warmth of a glowing fire. On the walls hung many pictures—not works of art but theatrical posters and old photographs.

While Octavia searched out a shawl to drape over her

shoulders, Derry was drawn to the photos. Many of the pictures featured showgirls of the fifties or sixties, and among their ranks was a young, very young, Octavia. Identifying her had taken a moment, but you couldn't mistake her eyes and the way she held her head.

'This is you?'

'Impossible to believe,' said the Dowager, settling on the chaise longue. 'How could what I was then turn into what I am now? At least I gave it a whirl. That's the great thing, isn't it? Giving it a go. In five minutes you'll be dead.'

Derry turned to look at the Dowager. Her words might have been grim, but she didn't wear a grim expression. Her eyes twinkled, and you had the powerful impression of a woman with a brain as agile as the dancer she had once been.

'Marlene told me you danced at the Palace,' said Derry.

'Wanted to be an actress. Thought I'd be rather good at it. But you needed training to get in. For dancing you only need the legs.' She smiled. 'Sit over here by me.' She pointed to a chair opposite. 'Would you like a drink? I've a nice claret, if you'd share a drop? You're not a ghastly teetotaller are you?'

Derry smiled. 'No. I try to be good, but I do have to try.'

'As long as being good isn't easy—that's the main thing,' said Octavia. 'Do me a favour won't you, and fetch over that tray. Bottle and glasses all laid out. Bottle is open already. Pop it on this little table.'

Derry retrieved the tray and its contents and sat them on the low table.

'Shall I?' asked Derry.

'Oh, do please,' said Octavia, indicating she should pour. 'And be as generous as you like. Everybody nowadays looks at me as if to say I suppose you could take a thimbleful or two, but are you sure that's wise?' Damn right it's wise. Stops me saying what I think.'

Derry smiled at the idea the Dowager Countess would ever refrain from saying what she thought, wine or no wine. Derry filled Octavia's glass but was less generous with her own. She was a guest, although after the day's journey and the strangeness of everything a drink was just what she needed. She wondered idly whether Bruce could be persuaded to jump in the van and search out the nearest off-licence. Probably not, seeing as how he hardly drank at all. Most likely he'd give her his concerned friend look.

'So the old place fell down,' said Octavia, when Derry had poured the wine and taken her seat.

'Just the ceiling over the stage, the flies. Part of the auditorium, I think. Nobody was hurt thank goodness.'

'Something to be thankful for, certainly.'

What Derry wanted to say was, you were a chorus girl way back, tell me all about it! But quizzing her hostess would be bad manners. Instead, she said, 'Thank you so much for your gift. The painting. It really was generous.'

'Will they rebuild?'

'I don't know. The auction went well, and we have lots of other fundraising planned. The hope is if we raise enough ourselves, the government will be embarrassed into chipping in.'

'Forgive me if I doubt the ability of politicians to be embarrassed,' replied Octavia. 'But tell me, before the accident, how was the theatre doing? What is the old place like now? They haven't done some kind of dreadful modernising, I hope?'

'No, not at all,' said Derry. 'They cleaned it up a bit back in the nineties, but everything looks just the same as it always did.'

'Something to be thankful for. When I danced there, I sometimes felt like the curtain would open and I'd see the audience for the first time, and they'd all be Edwardians—men with bushy moustaches and the women in lace collars.'

'You could still feel that,' said Derry. 'It hasn't changed.'

'I loved it. All of it. The routines were sometimes very good indeed. They worked us hard. But we were young, we lapped it up. I did enjoy Ireland.' She paused and sipped her wine. 'Marlene has told me a lot about you. And your friend—Bruce, isn't it?'

'Yes. He's a very special guy.'

'So Marlene said. Quite the action hero. Actor too, I believe?'

'Oh yes,' said Derry. 'We were at drama college together. Trinity. Dublin.'

'I remember Trinity well,' said Octavia, smiling. 'Those Trinity balls made theatre parties look like Sunday school.' She paused. 'But things were different in my time. More innocent. I used to worry myself sick over Charlotte when she started modelling. Charlotte was young when her mother passed away, and a young girl faces so many dangers. You see, in my day there was never real money involved. Models now are like cash machines. Everyone is making money out of them every moment of the day.'

'I can only imagine,' agreed Derry.

'Of course you can only imagine,' said Octavia, deadpan. 'You're an actress. No point anyone trying to make money out of you.'

Derry burst out laughing. Octavia grinned. They sipped their wine companionably.

'Now,' said Octavia, as if announcing the result of a prize draw, 'I have you all to myself. You'll be in demand for the next two days, I assure you, so I'm going to wring you dry. Apologies, but that's the way it is. I want you to do a reading for me.'

This was a surprise. Derry's beautiful Madam Tulip outfit was part of the show and was this moment hanging in a closet. Neither did Derry have her cards or her crystal ball. 'I don't have—'

'Nonsense,' said Octavia. 'Can you read ordinary playing cards? I'd imagine any fortune-teller worth her salt can do that.' She fixed Derry with a hawkish gaze. She was right, of course.

'In the drawer over there—left-hand drawer in that escritoire, you'll find a pack in a mother-of-pearl box. Bring it over here. While you prepare yourself to pull aside the gauze curtain of the future, I shall pour us another.'

Concentrating should have been difficult—being thrown into a reading, tired, in a strange place and without warning. But it wasn't. 'Let's see what the cards have to say, shall we?' said Derry. 'Would you shuffle the deck, please?'

She watched as Octavia shuffled. A rich gold bracelet gleamed on the Dowager's wrist. On her finger she wore a plain wedding ring. The Countess was surprisingly expert. She cut the deck into four parts before stacking them neatly in one pile.

'What knowledge does the seeker seek?' asked Derry. The old formula was comforting, like walking down a path known from childhood. 'You are enquiring for yourself or for another?'

'Don't be silly,' said Octavia, smiling 'It's not about me. What am I going to ask about? Career? Love? Health? At my age there are some things about my future I don't need a fortune-teller to predict.'

'Who then?' asked Derry. Often people asked about the futures of those close to them. Asking about others was natural. But answering was a different matter. Usually she let the cards decide.

'The girls of course,' said Octavia with a shrug.

'Very well,' said Derry. She dealt a spread, her hands settling into the familiar, fluid movements. As each minute passed, Derry O'Donnell, actress, faded further into the background. In her place, sitting poised at a low antique table, the cards spread in front of her, was Madam Tulip.

All at once, Derry felt unaccountably happy. Any sense of being at a disadvantage melted away. The Countess was just a woman, the stately home just a house. This family was a family like any other. Madam Tulip saw it all for what it was. 'Your question?'

'Bryony. She's taking a degree in estate management. Part-time. I've told her I think it's all too much for her—she works so hard. Will she… get through?'

Long ago, Derry learned that in a fortune-telling session the first question a person asked was rarely the one they most wanted answered—as if the questioner were gently pushing open the door to an unfamiliar room, wondering if they dared open a little wider, nervous about taking that step inside from which there could be no going back.

Derry turned the cards. There it all was. The story was plain—a kindly, good-natured girl. A challenge. A new beginning.

'The cards say... success will come.'

'I'm glad,' said Octavia.

Derry waited. If Octavia wanted to know more, she would ask. Inflicting unwanted information on someone was wrong. Once a thing was known it could never be unknown, and the person would have to live with that knowledge. But the Dowager seemed to be thinking of something else.

'The wedding,' she said. 'Will it come off alright?'

*And the door is pushed open a little further*, thought Derry. But Octavia hadn't yet stepped inside.

Another shuffle, another cut, another spread. The Dowager watched in silence. Derry saw no sign Octavia's heart was beating fast—no fumbling as she cut the deck, no telltale clutching of a handkerchief in a sweating palm. She seemed relaxed, sanguine, as if whatever the answer she would accept it.

And that, thought Derry, was just as well.

With shocking clarity, as plainly as if she had put a telescope to her eye and focused, a startling scene filled her vision. Shafts of coloured light played on the grey stone of an ancient church interior. Standing, her back to the altar, was a girl in bridal dress, her face veiled, a bouquet held in front of her. Derry was overwhelmed by the feeling she was intruding, that she shouldn't be watching, that what she was witnessing was something from which she should avert her eyes. But she didn't avert her eyes.

For a long time, the bride stood without moving until, in seeming slow motion, the bouquet in her hands drooped as though she were losing strength. From the flowers, petals fell one by one until only a single lily was left. Beneath her veil, the bride bowed her head. Her shoulders heaved in sobbing convulsions.

Derry looked up from the cards. Octavia met her gaze steadily. In Derry's mind, unbidden, came thoughts of her own loves. She shrugged them away impatiently. If Charlotte's future was a massive gamble, and if the gamble was lost, that was life, wasn't it?

'Love is never simple, said Derry. 'So much is… chance.'

Octavia nodded gently. Perhaps chance had intervened in her loves too.

'Tell me,' said Octavia, 'about the house.'

'This house?' asked Derry, surprised.

'This house.'

'Anything… special?'

'No,' said Octavia. 'Whatever you like.' Her gaze wandered, like she was looking clean through the walls of her grand sitting room out to the landscaped grounds and the spreading fields beyond.

Was this some kind of test? Often people did that. Instead of asking a genuine question, they would throw out a trick enquiry or a question to which they already knew the answer. Tedious. Derry hadn't expected a move so obvious from someone as sharp as Octavia.

Again Derry passed the deck for the Dowager to cut. Surprisingly, this time Octavia fumbled. She gathered the cards and tried again. Was the card that briefly showed an Ace of Spades? Derry couldn't be sure. She accepted the deck and dealt a simple spread. All the while, Octavia watched, leaning forward, expectant, uncannily still.

Derry turned the first three cards, the ones said to speak of the past. This time, no images came, and for that Derry was grateful. But neither did a meaning emerge that she could understand. Queen of Spades—a widow? The Dowager herself? Or someone else? Knave of Hearts—was that a young man? Or an opportunity? The cards of the present were no less confusing. A lie? Prosperity? As for the future—worry, fear. And that card again, the Ace of Spades. The card of obsession. Of death.

What to say?

Octavia's shrewd eyes assessed Derry's reaction to what she saw. But Derry's training as an actress came once more to her aid. She knew how to express no emotion whatever. If she had forebodings she knew how to hide them beneath a bland and reassuring mask.

'I see… worry,' said Derry. 'Anxiety. What cause, I can't say.'

'The outcome?' said Octavia. 'Those… fears. Are they justified? Do they come true?'

Since she had begun telling fortunes for friends, growing slowly more comfortable with her modest gift, Derry had meant only to bring happiness, even hope. The whole point was to help, wasn't it? And on the rare occasion she saw something dark, she reasoned that bringing fears to the surface could be a healing thing. But what about the self-fulfilling prophecy? How could a person be happy if they were told their future was unhappy? What strange tricks would the human nervous system play on someone warned to beware of accidents? Or told death was somewhere near?

'The cards show only one of many possible futures,' said Derry. 'Only when you look into your heart is the future resolved.'

Octavia bit her lip. Had she taken Derry's words—Madam Tulip's words—as a reprimand? Derry hadn't meant them that way. For a long moment, Octavia sat in silence. 'You're no fool.'

To that, there could be no answer.

'Marlene was right about you,' the Countess continued. 'You're nothing like any fortune-teller I've ever met.' Her look was appraising, but whether her words were meant as praise or criticism, Derry couldn't tell.

'Right-o,' said Octavia, briskly. 'James the head gardener wants to landscape the bunker—cover the thing in shrubbery and pretend it's not there. I say that's like painting Alcatraz pink and pretending it's Monte Carlo. Balls! So who wins? He might just walk, and then I'd be in trouble. Him or me?'

Derry tried not to smile. She handed the deck to Octavia to cut, dealt a spread, and there it was. The cards were in no doubt—Octavia triumphant. And not a rhododendron or resignation letter in sight.

'You will achieve your heart's desire,' said Derry in the time-honoured fashion.

Octavia laughed, rubbing her hands. 'Oh, jolly good. The old bastard will blink first. All I wanted to know!'

And the reading was over.

Octavia pressed more wine on Derry, but she was already

feeling pleasantly woozy and begged to pass. Octavia was having none of it. 'Don't be so damned bourgeois,' she said. 'If a countess asks you to pour, you ruddy well pour. *If* you'd be so good, dear.'

Derry smiled and obeyed.

# 10

'**H**i.'

He didn't explain who he was. Instead, he grinned and stood at the door with his hands in his pockets.

'Oh,' said Derry. 'Hi.' She was thankful she was up, dressed and breakfasted early despite the Dowager's generous hand with the wine. Bruce had gone for a jog, leaving a cheery note.

The young man was tall and dark, casually elegant. He wore a cream linen jacket, baggy trousers, and a silk cravat tied neatly at the neck. Attitude, thought Derry. But he was attractive. If you didn't hold long eyelashes against a man.

'I come from She Who Leads,' he announced.

'I'm sorry?' said Derry.

'Not a fan of old Nicky Roerich?' He smiled a challenging smile. 'One expects the masses to yawn, but I'd have thought given your paternity and your occupation, you'd have been a devotee.'

What was it with this man? The first time he meets you he quizzes you like a college professor.

'Hint—Russian? Painter?' He leaned idly against the doorjamb.

'Ah,' said Derry. 'New York. Roerich Museum. Sure, I went there once. Didn't go back.'

Roerich painted dreamy scenes of supposedly high mystical significance. The Russians loved him. But, surprising to those who didn't know her well, Derry wasn't much given to esoteric speculation.

'I like his mountains,' she continued. 'Makes you want to go to Tibet.'

'Suitably mystical. Not to Russia?'

'Russia? Maybe in summer. So long as the plane is American.'

'Please note I have refrained from suggesting you could visit on the *astral* plane. Points?'

No points. True enough, if he'd said she wouldn't need a ticket, being psychic, Derry would have closed the door in his face. Some jokes you only tolerate the first thousand times. Cleverly, this man got the satisfaction of saying what he wanted but without paying the price. Annoying.

'Can I help you?'

'Invite me in. Lady Bryony sent me.'

'Sebastian,' said Derry. Sebastian of the art gallery. Sebastian of the red sports car. She enjoyed his slight frown. It seemed Sebastian liked to have the initiative.

'At your service,' he answered, with a little bow.

Derry stood aside to let him in. He strode across the room, sat in the armchair in front of the unlit stove and crossed his legs.

'Do sit down,' said Derry, taking a seat at the table, signalling she had no intention of settling in for a long chat, however fascinating Sebastian thought he was.

'Bryony says why not do your business here for the party, save lots of faffing about over in the ballroom.'

Derry looked around, picturing how she might set the place up for fortune telling. And yes, the room could be arranged to make a fine fortune-teller's booth. She could sit at the round wooden table, have a fire lit, keep the blinds drawn.

'Your friend would have to keep a low profile, of course.' Sebastian's smile was knowing.

'Of course,' said Derry, resisting the urge to protest that Bruce wasn't her *friend* just a friend. She also resisted any remaining wish to be pleasant to this arrogant fop.

'I'm a great admirer of your father,' said Sebastian, idly examining his nails. Obviously, Derry was expected to say something in reply, so she didn't. Sebastian's statement hung in the air, faintly ridiculous, forcing him to continue.

'Your father is an exceptional talent—you must be proud.'

'I am,' said Derry. 'He is… himself.'

'And the world has so many imitations,' said Sebastian. 'Are you original?'

Tiresome. Derry's head was still muzzy from Octavia's hospitality, and the time was barely ten a.m.

'Bryony says would you mind giving her a reading this morning? She's keen, and she'll be busy once the beano gets going. Says she'll pop over in an hour, if that's alright.' He looked at his watch. Did he mean Derry to see it was expensive? 'She seems to think you'll tell her what's in store for us all. Will you?'

'I'll try my best,' said Derry, none too warmly. She stood. 'I'd better get ready. Sort things out.'

'I'll leave you to it then,' said Sebastian, getting up and moving to the doorway. As he reached the threshold, he stood waiting as if he couldn't simply turn the handle and let himself out. Derry opened the door.

'Goodbye,' she said.

'Oh, by the way, ' said Sebastian, 'Bryony says she'll phone you if she's held up. She has your number.'

Derry closed the door behind him. Then it struck her. If Bryony had her phone number—and there was no reason why she shouldn't, since all she had to do was ask Marlene—Sebastian hadn't needed to deliver his message in person. No need at all. But then, he knew that. And he wanted Derry to know it.

~

The shock on Bryony's face as Derry opened the door was hugely gratifying. Bryony took a step backwards, almost saying, 'Sorry,' as if she had come to the wrong address. Then it clicked.

'Oh my!' she exclaimed. 'Wow! Wait 'till Charlotte sees you!'

'If you come seeking knowledge,' said Madam Tulip, with the slightest of smiles, 'you are welcome. Do come in.'

Nothing is more satisfying to an actress than an audience being wowed when they first see her character in costume. Except an ovation, of course. But Bryony's reaction would do nicely.

'And the place!' Bryony squealed with delight.

The room was darkened, the shades pulled down. A lamp sat on a small circular table, casting an intimate pool of light while leaving the rest of the room in shadow. The fire gave out a warm glow, shifting, making shadows dance. Derry had laid her embroidered cloth over the table and placed her crystal ball in the centre. Her antique timer stood ready to measure out the session. Two decks of cards, a Tarot pack and a regular pack, sat side by side awaiting the client's choice. The setting was mysterious, other-worldly. You could easily forget it was eleven in the morning. Or that it was Berkshire. Or England, for that matter. Then there was Madam Tulip.

Madam Tulip looked nothing like Derry O'Donnell. Nothing like at all. Jasmine and Lorna were geniuses in the arts of makeup and costume, and they had created someone entirely new.

Madam Tulip had an unnaturally pale face. Her hair, a wig of the highest quality, was dark, with dramatic grey streaks. Tulip's bosom was ample, thanks to a padded corset, and her waist was thick—understandable in a mature woman of perhaps fifty. She wore glasses, emphasising her compelling green eyes. Her dress was calf-length—pale blue with a high collar, a low ruff at the throat and long sleeves with trailing lace cuffs. A twenties-style cord was tied loosely around her waist. About her neck hung strings of heavy beads, and on her head sat a delicate construction of three blue and two yellow feathers in an elegant cluster.

Derry invited Bryony to sit opposite her at the table. Bryony took her place, still shaking her head, speechless.

'Shall we begin?' asked Derry. 'Would you prefer the cards or the crystal?'

'Do give me a minute!' said Bryony, laughing. 'Let me be amazed. I had no idea.'

'Perhaps you'd like to make yourself more comfortable. Why not take off your jacket. Relax.'

'That would be good,' answered Bryony. 'I've been on the run all morning. Two coach parties already, and a child fallen off a swing. Grazed knee, poor dear. Our fault, of course.' She took her phone out of her pocket and put it on the table in front of her before removing her jacket and throwing it on the couch. 'Did you manage alright for breakfast? I'd have suggested you come over to the house, but no point really. All pretty random—everybody gets up at different times.'

Derry said she had indeed breakfasted, and all was fine. Although she didn't say so, a peaceful start to the day had been more than welcome. She would need her energy for her performances this evening.

'Just passed your friend Bruce,' said Bryony. 'He was jogging along beside Aunt Octavia in her buggy. The two seemed to be getting along good-oh. He looked like one of those Secret Service men who trot beside the President's motorcade, though I don't think they talk quite so much. He'd better watch out or Aunt Octavia will have him shifting boulders and digging ponds before he knows where he is. No able-bodied male is safe when Aunt has her gardening gloves on.'

They drank their tea, chatting comfortably. Beyond telling Derry that being an actress must be great fun, Bryony didn't seem much interested in showbusiness. But she was keenly interested in fortune telling. 'I hope you don't object, but I shall be watching how you manage everything,' said Bryony. 'I've always thought perhaps I could do it, if I studied. Haven't had the time, of course.'

'I'm sure you could learn,' said Derry. 'The important part is to have an open mind.'

Bryony laughed. 'I've got that alright. Sebastian says my mind is too open by far. I need to be a little more cynical, he says. Or is it sceptical? But it's like horses, isn't it? Anyone who knows horses knows they sense things we can't. Why should we be different?' She stopped, embarrassed. 'Sorry, I'm used to having to stick up for myself amongst the unbeliev-ers. Charlotte says I'm overcompensating for a boring life. She might be right.'

'Shall we start with the cards?' asked Derry. 'Afterwards, if you like, we can talk a little about how they might work for you as a reader.'

'I'd be so grateful if you would,' said Bryony. 'Shall I cut?'

Bryony knew what to do. She shuffled the pack expertly and cut the deck. Derry noticed her hands were strong and her fingernails short and a little grubby, but she didn't fumble or drop the cards.

Derry dealt a simple spread. Just as the last card landed on the table, Bryony's phone rang.

'Sorry!' she said, reaching for her jacket and fishing her phone out of a pocket. 'Yes?'

At first Derry paid little attention to Bryony and her call. She wanted to stay focused for the reading, maintaining that world of calm you had to enter if you were to sense anything of worth. So it took a moment for her to register that Bryony wasn't speaking. She was holding the phone to her ear, her mouth was open, but she was making no sound. At last, in a loud assertive voice, she spoke.

'Charlotte! Calm down! I'm coming now, alright? Right now. Yes, yes!'

Bryony ended the call. She sat motionless, staring at her phone. 'I'm sorry,' she said. 'Got to go. Explain later. Sorry.' She struggled into her jacket, and with the phone still in her hand rushed out, leaving the door gaping open behind her.

~

Derry's first thought on seeing Bryony's pale face and hurried exit was that she had heard bad news, perhaps of an accident. And if the accident had happened to a visitor, it must have been far more serious than a grazed knee. Derry's second thought would only occur to a fortune-teller—why don't I turn the cards and see what they say?

When difficult choices arose about how she might use what modest powers she had, Derry would mentally consult her grandfather and great-grandfather. She thought of them as the Grandads, and had always believed they would steer her through tricky dilemmas. She never felt guilty about bothering them, wherever they were—the Grandads were responsible for Derry having her gift in the first place, and she wasn't about to let them wriggle out of their responsibilities. But this time, as Derry sat with the tempting cards spread in front of her, she felt no need to consult her ancestors. She guessed that among the rules in whatever supernatural realm governs these things, was one clearly stating: Thou Shalt Not Use Psychic Powers When You can Pick Up the Phone.

Derry gathered the cards, careful not to peek, and replaced them in the deck. She automatically shuffled, burying whatever secrets they contained forever. She reached for her phone. Just as her finger was poised to call Bruce's number, the screen lit up and the phone trilled.

'Hi hon,' said Bruce. 'We've got a situation. Where are you?'

'Bruce, has something happened?'

'Uh, can't explain on the phone, but we could do with you right now—'

'Hold it!' said Derry. 'We? Who is we? What situation?'

'The girls are really upset. We need some calm, okay? Can you come? To the house. The breakfast room. Where we ate. Hurry. Like now, alright?'

Usually it took many minutes for Derry to get out of her Madam Tulip costume and put everything neatly away. Not this time. In seconds she was in the bedroom undressing. She took care to put the wig safely back in its box and her headdress in its container, but she left the rest—dress, jewellery, all of it—lying on the bed while she threw on her jeans and a sweater and grabbed her jacket. She checked she had her key and her phone, and pulled the door closed behind her.

As she crossed the courtyard to the house, a chill breeze sprang up. Gusts swirled around the old tower, raising miniature whirlwinds of dust. The yard was deserted. The builders' skip and cement mixer were gone. Only Marlene's SUV sat parked. She saw no sign of the Bentley or the red sports car. It seemed to Derry that everyone had suddenly abandoned the scene having heard a warning she had somehow missed.

~

The heavy back door to the East Wing was ajar, and even before she pushed it open Derry heard Bryony's raised voice.

'I told you. I explained that. Just come, will you!' Bryony was in the hall, on her phone. Her face was distraught but determined, her voice hectoring like she was taking control of the scene of an accident, telling everyone what to do, brooking no argument.

Derry stepped inside. Bryony motioned her urgently to carry on towards the breakfast room, down the long passageway.

She kept talking as she waved, and all Derry could do was obey. From somewhere down the corridor a dog barked frantically. Derry heard thumps as the animal threw itself against a door as if shut in a room against its will.

Even before Derry pushed open the door to the breakfast room, she heard the sobbing. At first the scene was so confusing she could make no sense of it. Marlene and Charlotte sat at the big dining table. Charlotte was the one sobbing—Marlene had an arm around her shoulder, comforting her. Beside Charlotte sat an unfamiliar young man looking helpless, but obviously concerned only for her. Derry guessed this was Torquil, Charlotte's fiancée. His face was pale. He looked as if he wanted to be sick.

Sitting on a small armchair by the window was Annie, the cook or maid who had served food the previous night. She was bent over in her seat, her head down like someone about to faint. Beside her, kneeling on the floor, encouraging her to breathe deeply, was Bruce, still in his sweatpants and running shoes. He greeted Derry with a look of intense relief.

'Take over here, will you. I have to do something. She's had a shock; she'll be fine. Explain later.' Before Derry knew what was happening, she was kneeling on the floor in Bruce's place, telling Annie to take deep breaths, assuring her that everything would be alright and having no idea whether it would or would not.

~

After Bruce left the room, nobody said anything, not a single word. He had gone through into the kitchen, pulling the door half closed behind him. Everyone's eyes were now fixed on that door as though something might emerge at any moment, something they couldn't bear to face. But all that emerged was Bruce's head as he peered around. 'Trash bag?'

'Drawer. Roll. Left of sink,' said Annie, gasping out the words.

Bruce's head disappeared back into the kitchen. Derry heard drawers sliding open and slamming shut. The room fell into an uncanny silence, like every sound that came from the kitchen was laden with some fateful meaning that no one expected to be good news.

A clatter made Derry jump. She knew instantly—ice cubes being poured into a sink. A ripping sound—Bruce tearing a refuse sack from its roll. Then nothing until Bruce emerged, his face grim.

At that moment the door to the hallway opened. Bryony ushered a dark-suited man into the room. He stood for a moment looking around warily, his face expressionless. Behind him entered two uniformed policemen and a figure in white coveralls.

# 11

The man in the suit announced himself as Detective Sergeant Cranshaw, Peter Cranshaw. The two uniformed officers stood uneasily, their hands behind their backs, trying to look as if being inside an earl's stately home was a matter of no special interest. At a word from the detective the two left, throwing regretful glances behind. Only now did Derry notice that the man in the coveralls had donned a mask and carried what looked like a plastic picnic box. A hood covered his head. His shoes were covered by little white booties. In silence, Bryony led the detective and the suited figure into the kitchen.

Derry sat on the arm of Annie's chair, still cradling her shoulders, but at least Annie was quiet now, staring into space. Charlotte, Marlene and Torquil were equally silent, as if by not mentioning whatever had happened they could somehow erase the event from history. And still Derry had no idea what was going on. If Bruce hadn't been in the kitchen, closeted with Bryony and the policemen, she would have pulled him to one side and demanded to be told, even if he had to whisper. The idea of asking any of the shocked faces around her to explain was unthinkable. So Derry waited.

The door to the kitchen opened. The coveralled officer emerged carrying his picnic box, followed by the detective and Bruce. Whatever the box held couldn't have been unduly heavy; the officer had no trouble carrying it. Bruce opened the hall door for him to pass, and he gave a nod of thanks. Bryony stood staring until the detective coughed tactfully.

'Lady Bryony, if you don't mind?'

'Of course,' answered Bryony. 'Please. Take a seat.' She indicated an empty chair at the table. The detective sat. He took from his inside pocket a small notebook and a pen.

The detective was a young man, younger than the constables who had come with him. He was pale-faced and fleshy, as though he spent most of his time at a desk or waiting long hours in parked cars. His accent was regional and he spoke slowly, enunciating every word in the way he might have addressed a room of foreigners. But his dark eyes were shrewd. Perhaps he was one of the new generation, with a law degree and a diploma in psychology.

'You've had a shock, I can see that, and I'm sorry. But I have to ask you some questions. I'll be quick as I can.' He opened his pad and scribbled something. Right away Derry recognised a piece of stage business. She would bet he had written nothing at all relevant to the case. Most likely he had scribbled a note to himself to pick up the dry cleaning on the way home. The detective leaned back in his seat, letting his gaze settle on them one by one. He turned to Bryony.

'My lady,' he said, 'if you could please tell me who was present.' Try as she might, Derry could detect no note of irony in his voice as he used Bryony's title. Nor did she sense the exaggerated respect that would signal disrespect.

'Annie was here. So were Charlotte, Marlene and Torquil. We came later,' she added, indicating Derry and Bruce, who stood against the wall with his hands behind his back.

'I'll take everyone's details as we go along,' said the detective. 'One more thing—the Earl. Is his lordship here?'

'No,' said Charlotte. 'He went to Fotheringham. About an

hour ago. With Sebastian. They'll have their phones on silent while they're there, of course.'

For the briefest moment the detective hesitated, failing to understand. Comprehension dawned. 'Of course,' he said. 'Naturally.'

You could see the detective couldn't help himself. He tried not to show it, but he was impressed. How could he not be? Derry knew Fotheringham belonged to the highest in the land. Not just aristocrats, but members of the Royal Family itself. Derry wondered at the extraordinary sensitivity of the English to class. They could place anyone in seconds, yet they pretended not to care. Many went out of their way to denigrate the *toffs* but still couldn't help being awed. So different from the States, where only money or showbusiness fame could get you on the A-list.

'Sebastian was going to London afterwards. Daddy was going on to Ascot—it's a big day, as you know,' said Bryony.

'Of course,' said the detective. Derry was certain he had not known.

'Daddy has two horses running today. He wouldn't miss it for the world. They'll all be going on from Fotheringham,' continued Bryony.

'All?'

'Perhaps not all; I don't think the Queen is going. I imagine preparations for the Prince's wedding will be distracting everyone, even from the racing. It's only a few months away now.'

'Ah,' said the detective. 'The wedding, yes.' Now he looked anxious, like a man who had breezily strolled into a flower-strewn meadow only to spot a sign saying Minefield!

'I tried to get Daddy,' said Bryony. 'I've left him a message to call me.'

The detective made a note in his book. 'I need to determine exactly where everyone was. If you don't mind.'

'I was over at the courtyard. With Derry,' said Bryony.

'You're Derry, Miss?'

'Derry O'Donnell, yes.'

'Address please?'

Derry noticed that the detective hadn't for one moment imagined she lived in the great house. And she'd only spoken three words. She gave him her address and phone number.

'And you, sir?'

'Bruce Adams.' Bruce gave his details.

'And where were you?'

'I came into the house with Lady Octavia. We'd been chatting, and I walked her to her apartment—'

'At the other end of the wing,' added Bryony.

'She was going to have a lie-down, but we ended up talking some more. And as I came back from her sitting room into the hall, I heard a scream from in here.'

'You didn't see the events, Mr…. Adams?'

'No sir,' said Bruce.

'I'll return to you later. You did a good job, by the way.'

Bruce only nodded.

Charlotte spoke. 'Marlene, Torquil and I were sitting waiting for our breakfast. Annie was cooking. Torquil had just arrived. We'd had a late night. Well, not really late—'

'And your name is?'

'Charlotte.'

'Lady Charlotte?' Had the detective done his homework on the way here? Or did everyone in the county know the names and titles of the family who lived at Sorley Hall?

'Yes,' said Charlotte. She gave her phone number and the upmarket London address she shared with Torquil.

And where were you, Annie, if you don't mind?' said the Detective. His tone was kindlier.

'In the kitchen, at the cooker. I'd just come out with the coffee pot and put it on the table—'

'I'm sorry—your full name Annie, please?'

'Fuller,' said Annie. 'I stay in a staff cottage here.' She gave her telephone number.

'Thank you. Can you say what happened?'

'Just as I'd put the pot down on the table—and thank goodness I had done—Percy came in from the hall.'

'Percy?'

'Our dog,' said Charlotte and Bryony at the same time.

'I see, thank you. And?'

'He was carrying something in his mouth,' said Charlotte. At that, Annie hid her face. Her shoulders shook. Derry squeezed her arm.

'For a moment we didn't know what it was,' added Marlene.

The detective gave her an enquiring look.

'Oh,' said Marlene. 'Sorry. Marlene O'Mara.' She gave her details, and the detective wrote them down.

'Then I saw what Percy had done,' said Charlotte. 'He'd never done it before.' She spoke as if she had explained everything. The detective waited, then gave up waiting.

'I'm sorry—done what, Lady Charlotte?'

'Picked up a package off the hall stand.'

'Ah,' said the detective.

'It was a Jiffy bag, like the biggest-size padded envelope.

But he'd ripped it apart. Torn it to pieces. He likes chewing things, but he'd never done that in the house. I was sitting right where I am now. I reached down to try to get it off him, but he wouldn't let go. Annie was standing beside me, and… it fell out.'

Derry felt Annie's back heave in convulsions.

'Did you recognise it… for what it was?'

Charlotte shook her head. She looked away.

For the first time, Torquil spoke. 'Um, can't speak for any-one else—'

'Your name, please?'

'Torquil Ormsby-Johnson.' He frowned. 'It's like your brain doesn't want to see what your eyes tell it. So it doesn't. Or it sees something else. To be honest, I thought the thing was a lamp.'

'A lamp?'

'Like a designer table lamp. It had plastic wrapping on it. You know, when you get electrical stuff from eBay it comes bubble-wrapped. I know that sounds stupid.'

The detective shook his head gently, as though he under-stood that what Torquil's brain had done to him wasn't at all stupid. It was doing him a favour.

'Then I saw it was a hand. An arm, really.'

Silence settled on the room. The dreadful thing had been said and couldn't be unsaid. Right here, an arm had fallen from a torn package dropped from the mouth of a curious dog. Or, thought Derry—trying both to picture the scene and at the same time not to picture it—a hungry dog. Nausea rose in the back of her throat. Into her mind, unbidden, came the image of a joint of meat on a butcher's block.

'Alright,' said the detective, answering a question nobody had asked. 'Presumably the… it was on the floor.' The three at the table nodded dumbly. 'So who…?'

'I did, sir,' said Bruce. His tone was matter-of-fact, as if he were reporting on a routine assignment completed according to standard procedures.

'Into the sink?'

'Yessir. The evidence was at risk of being destroyed. Seeing as how the pooch was uh—'

'Yes,' interrupted the detective. 'You did the right thing.' He paused. 'The package was stamped, presumably delivered by post in the normal way. Unfortunately, I couldn't see to whom it was addressed. Too badly damaged.'

Annie looked up, surprising everyone. 'It was addressed to his lordship.'

'You saw the address?'

'Yes sir. I took it in from the postman. He comes about quarter to ten, and he always rings the bell. I put it on the hallstand…'

She couldn't continue. Derry resumed patting Annie's back, not knowing whether it was helping or not. Perhaps it was herself she was comforting.

'There was nothing strange about the package?' asked the detective.

Annie shook her head. 'I saw it was for his Lordship. It was heavy, and I thought it must have cost a pretty penny in postage.' She burst out sobbing.

'I'm sorry,' said the detective. 'I'm afraid I have to ask you all, do you know of anyone who might have wanted to send… such a thing to his lordship? Any threats to his lordship or to anyone else in the house?'

'That's ridiculous! Of course not!' Bryony's reaction was instant. She seemed affronted, as though being threatened would reflect badly.

'Lady Bryony, I'm afraid there's nothing ridiculous about any of this. A serious crime may have been committed.'

'Of course, ' said Bryony. 'I'm sorry.'

'Somebody had a reason to send the… object to the Earl. I need to know what that reason was.'

'Someone crazy, of course!' burst out Charlotte. 'Horrible people are everywhere! If you saw the things I get called on the internet you wouldn't be surprised at anything. And anyway, aren't we forgetting something here? Like who did it belong to? I mean it's not like somebody's lost a pound of beef, is it!'

The detective was unmoved. He must have been accustomed to hysterical outbursts. And what Charlotte had said was true. The owner of the thing that had so shocked them was out there somewhere. And he was almost certainly dead.

'The next step is of course to establish who the… limb might have belonged to,' said the detective. And whether he is still alive.' He had no intention of being taught how to suck eggs, not even by lords and ladies.

'He?' said Bryony.

Derry saw Bruce nodding.

'Yes,' said the detective. 'The pathologist will confirm it, of course, but I would say the victim is male, yes.

'For sure, said Bruce. 'A guy.'

'Perhaps fingerprints will identify him,' continued the detective.

'Uh-uh,' said Bruce.

'I'm sorry?' said the detective, taking no trouble to hide

his irritation. Everyone turned to look at Bruce. Even Annie raised her head and stopped weeping.

'Uh, no fingertips.'

Annie's moan was like the lowing of a calf in distress. Until that moment, almost everyone in the room believed that what they had already experienced was the worst possible nightmare. But this was awful.

Bruce's simple statement earned him the detective's full attention. If the policeman was embarrassed by failing to notice this new and curious fact, his discomfiture was instantly displaced by professional interest. 'Are you sure?' he said, quietly.

'Certain,' said Bruce. 'Not the first I've seen like that.' He looked around apologetically. 'I won't go into details—ladies present.'

Torquil seemed disappointed. Bryony looked annoyed. Derry frowned. It seemed gays could be just as sexist as any other male.

'Fill you in later?' said Bruce. The detective was about to argue but never got the chance. The door to the hallway swung open.

'What on earth is going on?' The Dowager Countess stood in the doorway, supporting herself with her stick, her face a picture of outrage. She was smartly dressed, pearls around her neck, bracelets on her wrist. No scruffy gardening jacket or corduroys, Derry noticed. Octavia had taken some trouble getting dressed before she came to investigate the commotion. *Once in showbusiness, always in showbusiness.*

'I said, what is happening here?' The Dowager thumped her stick on the floor, emphasising each word.

Bryony jumped up from her seat. 'I'll explain Aunt, let's go to your apartment, shall we?'

'Certainly not,' said the Dowager. She pointed her stick at the detective. 'Who is this young man?'

～

The detective did exactly as Octavia ordered him to do. He recited the events as they had been described to him, consulting his notes and reading as though he were giving testimony in a courtroom. At first, Charlotte or Bryony interrupted, trying to tell part of the story themselves, but the Dowager insisted they be quiet and let the detective speak.

The policeman finished his account, leaving nothing out, not even Bruce's careful filling of the kitchen sink with ice-cubes, his laying a refuse sack on top, and on top of that another sack into which he had placed the horrid object and its tattered envelope. Derry saw that even the inscrutable Octavia couldn't hide her relief as she was told of the departure of the man in the white coveralls bearing away his prize in a plastic box.

Octavia remained stranding throughout, leaning on her stick, her face betraying no emotion. She's an actress, thought Derry. She may have worked as a dancer, but she's an actress through and through. Octavia was playing the stern and masterful countess, just as the detective was playing the provincial working-class cop. Then, all at once, Octavia abandoned the script. 'Alright, Annie dear?' she said, genuine concern on her face.

Annie sniffed. 'Yes m'lady. Thank you m'lady.'

'No point us feeling sorry for ourselves, is there?' said Octavia.

Derry found herself nodding with the rest. What the Dowager had said was true. The poor man who had lost his arm in some horrible way was the one for whom they should feel sorry.

Bryony spoke up. 'I'll get a cleaning company in this afternoon, Annie—how about that. Do the floor, the kitchen and so on. Give everything a good scrub. Alright?' She turned to the detective, 'Sorry, I'm making assumptions here. You're not going to cordon the place off or anything are you?'

The detective shook his head. 'No. You can clean up. I'll need to speak to the Earl as soon as possible. Can you give me his telephone number?'

Bryony scribbled on the detective's pad. He read the number back to be certain. Derry couldn't help admiring his thoroughness. The package had been addressed to the Earl, and he was the person most likely to know why anyone would do such a thing. And of course there was no point looking for forensics in the house. It wasn't as if anyone had chopped off someone's arm here, had they? There must have been blood. How much blood? A lot, surely.

Then it struck her.

She almost fainted. She must have swayed, nearly falling from the arm of the chair on which she was perched beside Annie, only just keeping her balance. Annie looked up in alarm, grabbing Derry's arm to steady her. 'Are you alright?'

'Someone get her a glass of water,' said Octavia. Nobody moved. 'Ah,' she added, as though reading everyone's mind. *Water. Kitchen. Sink.* And the horror that had sat in that sink wrapped in a plastic garbage sack. 'Perhaps better not. A bottle of mineral water?'

Bruce strode briskly to the kitchen.

'I'm okay,' said Derry. 'Sorry.'

But she wasn't okay. In her mind's eye the dream had returned in all its disturbing symmetry. The shield. The dog. The bleeding severed arm, fist held upright dripping with red blood—all now shot through with terrible meaning.

Bruce knelt beside her with an opened bottle of water—thankfully not the sparkling kind. All Derry needed was fizzy water up her nose, making her explode in coughs and sneezes in a room full of aristocrats and policemen. Somehow the ludicrous picture banished the nightmare vision of that fist from her mind. She smiled up at the others. 'Thanks. Sorry. Really, I'm okay.'

'What I want to know,' said Torquil, 'is why anybody would wrap up such an object and send it here. It's insane, like something from a gangster movie. I mean, will it be a horse's head next or what?'

'For goodness' sake Torquil! That's horrible,' said Charlotte.

'Just saying,' said Torquil. 'Maybe the thing wasn't even real. Maybe it was some kind of stage prop. A joke.'

Bruce shook his head.

'I'm afraid not,' said the detective.

'Who would do such an awful thing?' said Charlotte.

'Medical students having a laugh?' suggested Torquil. 'Dissections, all that? And why are we assuming the chap wasn't long dead already?'

'Hunt saboteurs?' said Bryony. 'Everybody knows I ride to

hounds now and again. But we don't even kill the damned foxes any more. Still, sabs do crazy things.'

'But Daddy doesn't hunt,' said Charlotte. 'Alright, he loves the races, but the sabs never seem to interfere with those.'

'Stop this now!' said Octavia, banging her stick on the floor, making them all jump. 'This is idle speculation. Ridiculous. There could be any number of reasons. Lots of people don't like us—you need to get that into your head, Charlotte. It's who we are. The world is full of resentful, envious people. Let the police do their job.'

As if taking his cue, the detective stood, returning his notebook to his inside pocket. 'That's it for now, I think. If you hear from the Earl before I reach him, please ask his lordship to telephone me at once.' He handed Bryony his card then turned to Bruce. 'Mr. Adams, would you mind stepping outside with me for a moment. A word.'

'Sure thing,' said Bruce.

'Inspector,' said Octavia. 'Tell me honestly, is there any chance of keeping this out of the papers?'

The detective shook his head. The world, he seemed to say, was a disorderly and uncooperative place despite the efforts of clever detectives. 'I'll be frank, your ladyship, I doubt something like this can ever be kept quiet. No reflection on the force, but there's the forensics lab. And the household here. People will have seen the patrol cars arrive. Folk will talk.'

'It will be all over Twitter in a couple of hours, I should say,' said Torquil, not looking especially troubled by the idea.

Bryony gave him a hard stare. 'Just the kind of publicity we don't need.'

'Oh, I don't know,' said Torquil. 'I imagine you'll have flocks turn up. People are ghouls. I bet I'm right.'

The detective apologised to the Dowager, promised to keep them updated on developments, said good morning, and left. Bruce followed, patting Derry on the shoulder as he went.

'I want everyone to promise they'll keep this quiet,' said Bryony. 'Whatever Torquil says, we don't have to help the story along.'

Torquil shrugged, and Derry wondered might the first tweet not come from Torquil himself? He seemed almost cocky now, enjoying the drama. But Mr. Film Director wasn't so brave when he saw that thing fall on the floor; he had left it to Bruce to handle the hard part. Torquil will make a director for sure, thought Derry. All bluster, and the sensitivity of an armadillo. She was surprised to find that thinking angry thoughts about directors made her feel better.

'What about our party?' said Charlotte.

'If you get me the list, I can text everyone for you if you like,' offered Bryony. 'Tell them it's off, unforeseen circs, all that.'

Charlotte nodded dumbly. Torquil didn't comment, as though his own engagement party was nothing to do with him.

Octavia spoke. 'Normally, I'd say carry on with your plans. But if you do, you'll end up telling the story to every Tom, Dick and Harry at the party. Better to let things quieten down.'

'Yes, Aunt,' said Charlotte meekly.

'Annie,' said Octavia. 'You must take the rest of the day off. You can walk me to my apartments on your way to your flat. Alright?'

'Yes, my lady,' said Annie, getting up from her chair. As she stood, she gave Derry's arm a squeeze.

'And no more guessing games. For your own sakes,' said the Dowager. 'Now I suggest you all get some fresh air.'

Nobody argued.

# 12

Bruce pulled up the bedroom's only chair, a delicate wicker seat that seemed far too flimsy for his impressive frame. A look from Derry made him change his mind about putting his feet on the bed.

'It didn't seem right to ask were they sure about cancelling, but I wish I had,' said Derry. 'Like should I pack away my costume or what?'

'Had a chat with Lady B.,' said Bruce, as if he and she were old friends. 'She says the party's off for sure—Charlotte can't face it, and anyhow the Dowager says no. Seems she gets the last call on most everything.'

'Makes sense, I guess,' said Derry. 'Hard to see how anyone could celebrate after this.' She remembered her card-reading with Octavia—was that only last night? She'd seen a dejected bride. A wedding come to nothing. Had that vision hinted at the disappointments to come? Derry dismissed the thought. This was a party being cancelled, not a wedding.

'Bryony says no need to rush away. We can stay until tomorrow. Only thing is, we'll have to get lunch in the visitors' restaurant 'cos nobody wants to go in the kitchen after what happened.'

Derry had no trouble agreeing with that. The idea of going into the breakfast room, never mind eating out of that kitchen, made her feel ill.

'We're to get the cashier to call her. The food's on the house.'

Bryony thought of everything. Even in the middle of

this appalling business, she remembered they'd need to eat. Charlotte was beautiful, but the man that married Bryony would be the lucky one.

'The detective,' said Derry. 'Cranshaw? What did he want to talk to you about?'

'He's okay, that guy. A lot of folks when they miss a trick they shut you down rather than take heed. Pure ego—ain't nothin' else. Ego can get ya killed. That's what they taught us in BUD/S.'

Derry nodded patiently. She had known Bruce long enough to understand that the valuable lessons taught in Basic Underwater Demolition training were not confined to athletic feats culminating in extreme violence. They included many nuggets of golden philosophy Bruce was keen to share.

'Fingers,' said Bruce. 'You heard me tell him the fingertips had been sliced off?'

'Yes,' said Derry. 'I guess that means whoever did it doesn't want the owner of the arm identified.'

'Sure, but what does that say?'

'Professionals? And the victim knew them?'

'Uh, yes,' said Bruce, frowning at being deprived of his punchline.

What was that about ego? Derry kept her smile to herself.

'Saw it with drug gangs in South America,' continued Bruce. 'Sometimes they needed to knock off somebody but didn't want the victim linked to them too quickly.'

'So the victim—assuming the victim is dead—'

'He's dead, alright.'

'—is connected to the killers in some way. If the body gets identified, they'll be identified.'

'Gotta be.'

Derry thought about that. It should have made sense. But it didn't.

It made no sense at all.

~

Lunch in the visitors' restaurant was good. The menu was based on the estate's own farm produce, emphasising the organic and the healthy. But the management had no intention of sacrificing cashflow to virtue. Strawberry jam and cream scones, Cornish pasties and shepherds' pie all paraded under the respectable banner of Traditional English Fayre. The message was clear—these were not calories; they were culture. Derry wondered if the hand she saw behind the business was Bryony's.

Derry and Bruce ate together, but neither again mentioned the events of the morning. In the afternoon Derry slept. By the time she surfaced to make herself some borage tea and sit quietly checking her email on her phone, the afternoon had slipped by. She had to turn on the lamp in the little sitting room, a reminder it was September. Should she revive the fire? A cheery blaze might dispel the gloom that had settled on everything.

Derry sat and sipped her borage. The heat from the open door of the stove was delightful. The flickering flames were soothing and hypnotic. But a difficult question refused to go away. How do you mention to a family of aristocrats that perhaps they should pay you something even though your show has been cancelled? And how to bring up the subject of money under such tragic circumstances? Was there a sensitive way of saying, sorry about the dead arm and all, but how about making with a few bucks for the gas?'

Bruce tapped on the front door before stepping inside, polite as always. He pulled his damp running jacket over his head. 'All change, hon!' he announced brightly. 'We're not leaving.'

'Oh,' said Derry.

'They're going to have the party next week. Saturday. We get to stay here 'till then.'

Derry frowned. The news seemed to call for action. At least, it seemed to call for not sitting cosily in front of a stove sipping borage tea as if her entire life wasn't being rearranged in her absence. 'Coffee?'

'Thanks,' said Bruce settling comfortably in front of the fire. 'I know what you're gonna say—what are we gonna do for a whole week?'

'No,' said Derry. 'That's not what I'm going to say. I'm going to say something completely different. I'm going to say, are you crazy? The place is coming down with body parts and weirdness, and I'm supposed to hang around waiting for the rest of somebody's bits to turn up! Or for the whole family to be arrested. Or for us to be arrested.'

'I called on her ladyship,' said Bruce.

'Which ladyship, exactly?'

'The Countess,' said Bruce, taking no notice of the sarcasm. Perhaps he liked the idea that Sorley Hall was a place with several ladyships from which to choose. Derry sighed. Maybe Bruce being impressed was understandable. In Texas you'd have to look long and hard to find even one ladyship. And they'd be working in a brothel.

'The Earl came back and he's real upset,' continued Bruce. 'He says he hasn't a clue who could have sent that thing or why they might have addressed it to him. But if you ask me, her ladyship ain't buying that, no sir. She says— "Bruce, in the City of London in all those shiny towers where the money is, there's more wickedness than in half the jails in England." That's what she says. And the Earl likes to bet on the races too, though her ladyship thinks racing people wouldn't be so vulgar about a little debt.'

'Hold it there,' said Derry. 'Is she saying—what's she saying?'

'I think she suspects the Earl has kept some unhealthy company, and she's worried. So she says, "Bruce, I've heard a lot about you from Marlene and Charlotte. How's about you keep an eye on his lordship until the party next week. Just watch out for him. Then we can think again what to do." '

'She offered you a job?' Derry's voice revealed every bit of the astonishment she felt. One moment Bruce was an out-of-work actor and van driver, next he was offered tough-guy jobs by royalty. Okay, not royalty, but good as. Then again, Bruce was eminently well qualified. 'Like a bodyguard?'

'Pretty much.'

'So what did you say?'

'I said no way.'

Surprising. How could there be much danger to anybody on a huge estate surrounded by walls and with the police already involved? 'I thought you could do that stuff. Wouldn't the pay be good?'

'I told her what she needs is a full protection service. Plenty of good companies out there with experienced veterans. The

Brits got the SAS, and they're pretty good. They're not SEALs, but they're okay as long as things don't get too hot.' He grinned as though telling an old joke. 'But her ladyship says the Earl wouldn't want the whole circus, and he wouldn't much want to pay for it either; close protection don't come cheap.

'Like how much?'

'Mmm, four guys? Plus vehicles and kit? Ten grand a week? Fifteen?'

'Dollars?'

'Dollars.'

If the Earl did have some business troubles or a gambling problem, he'd be in no position to spend that kind of money. And from what Bryony said, running a vast estate meant constant money worries. The Earl wasn't any kind of billionaire businessman.

'I told her I couldn't guarantee anybody's safety working on my own,' said Bruce. 'And anyhow, I'm not a bodyguard; I'm just a veteran with a few skills.'

A few skills sounded like extreme modesty to Derry. As far as she could make out, US Navy SEALs were one-man armies when they got going. But Bruce had no doubts about his decision.

'I kept telling her what the Earl needs is a team, and I ain't going to promise anything I can't deliver. No way. Then she changes tack and says okay, I can be her assistant. Help her out when she's in the garden or whatever. So I say, "Ma'am, I don't know nothin' about gardening." And she's like, "Neither do my gardeners, so don't you worry." What she wants is for me to keep an eye out for trouble. Maybe play chauffeur for a while. Check under the Earl's car. Take basic precautions. I said okay.'

'Won't the police give him any protection? Like, real protection?'

'Naw. They don't think the arm business is a direct threat against anybody. More a scare tactic. A psychological thing. Someone making a point. Anyhow, the Countess says the Earl doesn't want the cops involved. Says it would look bad for the family.'

'But she must be taking it as a genuine threat or she wouldn't be hiring you.'

'She's something else, that lady. She can joke about it. She says, "Bruce, we have to keep George safe or we'll be out of house and home, living in a caravan." I think she meant a trailer. "Some damned second cousin from Australia will be turning my gardens into a golf course." '

Derry smiled at the thought of the Dowager in a trailer park. But where did aristocrats go when they lost their estates? Derry supposed they worked in art galleries and interior decoration companies. They knew about art and antiques, that was for sure.

'I said to her, what's with the Australian?' continued Bruce. 'What about Lady B.? Wouldn't she be the new Lady Something Else?' The countess laughed and said ask the politicians.'

Derry smiled. 'She's talking about primogeniture, I guess.'

Bruce looked mystified.

'Primogeniture,' repeated Derry, allowing herself a small measure of smugness. Serve Bruce right for unfairly knowing about bodyguards, spooks and guns. 'Only male heirs can inherit British titles and estates. It's an ancient law.'

Bruce was shocked. 'But that's *sooo* sexist!'

'Sure is,' said Derry.

'So that's what she meant,' said Bruce. 'She said, "The politicians have promised to change it soon, but we have to keep old George breathing until then. After that he can pop off whenever he likes and leave it all to Bryony." '

'She said that?'

'She was laughing.' He shook his head. 'Man, these Brits are weird.'

# 13

Derry must have made up her mind while she slept. She woke early Saturday morning knowing all she needed to do was text her mother and tell Bryony.

She made her breakfast and packed her bag. She'd promised Jacko she'd go to London and speak to her mother about his pictures, and that's what she meant to do. While she was there, she'd talk Vanessa into giving her a week's paid work in her gallery. The tricky part, Derry realised, might be escaping again, but she'd deal with that when the time came.

Derry could think of many good, practical reasons for not wasting a week hanging around Sorley Hall. But as she sat, sipping her coffee, failing to get Bryony to answer her phone, Derry knew that none of those reasons mattered. She wanted to leave because an image of a severed arm she hadn't even seen wouldn't leave her mind.

A polite tap on the door. Bryony was standing politely waiting to be invited in, as if the cottage wasn't hers. 'Sorry I couldn't take your calls,' she said. 'Unbelievable crowds today. Do you think they heard what happened? I can't believe they did. We've had no reporters or anything. Can't last, though.'

Derry agreed the lack of fuss was unlikely to last. Marlene, Charlotte and Torquil had left the previous afternoon, and they were sure to dramatise their experience all over West London. The chances of Torquil staying quiet were zero.

'Coffee? Tea?' Derry motioned Bryony to take a seat. 'You look like you could do with a break.'

Bryony claimed not to mind instant coffee, so Derry made

her a cup and they settled down in front of the unlit stove. 'I'm going to London, if that's alright. Until the weekend,' said Derry. 'Will my costume be okay if I leave it in the closet here?'

'Of course,' said Bryony. 'And you don't have to ask to leave; I know it's been chaotic for you. That reminds me, I haven't forgotten your fee. That's why I came over. We can do something now, if you like. Or we can sort everything after the party next week. Extra, of course. We've really messed up your arrangements, I'm sure.'

Derry was just about to say the arrangements were no problem at all, and in fact she had no work lined up whatsoever, but her mother's voice rang in her ears. Make your clients appreciate you! You're doing them a favour!

'I was lucky things, um… worked out,' said Derry. 'I've managed to rearrange some commitments.'

'Really, I am sorry,' said Bryony. 'I can imagine how difficult scheduling must be for an actress. Especially filming and so on.'

Derry felt unspeakably guilty. The idea she was racing from film set to film set, barely able to keep up with the insatiable demand for her talents, was crossing the boundary from justifiable PR to certifiable delusion.

She came clean. 'Actually, things worked out quite well. I've a… break just now, and I wanted to visit my mother in London anyhow.' Time for a change of subject. 'I wanted to ask you what was the best way to get to London from here.' Derry already knew from a quick Google that Sorley Hall was a long way from any bus or train station.

'You're in luck,' said Bryony. 'Seb is going up to London

later on. You could go with him. I'm sure he won't mind. Likes to show off his car.' Before Derry had a chance to say anything, Bryony was dialling Sebastian and had made the arrangement. 'Done. He'll call here for you in say… two hours?'

For Derry, the thought of leaving Sorley Hall was like a dark cloud lifting. She hoped her bland smile of thanks hid her relief.

$\sim$

Derry had no wish to play the tourist, but she had two hours to kill before Sebastian called. Outside, the day was pleasant, but she had never been fascinated by flowerbeds. Neither had she any desire to tour the great house, though that probably meant she was a philistine. Derry reasoned she could claim exemption on the grounds that an actress did culture for a living, or nearly for a living. She was therefore entitled to avoid the culture everybody else felt compelled to consume. She felt no pressure, for example, to take War and Peace on vacation to read by the pool. Not that she could afford actual vacations or ever got to lie by an actual pool, but the principle was sound.

Instead, Derry checked her Facebook. Bella had just landed a part in a TV drama, and even her acting friends claimed to be thrilled for her. Derry added her congratulations, making them as hearty as she could, but deep in her soul she recognised that shameful stirring of envy and despair all actors know. She wondered which was more depressing, the endless disappointments of the business or the way you slowly, imperceptibly morphed into a small-minded, envious wasp.

Few comforts are available to the struggling actor, especially the single actor, who finds herself wallowing in negativity and self-criticism. Derry was proud of her emotional independence, and felt no need of a man to complete her life. On the other hand, out-of-work actors were known to benefit psychologically from the support of partners who plied them with unsolicited cheese-on-toast and a small glass of something nice.

The thought suggested to Derry an immediate course of remedial action—most likely the visitors' restaurant could contrive a toastie. Even more psychologically supportive would be a cream tea, with scones and indecent dollops of homemade strawberry jam.

~

Derry sat perched on the low, outside window ledge of the cottage, her bag at her feet, soaking up the warmth of the sun. She phoned Jacko, but got no answer. She left a voicemail saying she was going to London and she'd try to have a word with her mother about his pictures. Somehow, leaving a message felt like an achievement.

The courtyard was silent but had none of the oppressive atmosphere Derry had come to associate with the place. In the sunshine even the forbidding tower with its ancient armorial crest seemed harmless, the clenched fist and crouching dog an innocent coincidence.

Derry's idle thoughts were interrupted by the growling rumble of Sebastian's car as he nosed it between the gateposts and into the courtyard. The sleek red motor crunched to a halt right in front of where she sat. The door opened and out stepped Sebastian. He stood leaning his elbow on the car's low roof, appraising Derry with a grin.

'Venus In A Bower!' he said.

'More like Farmhand In a Byre,' answered Derry. She couldn't help smiling. The man had limitless confidence.

'Your conveyance, ma'am.'

If you were to fairly describe actors as a species you would have to mention their habit of driving cars at least ten years old. When it comes to expensive vehicles, all the creative classes are agreed. Flash cars are vulgar symbols of inequality, a crime against the environment and, on psychosexual grounds, thoroughly suspect. Coincidentally, for the average actor they are also less attainable than moonrock.

Derry tried hard to adopt the correct attitude of disdain. Swathes of the car's leather interior were yellow, for goodness' sake. The whole creation should have been disgusting and offensive. But this car was Italian, and the Italians, who had corrupted generations of popes without really trying, had found Derry O'Donnell to possess the average quantum of human weakness. The car was rather nice.

'Ars gratia artis,' said Sebastian. 'Art is the reward of art.' He smiled as if he had made some secret joke. Derry's newfound spirit of tolerance evaporated. What made this man assume she didn't know Latin? Okay, she did not in fact know Latin, but that wasn't the point.

Within seconds of sliding into that delicious interior, Derry had grasped the situation fully. The car was, admittedly, a beautiful object. But its function was not to be admired for itself. Its function was to ensure that its owner was admired.

Derry had no intention of admiring any man because of the tin box that carried him around.

Years of studying her craft had honed to perfection Derry's ability to hide her thoughts. She hid them now. She gazed blankly out front, not letting her eyes stray for one second around the car's opulent interior. Her expression of complete indifference was the face she wore climbing into Bruce's ancient van or Bella's old rustbucket. She pretended to be fascinated by a small black cat settling on the cottage windowsill. She took out her phone and checked for texts. 'Thankfully, I remembered to charge the thing,' she announced to no one in particular.

Sebastian frowned. He blipped the accelerator, making the engine roar throatily. Derry seemed stone deaf.

'The thing about a Maserati,' said Sebastian, ostentatiously executing a flawless three-point turn, 'is that it could only be Italian. The Germans could never create this.' He glanced sideways with a complacent smile.

'I think those old Vespas are really cool,' said Derry. 'They're Italian, aren't they? A little scooter would really suit me, but Irish rain doesn't agree.'

Did Sebastian give a barely perceptible shake of his head, that universal male gesture of despair at the failure of womanhood to grasp the essentials? Mentally, Derry took a little bow. *Applause.*

Sebastian changed the subject. 'I have to swing by the gallery; maybe you'd like to take a quick look? I guess you haven't had a chance yet.'

'Cool,' said Derry.

Their route to the gallery took them around the rear of the

house, passing yet more redbrick outbuildings and skirting the blank perimeter of the walled gardens. Meandering groups of visitors forced Sebastian to drive slowly. Tourists turned to stare at the car, bending to peer through the windows. Who knew but the occupants might be aristocrats, even minor royals?

'Lucky for you I'm heading for Town,' said Sebastian, avoiding the pedestrians like he was threading the car through a herd of sheep on a country lane. 'A dealer we've occasionally done business with wants to make an offer. His gallery is near your mother's place, in fact.'

'Thanks,' said Derry. 'I appreciate it.'

'Your friend Bruce—Bryony says he's an ex-military type and going to keep an eye on us, make sure nobody tries to blow up the Earl. Trustworthy chap, your Bruce?'

Sebastian's lightning change of subject took Derry by surprise. But the question was a fair one. And important. Time to be frank.

'I'd trust him with my life,' Derry said simply. 'Have done, in fact.'

'Not some kind of Rambo? No offence, but you Americans— how do I put it—can lack finesse.'

'No. He's cautious. Professional. Nothing to prove, you know? Anyhow, Bruce isn't going to play bodyguard; he's going to be helping Lady Octavia.' Even as she spoke, Derry was aware how ridiculous the story sounded. Bruce was to be a bodyguard and not-a-bodyguard at the same time. Was Bruce imagining a distinction with no basis in reality?

Sebastian stopped the car outside the gallery's front entrance. He parked by the flowerbeds where a sign said No Parking, but made no move to get out. 'One thing to be grateful for, at least. Lady Octavia wasn't in the room when the… when that package arrived. She's a game old thing, but she's not young. I don't like to think of the shock. Perhaps your friend Bruce will reassure her. Ease her mind.'

Derry was surprised—pleasantly surprised. Sebastian was right to be concerned about how an older person might be affected. The business must have come as a terrible shock to the Dowager—perhaps a far greater a shock than she admitted. 'Don't worry,' said Derry. 'Bruce is a terrific guy.' What she thought was, *perhaps you're alright yourself, Mr. Dandy.*

'Been an item long?' asked Sebastian.

At first, Derry didn't know what he meant. Then she laughed. 'Oh! I see! Just friends. At college together.'

Sebastian looked at her quizzically, raising an eyebrow in a way that Derry couldn't help think fetching.

'Didn't really see you as the West Point type. All that marching.'

'Haha. Drama college. And anyhow, the Navy is Annapolis.'

'Relieved, I assure you,' said Sebastian.

Derry tried not to smile.

~

'Meet Cassandra,' said Sebastian. He introduced a languorous blonde in an elegant tweed jacket and pashmina scarf, who managed to smile at Derry without showing any teeth. She wore her sunglasses on her head and sat behind the gallery's reception desk as though waiting to be served an expensive cocktail. 'She's a Bullingham-Smythe, great-great-and-so-on granddaughter of the Pre-Raphaelite. Knows a little art history, but don't let her decorate your flat.' He indicated Derry. 'Cassandra, this is Derry O'Donnell—her father's the awesome Jacko O'Donnell, no less.'

Cassandra cocked her head to one side, as if to say a star painter of the Pre-Raphaelites with a double-barrelled name trumps a contemporary colonial any day, however inflated his prices.

'Hi,' said Derry.

'Mmm,' said Cassandra Bullingham-Smythe.

'Come and look at the pictures, won't you, while I grab my things,' said Sebastian. 'Old Masters, portraits and whatnot are in the house by the hundred, but we've got some stunners here. Most of the Russians are upstairs, if they're your thing, but there's a fine Kandinsky over there.'

Derry had to agree the gallery was impressive. The main room was a long open space, most likely some kind of medieval great hall, but with tall windows added sometime later. Immediately her eye was drawn to four Matisses, and you could spot the Picassos from right across the room. And there, where Sebastian had pointed, was a magnificent Kandinsky.

Upstairs, as Sebastian had said, were the Russians—the Wanderers school from the 1870s, two Dobuzhinskys and a Bakst. Derry thought of Jacko, and how he would be entranced by what she saw here. When Sebastian emerged from a back office, laptop bag over his shoulder, he seemed to have forgotten he was supposed to be driving them to London. Instead of hustling Derry away, he joined her in front of the pictures and began to talk.

His knowledge was immense—Derry had grown up in a

family where the minutiae of colour, texture, brushstrokes and the chemistry of paints were the stuff of breakfast-time conversation, and this man knew what he was talking about. The pictures and the artists, the history and the theories of art that shaped them and that they shaped in turn—he ranged over it all. His understanding of painting technique and materials was amazing. No doubt about it, Sebastian loved his subject. Jacko would enjoy meeting him, Derry was sure of that. She wondered if Sebastian drank enough. Doubtful. But Jacko would forgive even a lamentable lack of interest in alcohol and the horses if someone knew enough about art.

'Dad would love to visit,' said Derry. 'Shame he's not here.'

'Any time he's in England, tell him to pop over,' said Sebastian. 'What you see here is only the tip of the iceberg. I could show him lots more. A good many moderns are in the house—it's not all gloomy old portraits. And we've a tremendous amount in storage at the back here. Matter of fact, I'm only just finishing the new catalogue.'

'A lifetime's work by the look of it,' said Derry. 'How many pictures does the estate have?

'To be honest, I'm not quite sure yet. During the war the art was scattered across several properties. Some was destroyed in the bombing of course. The catalogues were lost too. Had to start all over again. And of course we also have the furniture and ceramics, silverware and what have you.'

'But how many pictures, do you think?'

'So far, the new catalogue lists eleven thousand six hundred and three.'

The number was staggering.

'You're impressed,' said Sebastian, smiling. 'But remember, we've had fourteen earls altogether collecting for three hundred years. Look at it that way and it's not so many.'

'Where on earth do you keep them all? You could never display that number, surely.'

'That's true, I'm afraid. Most of the collection stays in storage.'

'What a shame. What's the point of a painting if nobody gets to look at it?'

'My sentiments exactly,' said Sebastian.

'Aren't you terrified the place will be robbed?'

'Not really. People think art theft is easy, but it's not. The stealing part can be easy, of course—although naturally we have sophisticated security systems. But the problem isn't how to steal pictures, it's how to sell them afterwards. A stolen work can't ever be seen in public again and won't fetch a fraction of its full value. There are always a few dealers who'll buy, of course, and some private collectors who'll hide their treasures in a secret room in their mansion. But not as many as people imagine. Let's face it, the mega-rich buy to show off what they've got, not to hide it away. Better to steal jewellery, I'd say. At least you can break it up and melt it down.' He looked at his watch. 'We'd best push off. Alright?'

Without another word he marched to the door, Derry trailing in his wake. 'Thanks,' said Derry to the Bullingham-Smythe as she trotted past. The receptionist frowned suspiciously, as though being thanked had implications she didn't like one little bit.

# 14

Sebastian kept more or less within the speed limits, seeming content to show off the car's looks rather than its horsepower. He drove confidently but seemed distracted and not much given to conversation. All Derry had to do was sit back in leather-bound, air-conditioned comfort and enjoy the beautiful English scenery and Mozart on the hi-fi.

Derry wondered how you attained that air of unassailable confidence all the English upper classes seemed to have? Anyone with money could go and buy a stupidly expensive car. The right clothes weren't a tough call either—you only had to patronize the shops whose names everyone knew, on the streets everyone knew. And a house was just a house, even if it did have a dozen bathrooms on every floor. Derry thought of Cassandra whatsit with her sunglasses on her head. How did she project the idea that she wasn't doing an actual job to make an actual living, but had instead volunteered in order to fill the time between society parties? There, thought Derry, was something to keep in mind if she ever had to play an upper-class Englishwoman—act as if life was one long sunny afternoon spent helping out at a garden fête.

'Preevyet,' said Sebastian.

'I'm sorry?' said Derry, before realising he wasn't talking to her. He was on the hands-free phone, making a call.

'Spaseeba preekrasna.'

Then she realised. Sebastian was speaking a foreign language. Swedish? Russian? Whatever it was, the call was short.

He frowned. 'Sorry. I'm supposed to be meeting a gallery

owner, but I can't seem to get him. I want to make sure he's remembered he asked me to call in. Supposedly he'll be back within the hour. I'm not betting on it.'

'Was that Russian you were speaking?' asked Derry. Okay, she was impressed.

'Yes. I studied in Russia. St. Petersburg. After graduating. Paid for by a rich relative, I hasten to add.'

Derry wondered if the same relative had paid for the car. 'St. Petersburg must have been wonderful,' she said. 'I'd love to go there. I've heard St. Petersburg has more beautiful things than just about any city on the planet. How come you didn't stay?'

'No jobs for foreigners, I'm afraid. Anyhow, that's when I got taken on by the Earl. The last Earl, that is—Lord Hugo. His curator was getting on a bit and not in the best of health. So I left Russia a year early. Been at Sorley ever since.'

'You never wanted to be a painter?'

'Oh, not me. Zero talent, I'm afraid. But someone has to do the appreciation part. Can't all be geniuses.' Sebastian smiled, his good humour returning. 'And what about you? I've always been fascinated by actors. The art of being something you're not. Intriguing.'

'I guess it is,' said Derry, smiling. 'Everybody else wants to be themselves, and we work our butts off trying not to be.' She paused. For some reason, she had suddenly thought of an ex-lover and the last time they had been together. 'Sometimes it's hard to remember to be real.'

Sebastian glanced at her as if he understood. They drove on in silence.

'What I'd like to know is, where's the art in performance

anyway?' said Sebastian suddenly. 'Is the art newly created for every show? Or is it just a copy after the opening night? If it's a copy, maybe theatres should charge less each time the play is performed? May I suggest a sliding scale?'

Derry laughed out loud. What an outrageous idea—charge less the longer the show's run goes on. Sebastian had a way of taking you by surprise, and Derry found she was enjoying the game. 'If you're right,' she said, 'A painting isn't even art once the paint is dry.'

'Or maybe the creation part doesn't matter, only the thing created,' answered Sebastian. 'Some say the art doesn't exist until someone engages with it. So all those thousands of unseen pictures at Sorley aren't art at all. And if someone thinks a can of tomato soup is art, it becomes art.'

Ahead, a giant sign loomed telling them they were heading for Central London. The traffic was thick, but Derry knew they couldn't be far now from their destination. Not much time to ask the question that really mattered. 'I don't mean to pry,' she said, 'but I'd like to know what you think about yesterday.'

If Sebastian didn't want to answer, he wouldn't. But Derry was sure he was in a better position than anybody to guess what was going on. He was close to the family, but as an outsider he might see things more clearly.

Sebastian bit his lip. 'I honestly have no idea,' he said. 'It doesn't make much sense, does it? Hunt saboteurs? Maybe. They do some crazy things. Perhaps whoever sent that package just hated lords.'

'It was meant to frighten the Earl, surely,' said Derry. 'But why? A threat says, "do what we want." So what do they want him to do or not do? Did they kill that poor man? Even if they didn't, and they got body parts from some morgue or something, who'd be so… callous?'

Sebastian hesitated, choosing his words carefully. 'I'll be frank. The Earl… how can I say this… Wealthy men who love gambling, who own racehorses and so on, can find themselves in difficult company. I… can't say any more.'

'Okay. I understand,' said Derry. 'Thanks.'

'Horse racing is a dirty business,' said Sebastian.

'Funny,' said Derry. 'That's what Dad says about art.'

# 15

The bustle of London was a shock after the tranquillity of a stately home in acres of manicured grounds. Hard to believe Sorley Hall was at most a couple of hours away from this vast, cosmopolitan metropolis.

'How about I walk you to your mother's,' said Sebastian, insisting on carrying Derry's holdall. 'I don't expect my meeting will take too long, and you must be hungry. Have you eaten?'

'Um, no,' said Derry, reasoning at lightning speed that cream scones in the late morning did not strictly qualify as eating and need not therefore be mentioned.

'Why don't I buy you a late lunch. Do you know Marples', round the corner from your mother's?'

Derry knew that restaurant. Not the most expensive but no burger joint either.

'Why not,' she said. 'Alright. What time?'

'Say three? Any problem I'll phone you. Swap numbers?'

'Sure thing,' said Derry. Meeting at three would give her an hour and a half with Vanessa, time enough to make some kind of plan for the week and bring up the problem of Jacko's pictures. Under the awning of a major auction house, she and Sebastian paused to exchange numbers. In the window was a notice announcing an international sale of minor Impressionists, most of whom, Derry noted, had died penniless.

London's most fashionable art galleries and auction houses lie in a warren of lanes behind the crowded main thoroughfares. Visitors to London are often surprised at how fashionable art businesses are so often tucked into backstreets. But when your gallery is truly exclusive, and its fame world-wide, anyone rich enough to buy knows how to find you.

The Caravaggio Gallery lay down a narrow alley opening onto a small courtyard, in a row of buildings once stables or workshops. As Derry and Sebastian approached the familiar premises, Sebastian stepped in front of Derry to hold open the door. He made a little bow as she passed.

～

Vanessa's gallery was a wide, white-walled space, expertly lit to display costly artworks to best effect. Stupendously valuable ceramics perched on plinths, making you nervous to look at them. The tone was subtle and low-key, nothing brash or overtly commercial. You saw no sign of the sophisticated alarms and shutters defending the building's precious contents from those unwilling to write the necessary cheques. Vanessa's gallery was so much like a temple to creativity you would scarcely guess the sole purpose of her establishment, and of every one of her neighbours, was to convert art into cash.

The reception desk was to one side of the main gallery space and about halfway down. As Derry and Sebastian entered the gallery, the pretty receptionist seated behind the desk paid no attention. She was gazing adoringly at an imposing figure in a broad-brimmed hat, brown leather top-boots and a green riding cape. He was obviously an artist holding forth on some high topic on which he was an acknowledged expert.

'Dad!'

The effect on Jacko was extraordinary. He jumped as if an electric shock had surged through his body. He looked as a person might who had been caught quietly slipping a Picasso into their briefcase.

'Ah,' said Jacko. 'Um.'

No doubt about it, thought Derry, middle-aged male artists were a menace. The trouble began with the shameless adulation of graduate students, who seemed to believe that by sleeping with the famously creative you could acquire both talent and an exclusive interview counting towards your grade average. For their part, men who should know better chose not to enquire too closely into the motives of their admirers.

'Where's Mom?' called Derry, projecting her voice more than strictly necessary.

'Ah,' said Jacko. 'Of course. Yes.'

'Hi Dad,' said Derry sweetly, giving him a kiss.

'In a meeting,' said Jacko, clearing his throat. 'In the office. There,' he added unnecessarily, pointing to a door just behind reception. 'Thought you couldn't get here 'till Monday,' he said, recovering his poise. 'Thought it best to come in person. Not fair to delegate.'

That Jacko was a master of the art of delegation, especially where difficult conversations with Vanessa were concerned, Derry let pass. Seeing Jacko always made her happy. She linked her arm through her father's and turned to Sebastian.

'Sebastian, meet my dad, Jack. Dad, this is Sebastian.'

'Delighted,' said Jacko, bowing. Sebastian bowed back.

What was it about today? The men were behaving like

pigeons. Was bowing a new trend? Usually, Derry was several years behind any fashion you could mention, so perhaps it was.

'An honour to meet you, sir,' said Sebastian. 'I'm a great admirer of your work.'

'Sebastian is Curator at Sorley hall,' said Derry.

Jacko's face lit up. The adoring receptionist was forgotten. Her mouth made a sulky pout.

'Ah!' said Jacko. 'Sorley! Fine collections I'm told. You know, I just lately bought a—'

To Derry's immense relief Jacko never did get to launch into the riveting lecture on Russian Modernists he surely had in mind. The office door opened. Framed in the doorway was a tall, well-built man with crew-cut hair, chiselled features and an expensive tan. He was deeply engaged in conversation with Vanessa. He kissed her outstretched hand.

The effect on Jacko was immediate. His brow darkened. He drew himself up to his full height. He clenched his jaw manfully. But the effect on Sebastian was even more marked. He stood staring, like a job applicant who had walked unknowing into another candidate's interview.

If the crew-cut man was as much surprised to see Sebastian as Sebastian was to see him, he concealed his feelings far better. After the briefest hesitation, his face broke into a practiced smile. He spoke, and this time Derry immediately identified the language as Russian. Sebastian replied in kind.

'What coincidence,' said the man in strongly accented English. His voice was deep and he spoke quietly, as though confident others would make the effort to listen. 'Forgive if introductions must wait for another time. I am late for appointment.' He turned to Sebastian. 'How fortunate. We can have our talk on way to my gallery.' He turned to Derry's mother. 'Vanessa, my dear. Pleasure as always. Thank you for your help. I will be in touch. Of course.'

Vanessa stood in the doorway showing to perfection her svelte figure and the marvellous cut of her Dior. She made her most dazzling smile. 'Always good to see you, Sergei. I'd introduce everyone, but you're in a rush. Such a shame.' She gave a little wave.

'Sebastian,' said the Russian, 'Come, please.' He strode down the gallery to the door without looking back. Sebastian followed, hurrying to keep up.

'Sergei is such a sweetie,' said Vanessa. She seemed to wake from a pleasant dream. 'Hello, darlings,' she said, offering her cheek to be kissed.

~

Vanessa's office was an office in name only. No computers or filing cabinets interrupted the seamless flow of designer furniture and fittings. But the place did boast a generous drinks cabinet, an artist's easel and a leather suite in impeccable white. In fact, the whole room was white, apart from the light grey of the carpet that Vanessa had once described, to Derry's amusement, as *dark* white. The room was a kind of nowhere, deliberately so—the merest splash of colour jumped right out at you, immediately justifying its exorbitant price tag.

'How nice,' said Vanessa, seating herself in a masterpiece of the furniture designer's art, a chair strongly suggesting its owner not only possessed impeccable taste and significant disposable income but could navigate to the far reaches of the galaxy if she felt so inclined.

Jacko sprawled on the couch without waiting to be invited, obviously sulking. Derry sank into an enveloping armchair, preparing to ride out the inevitable domestic scene. Pretending to silence her phone, she checked the time. To her surprise, she found she was very much looking forward to lunch with Sebastian.

'So glad you met Sergei,' said Vanessa to the room at large. 'We're such good friends. I'll admit, he adores me.' She laughed lightly. 'But you know what these Russians are, such charmers! Cultured, yet manly!' She glanced slyly at Jacko.

Jacko snorted.

'You should cultivate him, Jack. Sergei is Shirokov's right-hand man. Handles all his collecting.' Shirokov was a famous Russian billionaire, reputed to have made his fortune by being the only survivor of a consortium controlling seven oilfields, four provincial cities and the sole right to sell French lingerie in Moscow. Like many Russian billionaires with a healthy instinct for self-preservation, Shirokov lived in England.

'I doubt he'd be interested in my work,' said Jacko, a steely glint in his eye.

'And why is that?' said Vanessa.

'I might clash with his wallpaper. A tragedy, to be sure.'

'Do I detect a little envy, Jack darling? The success of others can be so… challenging.'

Why, Derry wondered, were families so infinitely depressing? And how come her parents' divorce so much resembled a marriage? Out of long practice, she executed a diversionary manoeuvre. 'I think Sergei is the gallery owner Sebastian was coming to London to meet. Isn't that a coincidence?'

With some other parent, Derry's comment might have sparked a lively and amusing debate on statistical probability and the nature of coincidence. But Vanessa was not to be deflected from the riveting subject of rich Russian art dealers. 'I've met Sebastian, dear. Sweet boy. Talking about coincidence,' she continued, turning to Jacko, 'it was from Sergei I acquired your Sorley Hall Sikorsky. He has such a fine eye. Small world, isn't it?

'Can I hope you paid too much?' said Jacko.

Vanessa brushed aside this pathetic thrust. 'What makes you think it wasn't a present, dear?' She smiled sweetly, her eyes twinkling. She raised her eyebrows in the way she had when hinting at the undying devotion of some male upon whom she may or may not have bestowed her favours. It was all too much for Jacko.

'What about my pictures!'

Vanessa's brow furrowed. She pursed her lips, as though the subject of Jacko's pictures was new and wholly unforeseen. 'Pictures?'

'You know perfectly well what pictures! The Corrib Series!'

Once more, Derry felt a pressing need to intervene. 'I hope you don't mind, Mom, I've agreed to meet Sebastian for a bite at three. Is that okay? I can come straight back after, and we can chat.'

'Of course dear,' said Vanessa. 'Your Sebastian—isn't he connected to the Marlowe-Stewarts? I'm sure he is. How interesting.'

'So what about my pictures!' insisted Jacko, his voice a strangled squawk.

'Fotheringham,' said Vanessa, casually. She turned to Derry, 'Coffee dear?'

'Um, please,' said Derry, getting up to pour herself a cup from a designer jug on the sideboard, prudently removing herself from the line of fire.

'What, where or who is Fotheringham?' enquired Jacko.

'Where have you been?' said Vanessa, genuinely surprised. 'Everybody knows Fotheringham. Your pictures are on loan. They'll hang there beautifully. Splendid gallery. Such a collection, and talk about good company!' She spoke as if Jacko's paintings were to be hung in heaven alongside the works of Michelangelo and the Angel Gabriel.

'Isn't Fotheringham where Prince thingy lives?' asked Derry. 'Not far from Sorley Hall. Isn't he going to be the next King of England or is it the one after that?'

Vanessa gave Derry a pitying look, as if wondering how any daughter of hers could have led a life so sheltered. 'Of course it's He. Didn't I tell you *She* came in? *He* was with her. He saw Jack's pictures, and we had a little chat. I sent them off to Castle Fotheringham next day.'

'Those pictures have been hanging on this gallery's walls for eighteen months,' said Jacko. 'I get a sale, and you tell me the pictures are lent out.' He looked like he was about to burst into tears. 'I have a German!'

Vanessa was unmoved. 'Really? See you one and raise you one.'

Derry was at a loss to know what Vanessa's riposte could mean. But her mother's pleased expression, her dry tone and the wry curvature of her perfect lipstick indicated she had made a joke—an exceptional event, as Vanessa's conversation tended more towards telling you what you thought, then telling you why you were wrong.

Derry waited. Jacko waited. Perhaps the explanation would come. Or perhaps it would never come, and instead Vanessa's observation would join the countless impenetrable statements made in our hundred thousand years of human conversation—statements still swirling around the ether, cluttering up history, as if history wasn't cluttered enough already.

'German!' explained Vanessa, exasperated. 'The British royals are descended from Germans! I thought all you Europeans knew that.' Vanessa said *Europeans* as one might say Yetis, a species known from the tales of adventurous travellers but probably mythical, and you certainly wouldn't want one at your dinner party.

'*Your* German,' she said, 'will have to wait. I have promised *my* German he can display the pictures in his new eco-gallery at Castle Fotheringham, and that's where they've gone.'

Jacko was silent and strangely calm. He turned to Derry, who hid behind her cup of coffee. 'Did you know,' he said conversationally, 'your mother is not only an insufferable snob but has the business sense of a rock?'

Having spent her whole life as an O'Donnell, Derry knew the statement was rhetorical, demanding no reply.

'If you have the time and wished to do me a favour,' continued Jacko, 'you might inform your mother she is a typical American—anything with a title and she swoons and grovels. *Sir* this, *your lordship* that. Their *lordships* oppressed the Irish for centuries, as you well know.'

Perhaps it was the barbed reference to the typical American that riled Derry. She loved her life in Ireland, but she was proudly and patriotically American and defended the honour of her country whenever it was challenged. Or perhaps Jacko's shamelessly selective view of history, a specialty of his, had offended her sense of fairness.

'Didn't you say our ancestors in the West of Ireland had zillions of acres of land and a couple of thousand peasants?'

'Sure weren't we their own?' insisted Jacko. 'A different case entirely.'

'He,' said Vanessa, 'has never oppressed anybody. Look what He does for the environment! For the Arts! Your pictures will hang In His Castle!

'I want my pictures back,' said Jacko, returning to the central theme. 'I'll go to Fotheringay and bloody well ask for them.'

'Fothering-*ham*,' corrected Vanessa. 'And I imagine his security detail would have something to say about that.' She turned to Derry, 'Would you mind stepping outside for a moment dear? I'd like to have a word with your father.'

Vanessa smiled her sweetest smile, the one she deployed when she was about to mention her staggeringly expensive lawyers.

~

Why do people whisper in art galleries? They don't whisper in car showrooms or furniture warehouses. You can understand why people whisper in a church—the other world might be listening, and there's no telling where that could lead. But in galleries everyone whispers, and that's exactly what a small group of patrons was doing in Vanessa's gallery now. They stood clustered reverently in front of a huge and incomprehensible painting by one Edgar Booth entitled The Ruins of Disneyland. The work was an oil in bilious green enlivened by streaks of orangey yellow.

Booth was Jacko's deadliest artistic rival, and Derry was thinking about sidling up to the group to collect choice quotations for her father's amusement, when the office door opened and Jacko himself emerged, carrying his holdall. His shoulders sagged miserably. His head hung in abject defeat. To Derry, the sight was deeply shocking.

Vanessa stood in the doorway, relaxed and smiling. 'Have a good flight dear,' she said. Her tone was kindly, even sympathetic. Her eye fell on Derry. She checked her Cartier watch. 'Darling, I have such an important meeting. I want us to talk, of course I do—how about coming back after your lunch with that nice young Sebastian.'

Vanessa waved and closed the door. Derry, Jacko and assorted art-lovers were left staring after her. Jacko collected himself, recovering sufficiently to harrumph and glare at the patrons, who hastily returned to studying The Ruins of Disneyland.

'D'ye see those dirty orange streaks?' demanded Jacko in the authoritative voice he used to denounce artistic charlatans and bookmakers. The astonished group waited, attentive. Here, obviously, was an Artist, perhaps the actual author of the magisterial work before them.

''Tis a revolutionary technique,' pronounced Jacko. 'You mix the acrylic with your own pee. Adds authenticity.'

The art lovers stepped hastily back, wrinkling their noses. Jacko paused. In his eye Derry detected a mischievous glint.

'Unless it's a fake, of course.'

# 16

'Mind if I sit with you 'till your beau comes along?' Outside Marples restaurant, Jacko and Derry stood together on the busy London pavement. Normally the idea of a parent playing gooseberry on a date would have appalled Derry, but this wasn't exactly a date was it? And Sebastian was certainly not her beau. This was no more than a casual, friendly lunch and some interesting conversation.

'He is not my beau,' said Derry.

'Sure,' said Jacko.

'Really,' said Derry.

'I believe you,' said Jacko. 'All the same, I'll leave you both to it when he arrives.'

Derry hesitated. 'Promise? He'll be here in ten minutes.'

'Promise,' said Jacko, unable to resist a smirk.

Derry had a sudden unaccountable vision of pink rose petals fluttering like confetti onto the London street.

'Stop it!'

'What?' said Jacko, innocently.

Several tables were free. Derry chose one by the window, and ordered two coffees. The frosted glass meant you couldn't see the street, but she had a good view of the door through which Sebastian would enter.

'So what was all that about with Mom?' asked Derry. 'I guess she doesn't mean to get your pictures back for you?'

'Worse,' replied Jacko.

'Worse than losing your pictures?'

'Almost.' He paused, as if the dreadful words wouldn't

come out however hard he tried. 'I've to give lessons. She says it was his idea.'

'She wants you to give lessons? To a Royal? That's crazy! She knows you'd say no.'

Once again Jacko wore that beaten look, hangdog and devoid of hope. 'I said yes,' he said weakly.

'But why?'

'Did I ever tell you how, when I was young and struggling, I had to teach watercolour to amateurs every weekend? The seven circles of hell, let me tell you, pretending they hadn't daubed an abomination that should go in the fire only it's still wet.'

'You don't have to do it. Say no!'

'Can't.'

'Why?'

Jacko looked around suspiciously. His voice dropped to a whisper. 'Remember that little episode where I was forced by unavoidable circumstances to sign my paintings in a… in an unusual way?'

Derry did remember. Jacko had tried to avoid paying Vanessa her agent's commission by signing his pictures in an unrecognisable variation of his name and selling to collectors for cash. When Vanessa found out, she was livid.

'I thought she'd forgiven you for that?' said Derry.

'That's what I said to her. She said she *had* forgiven me.'

'So? What's the problem?'

'She said that she'd forgiven me, but the taxman probably wouldn't.'

'Ah,' said Derry. 'It was cash, wasn't it? Quite a lot of cash? And no sales tax?'

'You can't keep track of every little detail!' protested Jacko. 'Sure how could you create if you had your nose stuck in the bookkeeping your whole life?'

Derry nodded sympathetically. Many an actor had failed to mention to Revenue the small matter of earnings from a theatrical fringe production and found the taxman's reach was long and his vengeance terrible.

'So I'm to fly home to Galway, get my stuff and turn up at his Lordship's castle on Wednesday, saluting and tugging my forelock.' His voice broke. 'For ten days!'

'Maybe it won't be so bad,' suggested Derry, trying to look on the bright side. 'Fotheringham could be a showcase for you. Distinguished pillars of the British establishment will be trooping through the place on their way to shoot pheasants or make documentaries. All you have to do is be nice to him and call him Sir, or Your Lordship, Highness—whatever.'

'Bollox,' said Jacko, making the couple at the next table stare. 'I call people *Sir* when I'm telling them they're talking nonsense. As in, "My apologies *Sir*, but you know as much about Art as the average sea-sponge." I do not—repeat, not— call any man Sir who isn't Michelangelo. Even then, from one man of Art to another, Mick would surely suffice.' He sniffed, resting his case.

'But it's the done thing,' protested Derry. 'You have to be polite. I don't see how you can't be.'

'I will not,' replied Jacko. 'An O'Donnell will never bend the knee! His ancestor cut the head off my ancestor. In fact more than one ancestor. And drawn! And quartered!'

'Dad, I'm hoping to eat.'

'Sorry, but a principle is a principle.'

'Hey, I'll be back at Sorley Hall by next weekend,' said Derry. 'I could come visit you—Fotheringham's not far away. Or you could come to Sorley. If he gives you his permission, of course.'

Jacko turned a glorious shade of red. Derry laughed. 'Joking! Joking!'

The more Derry thought about Jacko teaching painting to a royal amateur, the more amusing was the idea. In fact, so entertaining was her father's dilemma she had almost forgotten the time. She checked her phone. Three-fifteen. And no text or missed call.

'I asked her why she agreed to the lessons,' continued Jacko. 'My time and sanity may not be worth much to their highnesses, but you'd think my agent would be keen to have me shackled to my studio earning her a largely effortless living.'

'And what did she say?' said Derry.

'She said how could she refuse?'

'I don't get it,' said Derry. 'She knows she'd be due a fat commission from a big sale you've already made to your German, or practically. Why would she put that at risk?' Derry pondered the mystery. Vanessa pursued dollars like cats pursue mice. She was patient, but she always got her quarry. And now she was ignoring a valuable sale. 'The wedding!'

'Sorry?'

'There's a Royal wedding next year! I'll bet Mom wants an invite. The biggest society event in the calendar. Her friends would go crazy with envy!' Derry paused. The more she thought about it the more certain she was. 'I'm sorry, Dad. She won't give in. No chance.'

'Sunk,' lamented Jacko.

Derry often spoke to her father as if she and not her mother was his agent. Perhaps because they were both in the creative professions or maybe because of the peculiar gift they shared, the sympathy between them ran deep. The oft-repeated mantra of her friend Bella came instantly to mind.

'Say No to Negativity!' quoted Derry. 'Look on the positive side. The lessons are unavoidable, right? Giving him lessons is a way to get your pictures back. Schmooze him! Call him Your Highness or whatever he wants to be called. Then ask him for the pictures. Tell him you'll lend him something else instead.'

Jacko looked doubtful.

'And what's the urgency, anyhow?' continued Derry. 'You still haven't told me why you need to sell those pictures in such a hurry. Come on, Dad! If I'm supposed to be supportive you have to tell me what I'm supporting!'

Jacko looked around warily. He took his phone from his pocket, swiped the screen and slid the device across the table. 'What d'ye think of that?'

Derry looked through the pictures one by one. All were selfies of Jacko posing in front of anonymous ivy-covered walls. Others featured Jacko standing proudly by shapeless heaps of stones. Only the last picture made any sense—he must have cajoled someone into taking the shot from some distance away. It showed Jacko gazing purposefully into the distance against the backdrop of a looming tower, mostly hidden by yet more ivy. The tower was almost intact, if you discounted the vacant space where the roof should have been.

'What is it?' asked Derry, cautiously.

'What is it? 'Tis only your own ancestral home! The very castle of our ancestors for seven hundred years!' Jacko's eyes grew dreamy. 'Every time I set foot on that spot I feel our fore-bears calling to me, saying, "Jacko, restore to us our rightful legacy!" '

'Dad,' said Derry. 'How come I didn't know we had a castle? Did it like, slip your mind?'

'Ah,' said Jacko. 'True enough, it's been out of our hands for a little while now. The tides of history washed—'

'You said it had been in our family for seven hundred years.'

'No O'Donnell has ever accepted the injustices of the oppressor,' insisted Jacko.

'So we haven't owned it since—when, the Middle Ages?'

'Technically.'

'I don't believe it, you're buying a ruined castle.'

'No choice, dearest girl,' said Jacko. 'Fate has decreed. I buy or they bulldoze.'

'Surely, they can't bulldoze an ancient castle. Not even in Ireland. Isn't it a national monument? Doesn't it have a preservation order?'

'Of course it does. But only if it doesn't fall down by being accidentally bumped into by a JCB. Or find itself on fire because a bottle magnified the rays of the sun and set the place ablaze.'

'That's silly. Why would those things happen?'

'So a consortium of developers can create the Castle O'Donnell Theme Park. I can barely bring myself to utter the words.'

'Would that be so bad?

'Apart from outraged ancestors complaining every night, and me not getting a wink of sleep, no. And if you don't count the shame of the proud O'Donnell name being associated with fake medieval banquets, Finn McCool and mini golf.'

'Dad, that wreck will cost a fortune to restore. It's crazy. Only English actors and American film directors buy castles in Ireland.'

But Jacko had no interest in the buying habits of either species. 'Think of the parties!' he said, his expression dreamy. 'And I can have my own gallery!' He looked at his watch. 'The plane! I'd better go. They'll want to do an autopsy before they let me on board, seeing as how I'm wearing shoes and a belt and was born under Leo.'

'Call me when you get to Fotheringham,' said Derry. 'We'll meet over the weekend, okay?'

'Perfect,' said Jacko. 'I may need an alibi.' He gave Derry a shrewd look. 'Now, don't be puttin' up with yer man being late. Not gentlemanly. A bad sign. Tell him he's an arse.'

'It's not a date, Dad,' said Derry, smiling. She kissed her father goodbye.

Half an hour later, Derry ordered a chowder to keep the waiters and her stomach happy. Half an hour after that, she paid the bill and left.

❧

'How was your lunch, darling?' enquired Vanessa. Derry had returned to the gallery and was once more sitting in her mother's office. 'Was he too charming? He is handsome, I give you that.'

Derry wondered again whether she should have phoned Sebastian and demanded to know why he hadn't shown up or had the decency to call or text. But the memory of sitting alone in the restaurant under the pitying gaze of the waiters still brought a flush to her cheeks. Better to forget him. Eventually, he'd either explain or he wouldn't.

'He was… delayed. I had a nice chat with Dad.'

'I hope you talked some sense into your father,' said Vanessa. 'But I think he saw my point. Now, what about you?' Vanessa beamed, reached in a drawer and pulled out a sheaf of papers. 'So glad to have you aboard, darling! Sign wherever you see an X. One copy for you, one for me.'

'Mom, I wanted to ask you how you'd feel if I—'

'Nonsense dear, it's all arranged.'

Derry flicked through the contract on the table in front of her—twenty-six pages of Sections, Subsections, Paragraphs and Subparagraphs stacked one on top of the other like bricks in a prison wall. One especially troubling paragraph caught her eye—all statements containing the terms *employer, employee, anticipate, believe, imply, could, may, expect, promise, intend, should* or *will* were to be understood as meaning anything Carravagio Galleries said they meant.

'I always knew you'd come round,' said Vanessa. 'You're a late developer, that's all. Nothing to be ashamed of.' She smiled tolerantly, as though being a late developer was, with luck, a moral failing most would be too polite to mention.

'I can't sign this!' said Derry. 'What if I don't do what it says?'

Vanessa's face wore a puzzled frown. Not for the first time Derry was aware her mother suspected her only child of being a half-wit. 'Then I sue you. Obviously.'

'Mom, you can't sue your own daughter! This is crazy.'

'Oh, it would never come to that,' said Vanessa with her most charming smile.

'I'm relieved to hear it,' said Derry. Vanessa's threat had sounded all too believable.

'You'd fold before we hit the courtroom steps, dear.'

Derry remembered once standing on the top tread of a stairway at Dublin Airport, only for it to lurch into motion and reveal itself as an escalator. Such were conversations with Vanessa. All you could do was scramble backwards hoping somehow to end up where you should have started.

'How about I do a trial week? See if it works out?'

Vanessa ignored Derry's plaintive request. 'You're going to enjoy London so much! You'll meet such interesting people. Artists, of course. Captains of Industry. Diplomats. The right kind of banker! Let's start, shall we?' Vanessa reached for her notepad and her thousand-dollar pen. 'On Monday, you can alternate with Theodora out front. Be nice to her, she's a Chobham-Warner—one of *the* Chobham-Warners. Her father owns the building—the street, actually. Has done since eighteen-something. Not personally, of course. And when you're on the desk, remember this isn't New York or Dublin, where everybody is Mister or Mrs. We'll have to get you a Debrett's.'

Derry was tempted to say 'of course,' as if she knew perfectly well what a Debrett's was. But the only things conjured up were those forms you fill in at the bank.

'Debrett's, darling! The book! Debrett's tells you all you need to know about the British aristocracy. How else would you know whether somebody is a Sir, a Lady, a Countess, an Earl or a mere Honorable? Vanessa's voice dropped an octave.

She shivered with delight. 'For Princes, we don't need a book. We all know who *they* are.'

'Tomorrow is Sunday,' Vanessa continued. 'Sergei has asked me for a favour; he wants to store some pieces here. We do each other good turns from time to time.' Vanessa gave Derry her arch expression—the raised eyebrows and carefully modulated smile that said her conquests never quite got over her.

Derry was intrigued, as she knew she was meant to be. 'Mom! Are you and he really… you know?'

Vanessa smiled. 'All in the past, darling. Russians are so… emotional.' She shook her head sadly, as though inspiring excessive devotion had long since ceased to surprise. She allowed a nostalgic smile hover on her lips, savouring sweet memories.

'He *is* athletic looking,' said Derry. She was supportive by nature and by inclination, strongly believing it was important to see virtue in the object of another's affections, even an ex-object.

'He was Spetsnaz,' confided Vanessa in a conspiratorial whisper.

'Oh,' said Derry. 'I mean, is he okay now?'

'The Russian Army, darling! Spetsnatz are elite saboteurs! The most highly trained fighting men on earth. If World War Three had broken out, he'd have parachuted onto the roof of Buckingham Palace and taken the Queen hostage until she broadcast a message of surrender. That was before your time, of course.'

'And now he's an art dealer? Wow Mom, that's quite a career change. I guess his gallery customers don't often complain.'

Derry was pleased at her little joke. After the miserable events of the afternoon, she felt entitled to a laugh.

'His clients,' retorted Vanessa, 'are some of the richest men in the world. The fabulous things he finds for his collectors you would not believe! Though I have to say his main business is somewhat less respectable, and he really needs to be more discreet.'

'Mom, please don't tell me you've had an affair with a politician.' Derry tried hard to hide her amusement.

'Don't be silly dear. He furnishes ghastly hotels in Russia. He's got a warehouse full of reproductions—Degas ballet dancers; gypsies with improbable cleavages and roses between their teeth.' Vanessa shuddered. 'Thank goodness that's not what he wants to store here. We'd have to have an exorcism afterwards, a scattering of incense. Which reminds me, that'll be your first job, dear.'

'Scattering incense?'

'Helping Sergei move some things into the store. Paintings, sculptures, possibly some furniture. They've had a ghastly infestation at his warehouse, nothing contagious but he has to steam clean. He's stuck for space in his gallery until next week. We've got the room, but you'll need to make sure everything is properly handled. I don't know why he uses the men he does, they'd be more suited to moving washing machines. Tomorrow is the best day, obviously, as we're closed. You can manage that?'

'Why don't I take a look at the store right now,' said Derry. 'See how we can make some space.'

'Excellent!' said Vanessa. 'No time like the present. I knew you'd come round.'

And in a way, Derry realised, she was coming round. The practical, everyday tasks of a gallery assistant would be absorbing, a welcome distraction. At least here, unlike at Sorley Hall, life was normal. No one was likely to get horrible parcels in the post. And London had many other advantages. Not least, the city was entirely free of arrogant posers called Sebastian.

# 17

Vanessa's apartment in fashionable Chelsea was spacious and elegant. Derry had often stayed while visiting her mother but had always tried to avoid the parties and exhibition openings that came with the territory. That evening, she had an acceptable excuse—no party clothes, and a hint of a headache in case the first excuse lacked depth.

Vanessa was not pleased. 'You'll never succeed in this business, darling, if you're a complete misanthrope. Only collectors can be misanthropes; we dealers must be busy little social bees, gathering honey by night and by day.'

'Mom, bees don't—'

'Metaphorical, dear,' retorted Vanessa. 'Networking is the barge-toting and bale-hauling of the postmodern world. God forbid I raised a daughter afraid of a little work.' With that parting shot, she slung her Vuitton bag over her ostentatiously fake ermine and strode to the door, leaving Derry with her box set and a stern warning about the dangers of television as an immediate cause of excess pounds.

As Derry settled down in Vanessa's elegant sitting room, surrounded by a wonderful collection of pictures and ceramics, she found herself wondering whether a proper career wasn't worth thinking about. Normal life would be such a relief. A regular income. Somewhere nice to live. Derry tried to imagine not having to worry about paying the electricity bill but failed.

Why not give it a go? Many jobs were worse than working in a fashionable art gallery where your mother was the owner and the clients rich and sophisticated. Better than working the checkout in a supermarket. Derry knew, because she had done that job for two whole days before getting sacked for finding the till so complicated she did the sums in her head. The manager hadn't cared one bit that Derry got the answers right every time, he fired her anyway.

That night, as Derry lay in bed, cosseted by Egyptian Cotton sheets, she told herself she at least had choices, more than many people had. The most important thing was to keep an open mind, to relax, not sweat about it. And especially not when trying to get to sleep. So Derry did something she often did to banish worries before sleeping—she closed her eyes and imagined a blank canvas of nothingness.

Once, in a zoo, Derry saw an iguana sitting on a branch behind a glass window. The iguana could change colour like a chameleon, blending into its background so one minute you saw it and the next you didn't. The most remarkable thing about this strangest of creatures was the eye in the middle of its head. This third eye was outlined in a white circle like its two normal eyes but was now closed over, covered with skin. Derry tried to imagine the extra eye open like the others, a third eye blinking up at her. She was glad it was covered up. Eyes should be in pairs.

The eye that now jolted Derry awake gasping for breath and pouring with sweat wasn't paired with anything. It was the size of a golf ball, a golf ball made of white jelly that gazed up at her, blank and unseeing. She knew it was unseeing because it didn't blink. It didn't blink because it didn't have eyelids. Or a socket to sit in. Or a face to hold the socket. It was just an eyeball. Nothing like a gateway to the soul—more like a being in its own right. A thing. A thing that stared up at you without blinking.

In Derry's dream, the eye-thing squatted in front of her on some kind of table. The table's surface was smooth and white, not textured or grained like wood. An operating table? A mortuary slab? A kitchen countertop? The thought of a kitchen made Derry feel she would throw up. Why? In her dream, she remembered. That kitchen. The kitchen from which a man in white coveralls had carried another thing.

The eye's iris was blue. The thing seemed to fix her with its gaze, looking up helplessly, incapable of moving of its own volition. Now Derry felt sympathy for the eye. It seemed anxious that somewhere outside the periphery of its vision, anything could be happening. Anything at all.

In the centre of the blue iris, the eye's black pupil was like a dark tunnel through which you could just discern some other place. Derry looked harder, peering deep into the blackness, searching for some clue. Suddenly, unexpectedly, with no warning at all, the pupil flashed wide open as if startled by what it saw. The black disk swelled and contracted, swelled and contracted in a rhythmic pulse, like a code pleading to be understood.

Derry screamed.

## 18

Being all alone surrounded by fine artworks is normally the privilege of the very rich. But at noon on Sunday, as Derry wandered idly around her mother's gallery, she had the satisfaction of enjoying a rich person's pleasures without having to make actual money. Again she found herself wondering if life in the art world might not be a pleasant existence. More than pleasant.

A loud buzzer jolted her out of her reverie. Someone was at the rear entrance, where a wide, metal roller-door gave access to the secure storage and workshop.

'Gallery Rodina!' The voice on the intercom was impatient. Derry checked the video. All was as she expected. A white truck was parked in the back lane, as near to the entrance as it could get, its sliding side door gaping open. That the truck really did belong to an art gallery was obvious from the climate control unit sitting on top of the cab. Satisfied the visitors were who they said they were, Derry pressed the button to raise the door. As it slowly cranked upwards, the metal squealed and rattled.

Three men in jeans, leather jackets and sneakers stood by the side of the truck, waiting for their boss to step down. The man Derry knew as Sergei straightened his tailored jacket and approached, smiling and holding out his hand.

'I am Sergei Antonov,' the man said. 'I know you are Derry. Almost we met yesterday; my apologies for not introducing myself.'

'Hi Sergei,' said Derry, shaking the proffered hand. 'Nice

to meet you. I've made all the space you'll need, I think. Can you manage okay?'

'Sure,' said Sergei. 'You tell where, and I will instruct my men.'

Derry noticed he said *my men*, like an army officer. But of course, that's what Sergei had once been.

'An inconvenience for Vanessa, I am sure,' said Sergei. 'But my warehouse has some problems.'

'Mom said you had an infestation? I'm sorry to hear that; I know how destructive these things can be.'

He grimaced. 'Vermin, unfortunately. I am grateful to Vanessa. And to you also.'

Derry had already rearranged the space. All she had to do was make sure the men stacked everything in the right places, didn't knock over anything and didn't cause obstructions. There was little danger of damage—all the Russian's pieces were carefully packed in wooden crates or sheeted in boards, bubblewrap and clingfilm. Except for the most surprising artefact of all.

'Wow,' said Derry.

'You like him?'

The extraordinary object being manoeuvred onto a trolley by Sergei's men was the full-size wooden casing of an Egyptian mummy. The sarcophagus was brilliantly painted with the features of a bearded man, complete with robes and headdress. Sergei's assistants struggled to wheel the enormous coffin into the workshop, standing it against the last remaining area of vacant wall.

'Spooky,' said Derry, stroking the faded paint of the case. After its ride in the chill of the climate controlled van the surface felt unnaturally cold to the touch. 'What do collectors do with these things? I can't see one in my apartment, for sure.'

'People collect for the strangest reasons. Perhaps, in this case, a token of mortality. Perhaps they remind the rich to enjoy what they have while they still live.'

'Is there a mummy in there? Wouldn't you be afraid it's gonna, like, step out and start unwrapping itself behind you while you're watching TV?'

Sergei laughed a deep, throaty guffaw.

'No mummy,' he said. 'It would be worth so much more if there was, I assure you.'

'All the same, not for me, thanks,' said Derry.

The Russian smiled. Derry could see what Vanessa meant about him being charming and at the same time intensely masculine.

'You are an actress, I believe?' said Sergei.

'Sure,' answered Derry. 'When I can get the work,' she added, annoying herself. Why did she have to be so honest? It wasn't like she was testifying in court.

'I cannot believe a young woman so beautiful could have difficulties in that way,' breathed Sergei. He moved closer. Derry was sharply conscious of his height and the breadth of his shoulders. She was aware of a musky odour, not unpleasant, but heavy, somehow oppressive. She stepped backwards. Her retreat was blocked by the jamb of the door.

'Have lunch with me,' said Sergei. He spoke quietly, as if giving Derry lunch was a deep secret they would share only between themselves. But Derry had no intention of sharing any secrets with Sergei, deep or otherwise.

'Sorry, and thanks,' she said, smiling and sidestepping neatly into the street. 'I'm on duty here all day. Covered in dust. You wouldn't want to be seen with me. Hey! looks like your guys have finished waltzing with King Tut over there. You've another load to come?'

Sergei's face was expressionless. If he was offended, he was giving nothing away. 'I can order them to leave the second load until later. Much later.'

'I'm sorry, Sergei. I appreciate it, I really do. My mother would kill me if I walked off the job. You know what she's like.' She smiled, neatly reminding Sergei both of Vanessa's existence and her status as Mother.

'I will not take up your valuable time,' said Sergei, turning on his heel. He barked something in Russian. The men followed hurriedly. Sergei climbed briskly into the truck without a backward glance.

Derry pressed the button, lowering the steel door with a rhythmic clatter.

≈

As of nine o'clock Monday morning, Derry O'Donnell was officially an assistant at the Carravagio Gallery, London W1. By nine-ten, she had acquired a deadly enemy in the shape of Ms. Theodora Chobham-Warner of *the* Chobham-Warners. Derry's crime was, it seemed, first to have been born and second to have the boss as her mother. By nine-forty, the heinous sin of doing actual work had been added to her rap sheet, and Derry was happy to leave Theodora to the reception desk and retreat to the store-room.

Her first task was to package three paintings for shipment. First Derry took photos as proof the items had been despatched undamaged, then she set to work with the wooden battens, bubble wrap and sticky tape. She had been doing this sort of job since she was a girl and found it peaceful and relaxing. Only when she started working with the catalogue did she find herself ill at ease. She was checking and updating the vital details of each painting and sculpture—artist, title, date of work and date acquired—but random thoughts destroyed her concentration. She felt strangely like she should have done something but hadn't. Perhaps yesterday's incident with Sergei or Theodora's unpleasantness had disturbed her more than she realised.

Derry inspected the racks of paintings looking for any possible signs of danger from pests or mould. She remembered Sergei's story of vermin infestation and shivered. The damage mice or rats could do in an art gallery didn't bear thinking about.

As Derry worked, she realised she was happy. What would be so bad about living like this? Surrounded by beautiful things. No stress. Guaranteed pay. No waiting for the phone to ring or rushing out to an audition only to find the producers were looking for somebody younger, taller, thinner and Cockney.

∼

Tuesday was a quiet morning in the gallery, but pleasant enough. To Theodora's undisguised disgust, Derry sold two pictures before retreating to the peace of the store-room.

'Darling,' said Vanessa, poking her head around the store-room door, 'did you arrange Fotheringham?'

'Um,' said Derry, racking her brains to remember what, if anything, she might have been asked to arrange. Blank.

'You were to let them know what time Jack would be arriving tomorrow! What if he turns up and they think he's a terrorist? Or a door-to-door salesman? He could be shot!'

Derry had a sudden vision of her father in his green riding cape, wide-brimmed hat and top-boots, knocking on the palace door with a battered brown suitcase full of samples. What would he sell? Small pieces of Real Irish Bog in a cardboard cottage? Reproductions of his own paintings but with a genuine signature? Plausible.

'Darling! Wake up! Do I have to think of everything myself? Initiative! Be proactive! What use is an intern if they don't commit?'

It took a moment, but only a moment.

'Intern? Mom, you said intern. What is it with intern? You're employing me, right? That's what we agreed. Job. Not intern. Job.'

'Don't be silly dear,' said Vanessa lightly, as if Derry had amusingly suggested a spell doubling as her accountant or chiropractor. 'Everybody starts as an intern. Be sensible—nobody these days hires anyone until they're thirty. Theodora's an intern, and she's been here, oh, weeks. And you get to stay in a Chelsea apartment! How many interns can say that?'

'You never said it was instead of actual pay.' The awful realisation dawned on Derry that she had joined the ranks of Britain's volunteering upper classes.

'Think of your CV, darling. What valuable experience! We'll keep things under review, I promise. Start as an intern and gallery assistant, and move up to be my PA when you've gotten the swing of things and I know I can trust you. How does that sound?'

'Trust me? You've known me all my life! Mom, I need a paid job!'

'We can arrange some pocket money, of course—let's call it a stipend, shall we? Now, who can say fairer than that? Anyhow, we have a contract.' Vanessa slid a sheaf of papers across the table to Derry. 'You might like to check everything is in order.'

'I am not signing anything,' said Derry firmly. She felt moderately pleased with herself. Important to let Vanessa know that others could be assertive too. Derry leafed idly through the pages by way of stage business. Pity she wasn't perched casually on the edge of the boardroom table in the required posture for delivering lines triumphant yet corporate. Only then, as she flicked through the document, did Derry realise she was not being asked to sign. She was not being asked to sign, because she had already signed.

'Mom!'

Vanessa swept the document briskly back to her own side of the table.

'I did not sign that!'

'Of course you did,' said Vanessa.

'I did not!'

Vanessa shrugged, smiling. 'Black and white, darling.'

'Mom! You can't fake your own daughter's signature! This is illegal! I'll sue you!'

Vanessa's smile grew wider. She beamed, gazing at Derry with fond maternal eyes.

'Now, *that's* my girl.'

∾

Wednesday at noon, Derry was at the front desk covering for the absent Theodora. Ms. Chobham-Warner was urgently required at a gymkhana and had Vanessa's dispensation on the grounds that Certain People were sure to be there.

Derry's phone rang.

'Babe!' said Bruce. 'Missed you, hon!'

'Missed you too,' said Derry. She couldn't help smiling. Bruce always made her feel like she was snuggled up to a huge hairy dog curled on a rug in front of the TV.

'You sound the same,' said Derry.

'Huh?'

'I thought by now you'd be saying things like "jolly good, old chap," and "frightfully, frightfully." '

'They don't talk like that. That's the movies.'

'Alright, said Derry. How about, "Sorree!" '

Bruce laughed. 'Yeah, well they do say that a lot. Do they mean it?'

'How would I know? I never learned the language.' She hesitated, but the question had to be asked. 'No more surprises? All quiet?'

'Sure, no problems. Thought you'd like to know the detective guy Cranshaw came back and filled us in.'

It was a relief that no more awful things had occurred at Sorley Hall. And maybe by now the police were getting to the bottom of the story. Until they did, everybody at the Hall would live in fear that any day, any moment, something else dreadful might happen.

'They sent a cop to give the Earl advice on looking after himself, an anti-terror guy. I'd briefed his lordship on all that anyhow. The cop didn't seem too pleased; but hey, so what. Cranshaw was interesting. He said the business had all the hallmarks of an underworld threat—gangs, mafia, some kinda extortion—and the Earl should expect a follow-up. Another threat most likely, maybe some demands. Whatever, the bad guys aren't doing this for fun. When they spell out what they want, Cranshaw thinks he'll nail them right away. It's hard to stay anonymous when you want something, he said. I guess he's right at that.'

'But they still don't know who the… part belonged to?'

'No. The genetic ID stuff takes a lot of time, big backlog. And still no body. I asked about the arm. Seems the guy was dead before they cut off his arm and his fingertips.'

Derry tried hard not to picture the terrible things Bruce was describing, but the images kept slipping past her defences.

'Seems they didn't just cut off the fingertips; they broke his knuckles as well. While he was alive. I said maybe he broke them himself, like he was punching whoever, but Cranshaw said no. The knuckles were broken by a hammer or something heavy. Different kind of break.'

Worse and worse. Derry tried to overcome her revulsion by making herself think logically. Some instinct told her that being logical was the best way to banish those pictures in her head. And they had to be banished.

'Anything else? Can't they tell someone's job from their hands?'

'They came up with a few things. He was middle aged. Probably dark haired. They found some flakes of paint—they don't know what kind yet. He could have been an artist, maybe a housepainter. Could have been an ordinary Joe doing a bit of DIY.'

'What about the postage? Couldn't they work out where the package was from?'

'Yeah, they got that alright. The stamp has a code that tells you the post office. Churchill Place, London E14. Cops went there and checked the CCTV but didn't see anything suspicious. Seems if you put too many stamps on the package you don't have to get involved at the counter, you just hand it over. Could have been any one of thousands of people. And they could have been wearing a disguise. Dead end, basically.'

'So the cops have to wait for somebody to report someone missing, I guess. Or a body turns up.'

'That's about it,' said Bruce. 'Hon… tell me what you think about this idea. No pressure, you know?'

Derry wondered what was coming. It wasn't like Bruce to be so elaborately tactful. Usually whatever was on his mind, he came out with it.

'The Countess wants you to come back.'

'But I am coming back.'

'Like, now. Well, tomorrow.'

'Why? I'll be back Friday anyhow. What's the rush?'

'In fact,' continued Bruce,' she… uh… she said to say please, she would really like you to do that.'

'But why?' insisted Derry. ' I guess she wants a reading or something—but we'll have plenty of time Friday. What's a day?'

'She says it will make her feel better. She's not been herself.' Again Bruce hesitated. 'She says she'll pay an extra fee for a consultation.'

'She doesn't need to pay extra.'

Derry's head was spinning. Why the urgency? Was Octavia far more troubled by what had happened than she pretended? Even if she were, what could Derry do to help?

'Why not give the old lady what she wants,' said Bruce. 'She's pretty frail.'

Ah, thought Derry. There it was. Bruce had been conquered by his Countess. This wasn't fair. In fact, it was blatant emotional blackmail. Then again, Octavia *was* elderly, and she and her family had been through a horrible experience. Why deny her a little support? If something silly like a card reading helped her, who was Derry to say no? As long as she stuck to vaguely reassuring generalities, surely that would be okay. And escaping Vanessa's clutches for a while would be a welcome bonus.

'Okay. I'll come.'

'Aw, thanks hon. It'll mean a lot to the old girl.'

'If I get the train, can you meet me at the station and take me back to Sorley?'

'No need,' said Bruce. 'It's all fixed. Sebastian is coming into town. He'll pick you up at your mother's gallery. Fourteen hundred.' He corrected himself. 'Uh, two p.m.'

'No. It's fine, I'll get the train—'

'Hon, I won't be able to come get you at the station, I'm real tied up. Why not take the ride? What's the problem?'

What was the problem? Derry wasn't sure she knew. Whatever, Derry wasn't about to complain to Bruce that

Sebastian had stood her up in a restaurant. He'd laugh and say, 'chicks,' as if she had told him one more reason it was good to be gay.

'Alright, two o'clock,' said Derry. Why did she have the feeling everybody knew what was to happen except her? They hadn't even waited for her to agree before arranging her transport.

'Cool. I'm sending you a pic,' said Bruce. 'Bye.'

A ping from Derry's phone. She swiped. A selfie of two smiling faces.

Cheek to cheek, Bruce and a beaming Dowager Countess.

Five minutes before one, someone knocked on Vanessa's office door. Derry was sitting at the table, explaining to Vanessa a discrepancy she had found in the catalogue entry for a seriously pricey picture due to go on display next day.

'Sebastian! How lovely to see you,' gushed Vanessa. 'What have you brought for me?'

At once, Derry saw the change. Sebastian looked strained, older. Under his arm, he carried what appeared to be a medium-sized artwork, obviously well packed and padded, but otherwise undistinguished in its brown paper wrapping.

'I wanted to ask you would you mind holding onto this for Sergei to collect?' said Sebastian. 'It's for a client of his. I'm rather pushed for time, and the traffic is hellish.'

Only now did he look at Derry. She didn't feel like smiling any kind of greeting. He could make of that whatever he liked.

169

'I'm sorry Vanessa, I must apologise to Derry.' Sebastian turned to face her. 'Derry, I am so sorry. I apologise from the depths of my heart.'

Vanessa eyes widened at this surprising but deliciously exciting drama.

'We were to meet for lunch,' explained Sebastian. 'I got a call about a friend. An accident.'

Of all the possible explanations for Sebastian's behaviour, a real emergency had never entered Derry's mind. 'Is he alright? Your friend?'

'Um, yes. Will be. We hope. It was a shock.'

'Of course. That's terrible.' Now Derry felt guilty. She had nursed a grudge for days, and with no justification at all.

'I was completely distracted,' continued Sebastian. 'Then the phone number I had for you didn't work. Must have stored it wrongly. And then things…' he shrugged helplessly.

'Never mind,' said Derry. 'It was nothing. Honest. My dad kept me company. We had a nice time.'

Sebastian looked relieved. 'But genuinely, I am so sorry.' He checked his watch. 'We really must go. Bry says she'll fix you up with lunch when we get there.'

'Since it's to Sorley Hall, I won't blame you for taking her away,' said Vanessa. 'But it's too bad of you. I was trying to get her to stay here with me. But I believe she'll see the light.' Vanessa turned smiling to Derry. 'How about you come straight back after your weekend, darling. Oh, and while you're at Sorley, don't forget to look up your father at Fotheringham. Make sure he's behaving.' Vanessa darted a sly glance at Sebastian, making sure her reference to the royal residence had been noted. She seemed satisfied. 'Sebastian, you say Sergei is going to collect this?' She placed his wrapped picture flat on the table. 'I hope it isn't too valuable. Aren't you afraid I'll swap it for a poster of some tennis player showing her ass?'

Sebastian blushed and shot Derry a panicked look. Obviously he had no idea what to say.

Vanessa burst out laughing.

'Oh you Brits.'

# 19

'Shame we didn't meet somewhere else. Some other time,' said Sebastian. They had just pulled into the courtyard at Sorley, but instead of turning off the engine, Sebastian sat staring ahead. Derry could hear herself breathing.

'All the things that have happened…' He stopped, as if he hadn't an idea how to explain or where to begin.

To her own astonishment, and before her brain had any chance to consider, Derry said, 'Yes. A shame.'

Sebastian smiled, his mood changing like a switch had been flicked. He shrugged. 'Then again, who knows what the future will bring? If Madam Tulip finds out, please ask her to let me know.'

~

Sitting in the breakfast room of Sorley Hall was unsettling. Bryony had made the pasta herself, and followed with a salad she proudly pointed out came from the Hall's own vegetable garden. But even as Derry ate and made the appreciative comments demanded by good manners, she had the oddest feeling something was wrong, like she was eating sandwiches in a vet's clinic. Then she realised—in the air hung the faintest tang of disinfectant.

As circumspectly as she could, Derry asked how was Octavia, was she recovering from the shock. 'Fine,' said Bryony, seeming surprised at the question. 'She's a tough old boot. By the way, says she'll see you tonight and looks forward to a chat.'

Where was all the urgency? Derry had half expected to find the Countess waiting for her, desperate to confide. Instead, Derry's arrival had been greeted with a casual acceptance, as though she were some congenial cousin who occasionally turned up for the weekend. But she could hardly press Bryony for details, so instead they sat relaxed, chatting about stately homes and the business of running such a massive enterprise.

'Is it worth it?' asked Derry. 'It looks like a crazy amount of work. Don't you feel sometimes like giving it up? Doing something else?'

Bryony didn't seem to mind the direct questions. Derry liked the way she paused, giving her answer due thought.

'These places, they're part of who we are. They've been handed down. It's like a trust, and nobody wants to be the first generation to screw it up. I certainly don't. My father—'

Derry never did get to hear what Bryony was going to say about her father. The door opened, and the Earl himself stepped in. He stopped, surprised to see Derry.

'Oh, frightfully sorry.' His eyes didn't say sorry at all, they said irritated. 'Need a word with you, Bry.'

Derry noticed the Earl's maroon knitted tie was askew beneath his faded tweed jacket. He had thinning hair and dark circles under his eyes, but you could just see the resemblance to Bryony—that same strong jaw and those grey eyes. But there the resemblance ended. Where Bryony exuded ruddy health and boundless optimism, the Earl's face was pale and fleshy, his mouth turned down in a sulky, disappointed pout.

'Dad,' said Bryony, 'let me introduce Derry O'Donnell. She's going to be reading fortunes at the party. She's an actress.'

The Earl's expression said that fortune-tellers, and for that matter actresses, were the least interesting of the many uninteresting branches of the human tree.

'Derry's father is Jack O'Donnell, the painter,' said Bryony.

The Earl brightened. 'Ah! Always said, must get hold of some of his one day. Bit pricey now, though.' He looked at Derry with a mixture of renewed respect at her distinguished lineage and irritation at her father's prices. 'Well, you should do alright. Fortune-telling—lucrative trade, what? You'd think Octavia would have more sense, whatever about the others.' He frowned in Bryony's direction, leaving no doubt whom he meant by *others*. 'Fortune-tellers are charlatans the lot of 'em, begging your pardon.' He fixed a gimlet eye on Derry.

Derry wondered whether all earls were this bad mannered. Was being offensive a skill passed down from generation to generation? Something they learned at earl school? Or was it in the genes, the same genes that helped their ancestors kill enough people to get their castles and stately homes?

'Dad is so dogmatic,' said Bryony. 'No point arguing with him. His lordship's always right, aren't you Daddy?'

The faintest flicker of a smile at the corner of the Earl's mouth hinted at his fondness for his daughter.

'I'm inviting Derry and Bruce to dinner tonight, Daddy,' continued Bryony. 'Octavia is keen we should have a little get-together. Charlotte and Torquil will be back. Marlene too. A laugh will do us all good.'

'Who am I to argue?' answered the Earl, directing his comment at Derry. 'Women run bloody everything. Bryony, I need that word.'

Bryony patted Derry on the shoulder and stood to follow her father. 'You relax and enjoy your meal. Just leave the dishes in the sink; Annie will see to them later.'

Derry sat, her salad half finished. The smell of disinfectant seemed to grow stronger in her nostrils. She shivered, pushing the plate away. In the kitchen she emptied the remains into the refuse. She had meant to wash the plate and leave it on the draining board, but as she stood, the plate in her hand, she could think only of the thing that had sat in this very sink, wrapped in a refuse sack. Though she had never actually seen that grisly object, her mind had somehow decided she had. Like the universe had suddenly ruled that no petty distinction would ever again be allowed between seeing and imagining.

Derry could hardly bring herself to put the plate in the sink. All she wanted was to get out as fast as she could. She ran the tap, grabbed the little brush that hung over the basin on a hook, and furiously scrubbed. As she finished, rinsing the plate and placing it on the drying rack, it happened.

The sink was an ancient ceramic creation, off-white, deep and almost square. As the flow of water from the tap hit the bottom, the fall at first made almost no sound, none of the clatter made by aluminium. And where the water struck the base of the sink, the liquid spread in a smooth whirling circle before pooling round and gurgling down the plughole. So why was a gentle mist rising from the water just where it struck the surface? Why was a heavy miasma, white and dense, now collecting in the bottom? And why was the falling water now fizzling and spitting violently where it hit, as if reacting fiercely against the sink's hard white glaze?

Derry stared transfixed. Her eyes stung, and she found

however hard she tried she couldn't move to escape the acrid mist enveloping her senses. And all the while the fizzing foam rose, like the clean falling water was repelled by the very substance of that sink. As if, locked into the ceramic was an infinite quantum of fear and disgust. And from the swirling vapour random eddies drifted higher, and she was inhaling without ever meaning to. And with every breath she took, her mind darkened.

~

'Hon! You okay? You alright?'

For a moment Derry couldn't collect her wits enough to answer that yes, she was alright. Bruce was standing behind her, supporting her under her arms. She hadn't fallen, yet her befuddled brain seemed to believe she had. The tap was still pouring water into the empty sink. Bruce turned off the flow.

'Delayed reaction, babe.' He turning Derry around, letting her rest her back against the counter. 'Take deep breaths. It's just a kitchen, okay? Stuff happens in kitchens.'

And with that obscure but somehow comforting observation, Bruce put his arm around Derry's shoulders and led her out of the room and away from the Hall.

# 20

They called it the Red Room, but it was blue. Or what little wall space you could see around the paintings was blue.

'The room was redecorated in 1875,' said Bryony, as though she had read Derry's thoughts. 'Until then it was red. But to us it's still the Red Room.'

For the first time, Derry grasped how every stone of this old house, every piece of furniture, every picture, mural and carpet had meaning for the family whose ancestors had built the place and had lived out their lives here for generations. In New York, you got nostalgic about any place you lived in for longer than five years and pointed it out to your friend as you passed by in a cab.

Derry thanked her stars she had brought a decent party frock. Her nineteen-fifties velvet number with bare shoulders and a restrained glimpse of cleavage struck just the right note. She was especially pleased she had brought her Victorian green paste necklace, a real sparkler she never tired of being told brought out the colour of her eyes. The jewellery fitted the setting to perfection. Bruce had made an effort too, although men fit and clean-cut had only to put on a decent jacket and they looked a million dollars. He had done, and he did.

After drinks they processed down the full length of a corridor to what Bryony called the small dining room, which turned out to be anything but small. The table, set out with gleaming silverware, linen and sparkling glasses, was so vast only the top half was used. Derry felt for a moment that she had stepped onto the set of a British period drama, the effect heightened by the presence of Octavia seated at the head of the table, gorgeously dressed in embroidered silk, her necklace, bracelet and rings blazing with diamonds.

'Daddy sends his apologies,' said Bryony as they took their seats—Bryony opposite Derry, Bruce opposite Marlene, Torquil across from Charlotte. 'Some business in town. Unavoidable. I'm sorry.'

Bryony's apology on behalf of her father was casual, almost automatic, as if making excuses for him was a familiar habit, not at all embarrassing. Perhaps it was understood that if earls didn't want to show up for dinner, they didn't have to.

'And Sebastian never dines with us,' said Charlotte, her voice hinting she was going to make an especially droll observation. 'He says, as a family retainer it's better he doesn't get into the habit of being at the top table. He laughs like he's joking, but I don't know. I call that inverted snobbery.'

Did Derry notice Octavia frown at Charlotte's frankness? Perhaps some rule had been broken of which only Derry was unaware. She suspected many such rules existed and doubted you could learn them in less than a lifetime. The thought prompted her to check that none of the silver cutlery in front of her was unfamiliar. She had been brought up in a well-to-do family, but American well-to-do. Here, under the lazily watchful eyes of an English Countess and two Ladies, she felt a creeping dread she'd have to deal with some cross between a soup spoon and a fish knife, and be exposed as a peasant and an interloper.

≈

The meal was superb. Derry had been half hoping a butler and some footmen would appear to round off the scene, but instead Annie did the serving. She was helped by a younger woman, similarly dressed in a plain black outfit that came close to being a uniform but wasn't quite. Annie gave Derry a special smile, and Derry smiled back, feeling it strange to be waited on by her. Annie didn't seem to see it that way. A job, thought Derry. Acting a part. She plays the cook and the waitress and whatever else they pay her to play. Then she goes home to her husband or whoever, and they have a laugh about their employers. Of course, sometimes they wouldn't be laughing.

The dinner went well. Conversation was light and inconsequential. Everyone was cheerful and got more cheerful as their glasses were refilled. Even Octavia appeared to relax and was no longer distant in her benevolent but watchful way. Nobody made any faux-pas of which Derry was aware or betrayed any embarrassing family secrets. Torquil made outrageous comments but never crossed the line, leaving Charlotte unsure whether to be annoyed or amused. Marlene dazzled without having to do anything much at all. Bruce looked completely at home—maybe they taught them how to do these things at naval college, thought Derry. All those cute uniforms, white gloves and swords. Or maybe it was being gay—you learned not to care overmuch what people thought.

Derry was suddenly aware that Charlotte was commenting to the table at large, but to her in particular. 'Not so many years ago,' she was saying, 'after dinner, the gentlemen would stay for port and cigars, while we ladies retired to the drawing room to gossip amongst ourselves, show off our dresses and assassinate the men's characters.'

'Now we assassinate together. Gender equality, I'm all for it,' said Torquil.

'If Daddy were here, we'd still be doing things the old-fashioned way, you can be sure,' said Charlotte.

'Ridiculous,' said Bryony. 'He was practically a hippy until he was thirty.'

Derry remembered then that the Earl had inherited the estate late in life. Octavia, his uncle's widow, was the one who had lived in this house longest. But Octavia showed no inclination to revive the tradition of leaving the gentlemen to their port. Instead, she signalled they should all retire to the drawing room.

Derry was enchanted. A blazing fire in an elegant fireplace gave a warm, flickering light. Gilt mirrors reflected carefully placed table lamps. Two chaise longues, padded armchairs and a small occasional table made the place feel surprisingly homely and welcoming. A pair of tall windows were masked by pink velvet drapes. A gorgeous but slightly threadbare Persian carpet lay underfoot, a witness to generations of gentlemen's patent leather shoes.

'No candles allowed these days, I'm afraid,' said Octavia, settling herself in a high-backed chair near the fire and propping her stick against the white marble mantelpiece. 'The tyranny of insurance.'

On an ornate cabinet sat bottles of spirits, wine and a pair of cut-crystal decanters gleaming like miniature chandeliers in the firelight. Nuts filled small silver bowls. Annie circulated quietly refilling their glasses, before being told by Octavia she could go as she herself would take care of everything. Derry felt giddy. Had she drunk so much already?

'Derry, my dear,' said Octavia. 'We have you now. Captive at last.' She smiled. 'I admit to disgracefully bad form in asking a guest to sing for their supper. I do hope you won't take it as such, but I for one am not going to let the opportunity pass. Would you do us some readings? Please dear?'

'Say you will!' said Marlene and Charlotte together. 'Please-please.'

'The party will be so busy,' said Charlotte, 'we won't get a chance tomorrow, for sure.'

Bruce and Torquil obviously thought this a blatant female coup d'état, but kept their expressions as neutral as they could and accepted with good grace. All eyes were on Derry. All she could do was protest she had no crystal ball, no cards, nothing.

'Don't you worry, my dear,' said Octavia. 'I have cards here. Pure coincidence, I assure you.' Her eyes glinted mischievously.

Maybe it was the wine made Derry shrug and think what the hell. The atmosphere was friendly and relaxed, and she was confident she wouldn't be asked to pronounce on anything serious. Tonight was like when she used to tell fortunes for fun at her friends' parties. They'd all drink too much and laugh at each other's unlikely futures.

'So who starts?' asked Charlotte, slurring her words just a little. Octavia smiled indulgently.

'Bruce!' said Marlene.

'Oh no!' said Bruce, horrified. 'You can't do that!' He was blushing.

'Vote!' called Bryony. 'Who says Bruce has his fortune read first?'

One after the other, the girls raised their hands. Torquil

looked around, shrugged and raised his. Fully aware of his treachery, he made an apologetic face at Bruce. The final vote was Octavia's. She held up a languorous palm.

'Well Bruce, I guess you're it,' said Derry.

Bruce took his seat at the little table. The rest gathered round. Nothing about this was to be secret or private, but Derry didn't mind. Nor did she feel any sense of foreboding. Why should she? When the spirit was as lighthearted as this and the reading was a game for friends, nothing upsetting ever showed itself. Most likely, nothing true ever showed itself either, but that hardly mattered.

Derry suggested a palm reading instead of cards. Palm readings were huge fun, theatrical and easier to narrate to a group of onlookers. The fortune-teller could hold out the client's open hand and look astonished, intrigued, horrified and teasing by turns. Derry gave it the full repertoire. Would Bruce be rich or poor? Amazing—he would earn a fortune, partly by luck and partly by talent. And love? He would meet, not one, but more than one tall stranger. In fact, make that far too many strangers to be quite respectable. Bruce played along, grinning foolishly and being embarrassed, while the others hooted with laughter and told him he was irredeemably naughty.

After Bruce came Marlene, for whom a glittering future beckoned as cultural ambassador for the United Nations or perhaps a nuclear disarmament negotiator—the future was blurry about which. Vastly paid global modelling assignments would continue, of course. As Derry held Marlene's open palm in her hand, tracing the lines with her finger, Torquil took pictures with his phone. In twenty years' time, he claimed, Marlene, by then President of the USA, might want her biography written.

'I could ghost it for you,' said Torquil.

'Thanks, but no thanks,' retorted Marlene. 'Given the choice, I'd prefer to be ghosted by a real ghost. Much safer.'

Charlotte and Torquil were next. Charlotte insisted on their palms being read together as so much more romantic. This wasn't an approach Derry would normally recommend, as likely to cause the end of the relationship it was foretelling. But Derry saw little risk of discord tonight. As she held their outstretched hands in hers and let her eyes drift over the lines on their palms, she saw no trace of the troubling vision she once had—a despondent bride and a wedding abandoned. She hoped that was because the vision wasn't true. If the open affection between the pair was anything to go by they'd at least make it past the altar.

Bryony's turn should have been next. But however hard she was pressed, she refused to have her fortune told. 'I am not having you lot laugh at my pathetic little future,' she said. 'I'm a farmer and theme-park manager, and that's what I'll probably stay.'

'Listen to the poor relation, will you,' said Charlotte, laughing, while their glasses were refilled by Torquil at an indulgent nod from Octavia. 'We all know they're going to change the law. Then we'll have to call her m'lady and ask permission to visit. And we'll have to come in by the servants' entrance.'

'We already come in by the servants' entrance,' said Bryony. 'Now, stop it.' She was trying to be stern but couldn't quite manage. 'It's bad luck to talk like that.'

'Nonsense,' said Charlotte. 'It's not is it, Aunt?' she said, turning to Octavia.

'I doubt that anything any of us say will make the slightest difference,' said Octavia. 'Either it will happen or it won't. But change is devoutly to be wished.'

'Can't you tell us Derry? Can't you give us a little peek? We all want so much for it to happen.'

Even if Derry's head wasn't befuddled with wine, she would have had no idea what they were all talking about. 'I'm sorry, I don't understand.'

'Succession!' said Charlotte, obviously astonished that Derry didn't know. 'Rumour is they're going to change the law so a daughter can inherit the title and the estate. Just now the lot slithers off to some ghastly second cousin none of us have ever heard of, and we all get tossed into the street. Just because he's got *bits*.'

Derry remembered now. Primo... primo something. She knew the word perfectly well, but it refused to come to mind.

'We hope the government will change the law in this parliament,' said Octavia, gravely. 'They've promised. They've already changed the rule for the Royals so an eldest daughter can become monarch. It's only right they should go the rest of the way.'

'So will she inherit?' begged Charlotte. She looked to Derry with undisguised excitement.

'Really,' protested Derry, 'I don't know if I can—'

'Of course you can, said Octavia. 'Charlotte—cards in the drawer over there.' Charlotte stood unsteadily but obeyed.

They all gathered around Derry at the table, being careful to leave a gap so Octavia in her chair had a clear view. Nobody spoke, and Derry felt all eyes were locked on the cards as she shuffled. You could feel an edge of tension in the room that hadn't been there before. Derry wished she'd thought of asking for a glass of water instead of accepting the last refill.

Derry dealt the spread. And there was the answer—immediately, as if the cards were content to answer without fuss or argument. As clear as in a diagram, Derry saw the present order of things—the way the world was constructed, its institutions, rituals and customs. And there at the centre was the Queen of Hearts. But the arching structure that should have pushed her to the margins was turned on its head. No doubt about it. The rules would change.

'Yes,' said Derry. 'The change will come. Nothing about when, though.'

'Coolio!' said Charlotte, quietly. She turned to Bryony. 'Told you so. Congratulations. We'll have to call you La Chatelaine soon.' Was there a touch of something less than wholehearted in her teasing smile?

'I have to say, ' said Bryony, 'this is the most tasteless exercise in political punditry, shameless self-interest and downright bad taste I have ever seen, and that in a family noted for poor taste. In everything except houses. And paintings.' But she was smiling.

Octavia clapped her hands—one-two-three, like a flamenco dancer. 'No more of that now, girls. We have our answer. We can choose to believe or not, as our temperament or inclination dictates. Now Charlotte, why don't you tell us all about your party guests for the weekend. You may be as wicked as you wish.'

The Countess beamed benevolently on them all. And it seemed to Derry she bestowed on her a particular smile.

# 21

The party's end was prompted by some signal Derry missed, like a sound frequency audible to everyone but her. Almost as one, the others rose from their seats to make their goodnights and leave. Marlene claimed she had been up that morning at five. Charlotte and Torquil were already arm-in-arm and clearly needed no encouragement to leave early. Bruce rarely stayed late anywhere and was probably planning a twenty-mile jog in the morning. Bryony explained she was racing the following day and needed her sleep. She asked Derry would she like to come and watch, and Derry agreed automatically, forgetting to ask what kind of race, how they would get there or what time they would be leaving. She was just rising unsteadily to troop out with the others when Octavia put her hand on her arm.

'Would you stay with me a while and chat, dear? I won't keep you long, I promise.'

'I guess,' said Derry. 'Sure.' She sat, knowing she should be going back to the cottage and straight to bed.

Octavia gave a contented sigh. She wandered about the room, turning off lights one by one, until only a standard lamp and a single table lamp remained lit. The fire threw flickering shadows against the walls, and a friendly red glow made an intimate circle around the hearth. The Countess eased herself into her chair.

'Bring your glass here, and sit near me,' she said.

Derry did as she was told, settling herself by Octavia's seat. Beside her was a small table, and on it sat the wine bottle.

'Pass me your glass,' said the Dowager.

Derry murmured something about having had far too much already, but Octavia was brooking no argument.

'Don't be silly. You'll have a busy weekend, I'm sure. I know how professional you are, so I'm guessing you won't be indulging while you work. Relax. Enjoy yourself while you can, that's what I say.'

For a while they sat in companionable silence. Or near silence. A clock on the mantelpiece ticked loudly, and it occurred to Derry that this was the first dinner party she could remember at which no music was played.

'I must apologise for all the fuss about Bryony,' said Octavia. 'Inheritance and so on must seem so… grasping to outsiders. It's a strange world you live in, if you have family.'

She made the statement as though most people came into existence by magic, without parents or relations, but Derry knew what she meant. Seemingly, there was family and Family.

'Thank goodness George is healthy. Enough time for even the politicians to do what they've said.' She looked thoughtful. 'Too late for the rest of us, of course.'

What did she mean by that? For whom was it too late?

'Did I tell you my father had Barton Manor?'

Derry must have shown her puzzlement.

'The estate,' explained Octavia. 'Wonderful, wonderful place. Gardens by Capability Brown, just as here. Like growing up in Paradise. I was the only child, but female. When my father passed away the estate went to a cousin.'

Derry was uncomfortably aware she was finding it difficult to concentrate on what the Dowager was saying or follow the implications.

'Imagine the panic when they thought they mightn't be able to marry me off. Luckily, dear Hugo came along.' The Dowager's eyes, milky with age, grew distant, as if she were recalling a whole lifetime in one all-encompassing memory. 'This business is taking a terrible toll on George.'

The sudden change of subject roused Derry from her warm cocoon. By *this business* the Countess didn't mean inheritance or the likely actions of politicians. She meant... Derry found herself wanting to say this wasn't a subject for now. Really, not. But she didn't say anything.

'I often worry about his... associates. Especially at the turf. They call it the sport of kings—you can imagine why.'

What was Octavia implying? Derry knew she was in no state to think it through. Hadn't Sebastian said something about the Earl and wealthy men who love gambling? Some kind of sympathetic response was called for, but she couldn't think what.

'I want to ask you a favour,' continued the Dowager. 'A personal favour. I know you are the type of person who would help in any way you could.'

Derry wasn't at all sober, she knew that, but she was sober enough to hear alarm bells ring. Long ago she had learned that when anybody asked for a *personal* favour as distinct from any other kind of favour, she was likely to regret it.

'Obviously, I'll help any way I can,' she said, carefully, 'but I don't see how—'

'One reading,' said Octavia, quickly. 'Just one. I know these things don't always work out, but it could be so helpful, a kind of closure.'

Strange to hear the Dowager talk about closure like she was into psychotherapy or TV talk shows. Neither seemed likely.

Octavia leaned in close, her eyes soft. 'Do you think you could ask the cards something for me? For all of us?'

'I'm sorry, I don't know what I can do.'

'Ask the cards who that poor person was. If the police knew, they could surely put an end to the whole wretched business. Catch those responsible.'

No need to ask who Octavia meant by that poor person.

'Oh no,' said Derry, instinctively. 'No. Honestly. This isn't something I... I don't even know how.'

'Often people... like you... do help the police. I've read such stories many times in the press. Sometimes they even find the victim.'

'Really,' said Derry, suddenly feeling more sober than she had for an hour or more. 'I have no idea how to do that. Don't you need something that belongs to the person? Honest, this isn't the kind of thing I do.'

'I'm begging you,' said Octavia simply. 'I've been having terrible dreams. Perhaps if we knew more I could get some peace. Please. Try? Just once? If you see nothing, we'll leave it at that and I'll not ask again.'

Octavia took from the mantelpiece the pack of cards Derry had used for her reading earlier. She placed the deck on the little table, by the near-empty wine bottle.

If Derry had drank a little less, would she have thanked her hostess for a wonderful dinner and insisted on leaving? Perhaps. Then again, how do you point-blank refuse a hostess sincerely entreating the smallest of favours?

Derry picked up the cards and shuffled.

'Thank you,' said Octavia.

Derry dealt a spread.

She should have known she wouldn't find the cards easy. The hour was late. She had drunk too much. And she was far from wholehearted about what she was trying to do. She saw no clear pattern, as though the cards were as muddle-headed as she was. 'I'm sorry,' said Derry. 'I don't see anything that makes sense.'

'I understand,' said Octavia softly. 'I expected too much. I shouldn't have pressed you. We should probably leave it. Just one thing—can you see… what he looked like?'

Derry peered into the cards for some image of the person she was trying to imagine, but she saw no trace. How could you picture someone about whom you knew almost nothing? 'Honestly, I can't see. It's too confusing.'

Octavia contemplated the cards in silence. She looked up. 'Can you see his occupation at all? That would help a little.'

Automatically, Derry gathered the cards. She dealt once more. Nine cards, a full spread. And yes, this time, just possibly, she saw… something. 'Perhaps someone who works with his hands. Yes. I think so. But maybe I'm just going on what I've been told.'

'But not a manual labourer? Nothing like that?'

'No. I don't think so.'

Octavia sat bolt upright, as if struck by some sudden revelation. 'Oh!' she said, holding her hand to her forehead. She stared at the cards, transfixed. She swayed gently and seemed to have difficulty breathing.

'Are you alright? Can I get you something? Water?' Even as Derry spoke, she realised the only water jug she could see was empty, and she had no idea how to find the kitchen in this maze of a house. Worse, she was feeling distinctly unbalanced and in no state to wander off anywhere looking for anything.

'Why do I keep thinking of a priest?' said Octavia, her voice hushed. 'His arm. A priest waving his hand in a blessing. Dispensing incense?'

'I'm sorry? What priest?'

'I don't know. Really, I don't. The thought just came to me,' said Octavia quietly, almost nervously. For the first time since Derry had known her, the Countess looked her age—more than her age. A frail old lady. Tremulous. Easily frightened.

'But who would murder a priest that horrible way? And why?' Octavia's eyes were pleading, as though somehow Derry could answer the question. 'A parson,' whispered Octavia. 'Parson, parson, parson—'

'Are you okay? Octavia, are you alright?'

The Dowager slumped back in her chair. She seemed to wake from a dream. Her breathing came heavily, but the rise and fall of her narrow chest was steady. Whatever had happened to her, whether over-excitement or wine or both, the effects drained away as Derry watched. The Countess was again her old self. In command. Sharp-eyed. The helpless old lady was gone, like she had never existed.

'I'm alright. Please leave now.'

# 22

Charlotte parked her SUV in a muddy field somewhere near the village of Foxton. Several dozen well-used vehicles, many hitched to empty horseboxes, were already there. Across the field was an arched gateway in a high wall surrounding a stable-yard. Behind the wall you could see an ancient redbrick manor house, a random collection of tall chimneys and mismatched windows.

As Derry, Charlotte and Torquil joined the little knots of people trudging towards the house, Derry marvelled at how all the women she saw somehow managed to look elegant in tweed jackets and caps. She herself was similarly outfitted, but she doubted the effect was the same. Charlotte had lent her an ill-fitting brown tweed hat, gumboots and an ancient, green, wax-coated jacket that smelled of dog. In the pocket Derry discovered a bag of biscuits and a chewed rubber ball. Looking around, Derry realised that aside from the designer sunglasses everyone seemed to wear on their heads, everybody's clothes were just as old as hers. Maybe veteran country attire was some kind of proof the wearer wasn't a city upstart on a corporate outing.

The gravelled yard was chaotic, milling with people and animals. At least a dozen horses and riders were lining up in front of forty or so onlookers who stood chatting loudly, many with champagne glasses in their hands. The first thing Derry noticed was that all the riders were women. But it was the outfits that most surprised: black top-hats or bowlers; a few conventional riding hats—two with miniature cameras mounted above the brim; beautifully tailored jackets; white stocks and calf length skirts. All the riders sat sidesaddle on their horses.

'You're kidding me!' exclaimed Derry. 'They're going to race like that?'

Bryony had told her she would see something special this morning, and she had known there would be some kind of competition but had no idea what to expect. All Bryony had said was that she felt guilty about skipping off the chores but a girl had to have some fun.

'They're insane,' said Derry.

'Our Bry has nerves of steel,' said Charlotte, grinning. 'There she is.' Bryony was just visible in the crowd, perched atop a restless, prancing beast. She was exchanging words with a groom struggling to tighten her horse's girth straps.

'How many to post, Bernard?' shouted Charlotte to a ruddy-faced man in tweeds and black bowler, carrying a yellow folder under his arm. 'Seventeen,' he shouted back. 'Good show,' called Charlotte.

Torquil produced a camera and disappeared into the melee, cheerily photographing everything in sight and getting friendly smiles from people who all seemed to know him. Derry and Charlotte made their way out of the yard to a viewpoint from which you could see the racecourse marked by flags. The route stretched away across hedged fields and a series of high gates and fences. Along the whole length of the course, groups of onlookers positioned themselves for the best views.

Unbelievable, thought Derry. Dressing like a character from a period movie might be fine if you enjoyed a ladylike trot around the park, but none of the horsewomen she saw looked like they planned a gentle canter. The riders and their excitable mounts were gathering at the starting flag, posing raffishly for Torquil's photos. They raised their champagne glasses to each other and grinned. But in their eyes Derry saw a steely glint that seemed to say, *we're friends, but don't imagine for one moment I'm not going to ride you into the ground.*

Derry must have missed the signal. They were off.

'Oh my,' she breathed. Never in her life had Derry seen anything like this.

Charlotte handed Derry a pair of binoculars, never taking her eyes off the field. 'Our great-grandmamas used to do this. Like being let out of jail, I expect.' Through the glasses, in shocking close-up, the riders did indeed look as if they were staging a mass escape. Utterly careless of their safety, they showed no caution, no restraint amongst the thundering hooves. Horses and riders threw themselves at every fence, like sheer courage was all anyone needed to win and the instinct for self-preservation had never been invented. How anyone managed to keep their seat, mounted sidesaddle as they were, Derry couldn't begin to imagine. The ride must have been like sitting on the gunwale of a plunging boat in a hurricane. Through her lenses, as the field swung around to begin the return leg of the course, she could see clearly the expressions on the faces of the riders. Absolute, ruthless determination. And pure glee.

'Which is Bryony?' Derry was almost overcome by excitement and fear, although as far as she could make out no rider had yet fallen. She handed the glasses back to Charlotte.

'Second! She's second, see!' Charlotte was roaring wildly now. She handed Derry back the binoculars. Finding Bryony in the confusion of the close-up image took a moment. There!

'First!' cried Derry, caught up in the excitement in a way she had never been caught up in any sport before. 'She's leading!' Passing the glasses back to Charlotte, Derry found herself shouting and cheering with everyone else—the whole crowd was screaming, pointing, waving, insane with excitement.

'She's done it!' squealed Charlotte. 'Oh, Bry! You've done it!'

Now, Derry and Charlotte were clasping each other around the shoulders, hugging and jumping up and down. Yes, Bryony had done it. In what looked like a suicidal dash over the last fence, in a roaring of hooves she had beaten the second placed rider to the line by a neck.

Red faced, breathing heavily, laughing in relief, the riders pulled up in a confused mass of horses and spectators. Their mounts panted and skipped, showing no wish to stop now. Friends passed glasses of champagne to be swigged lustily. The noise level was tremendous as the crowd congratulated and complimented, guffawing at stories of near misadventure, and perhaps, Derry thought, wallowing in the sheer overwhelming relief that against all the odds no one was hurt.

'Amazing,' said Derry, finding she was hoarse and breathless. 'Absolutely amazing. Scariest thing I've ever seen. Shouldn't this be in the Olympics?'

'I doubt Health and Safety would let it through the door,' answered Charlotte, smiling. 'Might frighten the boys.'

Pressing through the milling crowd, they reached Bryony, still mounted, glass in her hand. She was talking animatedly to Sebastian. Derry was surprised. She hadn't known he was coming. But then why shouldn't he be here? Sebastian wore a wide-brimmed, black floppy hat and a trailing red scarf. An affectation designed to provoke the country set? Or did he simply not care?

'Isn't she a hero?' announced Sebastian. 'What a show! Valkyries ain't in it. She makes me feel such a wuss.'

'Me too,' agreed Derry. 'Bryony, congratulations. I am astonished.'

'It's how we got the Empire, dear,' said Bryony, laughing, patting her horse's flank. Derry wasn't at all sure she was joking.

As Bryony allowed her horse to be led away by her groom, and their little group, including Sebastian, wandered back towards the manor, a ripple of excitement passed through the crowd. The buzz of chatter was strangely hushed. A certain royal personage was coming. And not just any royal. The Queen was known to worship horses and admire horsemanship beyond any other accomplishment. Unannounced, she meant to hand out the prizes.

'Her Maj will be so pleased,' said Sebastian, speaking quietly to Derry as they walked. 'She's always had a soft spot for old Bry. Sees a kindred spirit, I expect. You know she tried to get Bryony to be a Lady-in-Waiting, but Bry was having none of it. Couldn't find the time, Bry said. You know about Ladies-in-Waiting?'

Derry did know that in England to be a Lady-in-Waiting to the Queen was an enormous honour reserved for the socially highest families. How well connected did you have to be for the Queen not to mind that you couldn't find the time?

'Oh, nearly forgot,' said Sebastian suddenly. 'Her ladyship asked me to give you this.'

Derry wondered which 'her ladyship' he was talking about,

but glancing at the envelope she saw stamped on the back a familiar crest—shield, fist and dog. And the legend, the Dowager Countess Octavia of Sorley Hall.

'Dear Derry,' the note read. 'So grateful. You really do have a wonderful gift. Thank you, dear.'

It was signed, 'Your friend, Octavia.'

～

'Can I have a word, Miss?'

Derry was standing at the back of the crowd with Charlotte and Sebastian, watching Bryony join the lineup for the prize-giving, waiting for the Queen to appear. Derry wondered why they hadn't gone nearer the front, but Charlotte explained that standing close risked embarrassing a winner by your presence. How British, thought Derry. In the States, your whole family would be right up there waving enormous banners with your name on. Pom-poms wouldn't be out of the question.

'Miss O'Donnell?'

Derry turned, puzzled at being addressed by name in a crowd of strangers. Pushing through the throng was a man in city clothes. His face was familiar, but for a moment, she couldn't place him. The detective. Detective Sergeant Peter Cranshaw.

'Oh,' said Derry. 'Sure.'

'If you wouldn't mind following me,' said the detective, turning and walking away without waiting to see if Derry followed.

They marched through the wide stone archway of the yard and on to the narrow country lane beyond. A white police car with its telltale chequered stripe and blue lights sat parked half on the road and half on the grassy verge.

'Perhaps you wouldn't mind sitting inside,' said Cranshaw, holding open the rear door. 'Looks like rain,' he added, squinting doubtfully at the sky. Instinctively Derry too looked up, but saw nothing remotely threatening in the few clouds sitting lazily in the blue.

In the driver's seat sat a uniformed constable who turned around and gave a friendly nod. He resumed staring vacantly ahead with the uninvolved air of a man on his lunch break. Cranshaw slid into the back beside Derry, pulling the door closed with a solid click.

'Sorry to drag you away like this,' said the detective. 'Didn't feel we could chat in the crowd. They all seem to know each other,' he added. 'Not very confidential.'

What could he want? Derry felt that unaccountable guilt she felt as a girl when a teacher accused her of something of which she was entirely innocent, and she would blush and stammer. She looked out the window. Some people were already leaving the event. Land Rovers were towing horse boxes out of the yard, nosing their way onto the road.

'No point asking you how you knew, so I'm not going to.' Cranshaw paused, as if that were Derry's cue to speak. But she had no idea what her next line was supposed to be.

'I guess I don't have to tell you that you were correct. Or probably correct.' Again Cranshaw paused. 'Look, this is not a parlour game. The facts, please.'

Derry felt as though she had stepped into a dream in which she had lost her memory but everyone else knew everything about her. 'I'm sorry,' she said. 'Of course I'll help. But I don't see how.'

'Her ladyship, the Countess, sent me a note first thing this morning. The victim whose body part was sent to Sorley Hall was one Philip Parsons.' He paused. 'She said you told her.'

He waited for a response, but Derry's brain was failing to process whatever it was he had said. His words made sense when you took them one at a time, but when you tried to put them together, nothing.

'Alright, let's take it from the beginning, shall we?' said Cranshaw. 'If I get anything wrong, do tell. Not everyone has psychic powers. Last night you held some kind of séance—' He held up his hand to silence Derry's protest that she didn't do séances. 'You did your thing, whatever you call it, and you told the Countess the name of a deceased man whose identity three neighbouring police forces have been struggling to determine for almost a week.

'Parsons, you said. Her ladyship says she was stunned; she hadn't given the man any thought for a very long time. It seems that Philip Parsons was an unsuccessful artist who tried to sell the Earl some bad paintings and later some doubtful heirlooms, probably stolen. This morning we went in search of Mr. Parsons, and the man has been missing from his studio and his flat for some time. Nobody remembers anything unusual, but there's some idea of a van making deliveries. Couldn't be vaguer, I'm afraid. But he's gone.'

Derry found her voice. 'Are you sure it's him?'

'Miss O'Donnell, I don't believe in coincidence. In any case, he left his toothbrush behind. We can match his DNA from the body part.'

'How long will that take?'

'Up to a month. The labs are short-staffed. Don't blame me, blame the taxpayer. He seems to have no family, so we don't expect a missing person's report from relatives.'

Derry's mind raced. Parsons. Hadn't the Countess said something about a priest? A blessing? Wasn't a parson in England some kind of clergyman? To her shame, Derry could barely remember. Yes, the Countess had seemed shocked by something. And yes, she had said Parsons. No, Parson. Derry racked her brains to discover what she herself might have said to make the Dowager react the way she had. Had she blurted out the name Parsons and now couldn't remember? Derry felt herself burn with mortification. How stupid! How lacking in judgement to drink all night then do a reading. In a party of happy friends, maybe. But in a house where a horror had appeared only days before? *Stupid, stupid, stupid.*

'I didn't say any name,' said Derry. 'I'm sure I didn't.'

The detective raised an eyebrow. His slow gaze lingered on Derry, challenging her to surprise a man whose job had left him incapable of surprise.

'I'd remember,' said Derry. 'We talked about who the dead man might be—presuming he was dead. Octavia said something about a priest.'

'What priest?'

'I don't know. A parson. Like a minister.'

'So you're saying you did not tell the Dowager Countess the victim was called Parsons?'

'No,' said Derry. 'At least… Yes, I'm sure.'

'Your natural modesty makes you reluctant to take the credit? Is that it?'

Derry didn't reply.

'If it's not that, then you're telling me her ladyship lied. That when she told me you named the dead man as Parsons, she was deliberately making a false statement to police. In writing, and in person less than an hour ago.'

'I did not name anybody,' said Derry.

'Her Ladyship said you were a proper psychic—the job I believe you're being paid to do. And now you're telling me you're not.'

Derry stayed silent. What was the point?

'My wife believes in all that,' said the detective, changing tack. 'I'm agnostic, myself. Then again, "More things on Heaven and Earth, Horatio," and so on.' He sat back and sniffed, as though giving the metaphysical all due consideration. 'To be fair, we have had one or two cases where so-called psychics have led us to bodies. But in ten times as many cases, they've wasted our time. You seem close to her ladyship. Know her before?'

'No. Of course not.'

'When did you intend leaving Sorley Hall—mind if I ask?'

'Sunday or Monday, I guess. We haven't booked a ferry yet.'

'I'd prefer you didn't leave before then. Understand where I'm coming from?'

Derry shrugged.

'I've already suggested the same to your friend Mr. Adams.'

Derry gazed out the car window, her mind blank. All along the verge, people were climbing into cars and jeeps to make their way home. At least half those people had been drinking champagne, but they didn't seem at all perturbed by the presence of a police car. An alien tribe, thought Derry—their own way of speaking and dressing, their own way of thinking. They all knew one another or were related. They had those ridiculous double-barrelled names, just so everybody saw them as special. How could an outsider understand what made them tick? How could anyone guess why a countess would lie to a policeman? The question circled around in Derry's head like a squawking mob of seagulls swooping on a seaside picnic. Noisy, insistent, frightening.

'I'm told your father is a famous artist,' said Cranshaw.

Derry waited. If the detective knew everything already, why answer?

'You'll know what a Fabergé egg is.'

What was he talking about? What had Fabergé to do with anything?

'My own upbringing was a little more down-to-earth than yours, I'm guessing. My father was a barman. Didn't even manage to own his own pub. Wouldn't have known a Fabergé egg from an Easter egg.'

If the detective meant to disturb Derry's poise with riddles, he was succeeding. A Fabergé egg was a jewel-encrusted bauble made for the Tsar of Russia's collection. Wildly valuable, extremely rare and owned only by museums and billionaires.

'Not a real one, of course,' said the detective. He waited, and Derry thought of how he might have made a fine actor. Mastering the timing of a pause was one of those indefinable gifts possessed by all great performers.

'Naturally, we have been intercepting all packages and parcels addressed to Sorley Hall. Nobody wants a nasty surprise. And lo, this morning a small parcel turns up addressed to his lordship. Must have been posted yesterday.' He paused again, a sad smile on his face. 'The parcel contained a strange item— a cheap Chinese reproduction of a Fabergé egg. Blue enamel with gold filigree. Fake jewels all over. Bloody horrible, if you ask me. The egg was wrapped in clingfilm and bubblewrap. And a page torn out of a magazine.' He cocked his head to one side. 'Maybe you can tell me what magazine that was? No? You sure? On the page was a photograph of Lady Charlotte.'

Derry's heart missed a beat. Charlotte lived a public life. Anyone wanting to do her harm would have no trouble finding her.

'You understand why we might view that as a threat.'

'Yes. I see.'

'Someone didn't,' said Cranshaw.

'I'm sorry?'

'*See.* Someone didn't.'

Derry shrugged. What gave this man the right to amuse himself?

'You know that Fabergé eggs are hollow and hinged on top? Like a little lid?'

No, Derry didn't know that.

'Naturally, we opened the lid. Carefully, of course—no sense in getting blown up by an egg, is there?'

Derry agreed that no, that wouldn't make much sense.

'But the egg didn't explode,' continued the detective. 'It wasn't meant to explode. Though it did achieve exactly what it was intended to achieve. Except in the wrong place.'

Derry tried hard not to ask the question she was being blatantly primed to ask. Then she asked anyway.

'Alright. What did it achieve?'

'We couldn't tell at first what was inside. In fact our dangerous-packages man thought somebody had been having a joke and filled the egg with… egg. But it wasn't egg.'

Derry swayed in her seat. Her vision dimmed. Nausea threatened to overwhelm her. She put her head between her knees and tried to breathe steadily. Her ears sang like she had entered a church tower just as the ringers went to work. Her mind was filled with a hideous eyeball staring up, helpless but horribly intelligent, its coal-black pupil encircled by an iris of vivid blue. *Please don't let me faint in front of these people.*

'An eyeball is a strange object, all on its own,' continued Cranshaw. 'Like a lump of jelly. Not nice. Not nice for our explosives man. He doesn't turn a hair at a powder that would blow your head off, but this one affected him much like it's affected you. Except he saw it, and you… didn't.' He waited, watching closely. 'Quite fresh. Pupil still blue. Not decayed at all, so the pathologist said. Rather like the… other relic. Are you alright, Miss?'

'Yes,' said Derry. 'Thank you. I just need a moment.' But she knew the damage was done. How could she have known the end of his story before he told it? If he were suspicious before, now he would doubt her every word.

'Take your time,' said Cranshaw.

'Charlotte,' said Derry, hoping to change the subject. 'Is she really in danger?'

'We can't be certain,' answered the detective. 'But the

package was addressed to the Earl not to her. Whatever pressure is being exerted, he's the target.'

'What about her party tomorrow?'

'We'll check the guest list, of course. Shouldn't be any problems. Everyone needs to stay vigilant, naturally. You had no contact with the family before this?'

Derry was no longer surprised by his sudden changes of direction.

'No. None.'

'Your mother is an art dealer, I believe?'

'Yes.'

'Done business with the family at Sorley, by any chance?'

'Maybe you should ask her yourself.'

Cranshaw ignored her little rebellion. 'I suppose we should be grateful to you,' he said. 'We know now who the victim was, and we know he did have some dealings with the family. But what dealings? That's the question.' He let his observation hang in the air, as though Derry could answer the puzzle for him if only she had a mind.

Derry's phone rang. She resisted the automatic urge to ask permission before answering. The caller was Charlotte wondering where Derry was and asking could she meet the others at the car in five minutes.

'Charlotte,' said Derry after the call had ended. 'Lady Charlotte. They need to leave now.'

'Of course,' said Cranshaw. 'I won't detain you any longer.'

'Thanks,' said Derry.

Cranshaw sat looking at her, making no move to get out of the car and let Derry past. The door on her side was useless as the car was parked on the verge and almost on top of the ditch. Was Cranshaw saying that for him detention was always an option? At last he opened the door, stepping out, letting Derry follow. He leaned back against the car, his arms folded across his chest.

'Did you ever feel some people weren't being frank with you—that they didn't feel they were under any *obligation* to be frank?'

Derry wondered was he talking about her or the family at Sorley Hall.

'You're here to do a fortune-teller's job. Or so you say. Perhaps you're the odd one out.'

'I'm sorry?'

'Perhaps you're doing exactly what you say you're doing.' He opened the front passenger door and climbed in.

'If you find the rest of Mr. Parsons, do let us know.'

## 23

Bruce was cooking. He turned around as Derry let herself into the cottage. 'Hey! How does it feel to be trending?'

'What are you talking about?'

'Twitter!'

It seemed to Derry that all day people had been speaking to her in a foreign language. They kept saying things in words that should have made sense but held no meaning whatever. How many times could you shrug, raise your eyebrows or say, 'huh?'

'I'm making us some noodles. Annie asked did we want to lunch with them in the house, but I thought you might prefer not. I made an excuse. Said you had to get into costume for Madam Tulip and prepare your mind for the other realm. Thought I'd go ahead and make us something.'

'Thanks Bruce, you're a star,' said Derry, stepping out of her muddy gumboots in the doorway and taking off her borrowed coat.

'One day, darling, one day,' said Bruce, smiling broadly. 'Laptop is on the table. Go on, check it out. I'll pour you a coffee.'

Derry had no clue what Bruce wanted her to see. But she prodded a key anyway and the screen came to life. What Derry saw made her stare. Right there on the front page of a news site was a huge picture of herself and an enormous black headline:

'PSYCHIC NAMES BODY PARTS MAN!'

'Madam Tulip, a famous American psychic, has identified a man whose severed arm was sent last week to terrorise toffs at Sorley Hall, home of the Earl of Berkshire. Police had failed to identify the owner of the limb until Madam Tulip was consulted on the case. Police will not say if Madam Tulip has told them a motive for the shocking act but hinted she may be consulted further. A spokesman said, 'We welcome any information the public can give us about the individual we have provisionally named as Philip Parsons.'

'Not a bad photographer, our Torquil,' observed Bruce.

And there was Derry in three-quarters profile, head and shoulders, green Victorian necklace. The expression on her face was intent, her forehead creased with a small frown. Now she remembered Torquil's camera flashing as she read Marlene's palm at dinner.

'Your best side, too,' said Bruce.

Derry felt like she had been mugged in the street. 'I can't believe he did this to me.' She slumped in her chair.

'Food, that's what you need,' said Bruce. He spoke as though a plate of noodles, albeit prepared with a superb sauce, was just the thing to erase any treachery you cared to name. He slid the laptop to one side and laid the plate on the table with a flourish. 'Eat now honey, you'll feel better.'

Derry ate. The noodles should have been delicious, but she couldn't taste anything. Bruce placed a coffee at her side and served himself a plate. He sat eating silently, tactfully leaving

Derry to her thoughts. Only when she sat back, sighing and sipping her coffee, did he speak.

'Better?'

'Better.'

'Want to tell me about it?'

Derry nodded. The shock was subsiding, but subsiding the way a tide falls—the further out the sea retreats, the more you see. The timbers of wrecked boats. Breakwaters encrusted in weed. Savage reefs you never suspected were there.

Derry told Bruce about Cranshaw interrogating her, and how Octavia had told him the body part belonged to a Philip Parsons and had claimed Derry told her.

'I thought you didn't do séances,' said Bruce.

'I don't! I did a reading, but I wasn't trying to do anything like that. And I know I didn't give Octavia a name, any name.' For the thousandth time, Derry struggled for an explanation that made sense.

'Maybe she, like, picked it up from you. Can't that happen? Like projection?'

'I guess,' said Derry, doubtfully. She thought about that. Projection, like when one person's thoughts are somehow communicated to another—call it psychic or say it's body language, either way maybe it could happen. But then, wouldn't Derry have had to create the thought in the first place?

'Bruce?'

'Hon?'

'I didn't project anything.'

Bruce looked doubtful. 'If you say so. You're the expert.'

'She set me up.'

If Derry had mimed what she was trying to say, like some

parlour game, Bruce couldn't have looked more confused. But Derry had no doubt. Projection could work both ways. And you didn't need psychic powers to make it happen.

'I was drunk. Stupidly. But I know what I did do and what I didn't do. We're invited to dinner. Lots of wine. Octavia gets me to do a reading, just the two of us sitting cosy by the fire. And she feeds me a name, not straight but sideways, all dressed up so the idea could have come from anywhere. Then she tells the police I told her.'

There it was. It had to be the truth. No other picture would fit.

'I made it easy for her.' Derry felt the shame of it. Not only had she let herself down, but she had been used. And she had never suspected a thing. 'Octavia gave the story to Torquil. He'd know journalists.'

Bruce was unconvinced. 'Alright, maybe. But the whole thing could be pure coincidence.'

'Bruce, somebody wants to scare the Earl into doing something. Or maybe not doing something. I don't know, maybe he owes somebody lots of money. If he's into gambling or whatever, he could get mixed up with some bad people. He gets into debt, and they're sending scary messages saying pay up or else.'

Bruce shrugged. 'Okay, I might buy that.'

'So how does he get them off his back without paying up? He needs the bad guys caught and caught real quick.'

'So why doesn't he tell the cops who the bad guys are? He's gotta know, right?'

'But he can't, because he's already told them he doesn't know. Maybe he's trying to hide something. We don't know what or why, but he's denied all knowledge and he can't go back on that. 'So in steps Little Miss Moron—me. And Octavia has a bright idea. Fill the dumb American bimbo with booze, feed her with the victim's name and get her to claim it was all her idea. Then tell the cops. And in case pressure from the cops isn't enough to knock the bad guys off their stride, feed the story to the press.'

'Okay,' said Bruce. He sighed. 'She might have done what you say. She's smart enough, for sure.' He inspected the ancient print of Sorley Hall on the wall behind Derry's head, as if the answer lay forgotten somewhere in its endless maze of rooms. 'She got the wrong woman, though.'

Derry sniffed. 'She got the right fool.'

'Uh-uh.' Bruce shook his head. 'What if Madam Tulip wasn't you?'

'Of course she's me!'

'I know she's you. What I'm saying is, say she was somebody else. Pretty well anybody else. She gets a juicy piece of intel, and she helps solve a crime. Her amazing talent is all over the papers. Wow! Would she say, "No sir, for I cannot tell a lie, it wasn't me?" Would she say, "oh no, publicity, take it away?" ' Bruce laughed. 'The heck she would.'

'Oh,' said Derry.

'Oh,' mimicked Bruce. 'You know, sometimes for a smart chick you don't get yourself at all.' He was beaming, like when a cute pet does something especially charming. 'You told the cop it wasn't you?'

Derry nodded. Now she thought about it, no wonder the detective was suspicious. Here was a fortune-teller and psychic disclaiming all knowledge of a correct prediction.

'Big problem for the family,' said Bruce, thoughtfully. 'The last thing they need is you telling the cops the Countess knew about this Parsons guy all along.'

'Well there's not much they can do about that. I don't imagine I'll be found in the ornamental pond anytime soon.'

'Not that kind of show. Still, not so good.'

'Why is it not so good? I told the truth.'

Bruce hesitated. 'Uh… I don't want to be alarmist, anything like that—'

'Okay,' said Derry. 'You're going to be alarmist, how do I know?'

'Just a heads-up. You… didn't do the bad guys any favours.'

'I didn't do anything.'

'They think you did. One day they're sitting pretty. They've got some kind of plan. It's working out okay. Then this crazy fortune-teller shines a big white spotlight on the whole business. Now they're all over the papers. Cops swarming over the victim's life. Not good.'

'Thanks for that.'

'All part of the service. Uh, did Mr. Detective mention another package?'

Derry nodded. 'Awful.'

'He told the Earl this morning. Made me think they must have used a fridge. Seems that eyeball was fresh like a plum straight offa the tree.'

'Bruce!'

'Sorry, hon. But you wonder.'

'Bruce, if it's right he was an artist called Parsons, why would anyone kill him and think the Earl would be frightened?'

'Some kidnappers cut off a captive's ear and post it to the family,' said Bruce. 'Pure terror. Says, look what we can do. We stop at nothing. Pay up.'

'But this guy wasn't kidnapped, he was dead. And if all the bad guys wanted to do was prove they'd killed Parsons, they only needed to send one proof. What's the point of two?'

'Who knows?' said Bruce. 'Maybe they made their demands and the Earl ignored them, thinking he'd just wait it out? Or maybe they were, like, angry? Mad as hell. Maybe they just wanted to scare the heck out of everybody.'

Derry was tired now. How many things could happen in a morning? She couldn't summon the energy to think anymore. So she stopped thinking. And saw the answer.

'Bruce, I know why.'

Bruce raised an eyebrow.

'Not two messages. One message. In two parts. A hand, right? And an eye. An artist, Bruce. An artist who can't be an artist ever again.'

# 24

'Thank heavens you didn't name the gallery! Say you didn't tell them!'

'Mom?'

Vanessa's voice was as insistent as a voice could be while still qualifying as a whisper. 'The paper! Front page! Dreadful picture. And look at your hair! Please say you did not tell them you worked for me.'

'I didn't tell them anything, Mom. I don't know what's going on.'

'Darling, you have never successfully lied to me in all the years since you were born. You are not succeeding now.' Vanessa's voice sank to a despairing moan 'Theodora has been smirking all afternoon. Sergei came in, waving the front page, asking was it you. Madam Rose—how could you be so... tasteless!'

'Tulip, Mom. And I did not talk to the papers. I didn't do any of what they said. I swear. You have to believe me.'

Vanessa hesitated. For a moment Derry thought her mother was going to concede that naturally she believed her very own daughter. But Vanessa had moved on.

'Whatever,' she announced. 'I suppose it's not material to where we are. That was then, this is now. Deal with the reality as it is, not as we wish it to be. Do I make myself understood?'

'I guess,' said Derry.

'Best we agree that for the moment things just aren't working out. Perhaps we should park the PA idea for the present? Nothing personal dear. If you need to come to London, that's

quite alright. Can't ask you not to visit the capital city, can I?'
Vanessa sounded vaguely regretful that she could not in fact
ban Derry from London. 'Next time you find you absolutely
must come to town, text me. No need to call at the gallery, you
can go straight to the apartment. Alright? I'll leave keys with
the concierge. Perhaps you could wear a hat?'

'Mom. I can explain how it all happ—'

'Must rush! Glad to have that straight, darling. We'll revisit
our little business arrangement some other time, I'm sure.
Don't forget now. Text. Apartment. Hat.'

～

Derry was still staring at her phone when the doorbell
sounded. Bryony had come to tell her that only a handful of
guests would be arriving tonight—most were expected next
day, the actual day of the party. For this evening, Derry should
make herself available as Madam Tulip, as agreed, but not get
into costume until Bryony texted to say someone wanted their
fortune told. If nobody was interested, Derry could call it a
day.

Bryony's offer was thoughtful. Someone else would have
expected Derry to stand by all evening, perhaps even in costume since she was being paid anyway. And yet, however
considerate she was now, Bryony had played along with last
night's charade.

'Mind if I sit?' she asked. She slumped in the armchair,
thrusting her booted feet towards the fire, and sighed. 'Thanks.
It's good to get away now and again.' She seemed to come
to some decision. 'Look here, I don't know whether I should

congratulate you or not. The papers have caused a hell of a stink. On the other hand, it might be for the best. Get the damned business over with.' She hesitated. 'You heard what the police found at the sorting office?'

Derry nodded but could think of nothing to say. A barrier had grown between them that wasn't there before, and Derry realised what she wanted was an apology or at least some explanation, some justification for what the family had done. But Bryony wasn't apologising, and slowly Derry realised it was because she hadn't the slightest idea she had anything to apologise for.

'You really do have an amazing gift,' said Bryony. 'Aunt Octavia says you positively radiated a connection. She says you have an astonishing talent. And Aunt doesn't hand out the bouquets easily, let me tell you.' She paused. 'Would you mind awfully doing a reading for me? Now? Before everyone arrives and I have to play host?'

Well now, thought Derry. How about that? Bryony too had been taken in by Octavia. Did the rest of the family think Bryony was too bluff and open-faced for subterfuge? Or was it that her interest in fortune-telling made her a useful audience for a carefully staged show? Was Bryony's unwitting role to trumpet the amazing powers of Madam Tulip, lending credibility to the whole creaky farce?

'I honestly didn't do anything,' said Derry. She hesitated. Did she really want to explain? Did she really want to say, this is all happening because your father lied to the police, is probably up to his neck in debt, has been mixing with gangsters and is, for all we know, a crook as well? And by the way, your aunt is mixed up in it too? Perhaps not.

Bryony smiled. 'Derry, you have to believe in your own gift.'

'Cards or crystal?' asked Derry. Why not? She had a job to do. Or Madam Tulip had. *The show must go on*, said Derry to herself in that hoariest and most true of all theatrical clichés. *Just make sure Bruce books a ferry home for first thing Sunday.*

'I'd be so pleased,' said Bryony. 'And perhaps afterwards you could explain a little about how you go about it. I know the basics, but I'm sure there's so much more.'

Bryony looked so frank, so certain that all you had to do was master the technique and you could do whatever you wanted, that Derry couldn't help feeling warm towards her. Bryony probably set about everything she did like that. Learn the right way to do a thing, practice conscientiously, then go for it wholeheartedly with no room for doubts—just as she had approached those hair-raising fences sidesaddle on her horse.

'Alright,' said Derry. 'Shall we sit at the table? Let me get the cards.'

'Why don't I make us some tea,' said Bryony.

As Derry set out the tools of her trade, she felt an unexpected lightness. Bryony too seemed more cheerful. Perhaps this was what they both needed. Life had become so complex, so unpredictable. Who says you can't just have a giggle, thought Derry. To hell with dowager countesses. To hell with earls and policemen.

'Okay,' said Derry, handing over the deck for Bryony to shuffle. Bryony did so expertly. Derry dealt a horseshoe spread—twenty-one cards laid out in that interesting shape.

'No point wasting time,' said Derry. 'We know you're going to get to be… what was it exactly? Countess?'

Bryony looked embarrassed but nodded.

'So what about a prince? No point having a crown without a prince. Do you get a crown?'

'Eh, a little coronet, I think. There's probably a tiara knocking about somewhere in a drawer.' She smiled.

'Right,' said Derry. 'Prince.'

'Doesn't have to be.'

'Why not? This is the future, you can have what you want.' That was often Derry's little joke. Nobody ever laughed, but she didn't mind. 'An aristocrat, surely.'

'Uh, no,' said Bryony in all seriousness.

'Okay, you don't want an aristocrat. Star of stage and screen?'

Bryony smiled, as if that idea was even further off the mark. 'You're supposed to tell me who I'll get.'

'Oh, so I am,' said Derry. She turned another card. Knave of Hearts. Why was the card familiar? But then, why shouldn't it be? 'Intelligent. Leaves you your independence.'

Bryony looked pleased at that.

'Calm and confident.'

'Good, that's the way I like 'em,' said Bryony. 'Athletic?'

'Uh-uh, don't see that.'

'Just testing,' said Bryony, grinning.

'He seems to like horses,' said Derry.

'Oh,' said Bryony, frowning. 'That's nobody I know, you saw what the horsey crowd looked like this morning. Fun guys, but more likely to have you mucking out their stables as wining and dining you. I've enough stable of my own to muck out, thank you very much.'

'Oh, said Derry. 'Okay, maybe not horses. I'm still seeing an aristocrat, though.'

'Mind if I ask what you're thinking there?' asked Bryony, inspecting the cards with professional interest.

'Okay, said Derry. 'I don't deal the spreads in the usual way, you'll have noticed that. And I don't much stick to the Past-Future-Present thing either. I like to keep it as open as I can, let the story come its own way. I mostly go with the normal kinds of meanings for the cards though—a place to start, even if they don't end up that way. Like, this seven of diamonds usually means some kind of surprise, though mostly it turns out to be about work. You have to see it in its context, then let the meaning come to you.'

'So what about this other diamond, the two?'

'Same idea. It all depends on what else is going on. The two often means some new business partner. But it could mean somebody not approving of your boyfriend.'

'I see,' said Bryony. 'So you have to figure out the bigger picture.' Bryony sat back. 'So... what about the future?'

Just as Derry settled down to think seriously about what the cards might be saying, there came a brisk rap on the door. Before either Derry or Bryony could get up to answer, the door was pushed open and the Earl stepped inside. He wore a beautifully tailored suit and polished brogues, obviously handmade. Behind him was Bruce, standing discreetly by the parked Bentley.

'Came to congratulate you,' said the Earl, smiling broadly. 'And to thank you.'

At first Derry imagined he was talking to Bryony about her win. But he was looking at her.

'Magnificent. Like I said, I don't hold much with all that voodoo. But who cares, as long as it gets the job done, hey?'

Congratulate her for what? Getting her name and his splashed all over the London newspapers?

'Now we know it was Parsons, the police can't be far from nabbing the culprits behind all this nonsense. Should make 'em keep their heads down. Make sense to you?'

His face was triumphant, a little flushed. Had he been drinking with his lunch? Yes, Derry could smell the heavy odour of wine on his breath. She made a noncommittal gesture.

'Bruce is going to run me into town,' said the Earl, addressing Bryony, 'I'll be staying the night, should get back lunchtime tomorrow. Thought I'd better let you know. In case you need me for anything.'

'Thanks Daddy,' said Bryony. Did Derry detect a slight smile that said the chances of Bryony needing the Earl's help for anything was the remotest of remote possibilities?

'Getting used to having a chauffeur again,' said the Earl. 'Just like the good old days. No more dodging the rozzers after a few swift ones.'

'Dad!' said Bryony.

The Earl leaned closer to Derry as if imparting a secret. 'Runs the place like the Chancellor of the Exchequer,' he said. 'Every damn thing you want to do she says no. I mean what's the point being a bloody earl if you can't have a chauffeur?'

'Pay no attention,' said Bryony to Derry. She didn't seem in the least embarrassed, as though the financial tribulations of the aristocracy were no kind of secret. 'If you'd prefer not to eat in the kitchen with us later, you can ask Annie for anything you want. You'd be perfectly welcome, though.'

To Derry that sounded like an invitation she was meant to refuse. Or should she take it at face value? Impossible to tell. 'You must have a lot of work to do getting ready for tomorrow,' she said. 'Is there anything I can do to help?'

'No. Thanks for offering,' said Bryony. 'Come on Dad, I need a quick word about tomorrow.' She propelled her father out the door, pulling it firmly closed behind her.

Derry returned to the table to sit and finish her tea. She thought of Bryony and her sweet insistence that no man in her future could be an aristocrat. Perhaps, like Octavia, she had little patience with the antics of the grown-up boys who had the right accents and went to the right schools. Derry found herself hoping that Bryony would find a good man. She deserved one.

# 25

'**M**eet Freddie. Derry—my bodyguard Freddie. Freddie—my favourite daughter, Derry.' Jacko beamed. Freddie was smiling too, as if delighted to be in on whatever act Jacko had contrived.

'*Only* daughter,' said Derry, laughing. 'Pleased to meet you, Freddie.' Derry shook his hand and kissed her father.

Derry had answered the door on the Saturday morning expecting Bryony with some last-minute instructions. Last night none of the few guests who had arrived at Sorley Hall had wanted their fortunes told, and Derry had a blissful night peacefully reading her book and listening to music. But today was the day of Charlotte's party, and outside the cottage window you could see the private courtyard filling with cars.

'Next time I'm forced to visit your mother, Freddie is coming with me,' pronounced Jacko. 'He's armed and trained to the highest standards. All the same, I'm not sure he'd stand a chance.' Freddie grinned. Boys together.

'Come on in,' said Derry. The two men sat by the stove, making themselves comfortable while she made the coffee. Freddie, she noticed, wore the country uniform of green shooting jacket and brown corduroys, but his city shoes were black and shiny. He took four spoons of sugar in his coffee.

'Meant to get back to you sooner,' said Jacko. 'Thought you'd want to know how your ol' Da was gettin' along. Security, don't you know. Can't be too careful.' Jacko tapped the side of his nose and wiggled his eyebrows as though, regrettably, the constraints of the Official Secrets Act barred further elaboration.

'Dad, am I missing something here? Have you been threatened?' Derry felt a sharp pang of anxiety. Hard to imagine that anybody would threaten her father unless in a barroom argument over politics, art and the influence of Blind Lemon Jefferson on the blues of the Rolling Stones. But given the appalling events of the past week, nothing any longer seemed too far-fetched.

Jacko laughed. 'The idea! Not me, my precious. Himself! Who knows what fiendish plots are this very moment being laid against a man who strives every hour of the day for the benefit of his subjects and the planet at large.'

'You mean—'

'Of course!'

Derry's head spun. What about the foreign oppressor and dauber of reprehensible watercolours?

'Himself asked me to deliver an engagement present to Marlene's friend Charlotte. Old chum of the family, and so forth.' Jacko's voice dropped to a conspiratorial whisper. 'But after recent unfortunate events the powers-that-be thought Himself had better not come in person. So yours truly was asked to hop over with Freddie and do the necessary. Sort of Ambassador, d'ye see.'

Derry tried hard to adjust to the startling image of her father as Emissary and Royal Messenger.

'So I handed over the loot to the happy couple. And Lady Charlotte said I should nip across and catch you before the party got going and you were too busy. She said you could show me around the gallery.'

'Sure,' said Derry. 'There's a beautiful little Kandinsky there. How about now?'

'Mighty,' said Jacko.

They finished their coffee, climbed into Freddie's black Range Rover and weaved their way through the dawdling flocks of tourists. The way was familiar to Derry from when Sebastian had driven her down this very path. To her surprise, she found she was hoping Sebastian would be at the gallery, but as they pulled up in front of the entrance she saw no sign of his car. She tried to pretend the emotion she felt wasn't disappointment.

≈

'Hi, Cassandra.' Derry introduced Jacko and Freddie. 'Is Sebastian around?'

'No, the swine,' said Cassandra. 'He's supposed to have let me off at eleven. He promised. He's not answering his phone.'

'Mind if we take a look around?'

'It *is* a gallery.'

Derry felt her blood rising, but resolved to let it go. 'Come on Dad, where will we start? Russians upstairs?'

'Kandinsky?' said Jacko, his eyes scanning the gallery walls with a practiced sweep. Jacko could recognise and name most notable artists of the twentieth century at a hundred yards.

'Over there... Oh,' said Derry. The Kandinsky was gone. For a moment, Derry toyed with the unlikely thought it must have been stolen. But if so, the thieves had carefully replaced the masterpiece with an ordinary Jules Breton of some peasant women. Or not so carefully. The substitute painting was much bigger and sat awkwardly in the space.

'It was there,' insisted Derry. 'Right there. Must have been moved.' Derry turned, meaning to ask Cassandra where was the Kandinsky now, but Ms. Bullingham-Smythe was engrossed in conversation with Freddie who was sitting on her desk. His jacket had somehow fallen open to show his holstered gun. Derry thought it better to leave them to their mutual fascination.

'Russians?' asked Derry.

'Sure thing,' said Jacko, and they headed upstairs. 'Ah! Another Sikorsky! The same series as mine, I'm sure of it. Haven't found a thing written about my own, but I've read about this one. A cracker.' He thought for a moment. 'Maybe you could mention to your friend Sebastian I might be interested in making an offer?'

'You can ask him yourself,' said Derry. 'I'll give you his number. My career in the art business is over. Fun while it lasted.'

'I don't like to interfere,' said Jacko, quietly. 'But the London press eventually penetrates even to Fotheringham.' He gave an embarrassed cough, looking around as if keen not be overheard by the paintings on the walls. 'I... hesitate to use the word vulgar, but you'll get what I'm driving at?'

Derry knew exactly what he was driving at.

'Are we letting the sins of show business creep in where arguably they should not?' Jacko paused. 'Just asking.'

'I didn't do it,' said Derry.

'Care to elaborate just a wee smidgen for the failing intellect of your old Da?'

Derry explained how she believed she had been manipulated and the story fed to the press. 'And no, I didn't put it into her head by thinking about it.'

'It can happen, though. Happened to me more than once. Embarrassing, I don't mind telling you. What we need,' said Jacko meditatively, 'is some class of helmet. Block out the waves.'

At some other time, Derry might have been willing to debate with her father the implications of living helmeted in the modern world. But not today.

'I was used, Dad.'

Jacko frowned. His protectiveness towards his daughter knew no bounds. 'A long and active life has taught me, child, that almost everyone is a complete bastard.' He smiled with the satisfaction of a prejudice confirmed. 'You're the generous sort. Naturally,' he added, seeing as how genes were involved. 'But we know how fallible are the small gifts we have. We know too there's a price. But others don't know. And they don't care. Just a word to the wise.'

Jacko pretended to be studying a colourful Bakst, but Derry could see he was watching her out of the corner of his eye. 'If you're sure you've been used,' he continued, 'tell them where to stuff it and move on. Perhaps delivering a smart kick up the arse as you leave?'

'I guess you're right,' said Derry. She shrugged. 'But I need the cash.'

'Nonsense,' said Jacko. 'Never let money get in the way of necessity. How much?'

Surprising. But Derry had no intention of accepting cash from her father. Far better to finish out the job here—she had only a night to go. The miracle was Jacko having cash to offer. 'Thanks Dad, I appreciate it. But no need, honest. Hey, how come you're flush? Thought you were stuck until your got your pictures sold?'

'Ah,' said Jacko. 'The Corrib Series, yes. Problem solved! Himself wrote a letter to my German asking him kindly to forbear for a couple of weeks. My German, wowed and awed by a personal letter from Himself, promptly paid over the cash regardless.'

'Wow, congratulations! You must be getting on fine with… um, Himself.'

'As I mentioned, our possible future sovereign is a man of taste and judgement.'

'Hey, hold on! Hardly *our* sovereign,' insisted Derry. Being both American and Irish, Derry felt obliged to make a mild protest. Citizens of neither polity held much with sovereigns unless found hidden in a wooden chest by the seaside. 'King of England, surely.'

'Some men's nobility transcends mere geography,' retorted Jacko.

'And what about the watercolours? Awful?'

Jacko adopted an expression indicating boundless tolerance for human failings even in the most elevated in the land. 'An earlier exposure to the fine points of technique would have been helpful, I admit. But real promise, I assure you.'

'You told him that?'

'A teacher must encourage his pupil. Praise is a legitimate instrument in the development of the creative personality,' added Jacko piously.

'And do you call him *Sire?*' Derry struggled to hide her amusement.

'Certainly not,' said Jacko. 'This is the 21st century. "Sir" does perfectly well.'

# 26

By Saturday afternoon, red and white barricades had cut off the walled gardens of Sorley Hall, barring entry to curious tourists. Behind the high redbrick perimeter had materialised a marquee, garden tables and sun umbrellas. From the vantage of her cottage window, Derry had a grandstand view of Charlotte's guests arriving, as each car tried to squeeze into the ever-diminishing space in the courtyard.

Derry was burning with curiosity to know what the Sorley Hall ballroom looked like decked out for the party. Idle sightseeing didn't seem polite, and she wondered if Sebastian was around. Maybe he could let her have a peek. At the same time, she should pass on the message from her father about his interest in buying a second Sikorsky. She took out her phone and dialled, but got only a network message saying Sebastian's phone was switched off or was out of range.

Bruce's van pulled into the courtyard, manoeuvring with difficulty into a space reserved by orange traffic cones. At once Bryony appeared, carrying a clipboard and accompanied by a girl helper. Bruce emerged from the van, slid open its side door and climbed in. Now Bruce was handing Bryony the costumes that had travelled all the way from Dublin, safe in their polythene sheaths.

Guilt made Derry get up from her chair, open the cottage door and step out. 'Can I help? I feel terrible doing nothing here.'

'Thanks. Things are getting hectic.' Bryony looked harassed. 'Maybe you could take this clipboard and check off each costume by the guest's name, hand it to Sarah and she'll take it to their room? That really would be helpful. I need to... I have to sort something out.'

'Sure,' said Derry. She accepted the clipboard and pen from Bryony and took her station.

'Hey,' said Bruce. 'Actors doing wardrobe. Don't tell Equity, right?'

Derry laughed. 'I won't tell if you don't.'

'Looks like six no-shows,' said Bruce, looking at Derry's clipboard. 'Shame to waste costumes after all that work. What'll we do with those?'

In the bustle and excitement, Derry had almost forgotten the shadow that hung over Sorley Hall and its inhabitants. Maybe some invitees couldn't reschedule after last week's cancellation, but most likely they had taken fright at the publicity.

'Leave the extra costumes in the van, I guess,' said Derry. 'Maybe Charlotte will know now who her friends really are.'

'Honey, that is so true.'

 ∼

An hour later, Derry wandered through the arched gateway from the courtyard into the walled garden. Inside the marquee champagne was already flowing, trestle tables were laden with food, and guests were helping themselves liberally to both. On a low stage, three musicians dressed in blazers and straw hats played Charlestons and rags, ignored by everyone though seeming not to mind. And all around stood characters looking like they had walked out of the most famous paintings on the planet. Now Derry saw what an astonishing job Lorna and Jasmine had done with their costumes.

The Girl With A Pearl Earring was loudly proclaiming that Mayfair was now far more desirable than Chelsea if you were single. The farming couple from American Gothic were demanding their champagne glasses be refilled, the man waving his pitchfork to emphasise the point. Magritte's Son Of Man, in suit and bowler hat, should have been wearing his green apple on his nose, but to avoid interference with the canapés and champagne, had rotated the fruit so it neatly covered his right ear.

The Barmaid at the Folies-Bergère looked wonderful. Her jacket was velvet and narrow-waisted, square cut on the chest over a lace blouse. A strategically placed floral detail neatly masked the cleavage, and she wore a beautiful locket on a black velvet choker. Lovely, thought Derry, vaguely wondering if she could contrive to get hold of something like it. Though the costume wasn't revealing in the least, its effect on the men was magnetic. King Philip the Fourth of Spain, in silver embroidered coat and lace shoulder panels, twirled his mustachios at the barmaid, while Tristan was shamelessly enraptured, peeving Isolde, who gave up looking mystical, folded her arms over her ample chest and sulked.

Torquil was circulating with a video camera, while a society photographer captured portraits like an entomologist with a butterfly net. No one was allowed escape his keen eye and easy charm, and he seemed to know everyone. Derry could detect no deference at all and guessed the man was himself some kind of aristocrat.

Derry declined an offer of champagne but tucked into the

canapés with a will, knowing she would be eating nothing until much later when there was to be a buffet in the ballroom. But then she spotted Torquil looking her way and saw with a sinking feeling he was pointing her out to the society photographer. Derry took it as her cue to melt away.

～

At four p.m. sharp, a hand-painted board proclaiming 'Madam Tulip—Fortune teller,' appeared outside the cottage. Beside the name was painted an enormous red tulip and a crystal ball. The art was amateurish but cute. On one side the sign said 'Free' to show Madam Tulip was available for consultation, and on the reverse 'Foretelling You'll Come Back Later.' Bruce's idea.

Derry's cottage sitting room had been transformed into Madam Tulip's salon, and now she sat resplendent in full costume—wig, jewellery and headdress—her cards and crystal ball laid out in front of her. One after the other, costumed guests trooped in for their readings. Derry was surprised at the turnout, but soon realised that notoriety was the biggest draw of all. A psychic who worked with the police on grisly murder cases was irresistible.

The afternoon passed quickly but pleasantly. The blinds were drawn, and the warm glow of the lamps and the flickering flame of the stove erased all sense of time. After the early rush of clients the pace slowed, and between sessions Derry could rest, have a cup of borage tea, even check her email. Three were from Jasmine and Lorna asking anxiously how the costumes had been received. Derry reassured them their work looked fabulous and everyone was bowled over. True professionals, thought Derry. They had probably been chewing their fingernails all morning, worrying.

A cheery rap on the door, and Bruce let himself in. 'Eight bells, Madam T.! Playtime!'

Derry checked the clock. 'It's seven.'

'Eight bells means your watch is over. You can hit your hammock, baby! Unless, that is, you want to join the social elite of Ingerland. Think I could nab me a nice dook with a castle?'

Derry laughed. 'Aren't dooks old and doddery and bad tempered?'

'Aw, I guess so. Why do I always end up with the poor but creative ones?'

''Cos you're poor but creative?'

'Dressing up time,' said Bruce, 'And no hogging the shower!'

# 27

As she stepped into the ballroom, Derry's first impression was of its enormous size. A gorgeous plastered and painted ceiling arched high overhead. Two huge chandeliers gleamed and sparkled, making you dizzy to look at them. The shining wooden floor seemed vast, way too big for tonight's modest gathering of thirty or so excitable guests. But, cleverly, the space had been divided in two—the top half was cordoned off for dancing, while a small stage had been readied for a DJ still nowhere to be seen. The lower part of the room was set out with tables and chairs, each table dressed with flowers. Along the walls, trestles draped in smooth white linen were laid for a buffet. Uniformed waiters from some upmarket catering company stood attentive and discreet, their faces impossible to read.

Derry took in the scene, imagining other waiters, other servants—the countless men and women who for generations had served their aristocratic masters and mistresses in this very place. She saw them now, stationed motionless against pillars or gliding through the room bearing silver salvers while blank-faced musicians played gavottes and minuets. Only yesterday, thought Derry. And now every one of those people was dead and long since rotted away.

Derry shook herself to banish the mood—this was an engagement, a happy occasion. A time for laughter, a time to be cheerful and optimistic. And there, across the room, was Charlotte, looking radiant. Cleverly, she had chosen not to wear a costume inspired by some painting, but instead a fabulous Versace. Around her neck was a glittering necklace of diamonds and on her head a sparkling miniature tiara. Derry smiled to herself. Compete with that.

Derry stood just inside the double doors watching until Marlene grabbed her by the wrist and dragged her to a table. She introduced Derry to everyone in sight and urged her to eat and have a glass of champagne. Derry refused the champagne on the grounds she had promised to tell more fortunes in the morning.

'Fortunes? No point,' said Marlene, laughing. 'We all have the same future—half a dozen aspirin and a lie-down.' Derry smiled. But she had no intention of drinking alcohol in this house ever again.

Bryony appeared at Derry's elbow. From a distance, Derry wouldn't have recognised her. She wore a beautiful twenties beaded dress of layered pink velvet and around her shoulders a short, white, feathered cape. So different from the businesslike estate manager Derry knew. 'Could you ask Bruce a favour?' she said. 'I need him to do something for me, if he would.'

'Sure, I'll ask him. But why don't you ask him yourself?' said Derry.

'I don't want to make a fuss. If I go over there, I'll have to talk to people.'

Derry looked, and sure enough across the room a smiling Bruce was surrounded by three women in various exotic costumes, all gazing up at him adoringly and talking at the tops of their voices.

'I can't find Sebastian,' said Bryony. 'He's not answering his phone. I've been texting since this morning. He's supposed to be here. 'She seemed stressed, at a loss. 'His car's not here or at the gallery. He might be at home—'

'Home?'

'He has a cottage on the far side of the estate, near the West Gate. Could Bruce drive over? See if there's been an accident or something? This isn't like Seb.'

Derry hadn't known Sebastian lived on the estate. At the gallery this morning, Cassandra had been annoyed at Sebastian not showing up. Had he eventually arrived? For some reason Derry didn't herself understand, she chose not to mention the incident with Cassandra. If Sebastian was at home Bruce would find him, and the mystery would be solved.

'Sure. I'll do it now,' said Derry. She nodded at Bryony and moved across to Bruce's little coterie.

～

Derry was enjoying herself. The food was superb. The company was jolly, and nobody mentioned the events of the previous week or Derry's very public role in that disturbing story. Had the guests been asked not to mention it or was their reticence simple good nature? Derry thought perhaps the last—Charlotte's friends seemed a genuinely pleasant bunch of people. And unlike parties dominated by actors, nobody was complaining.

The Dowager Countess Octavia made her entrance with perfect timing. Impeccably dressed and bejewelled, she took her place on a high-backed chair and held court as small groups of Charlotte's friends came to be introduced or remembered. Derry chose not to join them. And even when Octavia's gaze swept her way and Derry might have expected some kind of recognition, the Dowager's eyes drifted on as though she were invisible.

The Earl's speech was mercifully short and finished to noisy applause and robust cheering. Bryony, standing at the back beside Derry, whispered that her father was probably saving his worst jokes for the actual wedding. She was trying to be cheerful, but Derry could sense the strain. At the toast to the happy couple, Bryony mimed drinking from an empty glass.

As the Earl left the little stage, the DJ fired up his decks and introduced himself. Within minutes almost everyone was on the dance floor. My cue, thought Derry. She said her thanks and goodnights, and congratulated Charlotte and Torquil. Torquil waved his glass expansively, insisting that Derry should let him make a documentary about Madam Tulip. 'Fame all round,' he said, grinning. Derry smiled politely and took her leave.

She was crossing the floodlit courtyard, fumbling in her purse for the key to the cottage, when her phone rang.

'Derry? Can you come to Aunt Octavia's? Now?' Bryony's voice was urgent, panic-stricken, utterly unlike the capable future mistress of Sorley Hall that Derry knew.

'What is it? Has something happened?

'Please. Just come. Octavia's rooms. Okay?

'Bryony! What's going on?'

'It's Sebastian!' Bryony was shouting as if Derry should have known all along.

'Why me?'

'I don't know!'

～

Derry knocked on Octavia's door. Bryony let her in, standing aside so Derry was immediately confronted by the Dowager's hostile stare. The Earl paced by the window, agitated as if at any moment he might reach for some delicate objet d'art and dash it to the floor.

Octavia sat in her chair by the mantelpiece, her face pale. The glare she fixed on Derry should have been enough to send anyone scuttling away gabbling apologies. But Derry was in no mood to be intimidated by the Dowager. Octavia had used her mercilessly, not for a moment caring what the effect on Derry might be. She returned Octavia's haughty look with a coldness she hoped the Dowager would see and remember. Through the curtained window the sounds of Charlotte's party could be heard faintly drifting.

'Why did Sebastian insist you be here?' demanded Octavia.

Derry stood her ground. 'You'll need to explain.'

'Don't give me that, Miss Innocent!' The Dowager's hands were shaking.

'Aunt, please!' Bryony turned to Derry. 'He wouldn't say why he wanted you here. He'll call again in ten minutes.'

'Please tell me what's happening. What exactly did Sebastian say?' Derry kept her voice calm. The room was already on the edge of hysteria.

'He says he's in trouble,' said Bryony. 'Serious trouble. He wouldn't say what kind. He sounded frightened. He says Daddy has to give them some paintings. He says he was told to call, and if Daddy doesn't do what they say, they'll cut off Seb's ear and send it here to go with the… other parts.' Bryony could hardly get the last words out. She held her frame rigidly at attention, her head high, but her jaw trembled. 'He said I was to bring Daddy and Aunt together. And you too.'

Unbelievable. Derry had the dizzy sense of the world spiralling out of control, changing out of all recognition at breathtaking speed. Sebastian! And why her? Why was Bryony—no, Sebastian—dragging her into this? And what about the police? Surely they'd been called? But here was Octavia, seething as though she would tear Derry's hair out if some invisible thread wasn't restraining her. The Earl was red-faced, his straggling hair askew. He too looked as if he had a hundred accusations he wanted to shout at Derry but didn't know where to start.

'In front of strangers!' the Earl hissed. 'For heaven's sake, what is he thinking? Eh? Eh? I knew he was trouble. Ideas above himself. Never knew his bloody place.' The Earl fixed them with his bulging eyes as if inviting each to take turns at explaining the inexplicable.

'I'm sorry,' said Derry. 'You have to call the police. None of this has anything to do with me. As you say, I'm a stranger. I should go.'

'Derry, I'm sorry.' Bryony's eyes were beseeching. 'Nobody knows what to say or think. Please—Sebastian said you have to be here when he calls. He must have a reason. We can't call the police until we know what he wants!'

Before Derry could say anything more, her phone rang. Automatically, she answered, saying 'Hi,' like she was sitting in a cafe drinking cappuccino, instead of watching a family in agony.

The caller was Bruce. Sebastian's car wasn't at his house. Nobody seemed to be home; no lights were on. Would Derry tell Bryony he was sorry, no luck?

'Bruce, can you hold a second?' Derry turned to Bryony. 'I want Bruce here.'

Before Bryony had a chance to reply, the Earl was shouting across the room. 'Absolutely not! This is family business.' With an effort, he calmed himself. 'Bruce is charming and all that, but I hardly think a nightclub bouncer is going to be much help.'

Derry ignored him, speaking only to Bryony. 'If you want me to stay, Bruce comes too. I don't have to be here. Sorry.' She felt heartless saying it, but some instinct for self-preservation was telling her to be careful. Families have a mysterious power, like their spirits are connected in some magical way. Derry needed a friend. Bruce was her friend. Nobody in this room was her friend.

'Alright,' said Bryony. 'Okay. Whatever.' She glared at her father and her aunt, as though challenging them to fight. Earl and Countess fell silent. Bryony checked her watch. She spoke hurriedly, turning to her father, 'Daddy, please don't interrupt. Derry is here now, we have to treat her as part of the family. But you have to explain. The pictures they want—what pictures? Seb says you know everything. What is he talking about?'

The Earl gave a loud sniff and looked down at his highly polished shoes. He came to some decision. 'Thing is, this is not our problem.' He held his arms wide, as if everything were now explained—like this was a game of pass the parcel, and he had successfully rid himself of the inconvenience. 'I mean, obviously unpleasant—'

'Daddy! What pictures?'

'I don't know! I don't know what he's talking about.' The Earl's face was sulky, petulant.

'He said he'd give you a list. What list?'

The Earl shrugged.

'And why Sebastian? Why him?'

'Ha! Bloody fool should've stayed here. I told him.'

'Told him what, Daddy!'

'Those bastards threatening us.'

Derry noted the threats were against *us*, not him. *Us* meaning the family? Or *us* meaning the Earl and Sebastian?

'I told him, while this is going on, stay away from town,' insisted the Earl. 'But he would go in. Never paid a blind bit of attention to me anyway. Acted like he owned the bloody collection. Don't know why I put up with him. Wouldn't have,' he added obliquely. He glared at Octavia, who glared back.

'Didn't stop you going into town,' said Bryony, as if she well knew why her father went into London and might spell it out if she chose. The Earl was silenced.

'Please,' said Derry, 'when did anybody last see Sebastian?'

'Yesterday,' said Bryony. 'After the race. When I told him about the… the latest package. He looked ill. He said it wasn't anything, but I know Seb. The whole business upset him dreadfully. Now this.'

A knock on the door. 'Come in,' shouted Bryony, not waiting for Octavia's permission.

'Hi folks,' said Bruce, cheerily. Everyone in the room except Derry scowled. He shrugged. 'I guess we have a situation.'

Nobody was ready to explain from the beginning. The Earl acted as if Bruce wasn't there. Octavia wouldn't look at him. Bryony gazed up at Bruce with a pleading expression, like a person afraid at any moment they'd slip off a grassy slope and over a cliff edge. But she wasn't explaining either. Derry realised she herself had been delegated the job.

'Sebastian phoned,' she began. 'He's being held by whoever has been sending those packages. They're demanding paintings. We don't know which ones or why. He's going to phone back in a couple of minutes. He asked that I be here for some reason. I asked for you.'

'Okay,' said Bruce simply.

'So what do we do!' demanded Bryony.

'Wait,' said Bruce.

'We have to do something!' Bryony looked like she wanted to grab Bruce and shake him.

'Anybody know where he is?'

'Of course not!'

'Anybody know who has him?'

'No!'

'There we are,' said Bruce. 'Like I said, we wait.'

Octavia spoke up. 'It's extortion. Simple extortion. They know there's a valuable collection. So they take a hostage.'

'Well they've got another think coming,' said the Earl. One moment he was acting as if the whole business was no affair of his, the next he was outraged like he was the one kidnapped and held to ransom. He cleared his throat. 'Call the police now.'

'No!' Bryony was vehement. 'Seb said don't call the police or they'll hurt him.'

'Pure bluff.' The Earl took his phone from his pocket. 'It's a pity for Sebastian, but he is after all an employee. What possessed extortionists to think the family would hand over its most valuable possessions in exchange is quite beyond me.

They might as well have kidnapped the gardener. Better in fact, Octavia would stump up in no time. Ha ha.'

The Earl's supremely tasteless joke was met with a frigid wall. Octavia's face was a mask, but her eyes were like blades.

'No police,' she said. 'Not yet.'

'Nonsense,' retorted the Earl, scrolling for the number.

'No!' Bryony threw herself at her father, snatching the phone from his hand. 'You can't! I won't let you!'

The Earl was rigid with shock. He was breathing heavily but made no attempt to wrestle the phone back from his pale-faced daughter. 'What on earth has got into you, girl! You'll do as I say. Give me that!' He looked to Octavia, silently appealing for help, but the Countess sat stony-faced.

'So what is this about?' asked the Earl. He spoke quietly now. 'Don't tell me he's been charming you, Bry. Can't believe you'd fall for it.' He spoke dismissively, as if to say how foolish females are, how easily duped.

'We're engaged!' Bryony blurted out her words in a despairing wail.

A hush descended on the room. Everyone stared at Bryony.

'Child,' said Octavia, her voice barely rising above a whisper. 'Why could you not tell me?'

'No you're bloody not,' said the Earl.

'We are,' said Bryony, her voice firmer now. 'For two months.'

'What, some kind of state secret?' asked the Earl. 'Minor detail? No need to mention it to the family? No timid request for father's blessing? All that old-fashioned rot?' His voice was rising now. 'The damned little weasel, taking advantage of his employers. Came here without a bloody penny to his name and no family anyone's heard of. Bloody snake!'

'No, we didn't say anything. We didn't want to steal Charlotte's limelight, as it happens. And I doubt you'd care about his family if he were a banker or a hedge-fund manager.' Bryony's voice was rising. 'You pretend it's about pedigree, but it's all about money with you!'

'Don't you speak to me like that! And don't think I don't know where you're coming from. Or him. Bloody gold-digger! You both wait for me to pop off, and he's home and dry.'

'That's not fair! I'd never think like that!' Bryony was close to tears.

'The man is a hired hand who couldn't get a job in the real world if he were starving!'

The Earl struggled to collect himself, pacing in front of the window, hands clasped behind his back. He stopped, his tone matter-of-fact, an employer taking a harsh but balanced view of an unsatisfactory underling. 'Don't like to say it, but I'm not at all sure about his honesty. What about his connection with this painter fellow, Parsons? God knows what kind of company Sebastian was getting mixed up in. Now, give me my phone.'

The tears were streaming down Bryony's cheeks. Her usually tanned and ruddy complexion was ashen. Silently, she handed over the phone.

'George, a word, please,' said Octavia. She addressed the room. 'If you would all step outside for a moment. You too Bryony, dear.'

Meekly, without protest, they obeyed.

# 28

Standing outside in the gloomy hallway with Bruce and Bryony, portraits of the family ancestors glowering down at them, Derry struggled to pull her thoughts together. Sebastian engaged to Bryony. She had to admit it made sense. A hot flush rose to her cheeks. She had been a fool. Could she have misread the signals so badly? Of course she could.

Bruce took Bryony's shoulders in his hands. He looked steadily into her eyes, radiating calm. 'It'll be cool. Everything will be alright.'

Bryony didn't speak, instead she stared at Bruce as though he were speaking some obscure foreign language.

'These things are pretty simple,' continued Bruce. 'You give them what they want, and they've no incentive to hurt anybody more than they already have. They'll want to grab the beans and hightail it out. Just keep everything straight and do what they say. We'll help you, okay?' Bryony nodded, seeming desperate to believe any assurances Bruce chose to give.

The door of the Dowager's apartment opened abruptly. The Earl vaguely motioned them inside, walking away as though the invitation had nothing to do with him. They stepped inside and stood uncertainly, until Bryony realised it was up to her to be civil. She invited them to sit.

The Earl spoke, his back to the room, addressing his first words to the curtained windows. 'After discussion with her ladyship, I have revised my view.' He turned, but still didn't look directly at them. 'I may have spoken hastily. It is true the interests of the whole family are involved.' He nodded vaguely in

Bryony's direction. 'I also accept that I do have a duty of care to my employees. I shall therefore listen to whatever demands are made of me, keeping an open mind.'

Bryony ran to her father, enveloping him in a hug. He stood rigid, his jaw clenched, while she thanked him through her tears. Octavia looked on but showed no emotion. Derry wondered what the Dowager could have said to the Earl to have made him change his tune so suddenly. One more mystery. Even so, nowhere near as big a mystery as why Sebastian was kidnapped rather than Charlotte, Bryony or the Earl himself. And why the extortionists, whoever they were, chose to kill an obscure painter who may or may not have tried to sell stolen pictures to the Earl. Nothing made sense. Nothing at all.

As if she had read Derry's mind, Octavia spoke. 'Since you are all involved in this sorry business in one way or another, I believe you are owed an explanation. What I am about to tell you is embarrassing for the family but, given the seriousness of what is happening, we must be frank.' She hesitated, searching for words, as though finding it difficult to keep her composure.

'You will be too young to remember, but back in the nineteen seventies everything possible was being done to drive the old families out of their houses. Massive rates of taxation, all in the name of equality. I'm not asking you to judge what was done then or to take sides, merely to understand.

'The family's art collection is, as you know, large. Many thousands of pictures and objects. During the war, these were dispersed throughout the family properties to protect them from bombing, but several of our homes in London were damaged or destroyed. We lost many important works. We also lost both copies of the catalogue itemising and documenting the collection—a serious blow, as anyone who understands art will appreciate.

'I say a blow, but the loss of the catalogues was also an opportunity to, shall we say, soften the impact of the punitive taxation that followed the war—taxes on death, taxes on income, taxes on sales. When a new catalogue was compiled, some works—valuable works—were omitted from the record. And we... quietly sold them over the years.'

Bryony was listening with rapt attention. Obviously she knew none of this. The Earl stood with his hands behind his back, examining his shoes.

'You should have told me,' said Bryony, quietly. Octavia ignored her, as if the idea of including Bryony in illegality and tax evasion, perhaps to the tune of millions of pounds, was so absurd as to be undeserving of comment.

'I am telling you this now because it bears directly on our current situation,' Octavia continued. 'Certain buyers of the... let's call them unofficial works, would have known that part of the collection was undeclared. They must have judged that if they made extortionate demands, we would be reluctant to complain to the police. They involved Sebastian because, as the estate curator and with many contacts in the art business, he had managed several of the... transactions.'

'He never told me,' said Bryony. Her voice was hoarse.

'I'm sure Sebastian deeply regretted the need for confidentiality. He believed he was helping the family, and in the process helping you. Sebastian is a good boy.'

Silence followed Octavia's speech. The music from the distant ballroom could be clearly heard. Derry wished she was sitting someplace she could think, without the presence of the Earl and Octavia making her thoughts go round in futile circles. Only one thing made sense—this was about money. Perhaps large amounts of money. And she could understand now why the family hadn't wanted to tell the whole story to the police. But why had the Earl wanted to call the police now, until Octavia stopped him? What had Parsons the artist to do with anything? And so much for hints the Earl was losing money on horse-racing, mixing with the wrong people, mired in some kind of debt. A deliberate red herring, told to her by Octavia.

No. First told by Sebastian.

∾

'Bryony, you need to take the call,' said Derry gently.

Bryony seemed to wake up. The phone in her hand was ringing, a tinkling hunting tune, but she was staring at it making no move to answer. Every eye in the room was fixed on the phone, but still Bryony let it ring, as if by not answering she could prevent time moving forward.

Derry saw Bryony's jaw set and her face assume the determined look she had seen before, the fearless horsewoman who faced terrifying jumps without flinching. Bryony swiped the phone and held it to her ear.

'Seb,' she said, her voice steady. She stabbed at the screen. Speakerphone. Now they could all hear. Sebastian was weeping.

'You've got to do it!' he sobbed. The sound was thin, tinny through the speaker, but you could hear his voice breaking.

His breath came in gasps. If he had sounded frightened before, this was a whole new dimension of terror. Something had happened since he had last called. What had they done to him? What were they threatening to do?

'They're going to hurt me again!'

Bruce touched Bryony lightly on the shoulder, held his hand over her phone and whispered. 'Ask what they want. Time. Place to deliver.' Bryony nodded frantically.

'Seb, they want paintings right? Which ones?

'Derry, is Derry there?' said Sebastian.

'Yes,' said Derry, coming closer to the phone. 'It's me, here.'

'Pen and paper. Quick!'

Derry looked around desperately. Octavia, grim faced, was already on her feet and had opened a bureau drawer. She shoved a pad and pen at Derry, pointing her to the table. Derry sat at the table, pen poised, the others clustered around her.

'Okay, I have pen and paper.'

'I'm going to list catalogue numbers and names of pictures. You'll know most of the artists. Write them down.'

'But what—'

'Don't ask questions! Write!'

Derry wrote. The list wasn't long—thirty-five or forty works. But she could tell from the artists' names that all were extremely valuable, a carefully chosen collection worth many, many millions of dollars.

'Read them out!'

Derry recited the list.

'Outrageous! Bloody outrageous!' The voice was the Earl's, whispered under his breath but furious. Octavia fixed him with a savage glare, and he said no more.

Derry tried not to be distracted, to hear nothing but Sebastian's ragged breathing on the other end of the line. 'What next?' she asked, remembering Bruce's instructions. Time. Place. 'Where do we take them? When?'

'From the store. You know the bunker?'

'I'm sorry?'

'The nuclear bunker. Just ask!'

'Yes, alright.' Out of the corner of her eye, she saw the Earl turn away to stare blankly at the curtained window.

'You know how to pack pictures safely. You pick them out, protect them and load Bruce's van.'

'Say that again. Bruce's van?'

'Unless you have another van!' Sebastian shouted the words. He sounded enraged as if all his fear had been transformed into anger at Derry, and she had somehow become overnight his worst enemy.

'Alright, alright! Van, okay. I select the pictures and load them. What then? Who delivers?'

'You do.'

～

'Ridiculous!' the Earl's whisper was savage.

Sebastian must have heard. 'It's what they want! Derry, will you do it? Please! Say yes!'

Derry's brain was frozen. Impossible even to think about Sebastian's demand. The idea she should drive Bruce's van to a kidnapping was absurd beyond belief. It seemed Bryony thought so too; she was shaking her head and mouthing, *'No!'*

'When?' said Derry, unsure whether she said it to buy time or to change the subject.

'They'll give you two hours to load the pictures. I'll call then and tell you where to drive. You must come alone. Bryony—is Bry there?' Sebastian's voice was breaking again.

'Here!' Bryony snatched the phone. 'We'll do whatever you say. It'll be all right. I promise. I'll drive the van.'

Sebastian squealed. The sound was like a young pig being captured. 'Just do what I say!' he gasped. 'Derry drives! Don't let me down! Help me!' And he was gone.

Bryony stood staring at her phone. All colour had drained from her face, but Derry saw her hand was steady. Her own hands were shaking.

Bruce gave a little cough. All eyes turned to the tall, serious-faced man standing straight, feet apart, hands behind his back.

'Sorry, guys.' He addressed the whole room, speaking quietly, but he may as well have shouted at the top of his voice. The Earl and Octavia were as much startled as if the tall grandfather clock against the wall, instead of ticking monotonously, had suddenly made an announcement.

'Not on,' said Bruce. 'Cops. Call them. Right away.' He emphasised each word, like an admiral issuing quiet but definite commands from which no one was exempt.

Derry knew this wasn't the time or the place for irritation. Of course it wasn't. Irritation is a trivial emotion best kept for arguments about which movie to watch. But irritation was mostly what she felt now. Everyone in the room, including Bruce, seemed to believe today was some kind of Make-Derry's-Decisions-For-Her day. Like her own future was none of her business and consulting her not even an afterthought. 'Bruce, hold on a minute. We have to think about this—'

'No,' said Bruce. 'Nothing to think about. You asked what I thought—'

'I did not!'

'You were going to ask what I thought—'

'Please!' It was Bryony, imploring. 'I'll drive.'

'Uh, not that either,' said Bruce.

'Who the hell do you think you are?' shouted the Earl. He was trembling, all his anger and fear now directed at the upstart, insubordinate American with the insufferable confidence.

'We must consider carefully,' said Octavia. 'I am sure you, Bruce, will agree that in this situation one should try to follow instructions to the letter?'

Bruce nodded. 'Sure. With the advice of the cops. They have the experts.'

'We know what these dreadful people want,' continued the Dowager. 'Money is all they're interested in. Why would they want to attract more attention by hurting anybody? We want the same as they do. We want the whole business over with and forgotten. Move on, as they say nowadays.'

'Aren't y'all forgetting Mister Parsons, your ladyship? He won't be moving on anywhere.'

The Dowager's nostrils flared. 'A moment's reflection would tell you he had nothing to do with us. He must have been in dispute with these people over some other matter. He died who knows how or why. They used the opportunity, as anyone would.'

As anyone would? An extraordinary thing to say, but nothing about Octavia surprised Derry any longer.

'I don't believe there is any real risk,' Octavia insisted. 'Calling the police is out of the question. We cannot put Sebastian in more danger.'

'Her ladyship is right,' said the Earl. 'I can't see any risk to Miss O'Donnell. There would of course be inconvenience,' he spoke directly to Derry now, 'but I feel sure the family will compensate you most satisfactorily.'

And there it was. As far as Octavia and the Earl were concerned, Derry was to take whatever risk was to be taken. Some cash would be thrown her way for her trouble. No police, no awkward questions about millions of pounds in tax evasion. No fines or prison terms. Philip Parsons already forgotten.

But perhaps Octavia was right about one thing—another dead body could never be in the extortionists' interests. And the more Derry thought about it, the more likely it seemed that the first killing was unrelated, serving only to provide an opportunity to terrorise the Earl. The body parts, if they did indeed belong to Philip Parsons and not some medical school corpse, were an afterthought. An eyeball wrapped in a picture of Charlotte? Pure drama. Stage dressing. A grisly and effective prop.

But why did Sebastian insist that Derry be the driver? Why did his captors care who delivered the spoils? The answer came clear as day. A woman was unlikely to try strong-arm tactics. And they wanted a woman they knew, to make sure she wasn't a policewoman in disguise. They knew Derry—hadn't her picture been all over the London evening papers? But why not Bryony, a well-known member of a titled family whose picture could be sourced in five minutes on the internet?

Easy. Sebastian didn't want to put Bryony at risk. She was, after all, his fiancée.

*Thanks Sebastian. Thanks a bunch.*

~

'I know what you are thinking,' said Octavia. She fixed Bruce with a steady gaze. 'You imagine you can call the police yourself, like a good law-abiding citizen, because you think you know best. '

Bruce made no answer. Derry guessed that phoning the police was exactly what Bruce was planning to do.

'Make your call if you wish. We will deny everything you have heard here tonight. You will be reporting an incident that never happened.'

'Aunt! You can't say that!' Bryony was staring as if she had never seen her aunt before.

'Think, girl. Sebastian told us he would be harmed if the police were called. He told us they want Derry to deliver the goods. Who will you support, Bruce here playing boy scout or Sebastian who will pay the price if the police are as clumsy and stupid as they so often seem to be?'

Bryony's voice was hushed. 'I don't believe you give a damn about Sebastian. You're not afraid for him—you're afraid for yourselves.'

Octavia didn't flinch. 'Believe what you wish. But both Sebastian and your inheritance are at risk. I suggest, if you care for Sebastian and believe you are deserving of your inheritance, you show some spirit. And some sense.'

Bryony swallowed and turned away.

'And you,' said Octavia, addressing Derry. 'Will you claim to have heard a phone call that everyone except Bruce denies ever happened? I imagine your recent publicity will not be helpful.'

'I'll drive,' said Bruce.

Derry was stunned. Not because Bruce had volunteered—you expected that. The shocking thing was that he had so readily accepted defeat. A moment's thought told her why. Bruce knew if he called the police against the word of the family, time would be wasted in argument and cross-examination. Time that Sebastian did not have.

'No, Bruce,' said Octavia. 'I appreciate your courage and your chivalry as the only male volunteer.' The Earl's face reddened at the barb, but he could make no answer. He directed a look of pure loathing at Bruce.

'Derry, I hate this,' said Bryony. 'You must believe me. I don't care about the estate. I don't care about the pictures. I want Sebastian safe. It's not fair to ask, I know. Will you do it?' She turned to Bruce, 'We don't have to meet them, surely? Can't we leave the pictures somewhere safe? Choose a good place to hand them over? Tell them we'll leave the van somewhere?'

Bruce didn't answer. The decision was to be Derry's alone.

What makes self-pity the most seductive of all emotions? Derry felt an overwhelming urge to shout *why me?* Like the next few minutes were playing out in front of her eyes like some kind of movie trailer, she saw herself snuffling pathetically, insisting to anyone who would listen that none of this had anything to do with her; none of this was her fault. Except that it was her fault. Or some of it was.

Why had everything suddenly gone crazy with kidnapping and death threats? Because Philip Parsons had been named and the heat was on. And who was ultimately responsible for the dramatic naming of Philip Parsons? Not Octavia, for all her scheming. Not the Earl, in spite of his indifference to anyone's interests but his own. The person to blame was Derry herself. She had partied, felt herself the centre of attention, enjoyed her role, showed off a little, and gotten drunk. Recklessly, she had allowed herself and her precious gifts to be used. She had no excuse. Like the person who drinks and plays with a loaded gun has no excuse.

'Alright,' she said. 'I'll do it.'

# 29

Two hours to get to the gallery and load the pictures. What time had Sebastian called—ten fifteen? Expect him to call back at a quarter after midnight. Tight.

While Bruce fetched the van, Derry dived into the cottage to change from her party clothes into jeans, sweater and a warm jacket. She grabbed her handbag, throwing in a bottle of mineral water, a packet of biscuits and a wicked-looking kitchen knife wrapped in a dishcloth. Derry felt stupid and melodramatic—she couldn't imagine in a million years stabbing anyone. Then she thought of Philip Parsons.

Bruce was waiting in the van, the engine ticking over, the passenger door open. The night was dark. The wind had a September chill. As Derry scrambled inside, Bruce turned on the van's headlights. Derry checked the time on her phone. Of the two hours they had been given, ten minutes had already elapsed. At the bunker, the others would be waiting.

To Derry's surprise, Bruce didn't immediately gun the engine and sweep out of the courtyard. Instead, he turned to Derry and held out his hand, palm open.

'What?' said Derry.

'You know,' said Bruce.

'No. What?'

'Uh, let me guess. A short, but heavy poker? Corkscrew? Kitchen knife?'

Derry contemplated lying. It was no business of Bruce's. He was a man being bossy, that was all. Then some rational part of her brain reminded her how competent Bruce really was—she had seen what he could achieve in the most extreme situations. Bruce wasn't some male playing macho know-it-all. He was trained. He was experienced.

'Why?' said Derry.

'Because the quickest way to get hurt is to try and use a weapon you don't know how to use. All you do is annoy the bad guy. Then both of you do something stupid.'

Derry thought about that. 'Deterrence?'

Bruce shook his head. 'Zero.'

Derry reached in her bag, took out the wrapped knife and handed it to Bruce.

'Smart,' said Bruce. 'Trick is to stay out of trouble in the first place.'

Derry wondered how staying out of trouble was compatible with volunteering to drive into a den of kidnappers who might have murdered somebody already. But she said nothing.

'Uh, I'd say dump your bag,' said Bruce. No point losing it.'

He had a point. She might have to leave the van in a hurry, so why carry baggage? Derry took out the water and the biscuits and put them under her seat. Her pack of playing cards caught her eye, and without thinking she slipped it into her shirt pocket. The bag with the knife inside could be safely left at the bunker.

Bruce had just set the van in motion when the thought occurred to her. 'Maybe it's all a fake.'

Bruce had an attractive way of not interrupting until he had heard you out. Derry was grateful for that, because at this moment she wasn't sure what she was trying to say, like her thoughts were finding their way to her mouth all by themselves.

'They hurt, maybe kill Parsons, then say, "Hey do what we want or we do the same to you." It doesn't make sense.'

'Helluva roundabout way to put the frighteners on anybody,' agreed Bruce.

'Then Sebastian gets kidnapped, but he doesn't even own the pictures they want. First they kill the wrong person, then they kidnap the wrong person. '

'Now you mention it.'

'And why would they think anybody cares about Sebastian? Like the Earl said, they might as well have kidnapped the gardener.' She paused, certain now she was right.

'Bruce, the only person who knew the family would care what happened to Sebastian was Sebastian. He knows Bryony would make her father do whatever she wanted. The Earl dotes on her. Nobody else knew Bryony and Sebastian were engaged.'

'Meaning?'

'What if it's all for show? What if Sebastian is pretending to be kidnapped? What if the whole thing is an elaborate little drama meant to get the Earl to hand over a fortune's worth of pictures? Maybe they don't mean to hurt anybody. Maybe it's a scam.'

Bruce thought for a moment. 'There's logic in what y'all say. But you should maybe ask Mr. Parsons what he thinks. And if Sebastian was going to marry Bryony, and she was going to inherit the whole nine yards, he was going to get the pictures anyhow.'

'Unless he didn't mean to marry her at all.'

'Sounds like a TV soap.'

'What I'm saying is, maybe we're worrying over nothing here.'

'Maybe. But you know what? Worrying over nothing can stop you getting killed.'

As the van passed the great house, the headlights picking out the gravel roadway, Derry could see the tall windows of the ballroom brightly lit, as though the world contained nothing but love and happiness and parties. They drove on until they reached the featureless mound concealing what had once been a shelter against Armageddon. The bunker loomed like some Neolithic tumulus housing the dead. Except when this was built everyone expected the dead to be on the outside.

～

Two enormous metal doors, corrugated like an accordion, one gaping open, the other shut, were set into the concrete face of the bunker. From the maw of the doorway, light flooded out. Bryony's Land Rover and the Earl's Bentley were parked to one side, leaving the space close to the doors for Bruce's van. Derry felt her stomach clench. With every passing moment she felt her life's infinite options closing down, choices disappearing as if a million doors had slammed closed, leaving only one terrifying future.

'Let's do a recce,' said Bruce. 'See what we've got here.' As Derry opened the passenger door to get out of the van, he put his hand on her arm. 'I want you to remember one thing,' he said. 'This is their mess. Not yours, not mine.'

Derry nodded dumbly. Easy to imagine the whole business a charade; easy to theorise and insist nobody would get hurt. She felt horribly certain that in less than two hours' time the theory wouldn't seem half so neat.

'No matter what happens to Sebastian,' Bruce continued, 'whether it's a real kidnapping or a setup, something bad is going down. Whoever is responsible it's not you. That means you take no risks. No scenario like out of the movies where you hand over the goods and they hand over the hostage. That's not going to happen. We'll arrange a rendezvous—you leave the van, you walk away. I'll tell you where to head. Okay?'

'Sure.' Derry's voice came out husky, so she had to say it again. 'Sure, yeah.'

'No initiative.'

'Okay.'

'No bright ideas.'

'I said okay!'

Bruce let go her arm. 'You've a few more auditions in front of you yet, right?'

Derry smiled. 'Right. I hope. Parts too.'

'Plenty good parts. Name in lights, right?' His expression was again serious. 'You can still say no. Tell them solve their own problem. Nobody will think the worse of you.'

Bruce was offering her a way out, a way of saving face. Derry tasted blood in her mouth. She must have been chewing her lip. 'This is happening because I named Parsons. They're spooked.'

'You didn't name him,' said Bruce.

'You know what I mean. I let it happen,' said Derry. 'It's as much my fault as anybody's.'

Bruce shrugged. 'I can't tell you what to do or not do.'

Derry didn't answer, knowing more was to come.

'You sure it's not your ego taken a knock? You got tight when maybe you shouldn't have. So what? Okay, maybe you did wrong. Any of your friends ever say you were some kinda saint?'

Derry smiled. No. None of her friends had ever made that observation.

'So you screwed up. Get over it. Ego gets people hurt.'

Had any other man spoken as Bruce had, Derry wasn't sure what her reaction would have been. Men had a way of knowing best that drove her to distraction. But Bruce had no need to swagger or puff himself up. No need to prove anything. Was he right? Derry thought about that. Maybe he was. She thought some more. Okay, he was right. In fact, he had hit the target smack in the middle. Who was she trying to help here, Sebastian and Bryony, or herself?

'Okay,' she said quietly. 'I get it.'

Bruce nodded, satisfied.

'What happens if I don't do this?' said Derry after a moment.

Bruce shrugged. 'Has to be the cops,' he said. 'And yeah, I know, it'll take too much time.'

'Bryony will go,' said Derry. She was certain she was right. Nothing would stop Bryony going to Sebastian.

Bruce looked through the windscreen as if half hoping the cavalry would ride over the hill of the bunker and solve everything with one loud blast of a bugle.

'No,' said Derry. 'I'll do it.'

≈

'Come in. Hurry,' said Bryony, turning on her heel and vanishing through the metal doorway and into the hill. She had changed from her party dress into her estate-manager clothes of jeans, sweater and country jacket.

Derry expected the clammy, earthy feel of a place underground, a lair covered in thousands of tons of soil. But inside, in the narrow corridor leading deep into the building, the air was fresh. The bunker was built to keep out radioactive contamination and to circulate purified air. For storing tens of millions of pounds worth of art masterpieces, the place was perfect. All the sophisticated climate control of a high-end gallery.

The smooth white walls were harshly lit by a string of fluorescents. Massive ventilation ducts and drooping cable-runs hung from the ceiling, along with old-fashioned loudspeakers still waiting to announce the death of civilisation. Ahead, Bryony disappeared through a doorway to the left. Derry and Bruce followed, finding themselves in a wide-open space, perhaps once some kind of command centre. In the middle of the space stood Octavia and the Earl.

The transformation of the bunker was remarkable. Sliding mesh panels hung from the ceiling, familiar to Derry as the storage system used by art galleries everywhere. On each you could hang several pictures—slide the panel out to retrieve a work, slide it back to save space. But Derry had never seen a private store as big as this one. The racks ran the whole way around the walls and must have held many hundreds of works. In the centre of the room was a long table laid out with bubble wrap, cardboard, tape, clingfilm and labels.

'This is the main store. There are two smaller ones as well,' said Bryony. The plan was straightforward—they had about an hour and a half to find the pictures, pull them from storage, wrap them for protection and carry them to Bruce's van. Straight away Derry saw how thoughtful Sebastian had been—he had listed the works so they could be retrieved in the most efficient order possible.

'Can I see your phone?' said Bruce. Without question, Bryony passed her handset for Bruce to inspect. 'Thought so,' he said. 'No signal in here. Someone needs to—' But Bryony had already snatched the phone and was racing for the door.

Even without Bryony to direct, they knew what needed to be done. Derry worked the list and found the picture; Bruce pulled the work from its place; Octavia took command of the packaging. When the first batch of ten were ready to move, Bruce and Derry ferried them to the van, debating how best to load the space with its precious cargo. Outside, Bryony paid no attention, all the while pacing up and down, her phone in her hand.

'He might have gone to Salisbury,' she said suddenly. 'He has a house near there.'

Derry was surprised. 'I thought Sebastian lives on the estate?'

'He bought the house to do up and sell. It's still a building site inside, really. If he was scared, he might have gone there. We used to meet at the house. To get away from here.'

Derry thought how ironic that someone living on a ten-thousand-acre estate with dozens of buildings and countless rooms had to sneak away to another town to keep her secret.

'Even if he was at his house, he won't be there now,' said Bruce. 'Bryony, we need to get the plan straight. What I want to do is this—Derry drives the van. I hide in the back.'

'Won't that cause a problem?' said Derry. 'What if they see you?'

'No. Like I said, we're not going to do a handover. When Sebastian calls, he'll give us instructions where to go. We obey up to a point, then we abandon the van. The bad guys will either release Sebastian or not. Us being around would make no difference.'

'I could follow you in the Land Rover. At a distance,' said Bryony. 'Pick you up. Maybe pick up Seb if they leave him somewhere.'

Bruce thought about that. 'Okay, if you promise no heroics, no changes of plan?' Bryony nodded. 'Okay, you got a spare phone, not your own? Can you borrow somebody's?'

'I always carry an estate phone as well as mine,' said Bryony. 'Why?'

'I'll explain later. Better get the van loaded.' He checked his watch. 'Clock's ticking.'

Bruce cleared out everything personal from the van—he handed his binoculars to Bryony. Maybe she could use them if she were following and anything unexpected happened. Derry's bag joined the pile of assorted belongings left in a bunker storeroom. Derry noticed the only possession of Bruce's left in the van was a baseball bat tucked neatly behind the driver's seat.

Next to be taken out were the leftover party costumes in their cellophane wrappings and the rails from which they hung. Bruce quickly dismantled the rails, dumping them on the ground, but Derry suggested the dresses, cloaks and the rest would make serviceable padding for the paintings. Now the exquisite handmade costumes were put to use like so many old blankets. *Sorry Jasmine and Lorna, sweethearts*, thought Derry. *A higher cause.*

For almost an hour they worked steadily, pulling pictures, packing them, carrying them out to the van and loading them as carefully as they could. Derry slid the last of the paintings, one she knew beneath its anonymous brown packaging to be a small but gorgeous Monet, into what she hoped was a safe slot between bigger works. And that was it. They were ready. 'All squared away,' Bruce said. But for what?

～

Fifteen minutes after midnight—two hours gone by—and Sebastian still hadn't called. They were gathered outside, clustered around Bruce's van. The Earl stood stony faced, refusing to collaborate in his own loss. Octavia was rigid with tension, as though controlling her emotion was close to impossible even for her. 'Should we call Sebastian?' she asked, ignoring the Earl and addressing her question to Bruce. 'We could tell him we're ready.'

Bruce shook his head. 'Sorry, your ladyship. The bad guys are the bosses here. You can't hustle them. They'll call whenever they choose.' He turned to Bryony. 'You said you had a second phone.'

Bryony pulled the estate phone from her jacket pocket and handed it over.

'Can I have your personal phone as well?'

'What if he calls?'

'Don't worry. I'll give it back when he does.' Bryony handed over her second phone. For several minutes, Bruce did something with the phones that seemed to involve lots of swiping and prodding. 'There,' he said, handing back Bryony's own phone and keeping the other.

'See the new app?' continued Bruce. Bryony nodded. 'It can track the position of this second phone. I've switched off the sound and vibrate, so it won't give the game away. This one stays in the van. Problem is if I hide it too well it won't pick up the GPS signal. If I don't hide it well enough, the bad guys might find it.' After a few moments thought, he opened the glove compartment and took out a roll of carpet tape. He pulled off some strips, tearing them into short lengths and sticking them on the steering wheel ready for use. 'Okay,' he muttered to himself. He pulled down the sun visor on the driver's side and carefully taped the phone to its back. With the visor folded up into its normal position, the phone was invisible.

'Battery is good. And unless the sun comes out in the middle of the night, nobody should notice a thing.' He grinned at Derry. 'Don't try to check your makeup.' She let it pass.

Bruce stepped down from the van and took out his own phone. Derry could see he was checking that he too could track the van. 'Aren't you coming with me? You won't need a tracker.'

'Just a precaution,' answered Bruce, not looking at her. 'In case Bryony's phone quits, we can still track the van after we bail out. That's all.' Derry wondered did he fear things might go horribly wrong and they'd be separated? She found she didn't like that thought one little bit.

'Maybe you should put a tracker on my phone,' said Derry. 'In case we get split up. Then we could find each other.'

'No point,' said Bruce. 'If they caught anyone, first thing

they'd do is take their phone and trash it. Just make sure before we leave the van your ringtone is off. You don't want it giving away our position.'

'Sure,' said Derry. 'Obvious, right?' But it hadn't been at all obvious. Not once had it occurred to her that a phone could turn from saviour to deadly traitor in one ring.

∾

The Earl and Octavia sat in the Bentley, the Dowager with her eyes closed as if asleep. The Earl had rolled down his window, presumably so he could hear Bryony's phone ring. But it didn't ring. Instead the handset gave a muffled, tactful ping. A text.

'Directions,' said Bryony, glancing at the screen 'Why hasn't he called? Maybe he's hurt!' She was panicking, staring uncomprehending at her phone like the message was written in hieroglyphics. The Earl and Octavia were out of the Bentley now, alerted by the activity.

'Please,' said Derry, gently prising the phone from Bryony's grasp. 'Let me see.' Road numbers. A detailed route—several B roads, then the A4. From there they were to head south to the A338. No destination. Then the line that made Derry's stomach lurch—'next txt to Derry phone.' The message ended with an X, a kiss.

'The A338, where is that?' asked Derry.

'About twenty miles,' answered Bryony.

Good, thought Derry. Bryony was pulling herself together. 'Where does it go?'

'Salisbury.' Bryony seemed relieved, like Sebastian being

held hostage in his own house was better than being held someplace else. Maybe it was.

'How long to Salisbury?'

'To the city? An hour and a half, give or take. To Seb's house, maybe fifteen minutes less. Countryside, really. Outskirts of a small village. But why won't he talk? Why is he texting?' No one answered.

'Time to move out,' said Bruce. He climbed into the back of the van, threading his way past the stacks of packaged pictures and squeezing onto a little jump seat behind the driver's place.

Everyone was looking at Derry. She was absurdly conscious that she should say something meaningful, make some valedictory speech, even a joke. But she couldn't think of anything. She climbed into the driver's seat, started the engine and fumbled for the headlights switch. Bryony jumped into her Land Rover. Derry was to follow to the edge of the estate, then the two vehicles would change places.

As Derry pulled away, the beams of her headlights swept across the open mouth of the bunker. The Earl and the Dowager Countess of Berkshire stood as immobile as the carved stone statues gracing their vast estate.

They didn't wave.

# 30

Unlit, tree-lined roads gave way to the straighter A338. Roundabouts. More roundabouts. Why did the British think people were smarter than stoplights?

Derry's phone pinged a text. She handed it back to Bruce to read. She was to take the A303 signposted Exeter and Amesbury. Using his own phone, Bruce called Bryony with the update.

'What's down this way?' Derry shouted over her shoulder. Bruce relayed the question. The answer came back—Andover, Berwick St. James. Wherever they were going, it wasn't to Sebastian's house.

The road was well-surfaced and smooth but had only two lanes and no lighting. The clear white markings flew past Derry's headlights. In her rear-view mirror, Bryony's lights were reassuringly visible, never too close, never too far behind. A bright half-moon hung In the clear sky, enough light to show the land around was featureless apart from vague ridges and the occasional stand of trees.

Six miles further on, and the road began to feel somehow familiar. Derry wondered had she been this way before on some previous trip to England? If so, she couldn't place the memory.

Ping. Another text. 'Go to Solstice Park Services,' Bruce read. 'Fill tank. Park at Holiday Inn. Wait further directions.'

'Surely they're not going to do the exchange in a service station,' said Derry. 'Those places are lit like football stadiums.'

'No way,' said Bruce. 'They'll want someplace real quiet

or real busy. A service station is too orderly. Lots of CCTV. Likely they want a chance to check us out.'

'He says we need a full tank. Could mean we're going a long way.'

'Or they mean to take the van, and they're going a long way. Maybe they think we'd try to play smart and give them a van with a near-empty tank.'

'Shouldn't we get out at the services? Just walk? Leave the keys and take off into the convenience store? Plenty people there.'

'Could do,' agreed Bruce, but he sounded doubtful. 'We don't want to panic them either. Those filling stations are the perfect place for a police stakeout. We don't want them to quit and disappear. Better they get the goods and stay happy.'

Derry saw the sense in that. 'It says further directions, not instructions. To me that says we're to go someplace else. Wait and see what they say next?'

'Yeah. We should be safe near the service station and the hotel. But get ready to abandon ship real quick if I give the order, okay?'

Bruce called Bryony, again summarising what they'd been told. Bruce suggested she too get gas, but better she drove past this service station to the one beyond. They'd call her when they knew anything more.

Bruce hung up. 'She says she'll fill up at a place called the Countess Roundabout.' He paused. 'You think that's called after the Dowager?'

'I doubt it. What does it matter?' said Derry.

'I bet it is.'

'Naw.'

'But why shouldn't it be named for her?'

'I don't know. They'd have to ask her permission. She'd say, "No way am I having my name on a roundabout." Anyway, there's a ton of countesses in England.'

Bruce didn't seem to like that.

～

The sign said Solstice Park. Derry turned off the main road, following the red taillights of lumbering trucks and headed for the service area. The complex was big, boasting a burger restaurant, a coffee shop, a filling station and the Holiday Inn. The place was blazing with light, bustling with travellers. She checked the time—two fifteen.

Derry manoeuvred the van to the pumps under the forecourt canopy. In the back, Bruce sank to the floor out of sight of any curious passerby, both phones to hand. Derry got out and filled the tank, trying not to look conspicuous as she scanned the forecourt. But what was she searching for? What did hostage-takers, extortionists and murderers look like? The other customers were mostly doing as she was doing, sleepily filling tanks, averting their faces from the fumes and idly looking around. None seemed especially sinister. Derry looked for a parked truck the right size for taking a load of paintings—nothing too big, nothing too small, but she saw none. She replaced the pump, bought some pastries and was going to buy two coffees when she realised what an irredeemably stupid thing she was about to do. She had been told to come alone, and she had almost returned to the van carrying two coffees. *Well done, Derry. Take a bow.*

Derry climbed back into the cab, a single coffee in her hand. She passed the paper cup discreetly back to Bruce, remembering to keep staring ahead as though she were alone. She started the engine, eased the van off the forecourt and headed for the hotel. A sign said 'Holiday Inn,' and beneath in smaller letters 'Salisbury - Stonehenge.'

Stonehenge. Solstice Services. Was that why the road had seemed familiar? Years before, Derry had visited the ancient stone monument to see the famous summer solstice celebrations—an innocent gathering of would-be druids, pagans, witches and backpackers, playing guitars and imagining a past more congenial than their present.

In front of the hotel was a line of car-parking spaces. Derry chose one as far from the hotel entrance as she could and in the least well-lit spot. No doubt the area was covered by CCTV. No point attracting the attention of a curious night porter or a patrolling security guard. She killed the engine and doused the headlights. She shared the coffee and pastries with Bruce, still trying to avoid looking like she was talking to anyone. Only now did she notice how tired she was. Adrenaline had gotten her this far but that irresistible hormone was subsiding, leaving her washed out and dull-witted.

'May as well catch some rack time,' said Bruce. Derry heard him settling down on the van floor, leaning against the back of her seat. Soon she too was drifting away, her head against the door pillar, her arms folded for warmth.

In her dream, Derry danced in a circle of lights. Glimmering torches threw wild shadows on rough grey stone. The music grew louder, the drumming faster until the sound seemed to come from deep inside her body. In her dream, even as she danced, Derry wondered was this the past or the future?

And whose past? Whose future?

~

'What's the date? Bruce, what date is it?' Derry sat bolt upright, then remembered she was supposed to be alone.

'Twenty-second September,' said Bruce. He had snapped awake instantly. 'Why?'

'What time is it?'

'Uh, five thirty.'

They had slept for the best part of three hours. How had that happened? Derry groaned. She was stiff and cold. She started the engine to warm the van.

'No message?'

'No.'

Derry peered through the windscreen. The sky was dark, no sign of sunrise.

'Today is the autumn equinox. Day and night are the same length. That was a big deal for people way back, like thousands of years ago. A crowd would be good for making the exchange, right? But someplace with no CCTV. At equinox time, there's always a party at Stonehenge.'

'Like hippies?' said Bruce.

'Some,' said Derry. 'All kinds. Druids. Shamans. Witches. Ordinary folk there to see the sunrise line up with the stones. It's an amazing sight.'

'Won't there be, like, thousands of people? Cops everywhere?'

'That's the summer solstice. For the equinox, maybe a hundred. But it's still a crowd. I doubt the police bother. Maybe a few stewards to keep an eye on things. Can you check the time of sunrise this morning?'

While Bruce searched the internet on his phone, Derry kept scanning the area around for signs of anyone showing interest. Nothing.

'Sunrise 6.53.' Bruce read. 'Here we go, English Heritage run the site. Rules—autumn equinox. Accessible parking opens 5.00 a.m. at the Visitors Centre. Gates in fence open 6.15 to 8.00 a.m.'

Derry frowned. None of that sounded right for a secret handover. 'I don't remember having to go to any visitors' centre. They must have changed things. I don't know, maybe I'm way off.'

'They might as well do the handover right here as at some kinda tourist office,' said Bruce.

Derry heard her phone ping. Her heart skipped a beat. 'Is it them?' She realised she no longer thought of the messages as coming from Sebastian. Better not think too much about why.

'To Byway 12,' read Bruce. 'Park left side. Wait.'

'What's Byway 12?' Derry felt panic rising. The end must be close. She gathered her wits, trying to focus on pulling out of the hotel carpark without bumping into anything. On the filling-station forecourt, half a dozen vans and trailers ignored the designated parking spaces. Colourfully dressed people hugged and kissed. A druid in white robes and a red sash was filling the tank of a family hatchback.

'Bruce! Which way?'

'Slow down,' said Bruce. 'Hold on, I'm searching. Got it. They changed the roads. Byway 12 is a track, but public. Runs by Stonehenge. Closed for the summer solstice. Hey, wait, no! Open for the equinox! Head west.'

Derry swung onto the main road. The night was dark. The sky had clouded over. The only light piercing the blackness was from her own headlights and the glare of oncoming cars.

Bruce called Bryony. 'Byway 12. It's like a one-way track. Seems all the vans and campers go that way and skip the visitors' centre. You turn off the main road, go up the track, past Stonehenge to your right. Remember it's one-way, okay? To get out you carry on straight ahead. You come out on another main road. We'll be pulling up on the left of the track. Stay well behind us.'

Bruce hung up. 'She says she's only fifteen minutes away. She'll hang back until I call and say we're in. Can you see the turn?'

A primitive track like a farm lane between open fields suddenly appeared in Derry's headlights. Two yellow-jacketed stewards stood, flashlights in hand, watching them turn in, but made no move to stop them. In the lurching lights of the van, the rough reddish surface of the track was deeply rutted and potholed. Ahead you could see the taillights of other vehicles in convoy. On either side of the lane the grassy verge was barely visible in the gloom.

The track narrowed. Parked camper vans and trailers, mostly old and muddy, lined the left side of the lane, leaving just enough room for a single vehicle to pass. Ahead, small parties of gaily dressed pilgrims strolled on, picked out by Derry's lights or the lights of cars further ahead jolting their way over the ruts. Behind Derry, Bruce was reminding Bryony to stay well back and keep several vehicles between them. Bryony's response was businesslike, terse.

Now they were crawling in a slow procession of campers, cars and walkers all heading the same way—towards a gate further up the lane. The gate gave access to the field in which the stones of the great monument stood invisible in the pitch-black night.

'We should bail now,' said Bruce.

'You sure?' asked Derry. 'What if they want us to go some-place else?'

'If we were meant to drive somewhere else, they wouldn't have brought us into this. It's a traffic jam in a one-way street. Not good. Too few options. Pull us in the first space you see. We'll dump the van, head back to Bryony. She can carry on straight ahead and get us out of this.'

Bruce had hardly finished speaking when Derry's phone pinged in his hand. In all the years Derry had known Bruce, she had never heard him swear. He swore now.

'What do they want?' asked Derry. She had spotted a space on the left between two campers, big enough to manoeuvre into. She tried to get the wheels onto the verge while avoiding any ditch lurking in the dark beyond.

Bruce's voice was calm. 'They say park and wait.'

Derry felt sweat break out on the palms of hands. They should have abandoned the van earlier. For sure they were now being watched.

Bruce instructed Bryony to pull in now, wherever she could. She was to look out for them as they abandoned the van and walked back towards her. On no account was she to leave the Land Rover. To Derry he said, 'Leave your lights on. Full beam.'

Derry switched off the ignition but left her lights on like Bruce had said. At just that moment, the clouds parted and a bright half-moon bathed the scene in a milky light. Now she could see well beyond the arc of her headlights. Cars and vans were parked on the verge ahead for a hundred yards or more. Between the vehicles, small tents huddled together on the grass. And there, eight or ten vehicles in front, edging out from its parking place, a shiny, silver Mercedes. Clean. New. Out of place.

The Mercedes should have carried on crawling up the lane, following the vehicles in front. Instead it stopped, then manoeuvred like it was about to do a three-point turn. But it didn't turn. The silver limousine stayed where it was, at an angle across the track, blocking all progress.

Ahead, Derry saw drivers poking their heads out their windows to see what the obstruction could be. The doors of the Merc opened. Three men got out, clearly visible in the headlights. Now they were walking back, picking their way through the stalled traffic, ignoring the protests of drivers. Something about the way the men held themselves or the way they spread out to cover the width of the lane meant no one offered a challenge.

'Sebastian!' exclaimed Derry. You couldn't mistake his wide-brimmed hat and his trailing red scarf. 'Bruce, it's him!'

Bruce peered carefully through the windscreen, showing as little of himself as possible, not that anyone looking into the glare of Derry's headlights would be able to make out much. 'Doesn't matter,' he said, his voice low. 'We don't plan on introducing ourselves. We go now. Keys in the ignition, doors unlocked. Get out the passenger side. I'll do the same. Use the van as cover. Wait for my go.'

Derry heard Bruce pick his way through the stacked paintings. A pause while he cautiously peered out the back window. 'Bad luck. We may have a small problem.'

Derry's stomach lurched. Her gut felt like a wound-up rubber band. Of all the words you didn't want to hear, Bruce calmly announcing a small problem was high on the list.

'We got company behind,' said Bruce. 'Thirty yards. SUV. Blocking the track. Two guys getting out. Tracksuits and sneakers. Ain't no hippies, that's for sure,' he added. 'They're between us and Bryony. We'll need to face them down. I'll stall 'em; you make a run for it. They've no reason to follow.'

Derry heard Bruce threading his way back up the van. She knew what he was doing now; he was liberating his baseball bat from behind her seat. Bad.

'Hold on,' said Derry. 'Wait. 'She clambered across the gear lever into the passenger seat then wormed her way between the seatbacks to squat beside Bruce. 'The costumes. The packing. Drag some out.'

Bruce was quick. He scrambled around the back of the van, moving aside pictures in their bubble-wrap and cardboard, pulling out dresses, cloaks, three hats, a doublet. Anything he could persuade to come free he threw forward to Derry.

'Okay. Here,' said Derry. She threw him a long black overcoat coat and a peaked hat with a feather. The coat would at least hide the baseball bat.

'Your phone,' said Bruce, handing it back. 'Don't forget—silent.'

'Thanks.' Derry switched the ringtone off, pushed the phone into her jeans pocket and dumped her jacket. Over her head and shoulders she threw a lightweight, slate-grey cloak. She glanced through the windscreen. The three men from the Mercedes were now barely thirty yards away, unmistakeable in the full glare of the headlights. She could clearly see the one in the floppy hat and red scarf. He wasn't Sebastian. This man was broader in the shoulder by far, built more like a boxer.

'Go!' Bruce hissed. 'But *with* the crowd. Now!' He slid open the side door, took Derry by the arm and pushed.

Before Derry had time to argue, she was on the grass verge, trying not to stumble into the ditch. She glanced back to where Bryony must be waiting. The Land Rover had to be somewhere amongst the campers and cars, hidden in the confusion of headlights and the torch beams of pedestrians all walking towards Derry and the van. The two men in tracksuits and sneakers were now twenty yards away, no more. Anyone walking back in that direction, against the tide of people, would stand out like they were lit in neon.

Derry felt her way to the front of the van, careful to stay out of sight behind the bulk of the vehicle. Ahead, every few moments, she caught glimpses of the men from the Mercedes in the crowd. The three were closing fast, forcing their way through the gaggle of walkers, their hands raised shielding their eyes from the remorseless blaze of the van's headlights.

Derry took a deep breath. She breathed as she would before making her entrance onto a stage. Inhale. Exhale. Focus. Relax. She would have to bluff her way past. Between her and the approaching men, surging around the stalled cars, the crowd had formed an impromptu troupe, singing and clapping to a drumbeat and a jangling guitar.

Suddenly all was black. Or nearly black. Bruce had killed the van's headlights. His timing was perfect—anyone who had been peering into that glare would now be blind, as their eyes took precious seconds to adapt to the dark.

Derry moved quickly. Wrapping her long grey cloak tightly around her, covering her head so only her eyes showed, she stepped briskly into the weaving flock of chattering revellers. They smiled but didn't for a second slacken their pace. Derry was one more pilgrim come to celebrate the equinox.

With every step the crowd grew denser, the people packed more closely, their faces and costumes picked out in the fleeting beams of torches or headlights. A witch with flowers in her hair waved a homemade broomstick. Two druids in white vestments, with long grey hair and shaggy beards, tried to look dignified while being cheerfully jostled. Men in straw masks chanted like they were on the way to a football game. Almost everyone wore a headdress of some kind—tam o'shanters, deer stalkers, Viking horns and antlers. In the near dark, the effect was like some mad hallucination.

A man in a hooded monk's habit fell into step beside Derry, threw back his cowl and revealed a smiling red-bearded face and white teeth. He waved a slim wand in the air, as if to clear by magic whatever obstruction was slowing their progress. He introduced himself as Merlin and made some friendly remark, but the drumming was so loud Derry couldn't catch his meaning. And there, right ahead, were the men she feared.

Pulling her cloak tighter, Derry grabbed the astonished

Merlin by the arm. She dragged him to the side of the track, almost to the verge, throwing her arms around his neck and burying her face in his shoulder. At that moment, from behind, the headlights of Bruce's van blazed out once more. The engine burst into noisy life, revving furiously.

The effect on the men bearing down on Derry was instant. Shading their eyes against the ferocious glare of the lights, they bunched together, barging forward, knocking aside anyone who got in their way. She and the other outraged revellers were forced to stumble onto the grassy verge. Merlin shouted, 'Hey!' And Derry realised what had happened—Bruce had made himself bait.

Derry was overwhelmed by helplessness. Whatever was happening to Bruce, she could do nothing about it. She could only hope it really was true the extortionists wanted only the art. Behind, the van's lights still blazed, but now the crowd was even denser than before, pressing on irresistibly, and Derry was borne along with it.

'Well met, fair maid, on the Eve of Mabon,' said Merlin, as the throng surged past the empty Mercedes blocking the lane. Seeming to believe he and Derry were now formally an item, he slipped his arm affectionately around her shoulder.

'I guess,' said Derry, doubtfully. 'Mabon, sure.'

At the metal gates leading into the field of Stonehenge the crowd bunched together, almost overwhelming the three uniformed stewards standing guard. Derry was hemmed in by a press of bodies breathless with anticipation and excitement, but her own thoughts were elsewhere. Her mind was filled with fear for Bruce, for Sebastian, for herself.

The gates opened. As the crowd surged forward, five young men in black robes, cowls over their heads, snare drums at their sides, struck up a chaotic, deafening rhythm.

~

The drummers settled into a regular beat, spurring the crowd across the grassy field and along a roped-off avenue. Ahead, the brooding monoliths were only just visible in the darkness. Flashlights glimmered all round, and Derry took the opportunity to disentangle herself from Merlin. She gave him a friendly smile and a peck on the cheek, but still his face wore a disappointed pout. He frowned and waved his wand forlornly, as if trying to think of some counteracting spell but unable for the moment to remember the words.

In the anxiety of the last minutes, Derry had paid little attention to the enormous stone circle towards which they now trudged. But there it stood, the great grey stones looming massively in the darkness, picked out by the sweeping beams of the pilgrims' torches. The gigantic uprights towered over everyone, three times the height of a person and as wide as outstretched arms. Derry shivered. At the base of her spine she felt that prickly feeling she always got near these ancient sites. The revellers around her were smiling and laughing, but this was a place of the dead. Of that Derry was certain.

The drumming grew louder in a deafening crescendo. Jangly guitars joined in with gusto, playing nothing recognisable. Derry told herself to relax. Soon everything would come right. She pressed her back against the hard, chill face of one giant pillar, grateful for the anonymity. The celebrants were dancing now, skipping in a circle in somebody's idea of an ancient peasant ritual. Nothing orgiastic or Dionysian here, thought Derry. If this was ecstasy, it was polite, English ecstasy. She doubted that ceremonies in this place all those thousands of years ago were so sweet, so harmless, or so innocent.

~

Sunrise, the climax of the ceremony, was at least twenty minutes away, but the crowd was expectant. Flashes of light sparkled from phones. Selfies by the dozen winged their way around the globe. The most imposing of the druids took up a position in the centre of the dance and held up his arms. The music stopped.

Somehow, Derry had never imagined ancient Celtic druids making speeches, at least not in prose. But perhaps they had. The druid chanted in a booming cadence, a sort of blessing— something about peace in the East, South, West and North, and about Rebirth. Derry wondered idly if he could have gotten this far in Ireland without being heckled by some wag at the back demanding a verse of The Old Triangle. The cloying scent of cannabis drifted in the air. Unlike at the summer solstice, no police dogs sniffed the celebrants at the autumn equinox. In fact no police had showed at all. A pity, thought Derry, as she tried her best to blend into the shadows and swept the crowd for reasons to be afraid.

His sneakers gave him away. His black woolly hat looked anonymous enough; the parka was green and rural. But his skinny black jeans and designer running shoes marked him out—everyone else wore wellingtons or sensible hiking boots.

The man stood with his back to a giant stone almost directly opposite Derry, his figure obscured by the dancers and musicians. Every now and again she caught a glimpse. Somehow, he reminded her of Bruce, the chiselled jaw marking him out as someone fit by profession. At the same instant that Derry's brain registered his intense and watchful presence, his eyes locked on hers.

In the centre of the circle, the crowd now gathered around the druid was at least forty strong, with many more outside. The assembled warlocks, witches, bards and backpackers greeted each verse of his chant by raising their arms and intoning 'The Earth! Mother Earth!' Surely the watcher would never dare burst through the worshipping crowd? But the man in sneakers pushed his way through the celebrants, careless of the hostile looks and the protests.

Where to run? Moving out to where the crowd was thinner would leave Derry horribly exposed. Her only option then would be to rush blindly into the surrounding darkness of the field, easy prey for anyone with a flashlight. She ducked out of sight of her pursuer, rapidly skirted the circle of worshippers and without apology burst through the ring and into the centre of the stone circle. The druid stopped in mid-chant, his mouth open.

'Mother Earth!' intoned Derry, in a decent approximation of the druid's deep cadences. As her tones rang out, satisfyingly robust, she gave thanks for years of tedious training in the theatrical art of voice projection. Everyone paid attention. Expectant faces smiled encouragement in the torchlight. The druid frowned, disinclined to welcome an upstart co-presenter.

'Damsel!' shouted Merlin. 'The Earth! The Sun!'

'The Earth! The Sun!' responded Derry, seamlessly picking up her cue. The crowd raised their arms as one and took up the chant.

The druid cleared his throat loudly. Standing close beside Derry, he was an impressive figure, tall and corpulent in his splendid white robes. The limelight would not go uncontested. But Derry had delivered some of the finest speeches in the English language before many a discerning audience. She was not about to yield centre stage to an amateur.

'Shinne Feena Fawl' declaimed Derry, accompanying her proclamation with sweeping gestures. The crowd perked up. This was new. This was fresh.

'Athaw fay yowl in Ayring,' Derry added, confidently, as if proving a point.

The crowd were now fully committed. A trio of witches seemed especially impressed. If this wasn't ancient Celtic—the language everyone knew was tailor made for spells, incantations and folk singing—it was at least as good.

'Athaw Fay Yowl!' Derry intoned, raising her arms to what she hoped was the eastern sky.

This was the right stuff, the crowd seemed to say. This is what we came for. If you have to camp on a muddy grass verge on a damp September night, then what you want is the real thing.

The words Derry declaimed with such conviction came easily. They were indeed in the ancient Celtic language of Ireland. The occasion of her learning had been a notably drunken college party in her first week as a drama student in Dublin. She had asked a cute graduate student of historical linguistics what she could do to become more Irish, aside from learning to party at five minutes' notice. The handsome polymath had given the question serious thought, before suggesting she learn the national anthem. In Irish. There and then, he patiently wrote out in phonetic symbols the whole patriotic and surprisingly militaristic dirge.

Again Derry raised her arms to the heavens. Again she intoned, 'Shinne Feena Fawl,' repeating several times in the manner traditional, she hoped, amongst sun-worshippers. But even a national anthem has to end sometime. Even the most thick-skinned of karaoke performers eventually recognises when the game is up. If Derry had been using a microphone, she would have had to hand it back.

The druid gave a reasonable impersonation of an appreciative impresario, smiling a 'thank-you' through gritted teeth. Derry was hustled back into the audience.

The watcher was gone. Derry realised that sweat was pouring down between her shoulder blades. Stepping into the surrounding crowd, she found herself wrapped in the affectionate embrace of three witches at once, all exclaiming, 'Like, wow!' But soon the witches were distracted by the pressing need to do a kind of line dance with broomsticks and tambourines. Derry was left to lean against her stone once more.

Perhaps now was the time to phone Bruce or Bryony? Whatever had happened down on Byway 12, the business was surely over by now. The tension and the lack of sleep had left Derry wrung out. Dawn couldn't now be far away, and then she would have to leave the stones anyhow. All she wanted now was her bed.

He must have come from behind the massive bulk of the stone. Derry had taken her phone from her pocket and was about to dial Bruce when a hand closed over her wrist. In the din of wailing bagpipes and hammering percussion, the man had stepped out so lightly that Derry heard no movement. He was smiling, and Derry saw he wasn't the watcher she had been evading but the man in the black floppy hat and the bright-red scarf. The man who wasn't Sebastian. And now, from behind, her left elbow was gripped in a cruel pincer making her wince and gasp.

~

Of the sting in her arm, Derry would later have only the vaguest memory. As in a dream she saw the concerned face of a witch looking down at her, blond tresses beneath her garland strangely distorted. Someone—a man—said, 'Bad trip, she'll be okay,' and the witch left. Then Derry was stumbling, half dragged, half tripping across the grass, supported under each elbow by powerful hands. From behind came the swelling roar of the crowd, more chanting, and drumming so loud she couldn't tell whether from outside her head or inside.

The dawn of the autumn equinox was breaking.

But not for her.

# 31

For a moment, Derry thought she had fallen asleep in Bruce's van. Why Bruce was driving was a puzzle. She shook her head trying to clear her blurred vision. Why couldn't she move her arms? But she could move her head and saw that the person in the driving seat beside her was not Bruce but Sebastian. No, not Sebastian. He was wearing Sebastian's hat and his red scarf, and he was driving Bruce's van. But he wasn't Sebastian. And the van was speeding along a main road in the slowly strengthening daylight. And still Derry couldn't move her arms. She couldn't move them because her hands were tied together behind the back of her seat. And someone was gripping the tie between her wrists and pulling upwards promising excruciating pain and dislocated shoulders if Derry uttered a word or dared look behind.

The road ahead was narrow and straight, bounded by flat, open fields and the occasional small woodland. Few houses. From the direction the sun was rising, Derry thought they must be travelling south. It was hard to be sure, as the light was still dim and the sky overcast. How long had she been unconscious? Less than an hour? Maybe much less. Ahead in the gloom a few cars travelled their way, while almost nothing came towards them. Did that mean somewhere ahead was a town attracting early commuters? She was finding it hard to think, hard to be logical. What had happened to Bruce? Had he found Bryony? Were they following? Involuntarily, Derry's eyes flicked to the sun visor above the driver's head. Was the tracking phone still fixed in place or had it been found and discarded? Derry forced herself to look away.

The van braked hard. Derry lurched forward against the seatbelt she had no memory of putting on. The driver swung hard left, down a narrow track, a heavy growth of trees on each side. With a crunching of gears, he reversed into the gated entrance to a woodland. The gate was open, the track deserted. A sign on the gatepost said 'Private - No Trespassing.'

The driver threw his floppy hat and red scarf carelessly into the back of the van as though pleased to be rid of them. He seemed somehow familiar, but the memory wouldn't come. A voice from behind said, 'Nothing stupid. Understand? I am going to free your hands and undo your seatbelt. You will do as you are told.'

His accent was foreign. Something about his voice resonated in Derry's brain.

'Don't flinch or you'll be cut.'

Derry felt the cold blade of a knife between her wrists. A sawing motion, and her hands separated. Her seatbelt was unclipped from behind. She was rubbing the life back into her tingling wrists when the man in the driving seat shot out his left hand. His huge paw clamped around her jaw, holding her head in a crushing grip. 'No move,' he said quietly. 'Okay?'

Derry tried to shake her head to agree but couldn't. Behind her she could hear the side door of the van slide open and the man behind jumping out. The passenger door beside her was thrown open. A hand gripped the back of her neck forcing her head down violently, wrenching her out of the van. But not before she saw her captor's face. The Russian. The art dealer. Sergei.

Dragged by her shirt collar, Derry was hauled roughly to stand helpless by the side of the van. Only then did she see the white truck pulled up behind. A familiar type, climate control unit above the cab. The same van that had delivered Sergei's paintings and furniture to Vanessa's gallery.

Already, four men, two in overalls, two in jeans and black leather jackets, were transferring the contents of Bruce's van to the white truck. They worked with practiced efficiency. A little way down the track, a man in a bulky parka stood guard, facing back the way they had come. He held an assault rifle in a casual grip, its barrel pointing at the ground, the butt nestling beneath his forearm.

'Turn around,' said Sergei.

Derry did as she was told. Sergei released his grip on her shirt collar.

'Step forward.'

Derry obeyed.

'Further.'

Derry walked on.

'Stop.'

Now she was facing into the woods at the side of the track. At the edge of her vision, she saw the man with the assault rifle turn towards her. She was absurdly conscious of a light breeze rustling the leaves of the trees as her rational mind insisted they would never do anything so crazy. Still, her legs shook so violently she thought she would fall to the ground.

The gunman turned away, resuming his watch. Derry let out the breath she hadn't realised she was holding. In her mouth was a sharp metallic taste. Her palms were wet. But her legs stopped their trembling.

The pain was the worst agony Derry had felt in her life. No thought, no warning, no mild hurt turning to a pain more severe—one moment Derry was standing relaxed, anxious but herself once more, then she was a demented animal, rolling on the ground, moaning, 'Oh, oh, oh!'

'On your stomach! Now!' Derry obeyed without thinking, as if Sergei's voice was directly connected to her muscles and her limbs, by-passing her brain, short-circuiting her free will. But what free will? The excruciating, searing horror of the pain she had just experienced proved free will had never existed and would never exist again.

'You will do exactly as you are told, or you will get more of the same. I am sorry this is necessary, I assure you.' Sergei's voice was sympathetic, urbane.

'Okay, okay,' Derry gasped. She wanted to blubber and promise that she would do anything he said, but something stopped her, some vestige of self-respect more important than the pain. Perhaps it was the shameful knowledge that Sergei, a man, had watched her squirming powerless on the ground.

'I'm going to take the darts out now. Don't move,' said Sergei. Derry felt a sharp tug between her shoulder blades. She knew now what had happened. He had pulled out the needle-like points a Tazer had fired into her back. Now he was winding up the wires connecting them to the gun's fifty-thousand agonizing volts.

'Up,' said Sergei. A man grabbed her under the armpit. A second took Derry's other elbow. Together they hauled her to her feet and turned her to face Sergei. Derry was astonished that after such agony her limbs worked normally. Even her breath was normal. It seemed somehow wrong. A pain that horrifying should kill you or leave you a quivering wreck for life.

The two men dragged Derry to the white truck and opened the rear passenger door. They hustled her inside, Sergei following immediately to sit beside her. The cab of the truck was spacious, with a double row of back seats.

'On the floor,' said Sergei.

Derry lay crouched on the hard floor of the cab. Sergei put his foot on her ribcage but held onto one of her wrists. He looked down at her, his eyes expressing infinite regret. 'Do not try to cause a disturbance. A little pressure on the nerve… here.'

Derry couldn't stop the scream.

'Good. You are intelligent. Now, relax.'

What else was there to do? Derry breathed deeply—in through her nose, out through her mouth—the way she had been taught to deal with stage fright. And if the time-honoured method didn't work, what had she to lose? The absurd thought intruded—if she were to die, at least she would die calm and well-oxygenated.

Her phone! Her cellphone had been in her jeans pocket. But no longer. They must have taken it long ago. The doors of the truck slammed shut. She heard men climbing into the front seats, others behind. The engine roared into life. The rear wheels spun on the track, and the truck lurched forward. The mat on the cab's floor beneath her cheek smelled strongly of disinfectant. The Russian's foot pressed down hard into her ribs.

But she kept breathing.

That was the main thing, surely. Keep on breathing.

The drive wasn't long—no more than ten or fifteen minutes. The day outside had brightened; Derry could tell even from the floor of the truck. The surface beneath the tyres was smooth—a main road. Then it wasn't smooth, but not a rough track either. The truck stopped, then started again. A gate being opened and closed behind them? Once more they halted. The passenger side door beside Derry's face swung open, and again she was hauled bodily up and out.

To drag Derry the few yards across the tarmac took the men only seconds. But she had time enough to snatch a glance at her surroundings. Some kind of industrial unit, wide metal doors open. A yard surrounded by a high fence—a workshop or warehouse. No sign. No windows. In front, a shipping container, green and unmarked.

Through the doors into a wide space with skylights and hanging fluorescents overhead. Against one wall a long table with four men at work packing, barely pausing as Derry was hauled past, her feet dragging on the floor. On each side of the aisle, the walls were lined floor-to-ceiling with shelving and racks, paintings in reproduction gilded frames stacked like packs of cards—Van Gogh's sunflowers, Matisse's water lilies, Picasso's geometrical portraits, each by the dozen.

Now Derry remembered. Vanessa had said Sergei made more money from furnishing hotels with reproductions than he did from dealing in the real thing. Fake antique frames were stacked waiting for equally fake canvases. Enormous industrial-sized rolls of bubblewrap, clingfilm, cardboard and parcel tape lay neatly ordered. On the shelves were ranged an array of gilt mirrors, Ming vases and ormolu jewel boxes. And, right at the end, a row of gleaming Fabergé eggs.

Derry was still craning her head, staring at the eggs, as her captors halted in front of a sturdy metal door. One of the men tightened his grip in an unmistakable warning. The other slid back a bolt and swung the door open. Derry was roughly pushed inside. The door slammed shut behind. The bolt rattled home.

'Hi,' said Sebastian. 'Sorry.'

≈

Sebastian's hands were tied behind his back. He sat cross-legged on the floor, leaning against the bare wall. His normally smooth-shaven face was stubbled and grey. He looked exhausted.

'Really—sorry. Too late, I know.' He attempted a smile.

Derry said nothing.

'You've every right to be upset, naturally.'

What did he want to hear? Oh no, not at all, perfectly alright. Think no more of it?

Derry ignored him, looking around the bare room for inspiration, any glimmer of hope. Their prison was a medium-sized store, about the size of a largish bedroom. The walls were white, the floor vinyl-covered and unmarked. No windows. Metal shelving, empty, lined two of the walls. The ceiling was high and reinforced with a grid of steel mesh, typical of a secure store for antiques and paintings. The room contained no furnishings whatever and was uncannily clean. As clean and clinical as an operating theatre.

Derry slumped to the floor. A strongroom, clean, empty. The memory came almost before her brain registered the stark facts. Sergei had asked a favour of her mother. He needed to disinfect a storage area. An infestation. Vermin. Steam cleaning. And a climate-controlled truck for disposing of the remains.

'It happened here. Parsons—Sergei killed him here. Then…' She closed her eyes, but still saw the ranks of Fabergé eggs on the shelves outside.

'He says it was an accident,' said Sebastian. 'Says he wasn't around when the heavies wrapped Philip in clingfilm. Left him overnight to teach him a lesson. Seems your body temperature climbs and climbs. Basically, he cooked.'

'For goodness' sake!' Derry put all her fears and frustrations, all her panic and anger, into that one shout. She struggled to control herself. 'Where are we?'

'Off the Salisbury Road.'

'What happens now?'

'I have no idea.'

'Don't give me that! Octavia told us. Some kind of money laundering. Avoiding tax.'

Sebastian leaned his head back against the wall. He closed his eyes with a sigh. 'Derry, I am a minion in this. And so are you. We're the hired help.'

Derry remembered the Earl comparing Sebastian and the gardener.

'How is the Countess taking it?' asked Sebastian. 'And Bryony? Poor thing. Shocked I'd imagine. A bloody mess.'

What a strange man. As concerned about an employer who had led him into disaster as he was about his fiancée.

'Bryony is distraught,' said Derry. 'She told us about you and her.'

Sebastian bit his lip. He seemed about to say something but thought better of it. Derry could barely look at him now.

'Are they going to let us go?' She felt weak for asking, but couldn't help herself.

'Did they blindfold you?'

The implications shot straight to Derry's chest. No, they hadn't blindfolded her. They didn't care what she saw. They didn't care whom she might identify. A thousand questions surged around her tired brain but she could answer none, and Sebastian seemed in no mood to be helpful. To hell with him.

In the breast pocket of her shirt, Derry felt the solid bulk of her playing cards. No one had bothered taking them from her. For that small piece of meaningless luck she felt absurdly grateful. She slid the deck from its thin cardboard box and sat cross-legged. She dealt a hand onto the floor in front of her— not a fortune-telling spread, just a hand of Patience. Anything to avoid having to look at Sebastian's defeated face.

'I hope you're not going to tell my fortune,' said Sebastian. 'Ignorance is bliss, don't you agree?' Perhaps he was trying to sound brave. Derry didn't answer or look up from her cards. She wanted to think.

Had Bruce made his way back to Bryony on Byway 12? Could they have followed the van? If the tracked phone had remained undiscovered, perhaps they had. But then they would have found the van abandoned in the wood. End of the trail, unless they had somehow managed to follow the white truck without being noticed. But surely they'd have called the police by now anyway?

'Bryony will call the police,' said Derry. 'They know roughly where we are.' Roughly, as in *very* roughly, thought Derry.

But she didn't say that. Why had she said anything? Who was she comforting?

'No,' said Sebastian, opening his eyes. 'She won't call the police.'

'Why?'

'Because I asked her not to.' Just as he seemed about to say something else, the bolt outside rattled. The door swung open.

# 32

Sergei squatted on the floor, his back against the closed door. He seemed relaxed that way, at ease as if he had little regard for chairs or civilisation in general. Derry remembered he was a soldier, or had been. Something special. Like Bruce.

'I admire your sangfroid,' said Sergei, smiling at the cards laid out neatly on the floor in front of Derry. 'You are like your mother. Though she has more... style.'

Derry didn't reply. If Sergei was trying to nettle her for whatever reason, he was failing. Derry had lived her whole life being orders of magnitude less stylish than her mother.

'So... what do you see? Or did our young friend not have time to prompt you?'

Derry kept her eyes on the cards. She turned one, then another.

'I am wondering how long it will take for you to say that none of this is anything to do with you,' Sergei continued.

The thought of exchanging words with the man who had so casually inflicted such pain made Derry feel ill and furious all at the same time. But if she ignored him, would he lose his temper? No. He was too cool. Too professional. A problem solver. So what problem was he trying to solve? Again, Derry felt that cold churning fear in her bowels. She turned another card.

'Why did you involve yourself?' said Sergei. 'Identifying Parsons was a ridiculous stunt. You caused all kinds of trouble.' He paused. Oddly, his question didn't seem rhetorical, as if here was a puzzle he genuinely wanted to solve.

He glanced over at Sebastian. His look said the sight of the crumpled, pale young man on the floor disgusted him beyond endurance. He turned again to Derry. 'You were besotted like a foolish teenager.' He paused to let his judgement sink in.

Only by concentrating on her cards did Derry manage to hide her confusion. What was Sergei talking about?

'She had nothing to do with any of this,' said Sebastian. His voice quavered a little, then more firmly he said, 'She didn't even know Philip's name.'

'Quiet!' Sergei shot to his feet, his hand flying to his jacket pocket.

Sebastian threw himself sideways. As though obeying an irresistible reflex, he curled his body, bunching his knees to his chest. 'No! No! Please!'

Instinctively, Derry's eyes flew to the Tazer in Sergei's fist. As the memory of unspeakable agony flashed through her brain, all her muscles snapped tight, rigid with fear. That little black handset was an instrument of the purest coercion, and every nerve in her body remembered. How did she resist the overpowering urge to curl into a ball and beg? What savage core of pride gave her the power to hold the cards in her hands without a tremor? Somehow, Derry managed to take her eyes from the cringing form of Sebastian and the haughty man who stood over him smiling contemptuously. She dealt herself a card. Ace of spades. *Useless*.

Sergei burst out laughing. 'To give your Sebastian credit, twice I had to introduce him to my little toy before he begged for mercy and agreed to do as he was told.' He returned the weapon to his pocket and squatted once more, relaxed like his outburst had never happened. 'Where were we?' he said.

Derry wondered if Sergei had come for no better reason than he had time to kill. Presumably the Earl's paintings had to be loaded into the shipping container outside. Whatever was happening, the longer it took the better. Derry turned another card. She didn't look up. 'Parsons,' she said.

'Go on.'

'Painters don't steal paintings. Or deal in paintings, stolen or not.'

'Very good,' said Sergei. He was amused.

'Painters paint,' said Derry. 'You broke his fingers.'

'Tell me more,' said Sergei. 'Why would I do such a thing?' He was enjoying himself now. 'Has our young friend not explained to you? No matter—surely your cards can tell you everything.' He checked his watch.

'You broke Parsons' fingers so he couldn't paint.'

'And why would I wish to stop a man fulfilling his creative potential? How wicked of me.'

Derry shrugged.

'Your cards have nothing to say? I will help you out. Perhaps my little story will change your view of your Sebastian. Perhaps you will see he is a thief and a liar. And why he must pay the price.'

Out of the corner of her eye, Derry saw Sebastian turn his face away.

'Many years ago,' said Sergei, 'Sebastian, then assistant curator at Sorley hall, approached me to buy some interesting Russian paintings. Modernists. Not hugely valuable, but quality. The young man spoke excellent Russian and had a good understanding of the period. He said he had been given the pictures by a relative. I bought from him. Later, he brought me more pictures, two Picasso drawings. Again he claimed they were gifts. I asked for proof—they obviously came from Sorley Hall. He made excuses, and I resolved not to buy any more from him. But, later, he came back.

'Sebastian's old employer had died. The new Earl had promoted Sebastian to curator. Sebastian told me the Earl wished to sell a number of valuable pictures, but discreetly and over some time. I guessed the owner wanted to avoid the attentions of tax collectors. The buyers would need to keep the pictures off the market for some years, but that would not be a problem. These were not stolen works. They would figure on no international watch list. And the prices the Earl was offering were most attractive.

I met the Earl at his gentlemen's club in London. He confirmed that yes, Sebastian had his full permission and he trusted him completely. I was satisfied. And so, over several years, Sebastian brought me many fine works. And if his lordship neglected to inform the tax authorities, that was his affair. And if I didn't raise with him the subject of some small Picasso drawings, that was my choice.'

Derry had no doubt about Sergei's meaning. Sebastian had stolen from his employers. The thought was nauseating. Unbidden, something Sebastian had said about his precious car came to mind. Something in Latin—Art is the Reward of Art. How clever he thought he was. How much smarter than everyone else.

'Of all the sins a man may commit,' said Sergei, 'I truly believe disloyalty is the worst.'

Sebastian's eyes were pleading. He shook his head slowly but made no denial. Derry turned away.

'I trusted a thief,' said Sergei. 'Two thieves. Now I pay the price.'

Derry looked up sharply. Two thieves? And what did he mean about paying the price? Outside, his men were moving millions of dollars' worth of paintings.

Sergei smiled, giving Derry a fond look. 'Ah,' he said. 'I see our young friend has not told you everything.' He looked again at his watch. 'You see, I am a businessman. In Russia, to do business it is good to have the protection of someone powerful, someone with influence. We call such a man our roof. Perhaps in England, we should say umbrella.' He smiled, pleased at his joke. 'It is important to be helpful to such a patron.'

Sergei leaned back against the door and stared at the ceiling. He spoke again, quietly this time, so Derry had to strain to hear.

'Over the years, I sold many valuable works from Sorley Hall to my patron. He kept many himself, but sold others to his own circle—men of the highest standing, men of power. These men do not take lightly to being cheated and robbed.'

'Fakes,' said Derry.

The Russian nodded sadly.

'Parsons,' said Derry. 'He was a forger.' The answer had come as an absolute certainty. Parsons had been forging pictures. Sebastian had sold them to Sergei. And, somehow, Sergei had found out.

Sergei sighed, as though his faith in human nature had been forever shattered by this wholly unmerited betrayal. 'Forgeries,' he said, spitting the word out. 'Not copies—these were seemingly genuine but unknown works. Parsons could perfectly imitate the style of any modernist painter, and in the materials of the time. How Sebastian discovered Parsons I do not know, but here was an irresistible opportunity for his employer. Why sell real pictures, when you can sell fakes? Some were real, perhaps one in three. The rest were not.' He paused to let the infamy sink in. 'You understand provenance?'

Derry nodded. The value of a picture was in its history— who had owned it, where they had acquired the work and when. A picture from a famous historical collection, even if that information is discreetly conveyed, is a guarantee the work is genuine.

'Truly, the pictures were good. They would pass any technical examination. And because Sorley's catalogues had been destroyed in the war, who could doubt them?'

'You found a catalogue,' said Derry.

Her dream. The ledger with its entries, the familiar format of an old art catalogue. The falling snow. The scorching, and the snow quenching the fire, burying the book. Had the ledger been found? By whom? A servant? A member of the family scratching through the cooling ruins of a blitzed mansion?

'The pictures you bought weren't in the catalogue,' said Derry. It had to be true. A catalogue could prove a work existed at a certain time and place but could also prove a picture did not exist. Or at least, not in *that* collection. Not at *that* time.

Sergei scowled and stood, making to leave. 'You believe he has told you everything. I doubt he has.' His smile was cold. For him the business was personal. Delaying him was probably pointless, but it was all Derry could do.

'I thought the catalogue was burned,' she said quietly, forcing Sergei to strain in order to hear. 'In the snow.'

For a moment, the Russian stood motionless. Derry didn't look up, like she was interested only in the cards on the floor in front of her. In two steps he was back beside her, squatting, his back against the wall. The effect was strangely companionable. He stared down at the cards.

'Perhaps there is more to you than I thought. Yes, the book is scorched, but only its cover. During the German attacks on London, the family's houses were bombed. And yes, there was a snowfall the following day. So the newspaper reports have it. The catalogue must have been saved and sent from London to Sorley Hall.

'And you found it. After all these years,' said Derry.

'During the war, Sorley Hall was occupied by men of the Czech Resistance. One young officer had been a student of art history. He stole that only surviving catalogue or perhaps bought it from a servant. As far as he knew, he was to be parachuted into Nazi-occupied Czechoslovakia where he would certainly die. I sometimes think of him in his bunk at night, studying the lists, imagining the pictures he would never see. Can we blame him? Soldiers... some soldiers cling to civilisation like a wrecked sailor clings to a lifebelt. But our brave young fighter never was sent to his death. The war ended, and he returned home taking the catalogue with him.

'He died in Moscow last year, a very old man. Some weeks ago a dealer in rare books offered the catalogue to my patron, knowing his passion for art and his immense collection. My patron was overjoyed, being the owner of so many works from Sorley Hall. But as he searched the catalogue for the pictures he had bought for such very large sums, he saw only a handful had ever been in the Sorley Hall collection. That was a bad day for him. And a worse day for me.

'In such a situation, a man has two courses of action. No, three. He can kill himself. At least he can make it quick. He can protest his innocence and throw himself on the mercy of his patron—but believe me, the first course would be better. Or he can confess and try to make amends. That was the course I chose.'

'The pictures. In the van. They are for him, your... patron.'

'Of course. He or any one of the dozen powerful men who have been cheated would crush me like a beetle.'

'But your... protector need say nothing if he is the only one with the catalogue?'

'You are shrewd. He is compensated, and I return to Russia for a while.'

'The police won't rest now. Because of Parsons.'

'The assistants who... managed Parsons, were my patron's men. The aim was to extract from Parsons the full story and make sure he could never forge again. But they were over-zealous.' He gave a grim smile. 'Who would have thought an umbrella could cause rain?'

'The arm. Your patron's idea?'

'Melodramatic, I admit. I was in no position to argue. In any case, that is how we do things in Russia. We like to set the tone, to be sure we are taken seriously. Then we get to the point.'

'Compensation.'

'A consignment of selected works. Genuine works.'

'The Kandinsky. A down-payment?'

'Proof that his employer would cooperate. A gesture of good faith.'

Derry remembered a gaunt and depressed Sebastian arriving at her mother's gallery carrying a picture for Sergei to collect. He had said it was for a Russian charity. Some kind of grim joke? But easy to guess why he was afraid to deliver in person.

'He seemed to imagine that once compensation had been paid, he would be left alone. Touching simplicity. Then you named Philip Parsons to the police, and we had little time left. We found Sebastian at his house in Salisbury among the paint pots and the stepladders.'

Derry could only imagine the horror Sebastian must have felt when he realised the Russians had come for him. Had he believed they would accept his promises? Or had he, deep down, known all along that Sergei would seek a reckoning?

'We could not be sure the Earl would cooperate. We worried he would instead leave poor Sebastian to face the noise alone—'

'Music.'

'Thank you. Naturally, we thought of perhaps taking one of the Earl's daughters. But that would cause a storm. Dangerous for us—very dangerous. Happily, Sebastian solved our problem. No need to touch the daughters, he said, because one was his lover and would not see him harmed. She would intercede with her father. I hope you are not too upset by his faithlessness. But you must have known he was a liar.'

Time, thought Derry. Waste more time, please! Every minute Sergei spent talking was a minute in which something good might happen. *Bruce where are you!*

'You have the pictures now,' said Derry. 'You send them to Russia, right? Mixed up with cheap reproductions. That's clever.'

Sergei smiled. 'The British are sadly old-fashioned about valuable art works leaving the country uncontrolled. But nobody cares about Chinese copies—hand painted oils on canvas, sold amusingly as "genuine reproductions." At the port of Southampton, customs inspectors will see cheap frames and Van Gogh's sunflowers and will go back to their tea and their cricket. The method has served me well many times.'

'The police will be looking for us now.'

'I doubt it,' said Sergei. 'Sebastian has telephoned saying that to call the police would be foolish and all will soon be well.'

'And will it?'

Sergei shook his head. 'I am afraid not.'

# 33

The banging from the trunk of the Mercedes went on and on. Sebastian must have been hammering with his feet as hysteria triumphed over reason. Sergei's men had wrapped him tightly in clingfilm, like the pupa of a giant insect.

On the back seat, Derry sat between the two Russians she recognised as her Stonehenge captors. Her hands were free, but each man held one of her arms in a bruising grip.

Sergei sat in front, a large open coolbox on his knee. He was reading the label on a plastic carton. Derry glimpsed other containers neatly marshalled in the box. Twice Derry tried to ask a question. Twice, a vicious squeeze of her arm sent excruciating pain shooting into her shoulder.

The Mercedes swept along a smooth main road. Daylight, and the route was busy with rush-hour traffic. Onto a narrow lane—a familiar track, trees on both sides. A gated entrance to woodland. The van. Bruce's van.

Derry was sitting on the van floor, her back against hard metal. Steel protrusions banged into her shoulder-blades every time the van hit a bump in the road. Beside her lay Sebastian wrapped to the shoulders, hands clamped to his sides, feet bound, helpless. Sergei sat on the little jump seat opposite, the Tazer pointed casually in their direction.

The coolbox sat at Sergei's feet, its partly open lid revealing tightly packed, pastel-coloured plastic bottles. On the floor lay a roll of clingfilm perhaps a yard wide, a short wooden plank, a yellow plastic toolbox and, strangest of all, a green garden watering can—perhaps half the common size, but the usual shape, tall and narrow.

Up front, the Russian in the driver's seat wore Sebastian's floppy hat and his long red scarf. Beside him sat the second Russian, dressed in blue workman's overalls. To Derry's surprise, he turned around in his seat and winked, grinning broadly as if he and she were complicit in some hilarious prank. With a theatrical flourish he wound a brightly coloured shawl around his head, pashmina-style, so only his eyes could be seen. He turned away to look out front. Anyone observing the van and its occupants would see a woman in a shawl and a flamboyantly dressed man. Partners. Perhaps lovers. Collaborators.

Traffic lights. Roundabouts. Turns to the left and the right—too many for Derry to keep track of, though she tried desperately to memorise the sequence. From the floor of the van she could see only the roofs of houses and the canopies of trees. A sharp turn left then bumping—a rough lane? Ahead, the upper story of an old building. Slate roof. Redbrick facade, a pair of tall double doors, wooden, faded green. Some kind of coach house. Above the doors a first-floor opening, an arched window blanked off by rough shutters.

The van stopped, engine running. The overalled Russian in the passenger seat threw off his shawl and jumped out of the van. A grating sound. Again, grating. He was dragging open the big coach-house doors. The driver released the brake, nudging the van into the shadows. Silence as he killed the engine. Behind, more grating of doors.

Darkness.

≈

Somebody flicked on a light. The side door of the van slid open with a metallic clunk. Sergei gestured impatiently with his Tazer, signalling that Derry should get out. She eased herself shakily from the van to stand on the stone-flagged floor. Her legs were cramped and her back hurt. In front of her stood the overalled Russian. He too had a Tazer in his hand. He signalled her to step aside. Now she could see inside the van to where Sebastian lay cocooned on the floor. Sergei crouched over him. With a clasp knife he neatly slit the cling-film between Sebastian's ankles. The plastic fell away. Arms still bound to this sides, Sebastian was forced to wriggle and writhe to the van door, then stand awkwardly under the threatening Tazers.

Derry tried to calm her racing pulse. Every instinct in her body said run, take the chance. But run to where? Think! She needed to understand where they were and what was this place.

The coach house was old. Once it would have been part of a substantial residence. Derry tried to visualise a grand villa, perhaps Victorian, surrounded by lawns and a high bound-ary wall. The coach house would be built into the wall and connected to a rough lane and the road beyond. She looked around. Inside, the building was one big open space. Overhead, Derry could see all the way to the pitch of the roof, where bare slates and a grimy skylight were supported by rotten-looking beams.

On one side of the building a crude wooden stairway led to an open hayloft supported on a line of wooden posts. Beneath was a dark space packed with junk—an old lawn mower, rusty bicycle frames, broken garden tools. But not everything was decrepit. A bundle of fresh planking lay wrapped in plastic, along with a neat stack of slates and tiles. Unopened bags of cement were piled against the wall.

Of course. Bryony had said Sebastian was doing up a house somewhere near Salisbury. An old house. The house from which Sergei's men had seized him. Derry glanced at Sebastian, hoping for some signal confirming her guess. But Sebastian was staring at the floor, as though his and Derry's fate was of no further interest, a story to which he already knew the ending.

~

'Over there,' said Sergei, indicating with his Tazer the space under the loft. Derry and Sebastian were to sit on the ground with their backs against the supporting posts. The flagstone beneath her was cold, the post hard against her back. Sebastian never once let his eyes meet hers.

From inside the van, the driver emerged, carrying the roll of clingfilm. Sergei gave him his clasp knife. The driver and the overalled Russian set to work.

Around and around, wrapping tighter and tighter, Derry's torso was encased in clingfilm. Her arms were bound to her sides, her hands to her waist, her whole body to the post at her back. She felt herself losing all control. She wanted to scream and gasp, howl and writhe in a nightmare claustrophobia like being buried alive.

But she didn't howl. She didn't scream. She didn't even kick or wriggle. Somehow some small part of Derry's brain, some remote and hidden depth of her spirit stayed aloof from the terror. 'No need for any of this,' she said. She had meant her voice to be confident, relaxed. Her years of training should surely mean she could control her vocal cords. But she couldn't. Her voice trembled and broke in a humiliating squeak. She tried again.

'You have what you wanted. You have millions of dollars in paintings. Why attract more attention?'

'You are concerned?' Sergei sat perched in the open side door of the van, his face impassive, Tazer in his hand, watching the driver bind Sebastian to the post beside Derry. 'You know who to blame.' He waved the Tazer at Sebastian. 'It is over! You understand?' His voice rose to a roar of outrage. 'Finished!'

The Russian in the overalls climbed into the back of the van. He opened the yellow toolbox and began to do something to the insides of the doors. All the while, the driver stood over Derry and Sebastian, Tazer ready.

'When we have no choice, we need have no conscience,' said Sergei. He had collected himself, and his voice was again controlled. 'Apart from myself and my patron, only you, Sebastian and the Earl know of Parsons' forgeries. If that knowledge became public, my life would be worth nothing.'

As the implications of Sergei's words sank in, Derry fought an overwhelming tide of despair. Time. Winning time was all that mattered. Time for Bruce to find them. Time for the police to come. Time for a few more precious breaths of life. 'Whatever about us,' said Derry, her mouth dry. 'You can't harm an earl.'

'Correct,' said Sergei. 'Killing an earl would be dangerous indeed. In England, they care about earls. But his lordship will say nothing of forgeries. Why cast doubt on the worth of his collection? Why invite more questions?'

Inside the van, the Russian in the overalls was removing the door handles. Derry's heart beat faster. She had no idea what he was doing. But somewhere deep in her unconscious she knew that whatever it was, she should fear it greatly.

'Our story is sad and romantic,' continued Sergei. 'Sebastian, a talented young art expert, likes the high life. He drives an expensive sports car. He buys a big house in the country. And he can do this because he buys stolen artworks from a failed painter named Philip Parsons and sells them to wealthy foreigners. But Parsons is greedy, he wants more money. They fight. Sebastian kills him. Perhaps an unfortunate accident, perhaps not.

'This Sebastian, he has a lover and accomplice. A pretty young girl, an actress and charlatan fortune-teller. The lovers are afraid they will be found out. They resolve to flee to Russia—Sebastian has many contacts there. But first they mean to extort valuable paintings from Sebastian's employer. Sebastian takes gruesome souvenirs from Parsons' body and sends them to terrorise the Earl. To cover his tracks, he fakes his own kidnapping, persuading the noble family that he is the victim and that a ransom must be paid to save him. His lover will deliver the paintings to their hideaway.

'You rendezvous with Sebastian at Stonehenge. You think the crowds will hide your meeting and, as a devotee of the occult, you seek solace in drugs and pagan rites. No doubt the newspapers will enjoy that part of our story. The guilty pair flee to Sebastian's hideaway. Some passerby will remember them by their peculiar dress.'

Derry listened to Sergei's tale in numb silence. She remembered her own resolution to keep him talking. Don't think ahead. Don't think past the next sentence. He is a man, therefore he is vain and most likely pompous. Give him an audience. Let him take as many bows as he wants.

'Nobody will believe a word,' she said calmly. 'If we had killed anybody, why would I have named Parsons to the police?'

'A mistaken attempt to divert attention from Sorley Hall. Who knows what is in the mind of desperate criminals?'

'So where are the paintings? They won't be found, right?'

'The pair have hidden the goods to be retrieved later. Or perhaps in a panic they threw the paintings in the river Avon never to be seen again. A shocking act of cultural vandalism. But they keep three minor works that will later be discovered in their van. And ten thousand pounds.'

'Not much for a multimillion-pound art theft.'

'Enough to cover their escape. At least that is what Sebastian tells his lover. In fact he knows the only expenses will be funeral expenses.'

Derry tried to speak, but her voice came out as a hoarse whisper. 'You can't.'

Sergei's regretful smile said *necessity*. Nothing personal. Call it fate. *Your* fate.

'Sebastian knows he cannot escape the law,' Sergei continued. 'He means to end it all. Sebastian kills his lover, then he commits suicide. A tragedy.'

'It's crazy. The family will tell everything. Nobody will hide this.'

'Are you sure?' Sergei cocked his head to one side. 'Perhaps they will tell after a little time. But at first they will think why not let sleeping dogs lie? Why be dragged deeper into the mire? Who will the police believe is the criminal, an earl or a fortune-teller?

Into Derry's mind came the memory of sitting in the back of a police car and the detective's deep suspicion. Cranshaw would grab the story with both hands. Sergei had left little to chance. Now she realised why neither she nor Sebastian's wrists had been bound since they had left the warehouse—no chafing to arouse suspicion that an apparent suicide was a murder. 'The police aren't stupid,' she finished. But she knew her voice held no conviction.

'You misunderstand,' said Sergei, smiling. 'This… is *maskirovka*.'

~

'Maskirovka,' repeated Sergei with satisfaction. 'The most elegant of our Russian military doctrines. You might call it deception, but your English word fails to acknowledge its beauty. Move the left hand to distract from the right. Tell a lie to make your enemy doubt the truth. Confuse. Mislead. Surprise.

'And so we serve up an intriguing puzzle—a romantic tale of criminal lovers fleeing justice. For days the police will theorise, enjoying themselves enormously while failing to tell fact from illusion, truth from falsehood.

'I need forty-eight hours. No more. Then I shall be on a private jet courtesy of my patron, heading for the homeland. My container of worthless export reproductions will be in international waters bound for St. Petersburg.'

As Sergei finished speaking, the overalled Russian in the van climbed into the driver's seat. Derry heard the hum of electric windows. What was he doing? Some kind of mechanical test? If Derry's arms hadn't been so tightly bound to her sides her hands would have shaken uncontrollably.

Sergei stood. He barked something at his henchman in the van, gesturing across the coach house to a narrow door at the back, presumably leading into the garden behind. As the Russian strode to the doorway, he pulled from his overalls pocket an automatic pistol.

Sergei snapped out another order. The Russian shrugged and obeyed, slipping the gun back into his pocket. Had he been warned not to start any shooting outside? Derry wondered if that was good or bad. Shooting could mean rescue. Then again, shooting could get somebody killed. Somebody, that is, as well as she and Sebastian. The Russian left, dragging the door closed behind him.

To Derry's surprise, Sebastian spoke up. He was saying something in Russian, his tone defiant, vehemently insisting on some point. Sergei shouted him down, waving his Tazer. Sebastian didn't flinch or close his eyes. Nor did he stop remonstrating with Sergei. Now Sergei spoke quietly, smiling a tight little smile. Whatever he said silenced Sebastian, who slumped back against his post.

Sergei put his Tazer back in his pocket. He gestured to the driver to stand guard, while in a smooth athletic movement he stepped through the open side door of the van. Derry watched as Sergei dragged the coolbox, plank and watering can to the centre of the van's floor. From the coolbox he took four pink plastic bottles. Bleach? Cleaning fluid? Derry saw the brand was a household name but couldn't identify the product. Neither did she recognise two smaller, blue bottles. Next Sergei took from the box a pad of A4 paper and a chunky felt-tip pen. Placing the pad and pen on the van floor, he jumped out. Leaning into the opening, he took out the containers and put them on the ground beside him, before dragging the open coolbox to the centre of the door opening. From his pocket he took a pair of yellow washing-up gloves and pulled them on.

He reached in for the plank, carefully laying it flat across the open top of the coolbox, but not square-on. Instead he placed it across one corner of the box so part of the board stuck out of the van at an angle. Now he was balancing the watering can on the corner of the open cool box, partly supported by the edge of the box and partly resting on the plank. A nudge of the plank and the can would tip into the open box.

Sergei stood inspecting his handiwork and adjusting the position of the watering can. He stepped back and gently slid the van door as though closing it. As the door connected with the projecting end of the plank, the plank slid away. The tall, narrow can overbalanced, falling awkwardly into the box.

He seemed satisfied. He lifted the watering can from the coolbox and placed it on the ground beside him. He readjusted the plank, but did not reposition the can. One by one, Sergei unscrewed the caps of the pink containers and carefully poured the contents into the coolbox. Carelessly, he tossed the empty containers into the dim interior of the van. He unscrewed the cap of a blue bottle, pouring the contents into the watering can. He did the same with a second. This time, he didn't toss the empty containers away but carefully placed them on their sides on the van floor.

'We are ready,' said Sergei. 'Our maskirovka is prepared. But detail matters. I am sure you will appreciate my final touch.' He picked up the A4 pad and marker pen and set to work scribbling something. 'A little art work. You like?' He held up the pad to display the page beneath. A line drawing, thick, uncertain but unmistakable. A skull and crossbones. He flipped the pages to show an identical drawing, then another. Three pages. Three skulls. And beneath each skull the single word, *GAS!*

Derry barely registered Sergei pulling his knife from his pocket and carefully slicing through Sebastian's binding to release his hands. Under the Tazer of the driver, Sebastian was made to finger the pages, leaving his prints. But Derry saw only that one horrifying word, *gas*. Again she saw the kitchen sink at Sorley Hall. Fizzling liquid and rising vapour. An enveloping, choking cloud. Darkness.

'I too can play at the art of forgery,' said Sergei, holding up the fingered A4 pages in his gloved hands, admiring his creation. 'I too can create an illusion of truth.' He passed the pages to the driver along with a small roll of tape from his pocket. The man knew what to do. In minutes, the van's passenger window, the driver's side window and the rear tailgate glass bore the stark warning.

'You should be pleased,' said Sergei. 'A single breath of this vapour can kill even in the open air. Sebastian is a thief but he is showing some small vestige of honour—he is unwilling to put at risk the lives of brave policemen.'

Derry sneaked a glance at Sebastian. His head was bowed, his chin slumped on his chest, his eyes closed.

'Household cleaner and pesticide,' continued Sergei.

'Hydrochloric acid and a sulphide. Mixed together, Hydrogen Sulphide gas. The end will be quick—nine seconds in a confined space, a little longer in the open. I regret I could not add the final touch to this work. Instead of pesticide, the sulphide could have been supplied by... artists' oil paint.' He smiled broadly. 'How beautiful that would have been. But alas, artist's oils are not easily found at short notice. Even by a Spetsnaz.'

The driver was alert now, Tazer at the ready, as Sergei carefully picked up the watering can and with great delicacy balanced it on the plank and the edge of the cool box, just as he had practiced. For a moment he stood with his hands either side of the watering can, testing its stability. The can wobbled then came to rest. Content, Sergei turned away and again faced Derry and Sebastian.

'When you are discovered, the police will evacuate the neighbourhood. They will summon hazardous materials specialists, and they will wait many hours for the scene to be declared safe. Only then will they begin to speculate. Days will pass.'

Sergei stood back, gesturing to the driver to bring the roll of clingfilm. 'Until now, Sebastian's lover has imagined they will soon be together in Russia living happily in a sunny villa by the Black Sea or a pretty dacha in the woods. At last she realises what he has planned. Too late.' Sergei knelt beside Derry, took his knife from his pocket and snicked open the blade. Slashing expertly, he sliced through the clingfilm binding Derry to her post.

Sergei stood back, pointing his Tazer at Derry's chest, motioning her to her feet. He signalled to his henchman, and only then did Derry understand. Only then did she know the true meaning of fear. They meant to wrap her as they had wrapped Sebastian, neck to foot, making of her a squirming helpless larva, swaddling her in a plastic shroud.

Pointing his Tazer at Derry, again gesturing impatiently for her to stand, Sergei took his phone from his pocket. Most likely he meant to summon his henchman patrolling outside. One-handed, still wearing his yellow rubber gloves, Sergei made to swipe the phone to dial. As Derry watched, he swiped again. He peered at the phone, frowning. Again he tried to dial without success. Now he was peeling off one yellow glove and thrusting it into his pocket.

Irrational, absurd, but in Derry's heart, Sergei's trivial failure kindled hope. A man who had failed to dial a number on his phone couldn't possibly murder two people in cold blood. Illogical, but the thought made Derry smile. And as she smiled, another reason for smiling, equally illogical, presented itself in front of her eyes. Beyond Sergei's shoulder a light trickle of dust, a faint powder barely visible, drifted down from the roof.

Despite Derry's long training as an actor, all those years learning to control every muscle in her face and body, her eyes flicked upwards. Near the skylight, by the yellow plastic sheeting, something moved.

Sergei frowned. He swung around and peered at the rafters. The driver too gazed upwards. There! A trickle of dust, growing visibly sronger. Was that a shuffling noise? A creaking of ancient timbers? The crackle of splitting slate?

Sergei glanced at his phone. Whoever he had called was failing to answer. Again he inspected the roof. He rasped out an order in Russian. The driver instantly obeyed, leaving by the back door. *And now*, thought Derry, the phrase coming to her unbidden, *there was one.*

Sergei was watchful now, keeping a sensible distance between himself and his captives. He stood back almost as far as the van, his Tazer ready. On the floor beside Derry lay the fat roll of clingfilm, waiting for Sergei's helper to return. Then Derry would be wrapped head to foot and carried to the van, writhing helplessly as she was thrust into the passenger seat. Sebastian would be unbound and bundled in after her. He would hammer at the glass, scrabble for door handles now gone, and howl in frustration. Sergei would slam shut the sliding door. The tall can would topple its liquid load into the waiting acid. Billowing clouds of gas would fill the confines of the van, choking, asphyxiating, burning out their lungs.

Derry stole a glance at Sebastian. He was still bound to his post, but since his hands had been cut free only a few wraps of the plastic binding restrained his torso. He too was staring at the open side of the van and its deadly arrangement. His eyes met Derry's and he gave a rueful smile—strained, forced, but she was grateful all the same. Could he break free? And if he could, what then?

Derry focused every thought, every intention, every cell in her being on the Tazer in Sergei's hand. Even as she tried to muster all her willpower, even as she reached deep into herself to haul to the surface whatever pride she could muster, her body cringed with the memory. In her mind's eye she saw those wicked darts fly like arrows towards her chest, felt the agony, foresaw the inevitable thrashing and screaming, the craven supplication, the repeated merciless, searing jolts.

Someone was roaring—a savage howl like an angel thrown

from Heaven tumbling down to Hell. As every ounce of strength in Derry's thighs and arms exploded, propelling her at Sergei, Derry realised the howling voice was her own.

Sergei's eyes widened. His finger tightened on the trigger. The darts flew towards Derry. She saw their trajectory like a slow-motion film, the slender wires trailing behind. Then she was on the Russian, clawing and scrabbling at his face and his eyes, rolling on the floor, punching and hammering, and all the while wondering why any of this was happening. She should now be thrashing in agony, helpless and abject. Instead, Sergei was on his back, shielding himself from the raining blows of the madwoman on top of him, seemingly shocked into passive acceptance.

Where was Sebastian? A glance behind and Derry saw him wriggle and thrash against his post, grimacing and shouting in frustration but failing to escape his bonds. And now Sergei recovered his wits. In one massive heave, as though tossing a stuffed toy across the room, he threw Derry off and sprang to his feet. Derry was on her back, facing up at a raging bull of a man, fist upraised to smash her into the ground. All she could do was give one last lunatic shout of fury and defiance.

And the roof fell in.

Derry saw it happen. The skylight seemed to acquire a twin as a gaping rent opened in the slates. A deep creaking groan, a bulge inwards lasting only a split second, then collapse. Through the gash, in a shower of laths and slates, two men, thrashing and fighting, hopelessly entangled in a flailing mass of limbs, hit the ground and rolled.

The van rocked on its springs. Something had struck the hood a glancing blow making the van oscillate gently up and down. And through its open side-door Derry saw the tall watering can slowly sway—a rhythmic seesaw, back and forth as it tottered over the coolbox of acid. The can lurched once, twice, and stopped.

The shout of command was in Russian. Sergei stood amongst the debris, a gun in his hand. Bruce sat on the ground, covered in bits of broken slate and rotten timbers, his hands in the air. Beyond him lay the driver, holding one limp arm and rocking back and forth in pain. Sergei barked an order, and the man staggered to his feet. Another command, roared in English, and Bruce crawled towards Derry, under orders not to stand. No mistaking the savagery in Sergei's voice. Everything about him—his face twisted in fury, the agitated waving of his gun—all said it would take nothing for him to pull the trigger, and to hell with the consequences.

'You! Move!' Sergei jabbed the pistol towards Derry, herding her back to her place under the loft. As she shuffled backwards under Sergei's waving gun, she realised she was towing two thin wires. Behind her, dragging along the ground was the Tazer. Derry looked down at herself. The barbs of the Tazer were embedded in her shirt. They had struck her left breast pocket, embedding themselves neatly in her pack of cards.

～

'Hi babe,' said Bruce. He was sitting beside her, apparently uninjured, his hands clasped behind his head. He shrugged, as if he would like to apologise but saw the futility. On the other side, still bound to his post, was Sebastian. He sat slumped, slack-jawed, his mouth hanging open in despair.

Sergei barked something in Russian to his henchman, who stepped behind Bruce and, still clutching his injured arm, with one hand patted Bruce's pockets. He pulled out Bruce's phone, tossing it aside. Then he found the gun.

Derry guessed Bruce had somehow taken the pistol from the thug in overalls who had gone outside blithely unaware that Bruce was waiting. Why, oh why hadn't Bruce used the gun while he had the chance? Derry made herself see sense. This was real life, not the movies, and Bruce knew about gunfights. Bruce would be the last man to march in waving a pistol and hoping for the best.

The injured Russian stood, flicking the gun's safety off with his thumb. He said something in Russian to Sergei, gesturing at Bruce. Derry saw a muscle in Bruce's jaw twitch.

'Ah,' said Sergei, his eyes fixed on Derry. 'It seems our unexpected visitor is your friend from Stonehenge.' He came to come kind of decision. 'Our romantic tale must change.' He spoke as if reading from a sensational news story. 'The couple flee with their ill-gotten gains. But unknown to Sebastian, his fortune-teller girlfriend has another lover, a violent and passionate man. The lover discovers her betrayal with the despicable Sebastian, tracks the pair down and exacts his revenge. He shoots them both. And in despair shoots himself.

'I regret the lack of finesse, but our preparations will not go to waste. Your end will pose an even greater puzzle than before.'

From his pocket, Sergei pulled his clasp knife. Still wielding his pistol, he sliced through the plastic binding Sebastian to his post and dragged away the shreds.

'Turn around! Kneel!' Sergei was shouting now, barracking

all three victims. 'Turn! Heads down! Down!' Derry shuffled around, the cold hard flagstones hurting her knees. Now she was kneeling beside Bruce and Sebastian, facing back into the shadows beneath the loft. A savage cramp writhed in Derry's stomach telling her this really was the end. Her last sight on earth would be rusty bicycles, bags of cement and stacks of old grey slate. She could hear Bruce's breathing. Somewhere in the distance somebody was revving a chainsaw. In front of her eyes, dust particles hung in the air as though gravity were suspended.

In all Derry's life, she had never been as aware of anything as intensely as the invisible gun barrel behind her head. Her whole world had shrunk to a few square inches of scalp, every sensation in her body focused on that single point at the base of her skull.

Out of the corner of her eye Derry again saw a muscle on Bruce's cheek twitch. And with that twitch came a thought—not even a thought—knowledge, absolute certainty. Bruce would never quit. His training made him that way. Silently, Derry vowed in her heart that she too would never quit. She would die, but not with a Russian bullet in the back of her head. Not on her knees. And never playing a pre-assigned role in anybody's *maskirovka*.

Count to three. One... Two...

The crash was deafening. For a moment Derry imagined she must now be dead. But she couldn't be dead, because the stacks of slates and the rusty bicycles were still leaning against the wall. In front of her eyes motes of dust danced crazily in swirling shafts of light that hadn't been there before. And a thunderous, renting, ripping sound. An eardrum-bursting roar. And that chainsaw, now so loud as to seem inside her head.

The shock of the great wooden doors of the coach house smashing inwards sent Derry instinctively diving to the ground. As she twisted around, shielding her face with her arms, the shattered doors burst open with tremendous force, flung against the inner walls. Even as Derry watched, crouching, preparing to throw herself backwards to escape the violence, a Land Rover's green hood crashed through the wreckage, slamming into the back of the van.

Did time stop for the others as it seemed to do for Derry? Bruce, Sebastian and the Russians were frozen, rooted to the spot, their bodies crouched to absorb whatever catastrophe instinct screamed was unfolding around them. In that long moment, Derry seemed to see an event that had not yet happened—through the open side of the van, she saw the coolbox, with the tall can of sulphide balanced on its pale-yellow plank. She saw the van's sliding door. And in a perfect illustration of some half-remembered law of physics, she watched as the nose of the Land Rover slammed into the van's rear end, shooting the door forward on its rail as if from a gun.

Derry's leap must have taken time, a finite number of milliseconds. Yet no time seemed to have passed. Even as the can sloshed wildly into its acid bath and the liquid inside spat and foamed, Derry had both hands on the sliding door and was swinging with all her might. The door banged shut with a solid clunk and stayed shut.

'The glass!' The shout was Bruce. He stood behind Sergei holding him in a savage chokehold, clamping one of the Russian's arms in a rigid lock behind him. Sergei flailed and chopped with the other, but Derry saw he no longer held his gun. Sebastian was on the floor with the injured Russian standing over him screaming and pointing his pistol at his head. Bruce was still yelling. 'The rear! Smashed!'

He had to be right. The tailgate of the van could hardly have survived the battering-ram of the Land Rover. The crumpled rear would never contain the thickening vapours that must now be billowing inside seeking any means of escape.

'Out! Run! Go! Go! Go!' Bruce was screaming now, barely restraining Sergei who was writhing with savage, twisting heaves. Another violent twist and sidestep, and Sergei had flung Bruce to the ground and was racing for the back door, his injured henchman only yards behind.

The thought hit Derry like a blow. 'Bryony!' The green Land Rover was half buried under wreckage, embedded in the back of the van and completely blocking the coach house doorway. Derry launched herself past the rear of the van, scrambled over the twisted fender of the Land Rover and wrenched open the passenger door. In the driver's seat, Bryony was slumped over the wheel, conscious but dazed beyond comprehending. That she was alive at all must have been thanks to the stack of horse blankets she had piled between her and the wheel. A streak of blood ran down her cheek. She gave a weak smile. 'Sorry,' she said.

'Out! You've got to get out!' shouted Derry. Bryony seemed to understand, but she moved as in a dream, struggling weakly to open her driver's door. Hopelessly jammed.

'Here. This side!' Derry would never know where the strength came from as she reached in, grabbed Bryony under her arms and heaved her bodily across the gear lever onto the passenger seat. In a single violent movement she dragged Bryony's near deadweight half out of the land Rover. From nowhere, hands appeared grabbing Bryony's jacket, hauling as desperately as Derry was hauling. Sebastian! And now Bruce was with them, and the men each had one of Bryony's arms around their necks and were racing for the back door.

Derry was first, aiming to swing the door open so Bruce and Sebastian could hustle their burden through and out into the garden. She wrenched the primitive handle, pulling again and again. Locked. Bolted on the outside. In Derry's nostrils was an unfamiliar, acrid tang. Was it her imagination, fuelled by stark terror, or a foretaste of the killing vapour already seeping into the room?

'Heavier than air!' Bruce roared. 'Up! Upstairs! 'You first! Go!'

He meant Derry, and his voice of command brooked no questions and allowed no hesitation. Derry took the creaking rickety steps to the hayloft two at a time. She emerged into the loft gasping, launched herself at the wooden shutters of the window and fumbled with the simple wooden latch. She flung the doors open, breathing deep as though inhaling a magical antidote.

'No! Close it! Quick!'

Only now did Derry realise that the window she had thrown open so gratefully was directly above the shattered double doors of the coach house. Projecting below was the rear of the crashed Land Rover. In front of that was the broken glass and buckled metal of the van's tailgate, no barrier at all to the deadly cloud creeping and tumbling through every gap and crevice. A simple change of wind direction, a random gust, and they would all die.

Derry slammed the shutters closed. Bruce had set Bryony on her feet and had opened an identical shutter in the rear wall. Bryony was unsteady, swaying a little, but she was standing. Bruce was shouting. 'I'm gonna jump out, then catch y'all. Then run like heck. Do not stop. Okay, go!'

Obeying his own command, Bruce leapt from the window. He hit the ground, rolled and sprang to his feet shouting, 'Bryony, now!'

Bryony hardly hesitated, throwing herself off the ledge without a thought. Bruce staggered as he caught her, but he broke her fall, and the two rolled on the grass below.

'Sebastian!' shouted Bruce.

Derry knew why Bruce had chosen Sebastian to go next. He could help Bryony get away if she couldn't make it by herself. Bruce caught him too, and then Sebastian had Bryony by the arm and they were on their feet in a staggering run.

Derry sat on the window ledge, paused for barely a second and pushed herself off. Bruce caught her, both of them rolling and tumbling. Bruce was gripping her elbow, dragging her to her feet. Now they were racing, racing, as if the Devil and all the legions of Hell were at their heels.

# 34

You might imagine that barely escaping with your life from attempted murder by Russian gangsters would earn you some sympathy. But Detective Sergeant Peter Cranshaw wasn't at all sympathetic. He and his boss, a Detective Inspector, seemed barely able to contain their irritation. Derry supposed having to evacuate the wealthy properties adjoining Sebastian's house was part of it, and catching only one of the Russians hadn't helped their mood. She guessed too that both detectives had a nagging sense they weren't being told the whole story. Not by a very long way.

Derry, Bruce, Sebastian and Bryony sat on hard plastic chairs at a conference table in a police station interview room. The two detectives sat opposite, along with a constable who took notes and occasionally prodded a voice recorder that didn't want to work.

Derry was so far beyond exhaustion she felt skittish, even cheerful. The urge to smile at everyone no matter what they were saying was irresistible. She caught Bruce peeking at her fondly. The detectives seemed to approve of Bruce, perhaps because he'd insisted they call a specialist team to deal with the gas and had probably saved police officers from death or serious injury. And it was thanks to Bruce they did have one of the Russians, the man Sergei had first sent into the garden. Bruce had disarmed him and tied him up in a garden shed. Luckily for the Russian, the shed was some distance from the coach house and its deadly vapours.

Beside Bruce sat Sebastian, his face drawn, stubble making

him look ten years older. Not once did he smile or show any sign of relief at their near-miraculous escape. He seemed to accept his rescue with the same fatalistic indifference he had accepted his captivity. Bryony sat next to him, a plaster on her forehead but pronounced by the police doctor fit or at least not concussed. She was clasping Sebastian's hand in hers as if she would never let him go.

The sight was sobering. Suddenly, Derry didn't feel like smiling anymore. Perhaps Bryony wouldn't care that Sebastian was a forger. But how could she not care he was a thief? Derry imagined that on the table between the couple, invisible to Bryony, lay two small Picasso drawings stolen from Sorley Hall. Stolen from Bryony.

Derry realised she was chewing her lower lip. Detective Cranshaw fixed on her a considering look that said, *you don't fool me. I know you know something.* True, of course—Derry was acutely aware she was the only person in the room other than Sebastian who knew the whole story. And it was obvious Sebastian didn't mean to tell.

'You say the paintings these Russians extorted were worth several thousand pounds? You said several thousand?' The Detective Inspector spoke in measured tones, obviously aware his voice was being recorded for posterity.

'Yes,' said Sebastian. 'Several thousand. Hard to be precise, of course. Artworks really have no fixed value. Fashion, mainly.'

If Derry had been drinking coffee, she would have spluttered and choked. The value of a sizable chunk of the famous Sorley Hall art collection had been reduced to peanuts. Derry sneaked a glance at Sebastian who sat straight-faced. Bryony was equally expressionless. But she must have known roughly what the pictures were worth. Well, well, thought Derry. *Team Sorley sticks together.*

Detective Cranshaw briefed them on events since their escape. 'We sealed off the warehouse, but the container you describe wasn't there. I wouldn't worry too much—a container of reproduction art works was listed to sail from Southampton today. It's probably sitting in the container park right now. We'll have it soon enough.' He turned to Bryony, 'I'm sorry your ladyship, but the paintings will constitute evidence, so you may not get possession for some time. Can't be helped, I'm afraid.'

Derry wondered what exactly *for some time* might mean. Never? Confiscated to pay enormous back taxes? Or frozen in legal limbo until someone could prove ownership. And what then? Derry realised she was far too tired to care. And too depressed. In her mind's eye she saw Bryony's face crumple into tears when she discovered her fiancée was a thief and learned the awful extent of his betrayal. Then she remembered. Shafts of coloured light from a stained-glass window. An altar. A woman in bridal dress holding a drooping bouquet.

Petals falling one by one.

# 35

Derry didn't know where she was. Then she recognised her little bedroom at Sorley Hall. What time was it? Where was her phone? Then it all came back.

She waited for her body to start shaking with delayed reaction. Nothing happened. She felt hungry, that was all. And numb. Disconnected. She got up, dressed, made some toast and was pouring coffee when Bruce emerged from his room. He was limping.

'You okay?'

'Sure, hon. Living is the part I like. The rest is a bonus.' He gave an involuntary groan as he settled into a chair.

Derry poured him a coffee. She only vaguely remembered their return to Sorley Hall. They had been met by the shocked household, fussed over by Charlotte and Marlene but had insisted all they needed was sleep. She had made Bruce shower and she had put salve and plasters on a dozen scrapes and small cuts. He was a mass of bruises. 'If the SEALs couldn't kill me no Russian is going to do it,' he'd said, smiling. 'All hat 'n' no cattle.'

They sat in silence, lost in their own thoughts. Outside, a car revved its engine in the courtyard and pulled away. The last revellers from last night's festivities? Another planet. Derry wondered what story the guests had been told. She wondered too what the Dowager and the Earl had told Cranshaw and his colleagues. No more than half the truth, of that she was certain. Mostly she was thinking about Bryony. Was Sebastian at this moment confessing his theft and breaking her heart? Or worse, was he still telling lies—lies to which Derry would soon become party if she chose to say nothing of what she knew?

The door-knocker gave a light tap, as though apologising for its existence. Derry stirred herself to answer. The caller was Marlene, dispensing hugs, wide-eyed sympathy, limitless admiration for their bravery and a stream of questions. Derry described how Bruce's van had been impounded by the police as evidence, and was smashed up and probably still contaminated with chemicals. On top of everything, Bruce had lost his phone. He guessed he'd get it back when the coach house was declared safe but not until the police had copied all his phone numbers and photos. 'What treats in store, darlings,' he said in his campest voice, grinning wickedly.

Marlene showed practical good sense. First she offered Derry her phone—for a model to part from her phone for longer than it took to make a circuit of the catwalk was beyond mere friendship. All the same, Derry refused the offer. She didn't want to phone anyone, even if she could remember anybody's number. What was she supposed to say—hi, just wanted to let you know I'm not dead?

Marlene insisted she arrange flights home for Bruce and Derry and meant to organise getting the van released and repaired—she knew a little garage where the boys would do anything for her. Most surprising of all, she undertook to chase up the fees Derry and Bruce had been promised. 'And by the way, Octavia says can you both come to her apartments at five.' She looked at her watch. 'Pretty well now, actually.'

Why not refuse? Something in Derry resented being summoned peremptorily as if to an audience with royalty. The Dowager had used her without mercy, not once but twice. Yet so many questions were still unanswered, questions Derry knew would never let her rest. Promptly at five p.m., Derry and Bruce knocked on the door of Octavia's apartments.

The surprise was that the whole family was there. Octavia sat in her customary place by the fire, beneath the pictures of her young self as a dancer at the Palace. Bryony and Sebastian sat together on a chaise longue, but not close Derry noticed, and not holding hands. They sat stiffly, upright, as correct as you could be on a chaise longue.

Charlotte sat to one side at the little table. The Earl stood at the window, his hands behind his back. The curtains were open, the September light still strong and warm. Motes of dust danced in the sunbeams, and Derry shivered at a memory.

'I wanted you all here so you could understand,' said the Dowager. She spoke as though her listeners had waited their whole lives for the privilege. Derry wondered if she hadn't made a mistake letting her curiosity bring her here to be condescended to. Who did these people think they were?

'Everything I have done has been for the family,' said the Dowager. She corrected herself. 'Everything we have done, all of us, has been for the family. I want you to understand that.' She directed her words at Derry and Bruce, but especially at Derry. Was she asking for some kind of forgiveness? The whole family, Sebastian too, was watching to see how the two outsiders would react. A show, thought Derry. *All for little us.*

'Would you stand, please Sebastian.' Octavia spoke loudly, her voice firm.

Derry was jolted from her resentment. What was this? Some kind of therapy session? Was Sebastian going to confess he was a thief in front of everyone? At least that would put an end to the secrets. Perhaps he had already told Bryony. Was that why they were sitting a foot apart on a couch made for lovers, each staring straight ahead as if the other wasn't in the room?

'I want you all to meet my grandson,' said Octavia.

If a genie had appeared in the middle of the room, rising in a cloud of smoke from the bowl of potpourri on the table, Derry could hardly have been more astonished. Everyone— the Earl, Bryony, Charlotte, Bruce and Derry—was staring at Octavia. The Dowager sat expressionless, having done what she had set out to do. Sebastian too betrayed no emotion. His face mirrored the woman who, Derry realised with a shock, was indeed his grandmother. How had she never seen the resemblance, the finely curved mouth now so obvious?

The Dowager recounted her story efficiently and without emotion. Her career as a chorus girl at the Palace Theatre in Dublin had ended abruptly when she discovered she was pregnant. She returned home and had a daughter, quietly adopted by a well-to-do family with good connections. A couple of years later, Octavia married her Earl, who knew nothing of her indiscretion. The years passed, and the daughter had a son, Sebastian. Being a lone parent, she used new laws to discover her mother's identity. The girl had no intention of embarrassing anybody with her history and asked for nothing, but Octavia wanted to help. Secretly, in the guise of a family trust, Octavia paid for her grandson's education at the best school, funded his degree, his sojourn in Russia, and—without ever revealing his identity to her husband—contrived to land Sebastian a job as assistant curator of the Earl's art collection. In exchange, Sebastian was sworn to secrecy.

With the death of her husband, the estate passed to Octavia's nephew the present Earl, and Octavia got Sebastian promoted from assistant to full curator. She made him small but valuable presents of minor paintings from her own collection, but she could do little more for her grandson. Sebastian was of the female line, as well as being illegitimate in the eyes of the law, and was entitled to no inheritance. He would have to make his own way.

'Sebastian kept his word,' Octavia finished. 'He was discreet. He is a good boy.'

The relief that swept over Derry was almost unbearable. Sebastian was no thief. He had been given presents by his grandmother but could never prove it or defend himself by identifying her. Not even to Sergei.

The Earl, Charlotte and Bryony, sat silent, visibly stunned by Octavia's revelation. But Derry found she was smiling as broadly as if she had won an Oscar. She couldn't help it. Sebastian saw and caught her eye. What did she see in his expression? A softness? Gratitude? Perhaps he was saying he had hated being misjudged by her, hated not having her respect. Wanted her to think well of him.

The rest of Octavia's story hardly interested Derry at all. Why had Octavia kept the secret for so long? Things were different in those days, she said. To reveal her past would have opened the door to intolerable gossip.

'I am proud of Sebastian,' said Octavia as if her judgement and hers alone mattered. 'He acted for the good of the family.'

Derry wondered what the Earl was thinking. His employee could no longer be treated as an opportunist without family who meant to make off with his daughter. He must be remembering his willingness to call the police and throw all the blame on Sebastian even though he himself had been the main beneficiary of the fraud. But if the Earl felt shame, he showed nothing. The trick, it seemed, was to wait out the problem until it went away and everything returned to what it was before. Perhaps his ancestors rode out the vicissitudes of history the same way.

Sebastian stood. 'I'm sorry, your ladyship... grandmother.' He said the word like he was using the term for the first time. 'I'm not proud of what... happened... what I've done.' He glanced at the Earl, 'We persuaded ourselves nobody would get hurt. And I admit I thought the idea amusing. Picasso said he would himself sign a very good forgery. I thought what was good enough for Picasso was good enough for me. All so very postmodern. But a man was killed. My fault.'

Bryony cleared her throat and stood. She spoke to her family. 'Sebastian and I have agreed to call off our engagement. I will always love Sebastian, but what he did... what you all did, was wrong. I won't be part of that. What I have learned just now, about his... origins... changes nothing.'

Octavia closed her eyes. Whether she was pained at Bryony's condemnation or at seeing a dream so recently born vanish into thin air, Derry couldn't guess. For the Dowager, the wedding of her grandniece by marriage to her grandson by blood must have seemed like a fairy tale. Now that dream was shattered.

'That's all I have to say,' said Octavia. 'Thank you. Bryony, we need to talk. In twenty minutes?'

Bryony nodded. It was as though Octavia had called a board meeting, with herself the chairwoman and Bryony the chief executive.

'Derry dear,' said Octavia, 'and Bruce. Could I ask you to stay a few minutes more? I have one or two matters I would like to discuss with you.

∼

The Dowager Countess of Berkshire made no apology, and Derry hadn't expected one. Instead of saying sorry for almost getting them killed, Octavia was effusively grateful that Derry and Bruce had saved her grandson. Nor was Derry surprised that Octavia appeared to see nothing wrong with defrauding wealthy foreign art buyers she considered as shallow and fake as the pictures they were buying. But Octavia did make an admission she had chosen not to make in front of Bryony and Charlotte. She had known about the forgeries.

Octavia was painfully aware the Earl was selling valuable pictures to fund his horses, his gambling and his women—threatening to bleed the Sorley Hall collections dry. She believed those pictures did not belong to him, but to the estate that would one day be Bryony's if the law changed as they all believed it would. Sebastian had seen the possibilities presented by Philip Parsons. Octavia had crafted the plan. The Earl had thought the whole scheme rather clever.

'I have spoken to George, you may be interested to know. He will step down in favour of Bryony as soon as the law is changed—next year we expect. We will come to some arrangement with the tax authorities if we must, and in any case the business will take years. Meantime, all sales from the collection will be controlled by Bryony alone. With my guidance, naturally.'

Octavia hesitated. 'That dreadful man, the art dealer—the Russian—will he seek revenge? I am concerned for Sebastian. And George too, of course.'

'We've thought about that,' said Derry. 'Whether Sergei gets to Russia or stays here, he'll have a big enough problem looking out for himself.'

'Most likely he and his boss have already hightailed it,' added Bruce. 'Private jet to Finland. On to Mother Russia. England will be too hot for those boys for a long time.'

'I'm relieved to hear it,' said Octavia. 'I am going to suggest to Sebastian that he stay with friends of mine in the States. As it happens, I have a relative in a senior position in one of your major galleries—we may be able to find a post for him there.

'I hope you won't be embarrassed if I say I would like to recompense you both in some way, above and beyond our agreed fees, for the trauma you have suffered. I'm sure you would think it vulgar of me to speak of money under the circumstances, and I won't insult you by making such an offer.'

Derry and Bruce were different people in as many ways as you could imagine. But they were both actors. To be insulted by offers of money was, therefore, an existential impossibility. As one, they made a range of indeterminate noises meant to convey that Octavia shouldn't worry one bit about insulting them, and she wasn't to imagine for a moment they would see hard cash as in any way vulgar or beneath them. But Octavia had moved on.

'So in recognition of both of you, I'm going to make a donation to the Palace Theatre restoration fund. A couple of small Picassos, perhaps a Matisse should be helpful, don't you think? Real ones, of course,' she added, smiling.

The Countess has made a joke, thought Derry. How about that? For the hundredth time, she wondered what strange material these people were made of. But no doubt about it, Octavia had offered something wonderful. And maybe, thought Derry, just maybe Octavia was right. Paying them for what they had done would cheapen everything. She and Bruce had acted the way they had for their own reasons. They were nobody's servants or loyal retainers.

'Such a pity about Sebastian and Bryony,' said Octavia. 'Such a very great pity.'

～

Derry was sitting on the cottage windowsill soaking up the late evening sunshine when a black SUV swept into the courtyard, spraying gravel as it skidded to a halt. The driver leapt out. Over a city suit he wore an incongruous green parka, his only concession to country life. He was plainly a policeman, and if the hand thrust under his jacket, his alert stance, his sunglasses and his earpiece said anything, he was an armed policeman.

'Hi Freddie,' called Derry. Freddie nodded, but obviously felt smiling was incompatible with whatever state of alert was currently in force.

A second man leapt from the passenger side, similarly attired, equally fit, and strikingly handsome. He too had his hand inside his jacket. Satisfied that neither Derry nor the cat sitting on the windowsill posed any threat he couldn't handle, he swung open the rear door of the SUV. Out stepped Jacko.

'Dad!'

'Light of my firmament!'

They hugged like they hadn't seen each other for a year.

'Oh, Dad!' A lump formed in Derry's throat. Tears filled her eyes. She couldn't speak.

'You're alright now,' said Jacko, enveloping her in a mighty hug. 'You've done well, by all accounts. Why don't we sit ourselves down in the sun. No need to say a thing.'

They sat side by side on the window ledge.

'We heard of the… incident,' said Jacko tipping the side of his nose conspiratorially. 'Himself suggested I pop over. His people are notably well informed.'

Derry had to wipe her eyes with her handkerchief. 'So what's all this?' she asked, indicating the bodyguards.

'No idea,' said Jacko. 'These kind and capable gentlemen seem to have taken it into their heads to guarantee my welfare. I think Himself had a wee word. Not complaining, I can tell you. The world is a dangerous place.' His tone said he was now privy to matters of such importance to national security that if people knew what he knew, they would never sleep at night.

Jacko's phone rang. Somehow Derry knew the caller was her mother. But why did Jacko seem pleased? His usual response to a call from his ex-wife was the panicked look of a hunted sheep. 'She's right here,' he said. He handed Derry the phone. 'For you.'

'I told them it was empty!' said Vanessa. She was trying to whisper and shout at the same time. 'They opened it anyway. Of course the thing was empty! It'd be worth a fortune if it weren't!'

'Mom, what's empty?'

'Sergei's sarcophagus! They said they were looking for a dead body! Now they're taking away all Sergei's pieces! Pictures! Everything! Look! Look!'

Even if Derry could have looked, she had no need. Of course the police were seizing everything of Sergei's. More than once over the last day, she too had wondered if the sarcophagus Sergei had stored in Vanessa's gallery held the mortal remains of Philip Parsons. She had dismissed the idea as lacking the elegance Sergei seemed to value so highly. Most likely Parsons would be washed up on some shore or be discovered buried in a woodland. She hoped the police would soon find him.

'They won't say why they're doing all this!' said Vanessa. 'Please tell me we're not going to be in the papers again!'

Derry noted the *we*.

'Has something happened?' said Vanessa. 'I've been trying to phone you!'

How do you explain to a more than usually excitable mother that you have just escaped death by poison gas and shooting?

'Nothing much,' Derry lied. 'I'll tell you all about it over coffee some time. We're back to Dublin tomorrow, I think.'

'Oh well, have a nice trip dear,' said Vanessa, sounding relieved. 'But honestly, this publicity-seeking has to stop!'

As Derry handed Jacko back his phone, she remembered his Sikorsky. Her father had paid ten thousand euro for that painting at the Palace Theatre auction, and the work had come originally from Sorley Hall. Had her mother sold her father an expensive fake? Best have that conversation some other time.

'You're pals with royalty now, right? Is Mom going to get her invitation to the big wedding?

Jacko smiled enigmatically. 'Yes… and no. She may of course be present.'

'Come on Dad. Give over.'

'Plus one,' said Jacko.

'Dad!'

'Courtesy of Himself, I already have the wedding invitation so coveted by the female of the species. Plus one. In other words, with the companion of my choice. I emphasise, *my* choice.' Jacko grinned, delighted. To have one's ex at a social disadvantage was the ultimate in post-marital bliss. 'She may have to be civil,' he added. 'She may have to withdraw certain scurrilous allegations concerning a person's tax affairs. She may also have to take a more enlightened view of her daughter's artistic endeavours, abandoning her foul ambition to recruit an innocent and creative soul to her infernal trade.'

Derry and her father sat in comfortable silence. Freddie idly stroked the cat on the windowsill. Bruce had emerged from the house and was chatting amiably with the good-looking bodyguard. Derry wondered were they exchanging war stories or telephone numbers. With Bruce, you could never be sure.

'Come and stay at our castle,' said Jacko. 'Home of the ancestors. Feel the vibrations.'

Derry remembered the photos of Jacko posing in front of various shapeless masses of ivy somewhere in County Galway. 'It's a pile of rubble!'

'Um… a caravan? Could be draughty this time of year, but we O'Donnells are made of stern stuff.'

'Dad! I am not staying in a trailer. Ever. Even if it is hitched to a castle.'

'Ha ha! Joking, my dearest. How about Fotheringham? Nice little place. Invitation that can't be refused, I'm afraid.' He paused for effect. 'From *Herself.*'

'I'm sorry?'

Jacko leaned his head close to Derry's. He whispered out of the corner of his mouth like a ventriloquist. 'Herself!' He glanced around suspiciously, as though concerned the cat on the window-sill might hear and take some sinister advantage of a lapse in security.

'Herself heard of your little adventure. Herself has a soft spot for the Lady Bryony. Treats her like a godchild. Herself has heard how brave you and Bryony were. And your friend Bruce, of course. She said of you, and I quote, 'I love a horse of pluck and intuition.'

Derry wasn't sure what she thought about being compared to a horse, however favourably.

'Herself wants you to pop over to Fotheringham and stay for a few days to recuperate. No social requirements. In your own time, she would like you to give her a card reading. In complete confidence, of course. If it's ever mentioned, it never happened.'

'I didn't know she was… interested,' said Derry, astonished.

'I doubt anyone does,' said Jacko. 'So what about it? The food is superb. Chef from the Dorchester.'

Derry wouldn't have been more surprised at an invitation

to play golf with the President of the United States. But this was the more exclusive invite by a long way.

'So what do you say?' said Jacko.

'Um… I guess so. I mean, I suppose I could. Oh no! What will I wear!'

'Don't you worry about that,' said Jacko. 'Just make sure its old and green.'

'Wait a minute. What if Mom finds out?'

'So what if she does?' said Jacko, grinning from ear to ear.

'She'll have By Appointment on a huge sign over the gallery door and the royal crest on her dinner plates! She'll be impossible. Promise never to tell?'

'Hmm,' said Jacko, his eyes glinting wickedly.

'Promise!'

'She would so very much want to know.'

'Dad!'

Jacko only smiled.

63054105R00214

Made in the USA
Charleston, SC
27 October 2016